The Silent Tide

Also by Rachel Hore

The Dream House
The Memory Garden
The Glass Painter's Daughter
A Place of Secrets
A Gathering Storm

The Silent Tide

RACHEL HORE

WITHDRAWN FROM DÚN LAOGHAIRE RATHDOWN
COUNTY LIBRARY STOCK

BAINTE DEN STOC

**SIMON &
SCHUSTER**

London · New York · Sydney · Toronto · New Delhi

A CBS COMPANY

DUN LAOGHAIRE-RATHDOWN LIBRARIES	
DLR20001022537	
BERTRAMS	29/08/2013
	£19.99
CA	

BAINTE DEN STOC

WITHDRAWN FROM DÚN LAOGHAIRE-RATHDOWN
COUNTY LIBRARY STOCK

First published in Great Britain by Simon & Schuster UK Ltd, 2013
A CBS Company.

Copyright © Rachel Hore 2013

This book is copyright under the Berne Convention.
No reproduction without permission.
® and © 1997 Simon & Schuster Inc. All rights reserved.

The right of Rachel Hore to be identified as author of this
work has been asserted in accordance with sections 77 and
78 of the Copyright, Designs and Patents Act, 1988.

1 3 5 7 9 10 8 6 4 2

Simon & Schuster UK Ltd
1st Floor
222 Gray's Inn Road
London WC1X 8HB

www.simonandschuster.co.uk

Simon & Schuster Australia, Sydney
Simon & Schuster India, New Delhi

A CIP catalogue record for this book is available from the British Library

HB ISBN 978-0-85720-974-0
Ebook ISBN 978-1-84983-291-5

This book is a work of fiction. Names,
characters, places and incidents are either a product of the author's
imagination or are used fictitiously. Any resemblance to actual
people living or dead, events or locales is entirely coincidental.

Typeset by Hewer Text UK Ltd, Edinburgh
Printed and bound in Great Britain by CPI (UK) Ltd, Croydon CR0 4YY

David's

'Women were wanting to escape the net just as men were climbing back into it.'
Only Halfway to Paradise: Women in Postwar Britain, Elizabeth Wilson

'Oh, I am nothing without you,' she said. 'I should not know what to be. I feel as if you had invented me. I watch you inventing me week after week.'
Elizabeth Taylor, *The Sleeping Beauty*

Prologue

Isabel

She couldn't say at first what woke her.

It was dark, very dark – and cold, a penetrating icy cold. Even under the bedclothes she shivered. Something was different; all her senses told her this. Outside, the wind was up, scuffling about under the eaves of her wooden beach house, shaking the glass in the windows, setting off strange creaks and sighs around her, as though the house was shifting and muttering in its sleep. There was an odd smell, too, of something dank and salty, and a trickling sound like rain in the gutters. She threw back the blankets and swung her feet to the floor – only to snatch them back as they met several inches of water.

She reached for the switch of the bedside lamp and at once lit up a scene of devastation. The whole room was flooded. Water had risen above the level of the skirting boards, opaque, swirling. It seeped in through the windows, dripped down the walls, flowed in under the door.

The lamp flickered urgently, compelling action. She hitched her nightdress up over her knees, drew breath and stepped down into an icy sea. Wading to the door, she turned the handle and had to hang on, gasping, as the door burst inward and a surge of water almost knocked her off her feet. Under her hands, she felt the house give a shudder of complaint. At the same moment, the light gave a final flash and went out.

Alone in the dark, knee-deep in seawater and numb with cold, she cried out in terror. For a moment she couldn't think what to do. She daren't try the front door, fearing the full strength of the incoming tide. The back perhaps. She felt her way round the corner into the hall and cloth brushed against her cheek. Her coat was hanging on the hooks there. Quickly she took it down and pushed her arms into the sleeves, wrapped it around her. The act gave her courage.

Now she was used to the darkness she saw that the door to the kitchen stood open. A faint trail of moonlight from the window shimmered on the water. She struck out, her progress assisted by the force of the tide.

She spotted her handbag, standing primly upon the kitchen table where she'd left it when she went to bed, snatched it up, then looked for Penelope's letter. There, propped on the dresser. She slipped it into the bag.

There was no time to think what else to rescue. She had to get out. But when she unbolted the back door and shoved, it would not move against the weight of the water. The window then. She'd have to climb on the roof.

She seized a floating chair, set it by the sink, stood on it, and after testing her weight, hoisted her bag onto her shoulder and stepped onto the draining board. The window opened with a squeak and she eased herself out onto the sill. There she crouched, looking out in amazement.

A huge moon, veiled in storm cloud, presided over an alien landscape. What yesterday had been a peaceful scene – bleak marshland stretching into the distance, cows grazing, the sail of a distant windmill moving against the sky – was now a rolling sea, the waves crested with foam. Some way to the right, mercifully above the level of the water, lay the silhouette of the town, church towers, a lighthouse, which from time to time bathed the watery scene in a patient yellow beam. Suddenly, the house gave another lurch, like a tooth loosening in its socket, as a great wave swept round it. Water surged up to the edge of the sill.

She straightened, twisting awkwardly, straining to see where she could go next. There was a flat roof over the kitchen. Terror helped her scramble up on to it. There she perched for a moment, feeling with alarm the house rock under her. Gradually, it was being eased from its foundations. The land was becoming the sea and the little wooden house a boat.

She was shivering now, as much from fear as cold. Rain was beginning to fall, huge, heavy drops slapping down on the roof. Another wave smashed against the house, which shrieked at the onslaught. Suddenly she felt it lurch free altogether, and as it bumped along the ground she had to scrabble for handholds. The thing to do, she saw, was to mount the sloping roof and sit astride it. There she'd be further above the rising water. She tried, but the surface was too slippery and she kept falling back. The house bumped along some more, then caught on something and began slowly to revolve. With the roof at a gentler angle she took her chance and crawled up. Just in time, for the house then righted itself. The best thing, she found, was to lie flat with her legs on either side of the ridge and clutch the top of a gable.

The view was better up here, too, but as she looked towards the sea, her courage almost failed. The sand-dunes that once sheltered the house had been wiped out so the full force of the North Sea poured down on the marsh. There was sea where the river used to be, and the boat sheds and fishermen's huts that lined the bank had been submerged or swept away. There was no sign of life anywhere. She was completely alone.

She tried shouting anyway, but her voice was blown away by the wind. The house bumped a final sickening time and tipped, and now it was afloat, listing as it turned at the mercy of the waves, the nails in the framework screeching as they were torn from their beds. Slowly but surely it was breaking apart. Still she clung to her perch. There was nothing else to be done. She was soaked through now and frozen almost beyond endurance. Shivers rattled her bones, but still she clung.

She was clutching the edge of the roof when first one wooden elevation, then another, parted company from the roof, hanging wide, to catch like sails in the wind. It was odd how warm she was feeling now, warm and drowsy, so drowsy. It would be lovely to let go and sleep, but she told herself to cling on. The rain was slackening, and as she watched the moon began to shine again, making a shimmering pattern across the water. How beautiful it was, that silvery light, how comforting. She must be the only person left in this dark, chaotic world, but she didn't mind any more. She was thinking of a picture she used to study in a children's Bible, of a mystical light brooding over the surface of the waters at the Earth's beginning. She'd always liked that picture. It made her feel safe, knowing the light would overcome the darkness.

This was her last thought as her fingers opened and she slid down into the water.

PART I

Chapter 1

Emily

London, the present

Berkeley Square, Mayfair. A November evening, twilight
fading into darkness. Street lights glowing in the misty
air. In the garden at the centre, the branches of great trees
formed filigreed shapes of black and silver, from which
cries of roosting birds contended with the grind and roar
of traffic. At this hour people passed through the square
on their way somewhere else, huddled warm in coats and
scarves, or shivering in short skirts and too-thin jackets.
Those heading for Tube station or bus stop walked
purposefully, eyes down, dodging the laughing groups
that drifted towards wine bar or pub. It was a Friday
night and London's offices were emptying fast.

On the east side of the square, next door to an art
gallery, stood a Georgian building, five or six storeys of
dark red brick. If any of the people passing had glanced
up they'd have seen the slender figure of a young woman
sitting at a second-floor window. The light from her desk
lamp picked up fiery glints in her feathery brown hair.
She was reading a manuscript and eating an apple. From
time to time she glanced out across the square. But she

did not see the slumbering garden or the lambent lights or the delicate rain beginning to streak the window. Her thoughts lay in a far country of the imagination.

There was something timeless about this girl, this scene. It might have been the present, or it might have been many years ago, sixty or seventy perhaps, for there was a 1950s feel to the round collar of her ivory blouse, the pretty cardigan and the stylish cut of her high fringe. She finished the apple and turned from the window, and for a moment it was impossible to tell whether she was typing on a computer keyboard or an old manual type-writer. Her small pointed face was grave, full lips parted, kohl-lined blue eyes dreamy, her gaze intent as she concentrated on her work. It was an expressive face: she frowned as she read, shook her head, wrinkled her short straight nose, then leaned back in her chair, hands clasped behind her head as though lost again in a world beyond the confines of office walls.

Emily was actually thinking she was hungry.

Her office at Parchment Press was deserted, she alone still at her workstation, one of several pens in the square high-ceilinged room. She'd been lucky to be given a desk by the window, especially since she was new. Many of the other editors strained their eyes under artificial light, and only a few, the most senior, had offices to themselves.

Everyone at Parchment was overworked and often stayed late, though rarely on a Friday. Emily, however, was waiting for her boyfriend, Matthew. He had prom-ised to meet her at six-thirty, but it had already gone seven and there was still no sign, which meant they'd have no time for a snack before the poetry book launch.

Her mind began to thrum with anxiety. This was not unusual these days where Matthew was concerned.

She reached down for another package from the untidy stack on the floor and glanced at the label. It was her turn this week to deal with the unsolicited scripts. Most aspiring writers sent them by email these days, and she wondered why these few still bothered to send them in the post. Perhaps they sensed it was too easy to delete an email. A parcel was unignorable. This one was addressed uninspiringly to *The Parchment Publisher* in sloppy block capitals, and when she pulled out the manuscript inside, her nose wrinkled at the reek of stale smoke. She scanned the writer's covering letter with distaste, balked at the trumpeted self-praise picked out in luminous green pen, then turned without hope to the first page, thinking maybe, just maybe, she might catch a voice, some pulse of life in the prose. There was none. She skipped to the middle to confirm that her search was in vain, then laid the script on the desk and began to type. Five minutes later, the offending item was back in its padded bag, readdressed. The author's own postage stamps appeared to gleam at her accusingly.

A picture came into her head of an ill-nourished man with nicotine-stained fingers reading her polite but firm refusal and uttering a cry of despair. At twenty-eight, after six years in the business, she still hated turning books down. She knew about the months, even years, some writers put into their work, the tender yearnings with which they sent it out into the world. But so many were not destined to succeed. She brushed some dust off her skirt and picked up the next package, resolved to harden her heart.

After sealing the final parcel she checked her phone. Seven-thirty. Still nothing from Matthew, no answer to her enquiring texts. She slicked on some lip gloss, pulled on a red coat, then went to the window, leaning her forehead against the cold glass as she peered out into the darkness, hoping to see a tall lean figure, long scarf flying, striding across the square, but there was only an old man taking an elderly Labrador for its evening constitutional.

She sighed, slipped her tote bag on her shoulder and scooped up the parcels for posting under one arm, which left her free to haul open the heavy fire door with the other.

Out in the lobby, the dim light from an antique chandelier flickered like candleflame, casting sinister shadows on a row of closed doors. She must be the only person left in the building, she thought uneasily. An empty post trolley had been abandoned by the lift and she stowed the packages in it. If only Matthew would hurry up. She would nip to the loo, then go and wait downstairs. As she walked across the lobby, she gave the wire post-racks an automatic glance, but the compartment with her name on it was empty.

When she emerged from the cloakroom a moment later, she was surprised to see the lift doors open. She caught a sideways glimpse of a woman inside – middle-aged, laden with bags – before they shut. Whoever she might have been, and there was no spark of recognition, it was plain that Emily wasn't the only soul working late after all. The thought was comforting.

Passing the pigeonholes on the way back to her desk, she paused. There was something in hers after all, pushed to the back. Common sense told her to leave it till Monday, but something made her reach in and pick it up.

It was a book, a small, worn hardback with yellowed, rough-cut pages and a jacket of cheap, unvarnished paper. It felt light and warm to the touch and she liked the way it fitted snugly in her hand. Who had left it for her and why? The picture on the front was a simple line-drawing in white on a dark, patterned background. It was of a heraldic shield with a plane flying across it. The plane must be in trouble, for the lettering of the title had been forged out of smoke swirling from the fuselage. Now she could make out the words *Coming Home*, which the damaged plane looked as though it wouldn't be. The helpful words *A Novel* were printed beneath the shield, but the jacket had been ripped at the bottom and the author's name was unreadable.

Emily was puzzled. Perhaps the book was meant for someone else – Gillian, her boss, for instance, whose cubbyhole above hers was, as always, overflowing? But when she angled the book to study the spine, she knew with a little shock that it was for her, after all. The author's name was Hugh Morton.

She moved nearer the chandelier to study the photograph on the back of the jacket. It was a monochrome portrait of Morton as an attractive young man; hard to believe he'd once looked like that, given the cragged-up, bulldog personage of his later years in the images that had dominated the obituaries of him. This portrait must have been taken in his late twenties, before he became well known, maybe before he published the phenomenal bestseller *The Silent Tide*. She considered the title again, *Coming Home*. He had written so many novels, but she didn't recall this one. She checked the publisher's logo on the spine – an M and an H, intertwined. *McKinnon & Holt*, it said underneath. She'd never heard of them. One of many publishers that had come and gone over the years.

She turned to the first page and stared. Under the title and the author's name was something scrawled in bold, black pen strokes. In the dim light it took a moment to work out what it said.

' "To Isabel, who makes everything possible," she read out loud. "With kind regards, Hugh Morton."'

Isabel. As she said the name the light overhead flickered, making the shadows dance. She wondered who Isabel might be.

Her eye moved to the bottom of the page where there was a date, 1949. Several years before *The Silent Tide* then, which she vaguely remembered was 1953. That was the book everyone spoke of when Hugh Morton was mentioned, the novel that made his name and his fortune. She'd read it a couple of times, the second quite recently when she'd joined Parchment, because it was one of the most famous books in their catalogue. It was the story of a woman, Nanna, who wanted to make her mark on the world but who ended up overwhelmed by circumstance. Somehow it struck a chord at the time it was published, and went on, unusually for a literary novel, to be a huge bestseller. It was also the book that became a curse for Hugh Morton. He could never again quite emulate its success in the whole of his long literary career. A not unfamiliar publishing story, but Emily couldn't imagine how it must feel for a writer to know his future was behind him.

And now her thoughts flew to the editorial meeting of the day before, in the old Regency boardroom with its views across Mayfair and its awful modern features – the long table of pale ash wood, the sleek plasma screen for presentations of budget figures and marketing plans.

The Publisher, Gillian Bradshaw, a tall, willowy woman who ran on nervous energy, had glared round the table at the half-dozen editors present and asked whether any of them knew Hugh Morton's work well. 'We're all familiar with *The Silent Tide*, of course. It's a staple of our classics list. But what about the others?'

'I've read *The Silent Tide*, naturally – find me some-one who hasn't,' one of the fiction editors said in her sophisticated, world-weary fashion. 'A TV adaptation is coming with Zara Collins playing Nanna. The fifties are still so popular.' A couple of other editors murmured that they'd read *The Silent Tide*. After all, it was on schools' reading lists. In the 1950s it was considered ground-breaking. 'That's the only one of his titles we own, isn't it?' she asked.

'I'm not sure,' Gillian replied. 'It's the only one in print, anyway. Morton had so many different publishers.'

'And kept falling out with them, I gather.' The fiction editor gave one of her amused smiles and began to exam-ine her long blue-polished fingernails.

Emily, still feeling very new and needing to prove herself, said, 'I've read three or four of the others. Our English teacher gave us an assignment. There was one set in the sixties, I remember, about a writers' retreat on an island . . .' She stopped, seeing that everyone was staring at her. She felt her face grow hot.

'We'll have to believe you there,' Gillian said, looking over her glasses at Emily in a not unkind fashion. 'I must admit that I, too, have only read *The Silent Tide*.' She with-drew a crisp, cream-coloured sheet from her pile of

papers and smoothed out the folds, then paused dramatically before continuing. 'As you all know, Morton died
two years ago. The funeral was just family, but I wrote to
his widow, Jacqueline, to offer our sympathies. She's sent
me what I think is an interesting proposal.'

She frowned as she scanned the letter. 'Here we are:
"You might know that my husband always resisted
approaches from biographers, disdaining the modern
lurid obsession with the purely personal. I have, however,
been approached by a young man who has, I believe, the
appropriate attitude to a writer of Hugh's stature, and
have allowed him access to Hugh's private papers. The
project being somewhat advanced, I should accordingly
like to arrange a meeting with you. As the current
publisher of *The Silent Tide,* I feel that you are the most
appropriate home for Hugh's biography.'

Gillian stopped and looked directly at Emily. 'Emily,'
she said, like a cat pouncing on a mouse, 'since you've
read more of the novels than the rest of us, I'd like you to
follow this up. La Morton clearly wants someone to go
and see her in Suffolk and I simply can't spare the time at
the moment.'

'Surely a life of Morton wouldn't exactly be a bestseller,' said a young man with curly blond hair, tapping
his pen on the table's edge. Emily found his arrogant
drawl irritating.

'You're possibly right, George, ' Gillian said, unruffled.
'But I still think there's more interest in him than you'd
expect, and the TV adaptation will add to that. By the
way, does anyone else remember that brilliant programme
about Morton in the eighties?' A couple of the older
editors nodded. 'You, George, would have been in

nappies at the time.' Everyone smiled and George gave a self-conscious snigger.

'You'll find the house absolutely fascinating,' Gillian remarked to Emily as she pushed the letter across the table. Emily took it, glancing at the address – Stone House, Salmarsh, in Suffolk – not sure whether the job was prestigious or a nuisance, and wondering if George was jealous that she'd been given it. Since he always spoke as though he knew best, it was difficult to tell.

'Biography of Hugh Morton, Becky,' Gillian told her assistant, who was taking notes. 'Put Emily's initials on the minutes.' She shuffled her papers and sighed. 'I'm sorry to be shifting so much of my work on you all at the moment, but with my Australian trip brought forward I've no alternative.'

Now Emily stood in the gloomy lobby examining the book, wondering if Gillian had left it for her. She hadn't managed to get through to Jacqueline Morton yet. She was just thinking that she must try again on Monday when her phone vibrated with a message: *Here now, Em. Where you? xx* She smiled and wrote back, *Coming.* Her mind now full of Matthew, she reached to replace the book in the pigeonhole, then hesitated. She ought to look at it properly.

She pressed the button for the lift and when its doors slid open, recalled the brief sight of the woman with the bags who'd left a few minutes ago. Like Isabel in the little book, her identity was a mystery.

Chapter 2

Isabel

London, November 1948

The petite redhead dressed in sherry brown hefted her suitcase off the bus on Earl's Court Road and shivered as a bitter wind caught her. She stopped to wrap her scarf more tightly round her neck and glanced about, unsure of her way. People flowed round her with eyes cast down, too busy picking their way across fractured pavements to stop for yet another refugee. Above, pewter-coloured clouds hung sullen with rain.

Nearby, a skinny youth selling newspapers breathed into his cupped hands to warm them.

'Excuse me, do you know Mimosa Road?' she asked him.

'Nex' left, Miss, and along a bit,' came the mumbled reply.

Thanking him, she picked up the heavy case and set off in the direction he had indicated, but the labyrinth of side streets where she found herself had no signs and she had to ask the way again, this time of a young mother with a toddler straining on its reins. Eventually she found herself on the doorstep of a handsome red-brick Victorian villa, one of the few still whole in a bomb-damaged terrace. It had to be the right house: someone had fastened a strip of card with a hand-scrawled 32 above the door, where a glass fanlight must once have been.

She hesitated, wondering not for the first time if she'd been rash to come. Since the alternative was to return home defeated, she raised the door knocker. It fell with a loud bright sound. While she waited, the worries chased through her mind. Suppose her aunt was away? Or didn't live here any more? She wished she'd had the sense to telephone ahead.

The door flew open to reveal not Aunt Penelope, but a wiry, flat-chested woman in a shabby overall, wielding a carpet beater. She had clearly been interrupted in her task for she was breathing hard, and strands of thin, iron-coloured hair escaped an untidy knot at her nape. From the expression on her face, it was plain that finding a strange young woman with a suitcase on the doorstep was an unwelcome interruption.

'Yes?' the woman snapped.

'I'm looking for Mrs Tyler,' the girl said, in as firm a voice as she could muster.

The woman studied her with a suspicious eye. 'You sellin' something?' she asked.

'Certainly not,' said the girl, drawing herself up to her full five feet two, glad that she'd taken trouble with her appearance before setting out. Not only had she purloined her mother's best hat, but also the precious remnants of a coral lipstick. This, she had been pleased to see in the mirror of the Ladies at Charing Cross station, suited her creamy skin, auburn hair and brown eyes to perfection.

The woman's mouth set in a hard thin line. 'This is Mrs

Tyler's residence,' she said, 'but she ain't here. Who might you be, Miss?'

'Isabel Barber. Mrs Tyler's niece.' The woman's eyebrows shot up in surprise. Isabel added less confidently, 'Please, may I come in? It's awfully cold.'

'I s'pose you'll 'ave to,' the woman sighed, opening the door wide. 'Wait in the parlour with the other one.'

Wondering who 'the other one' might be, Isabel left her case in the hall and the woman showed her into a chilly, over-stuffed sitting room at the front of the house that smelled strongly of coal-dust and wet dog. There, a small dapper man was struggling to secure a sheet of news-paper across the fireplace. He looked round at her entrance with an expectant expression, but seeing only Isabel, rearranged his face into a polite smile.

'Herself shouldn't be much longer,' the woman announced. She went away, pulling the door shut, and Isabel, to her alarm, found herself alone with the stranger.

'I'm afraid the coal is damp,' the man explained in heav-ily accented English as he held the paper, waiting for the fire to draw. She nodded, wondering who he was, and, what piqued her curiosity more, why he was wearing a dinner suit at half past eleven in the morning. The suit needed pressing, and though his smooth dark hair with its threads of grey was combed back neatly, his skin was drained of colour, his jaw unshaven. It struck her that he couldn't have changed since the night before, a thought she found shocking and thrilling at the same time. His undernourished appearance awoke her pity, though, and his expression was friendly.

'It is very cold today, yes?' he said, peering over the paper at the fire, which was beginning to roar.

'Very,' she agreed.

She sat gingerly in one of the two armchairs, pulled off her gloves and rubbed her hands together as she looked about. The room was dark, even for a day without sun, owing to a great honeysuckle that grew across the window outside, its tangled tendrils knocking on the glass in the wind.

Her aunt, she guessed, was fond of ornaments, and must be very sociable, for correspondence cards and invitations fought for space with china dogs and shepherdesses on the mantelpiece. There was a crowded bookcase against one wall. A slim book had been left open face down on a side table. She craned her head but couldn't make out the title or author.

'There,' said the man, lowering the newspaper and stepping back. In silent satisfaction they watched the fire, now leaping merrily. Soon the room started to feel cosy, rather than gloomy. Isabel unbuttoned her coat.

'Good.' The man tossed the folded paper into a box and balanced himself on the arm of the second chair, where he mopped his shiny face with a handkerchief. Finally he extracted a cigarette packet from his inside pocket and offered it to her.

'No, thank you, I don't,' she said, touched, for though he sought to disguise the fact, only one was left in the packet.

He took it himself, then paused, changing his mind. 'Save it for later,' he said with a shrug and put the packet away.

The lilt of his speech reminded her of someone. At the end of the war, three or four years ago, a Polish family had come to settle in the small Kent town where Isabel's family lived. It was the eldest boy, Jan, she came to know, a tall, narrow-framed lad with passionate eyes, who gave her a lift home once on the back of his bicycle. She smiled, remembering their laughter as they'd clattered down the hill, then frowned at the memory of her father's angry face at the door as the bike wobbled to a halt outside their pretty cottage. She still wasn't sure whether it was her hoydenish behaviour that had annoyed him more, or her association with a foreigner. All she knew was that her father had returned from the war a different man. Three cruel years in a prisoner-of-war camp in Bavaria had soured all his sweetness, making him prone to bouts of furious temper. She'd not seen Jan since last year, when her father found a better job and her family had to move near it. The ugly pebbledash house on the pre-war housing estate was only a dozen miles from her old school and the friends she'd grown up with, but it might as well have been a hundred.

The stranger was watching her now with an interest that was sympathetic rather than discomforting.

'It seems that we must make our own introducings,' he said. 'I am Berec, Alexander Berec.' He rose and offered her his hand with a gracious little bow that charmed her. Close up, she saw that, less charmingly, his eyes were puffy, with violet shadows beneath.

'I'm Isabel Barber,' she said for the second time that morning. Not Izzy, no more Izzy, she decided. 'You are waiting for my aunt? Well, of course you must be.'

'Mrs Tyler is your aunt?' Berec said, sitting down again. 'Ah, she is an admirable woman, is she not?'

'Is she?' Isabel said, breaking out in hope. 'You might think this odd, but I don't know her very well.'

She couldn't remember when she'd last seen Penelope. Five or six years ago, perhaps, soon after Isabel's grand-mother had died. Her elegantly dressed aunt had arrived by taxi in a cloud of scent with some paperwork for Isabel's mother to sign. Plainly ill at ease in the cramped cottage kitchen, she hadn't stayed long, but Isabel often thought of her and she came to represent the life she longed for, a life less ordinary than hers with its routine domesticity, her anxious mother's scrimping and saving. It made Isabel feel better that Berec thought Penelope admirable. Her parents certainly didn't seem to think so.

Berec looked curious, but before she could muster an explanation about the icy wastes that lay between the two sisters, they heard a frantic tripping of high heels on the path outside, then the front door banged and sounds of commotion came from the hall. Berec and Isabel jumped to their feet as the sitting-room door flew open and a large, slavering beast burst into the room, dragging a beautiful auburn-haired woman in its wake. Isabel backed away from the beast and into the shadows.

'For goodness' sake, Gelert,' the woman cried, losing her grip on its leash. The animal, a sort of big hairy grey-hound with a comical-looking bandage round its head, galloped over to Berec and greeted him rapturously. Isabel's attention, however, was fixed on the woman. Aunt Penelope's presence lit up the room. Expensively dressed, perfectly made-up, she was every bit as Isabel remembered: a younger, more glamorous version of Pamela Barber, Isabel's mother.

Penelope, pulling off her gloves, didn't appear to notice Isabel. 'Dear Berec, what a lovely surprise,' she said. 'We've been at the vet's. Gelert's been fighting again. Not his fault, poor boy, it's that awful pug at number four. It simply attacked him, with no provocation.' Gelert's tail whipped the carpet.

'Mrs Tyler, my dear Penelope, I'm so sorry about your poor animal,' Berec said, looking as hangdog as Gelert. 'I have come once more, I'm afraid, to throw myself on your gracious mercy. I returned home very late last night after dinner with friends, and Myra, once more she has locked the door against me. If you have a little money to lend me, only until Friday . . .'

'Oh, Berec,' Penelope Tyler said, folding her arms, as though admonishing a small boy. 'I must say, you do look a little . . . well, did you sleep on Gregor's floor again?' He nodded and she tutted. 'You're welcome to use the bathroom, of course.'

It was then that she saw Isabel. 'But you'd better introduce me to your friend.' Looking at her properly for the first time, Penelope's expression altered from polite interest through dawning recognition to blank amazement.

'H-hello,' Isabel said, stepping forward.

'She says she is your niece,' Berec said, looking from one to the other, bewildered.

'I know exactly who Isabel is, Berec,' Penelope told him. 'My dear child, what on earth—?'

'I had nowhere else to go,' Isabel interrupted, her voice quavering with emotion. 'They don't want me at home. Not really. I can't seem to do anything right and they're always cross with me.'

Now both her aunt and Berec were gaping at her in astonishment. Penelope broke the spell by moving close to place a finger beneath Isabel's chin and study the girl's face. 'Mmm,' she murmured again, releasing her. 'So you came to me. How very flattering.' She stepped back to take a longer view of her and did not seem pleased by what she saw. 'So it's your suitcase I tripped over in the hall. What have you got in it? Bricks?'

'Books,' replied Isabel.

'Ha!' Berec looked delighted at this.

Penelope frowned him into silence and said, ' Does your mother know you're here?'

'No,' said Isabel in a tight voice. 'I left a note, but didn't say where I'd gone.' They'd drag her back, she knew they would. She remembered the shouting match with her father at breakfast that morning, how he'd called her an 'idle slut'. After he'd stormed off to work she'd run upstairs and cast herself weeping on her bed. There she'd lain listening to her mother hustle Isabel's twin brothers off to school, then little Lydia being buckled into her pushchair, howling, for the daily trip to the shops.

Her mother called up the stairs, '*Izzy, washing-up!*' as she left the house.

Isabel had sat up, fuming. She was not an *idle* slut. Housework, child-minding, washing! That's all her parents thought she was good for. Well, she wouldn't put up with it any more. It was time to carry out her plan. She'd got up and flown furiously about, packing clothes and books and the little money she had. Casting one final look round the featureless house that had never felt like home, she tried to ignore the unwashed bowls, the toast crumbs on the floor, the basket of clothes for ironing. On the way out she had slammed the front door so hard that the last of the summer's geraniums shivered in their window box.

'I found you in Mummy's address book,' Isabel told

her aunt now. 'You were the only person I could think of to come to.' She tried a pleading look, but she found no sympathy in the other woman's face and the look faltered.

Isabel had never been sure why her mother disapproved of her younger sister so much, but supposed it was something to do with the fact that Aunt Penelope had somewhere along the way dispensed with her husband Uncle Jonny, though the exact circumstances had never been explained to the Barber offspring. She did know that Penelope lived in London and liked clothes very much, and going out, and that she didn't have any children. It all sounded so interesting and exciting, and the disparaging way her parents spoke about Penelope only lent her extra mystique in Isabel's eyes: references to 'the odd kind of people Penelope might know' or 'Penelope's idea of a good time'.

'I thought you had stayed on at school,' Penelope said severely. 'Last time I telephoned your mother, she told me you'd passed your exams with flying colours. How long ago was that? I've hardly spoken to her recently.'

'When we moved,' Isabel said, 'I'd just finished school. Now we're living in the middle of nowhere and there's nothing for me to do. That I want to do, I mean,' she added hastily. 'I won't be their skivvy any more, I just won't.' Her voice rose to a squeak. 'Please, can't I stay here with you, Aunt?'

'Goodness me, child, I can't have you living here. It's out of the question. But never mind that now. The most important thing to do is to telephone and let your mother know you're safe.'

'No!' Isabel cried. 'They'll only tell me to come home. I left a note. I was going to write to them – in a little while.

When I'd found a job and somewhere to live.' She sounded braver than she felt. In truth, she was in turmoil. If her aunt wouldn't have her, where could she go?

'And you imagine that these things will happen instantly?' Penelope said in a quiet voice. 'Isabel, we must at least assure them that you haven't been murdered or worse. I should be sorry to learn that you had grown up cruel.'

Isabel turned her face away, her mouth quivering. After a moment she mastered herself sufficiently to mutter, 'All right, you can telephone. But I'm not going back.'

'We'll see. I suppose, thinking about it, I could keep you here for a few days. Just a few days, mind. That would give everyone time to calm down. '

'Could you? I'm not . . .' Isabel started, but Penelope was already sweeping from the room. 'Ohhh,' the girl cried. She sank onto the sofa, arms crossed, her small face cast in misery.

'Do not despair.' She'd forgotten that Berec had been listening all this while. He was sitting by the fire, silently stroking the dog.

'How can I not? I've nowhere to go. I need a job – any job. What is it you do?'

Berec shrugged. 'This thing and that thing,' he said. 'I have to be free to write my poems. People like your aunt are very kind to me.'

'You're a poet, really?' she gasped, for a moment forgetting her troubles. He gestured to the book on the table before her and she reached and scooped it up. Sure enough, *Alexander Berec* was printed on the jacket. '*Reflections on a Strange Land,*' she read aloud. 'Is that this country, or where you came from?'

'You'll have to read and see,' he replied with a smile. She turned the pages, glancing at the poems. Decidedly melancholy, she thought them.

'My first collection,' Berec murmured. 'You will see, here.' He leaned forward and showed her a page near the beginning. A line read, *My thanks to Mrs Penelope Tyler for her generous support.* 'Your aunt,' Berec said proudly, 'she is my patroness.'

Isabel's mouth formed an O. Her aunt knew a poet and she, Isabel, had met him, this gentle, charming man. She looked up at him, her eyes shining. 'I love poetry,' she said. 'And books and reading. I wanted to go on to university, you know, but my father said it would be a waste of time.'

Berec clapped his hands together. 'I guessed you were an intellectual young woman,' he said, amused. 'Why, I tell you what, I will introduce you to some people. Come along tonight. Wait.' He fished the newspaper out of the coal-box, tore off a corner, then using his own book as a rest, scribbled an address.

'Six o'clock this evening,' he whispered, passing the piece of paper to Isabel just as the door handle turned. 'I'll wait for you outside.'

Isabel thrust the precious scrap deep in her coat pocket just as Penelope re-entered the room. The girl looked up eagerly, but something sombre in her aunt's face alarmed her.

'What did my mother say?' she asked, rising to her feet.

'It wasn't she who answered,' Penelope said, biting her crimson lower lip.

'Not my father?'

'She found your note and panicked, called him home from the office.'

'Oh.' He'd be furious.

'What he said was . . . well, I'm afraid you're to return home immediately. He is, I think, a little upset.'

Isabel took a step back. 'I won't go. He can't make me.'

'And if you don't go, he says – my dear, I'm sure he doesn't mean it – that he doesn't want you back at all.'

'Oh,' Isabel repeated, full realisation of her situation dawning.

'I'm unsure what to advise. Can you really not go back?'

'I can't, it's simply impossible.'

'I see. Well, I suppose you may stay here for a night or two. A short while. Until you find work, perhaps.' Penelope was reasoning with herself.

'Could I not live here if I paid my way? I'd not be any trouble.'

'Isabel, it wouldn't work.'

Though wrapped up in her own concerns, Isabel caught a sudden glimpse of secrets her aunt kept close.

The address Alexander Berec had given her took her north of Oxford Street, to a tall, narrow Georgian house in Percy Street, on a corner at a junction where the road curved in a sort of elbow. A painted sign, palely visible in the lamplight, announced it to be the offices of McKinnon & Holt Publishers. Curtains were drawn across the ground-floor windows, but chinks of light, snatches of voices and laughter betrayed a party going on within. There was no sign anywhere of Berec, but as she hovered outside, mustering the courage to ring the bell, he came hurrying round the corner. 'Isabel,' he cried, kissing her cheeks. 'I am so pleased you came. Mrs Tyler . . . ?'

'I'm afraid I told her I was going to meet a friend.' Isabel was relieved to see that he looked more spruce than he had that morning.

'Why, that is exactly what you have done,' Berec replied, going up the steps and pressing the bell. 'I am your good friend.'

'What is the party for?' Isabel asked, as they waited to be admitted.

'It's not for anything, I don't think – just a literary party,' he replied.

The door opened to reveal a solidly built, pleasant-looking man of around thirty with fair hair brushed to one side and a fresh, sensitive face.

'Come in, both of you, come in,' he cried. 'Berec, the ladies had almost given up on you.' He ushered them into a big, shabby hallway lined with piles of cardboard boxes where half a dozen people hung about talking. It smelled excitingly of cigarettes and alcohol.

'And this must be . . . Mrs Berec?' The man put out his hand to shake Isabel's, his expression polite but uncertain.

'No, no,' Berec said, with a laugh. 'Myra conveys her apologies, but she is once again indisposed. Stephen, may I introduce my young friend, Miss Isabel Barber? Isabel, this is Stephen McKinnon, my publisher – the best, may I say, in London.' These last words were spoken with one of his gallant little bows.

'Miss Barber, enchanted,' Stephen said, looking askance at Isabel.

Berec rushed on. 'I see I must explain. Stephen, Miss Barber and I met at Penelope Tyler's home this morning. She is Mrs Tyler's niece, a most intellectual sort of girl.

Isabel has only recently arrived in London and needs to find suitable work. I immediately thought of you.'

'How very considerate,' Stephen McKinnon murmured.

'I'm sorry,' Isabel said, feeling far out of her depth. 'You must think it awfully rude of me, turning up like this.'

'Not at all,' Stephen said. 'I know your aunt and am glad to have you. Come in and meet everyone. Excuse us, gentlemen, please,' he said to a group being lectured on politics by a short stout man with fiery eyes and a low, passionate voice. Stephen led Berec and Isabel past them into a noisy room packed full of people.

At once, a chubby, middle-aged woman with a low-necked dress and too much face powder came to meet them. 'Ha, Berec,' she said. 'You're just in time to settle an argument about great Czech poets. There's a man here says there aren't any.'

'That's perfidious, Mrs Symmonds! Isabel, please excuse me,' Berec said, as the woman dragged him away.

Beside her, Stephen chuckled. 'Berec gets on with everyone, but particularly the more mature ladies.' He handed her a glass of whisky. 'They like to mother him. Your aunt is a case in point. A truly nice woman, and very generous to impoverished writers.'

'Why doesn't his wife look after him?' Isabel asked. She'd liked Stephen immediately, sensed there was some-thing very straight about him. She didn't mind that he regarded her now with amusement.

'I have never met Myra Berec and am not even certain that they have, er, exchanged marital vows,' Stephen said gravely. 'But I've not enquired too closely into Berec's past or indeed his present. He is a man of great talents and has a gift for friendship that proves very useful on occasion. Him bringing you here is typical.' He smiled.

'He meant me to ask you about a job,' Isabel rushed in, taking advantage of the smile.

'I'm afraid that, too, is typical Berec,' Stephen said, the smile turning regretful. 'Sometimes he acts before he thinks. I can't afford to employ anyone else at the moment. Business is very tight. There are too many writers and not enough people who buy their books.'

'Oh,' she said, crestfallen.

'I hope something turns up for you soon,' he said. 'If I hear of anything, of course . . . Ah.' A large man of about sixty, with sad eyes and an untidy moustache, had shambled through the door. 'That is the great William Ford,' he whispered. 'Or so he likes to think of himself. I'm afraid I must ask you to excuse me for a moment.' Isabel watched him greet the man and pour him a drink. For a while she was completely alone. She didn't mind. It had been a long day, a momentous day, and not without its disappointments. She was too tired for bright conversation with strangers. She took a tentative sip of the whisky and screwed up her face. It tasted like castor oil. She swallowed it hastily and it burned her throat, but she liked the warmth it spread inside. The second sip was a little better and she allowed herself to relax and take in her surroundings.

This room must once have been a reception room, but was now furnished as an office, with a big mantelpiece above a blocked-up fireplace, and windows on three sides hung with blackout curtains. The twenty other people in the room were about all it could accommodate amongst several large desks, an elderly dining table on which bottles and glasses were laid out, bookshelves, piles of paper, potted plants and other assorted paraphernalia. A delightful, messy collage of book covers and newspaper cuttings decorated the wall by which she stood. These she perused eagerly, without recognising any of the titles and hardly any of the authors. There were lists and notices: mysterious charts concerning paper and typesizes; handwritten instructions regarding petty cash and returning the key to the lavatory. There was a poster printed in clear capitals to simulate carving in stone. She began to read it with a deep sense of thrill:

THIS IS A PRINTING OFFICE, it said, CROSSROADS OF CIVILISATION, REFUGE OF ALL THE ARTS AGAINST THE RAVAGES OF TIME, ARMOURY OF FEARLESS TRUTH.

'Isabel, did you speak to Stephen about employment?' She swung round to see Berec.

'Well, yes,' she said, touched by his persistence, 'but he said there isn't anything. He can't afford to pay.'

'What nonsense,' Berec growled, his normal good-temper ruffled. 'You must speak to him again. We will *both* speak to him.'

'But if he has nothing, what is the point?'

'Nonsense,' Berec said again. 'He has some successes. Maybe not with poetry, but Miss Briggs's romances sell well. He must expand. He needs another editor, he can't rely on Trudy Symmonds for everything.' He bent close and whispered in her ear, 'I don't care *who* she's married to, the woman has no soul. Not like you. You have soul. I can always tell in here.' He struck his chest with a clenched fist and said something resonant in his own language.

'I can't be an editor,' Isabel said. 'I know nothing about it. I mean, I read and read – but that's all.'

'Read widely and believe in your judgement. One day you will be an editor. You are an intellectual, I tell you. I always know.' He gave a broad smile.

'You are kind to me, Mr Berec,' she said, her voice trembling. 'Nobody has ever said encouraging things like that to me before, certainly never my parents.' Was it only this morning that she'd been living at home, being ordered to wash up? 'Why do you say them? You don't know me at all.'

'I know Mrs Tyler. I would do anything for her. You are her niece. Come, I want to help you. We will speak to Stephen together, when he finishes with that bitter old man Ford. Twenty-four novels, ha. The same novel twenty-four times, is what I say. Give the money to some-one who deserves it.'

'Shh, he'll hear you,' Isabel said, giggling, but the big moustachioed man was rambling away to Stephen, impervious to distraction. Finally, Berec persuaded Mrs Symmonds to intervene.

'Stephen,' Berec said, catching his sleeve, 'come, I must speak to you seriously. You have an opportunity. This young lady, you can't turn her away.'

Isabel, seeing the expression on Stephen's face turn from polite good humour to annoyance, couldn't help bursting out, 'Please, Mr Berec. Mr McKinnon isn't inter-ested, it's quite clear. And I couldn't work for anybody who didn't really want me. I would simply die.' She spoke with such passion that she found both men silent, staring at her. 'I'm sorry,' she mumbled. She put down her glass clumsily, so Stephen had to steady it. 'Perhaps I should go home now. I'm really quite . . . exhausted.'

She started to move away, but Stephen touched her

arm. 'Wait.' He was perusing her as though he hadn't seen her properly before.

'I want to help you,' he told her, 'but I stand by what I said. There is no position at the present time that I can offer you. I simply have no spare money. I rely on the financial support of a gentleman whose factory makes ladies' shoes. Every book I publish seems to lose money.'

'Except Miss Briggs's romances.' Berec put in.

'What the *Daily Mail* calls Maisie Briggs's "enterprising heroines" may indeed prove to be our salvation,' Stephen McKinnon said, his eyes twinkling.

'My mother simply devours Maisie Briggs,' Isabel told him, cheered by this change of mood.

'Devours her, does she?' Stephen grinned. 'And what is it that you *devour*, Miss Barber?'

'Oh, I like anything,' Isabel said, filling up with happiness at his attention. 'I mean, I'll try anything. My parents don't understand at all. If my father sees me reading, he tells me to go and do something. I say *I am* doing something – I'm reading – but he thinks that's being pert.'

At this, Stephen threw his head back and laughed, but Berec's expression was horrified. 'You poor child,' he breathed. 'Stephen, you must do something. The forces of ignorance must not be allowed to triumph. '

Stephen assumed an expression of amiable defeat. 'Look here, I must go and speak to my other guests,' he said. 'Miss Barber, please. Would you come and see me tomorrow? I can at least give you some advice. Audrey,' he called. A poised young woman with a pretty upturned nose pushed herself off the desk she was sitting on and sauntered across. 'Audrey, what am I doing tomorrow morning?'

'Chuck over my diary, someone.' Audrey consulted a black notebook and read out, 'Mr Greenford with the quarterly accounts at ten, the man from Unicorn Printing at eleven-thirty, lunch at La Scala with James Ross's agent.'

'Eleven then, does that suit?' he asked Isabel, who nodded. 'Audrey, this is Miss Isabel Barber. Put her down for interview at eleven.'

'Interview?' Audrey gave Isabel a cool up-and-down stare, then scribbled what looked like *Isabelle Barba* in the diary. Isabel didn't dare correct her.

'You see?' Berec said later, as he put her in a taxi and pressed into her hand the ten-shilling note he'd just cadged. 'I knew Stephen would see sense.'

Isabel, riding the cab through the dark, unfamiliar streets, was not so sure. Mr McKinnon was humouring Berec. It seemed that everyone succumbed to his charm. As for her, she was wound up to a pitch of intensity that only a very young person can feel. In that untidy office with its interesting posters, all those people and their talk about books and ideas, things she thought really mattered, she had seen something she wanted. Not just wanted: she had set her heart on it with every drop of feeling she possessed.

Chapter 3

Emily

London, the present

'Matthew, how did you get in?'

The street door of Parchment Press was kept locked after hours, so Emily stepped out of the lift unprepared to see Matthew in the hallway, the wings of his thick black hair glistening with mist. In the low light, with his shadow of beard and his eyes glinting like chips of blue granite, he looked like an exotic pirate. Then he smiled in that vulnerable, lopsided way she loved as he came forward to greet her, and he was Matthew, nice and familiar again. For a moment she forgot she was cross with him for being late. His kiss tasted deliciously of spearmint and rain.

'Some woman let me in on her way out,' he explained as he pushed the button to release the door. 'No idea who she was, but she seemed to know me.' He hung back to let Emily through first. The world outside was cold and shiny, but the rain had thankfully ceased.

'She must be mad, letting riffraff like you into the building,' she teased.

'I expect she knows a promising poet when she sees

one,' he retorted and Emily laughed. 'Sorry about being late, Em. I was in the library and didn't notice the time.'

'For a whole hour?' she asked severely, but he was already bounding down the steps and didn't hear. She followed more cautiously in her high-heeled ankle boots. It was difficult to be cross with him for long.

'Come on, cutting across Bond Street will be quickest,' Matthew said, taking her arm. 'We can look at the Christmas lights.'

Tonight's event, the launch of a poetry anthology to which Matthew had contributed, was taking place in an old pub in Soho. Emily, who always felt guilty that she was earning a proper salary when he was managing on bits and pieces, bought drinks and crisps at the bar and they carried them up a narrow staircase to a spacious room at the top. The place was filling up fast. Whilst Matthew went to check his place in the running order to read aloud, she looked about uncertainly, feeling a bit on the sidelines.

The room must have been intended for night-time use. It was painted black from floorboards to ceiling, which in daylight would feel oppressive, but which now merely conveyed an impression of dark intimacy. She inspected the photographs that flanked the walls – bizarre shots of pets and farm animals in gothic costumes that made her feel uncomfortable. Above the hum of voices, electronic whistles and wailings assaulted her ears as someone tested the sound system.

Finally the racket ceased and Matthew reappeared. 'I'm on first,' he said, with a grimace, 'so I'll see you later.'

'At least you'll get it over with,' she pointed out.

'There is that,' he replied with a smile, and disappeared into the crowd.

Emily moved over to a table where piles of the anthology lay on display. She'd already seen Matthew's copy, of course, but she wanted to buy her own, though there was nobody to take her money. She picked up one of the books, studied the Contents page and turned to Matthew's poems, taking a professional pleasure in how attractively laid out they were.

'Sorry, I'm here now,' came a light female voice and Emily glanced up to see a nut-brown wisp of a girl with gypsy-black eyes standing before her clutching a foaming pint glass. 'The queues at the bar were really bad. I hope no one's nicked any books. Did you see?'

'I don't think so. I want to buy mine. '

'Only seven pounds tonight. Or two for thirteen, unlucky for some.' She gave a little laugh. How perfect her white embroidered shirt looked against her complexion, Emily thought as she slid a banknote out of her purse. 'I'll have one. Do *you* have anything in it?' she asked to be polite.

The girl managed to nod as she drank the head off her beer then licked foam neatly from her upper lip like a cat. 'A photograph. Page nine. Lola Farrah, that's me.' Her smile revealed small, even teeth. She put down the glass and rummaged in her shoulder purse for change. 'A group of us put the book together. It was Matthew Heaton's idea. Do you know Matthew?'

'I'm Emily Gordon,' Emily said. 'And yes, I do know Matthew.'

'He's lovely, isn't he?' the girl sighed. 'I adore his poems.'

'So do I,' Emily said, feeling a touch possessive. She was wondering how to hint at her relationship with Matthew, when a voice came over the sound system.

'It's my pleasure to introduce the first of our readers this evening.' The speaker was Matthew's tutor, Tobias Berryman. Tall and balding, with piercing eyes, he commanded the room.

Matthew moved to the microphone and as he read, Emily tried to concentrate on the words, rather than the beguiling timbre of his voice. She knew the first poem by heart because she'd helped him practise: 'No one tells the rain where it may fall' was how it began. It was about the random nature of where we love, and she always found it very moving.

Tonight he was nervous and read a little too quickly, but the applause was enthusiastic. She watched with pride, seeing his pleasure at the response before he bowed his head and stepped down. As the next reader took his place at the microphone she sensed him return to her side. 'You were great!' she whispered in his ear and he smiled.

There were more readings, and lots more drinks, and the conversation grew livelier, the laughter louder, the room hotter. Standing on the fringes, Emily espied the slender brown girl, Lola, curl her arm round Matthew's neck in a hug, but then the big, moleskin-jacketed figure of Tobias Berryman insinuated itself, blocking the view. 'Emily, it's good to see you,' Tobias said, in his warm, suave way. Now in his early forties, Tobias was a prize-winning poet. She'd met him before, at similar occasions, and Matthew often talked about him, sometimes with admiration, sometimes with fury, depending on how a tutorial or a workshop had gone.

'It's been a wonderful evening,' Emily told Tobias. 'They're a really talented bunch, your students.'

'They are a strong group this year. And what do you think of our little book? Published on a shoestring, of course, but I don't think Matthew and his team have done too badly.'

'It's beautiful.'

'And you're meeting a few of the poets, I expect. Anyone I can introduce you to?'

'No, really, I'm here for Matthew. And Parchment doesn't publish poetry, so I'm off-duty tonight.'

'I know that, but I'll bet you're always keeping a look out,' he said. His eyes twinkled like a roguish uncle. But suddenly he became more confidential. 'In fact, I'm having a stab at a novel myself. I was wondering if I might send you my first draft.'

'Yes, of course,' she said, rather surprised. 'May I ask what sort of thing?'

'Oh, it's very noir. Echoes of Marlowe. Anyway, see what you think.'

'How intriguing.' Emily wondered what on earth 'echoes of Marlowe' meant. 'It sounds highbrow.' She privately feared it would be unreadable.

He laughed. 'I sincerely hope so. Of course, perhaps it won't suit a commercial firm like Parchment.' She realised that under the charm he was nervous.

'I'll happily take a look,' she promised. 'I can advise, at least.' Tobias had shifted slightly and now she could see Matthew again, though his back was turned. Lola, she noticed, was still standing close, but they were part of a larger group of students all laughing and chatting as they signed each other's books.

She tried to concentrate on what Tobias was saying – something about needing to acquire a literary agent – but now, out of the corner of her eyes, she became aware that she was being watched. Standing beyond Tobias, near the door, was a man she'd never seen before. He was a year or two older than her, thirty perhaps, with shoulder-length tawny hair and a certain ease of presence. He was standing on his own, but he didn't look as though this bothered him. She met his eye and he smiled a secretive smile. She smiled back and for a moment it looked as though he was about to come over and speak to her, but then someone else touched his arm and he turned to speak to them instead.

'. . . so do you have any hints about agents?' Tobias was asking her, and once more Emily attempted to focus on him, but was still intrigued by the man who had smiled at her. She didn't know why, there was just something about him. Later, she happened to glance up and saw him leaving. Interestingly, he was with Tobias.

It was almost midnight when they got home to Matthew's flat. 'I'm absolutely shattered,' Emily said, resting against the peeling wallpaper of the upstairs landing, while Matthew wrestled with the lock. 'And *sooo* hungry.'

'Tea and sushi coming up, Miss,' Matthew said, shoving open the door. They'd stopped at a takeaway bar near the Tube station.

After leaving the pub they'd argued amiably about whose home to go to – the two-room upstairs flat of this shabby Victorian cottage in South London, or Emily's more up-to-date apartment in the better part of Hackney. Matthew had won because, although tomorrow was

Saturday, he needed to get up early and work on an assignment.

Inside, he laid down his bags. 'Sorry about the mess,' he told her. He went round the little living room switching on lamps and closing the curtains that never did quite meet in the middle, then took the takeaway into the kitchen where he could soon be heard clattering about with plates and cutlery.

Emily kicked her ankle boots off with relief and sank onto the sofa. She glanced about. 'Mess' was the right word. Everything spoke endearingly of Matthew. Random piles of books and paper covering every surface. A laptop left open on the floor by the telly, its blue battery light winking. Half-empty coffee cups. He used this room to work in when he wasn't at college, supplementing his meagre grant by writing articles for newspapers and websites. Sometimes he drafted marketing blurbs for a small PR consultancy, in whose offices he'd been employed at one time; it paid better, though the work no longer engaged him. Emily knew he'd muddled along in this way for several years after university before deciding to return to his old college to take a part-time Creative Writing Masters. Poetry was his passion, it always had been, but he would be very unlikely ever to make a living from it. If he was good enough, he'd told her, and went on to make his name, he'd at least be able to stitch a patchwork career around poetry, doing bits of teaching, journalism or arts administration, and he'd be happy with that. Whatever he ended up doing, it would be vital to be able to fence off time to write.

She went to see what was happening. 'I'll make the tea if you like ... My God, Matthew.' She surveyed with horror the stacks of dirty plates and saucepans that littered the surfaces of the galley kitchen. Strands of sodden spaghetti snaked out of the pedal bin.

Matthew, opening plastic takeaway boxes in the only clear space, said sheepishly, 'I didn't have a chance to clear up.' Two of his brothers, she remembered, had come round for supper the previous night to watch the match on the telly.

She sighed as she unplugged the kettle.

'No, Em,' he said, taking it from her. 'I'll deal with everything – you relax.'

'I can wash up,' she said brightly.

'No, it's midnight. I'll do it tomorrow after you've gone.' He went back to serving out food. 'If I hadn't been so busy . . . Tell you what, fancy swapping one of your temaki for my nigiri?'

'Yes, OK,' she said. 'You *are* busy, you know.'

'Busy is what I do at the moment,' he said, turning to switch on the kettle. 'I have to get through the next ten months and then it'll be easier.' September was when he had to hand in his final dissertation.

'It's a shame if it gets in the way of us.' Ten months seemed an age.

'Hey, you're not still cross about last weekend?' he asked gently. 'I thought we'd got over that one.'

'It's not that.' It was in part, though. She bit her lip as she recalled their argument – well, it wasn't an argument, she told herself, more of a disharmonious episode. The previous Saturday, her sister had turned thirty and their parents had organised a family dinner in a hotel near their home in Hertfordshire. At the last moment Matthew had said that he couldn't come, since he had a long newspaper article to research and write. Her mother and father were quite put out, and so was she. When she'd tried to talk about it, Matthew had been defensive and now she sensed it wouldn't do to dwell on it. After all, they hadn't known one another very long.

It was only five months ago that they'd each found themselves out-of-place singles at a supper party given by some very smug married friends and had stuck together all evening. When he'd described what his life was like, she'd thought it marvellously bohemian. Now she saw the reality, and she couldn't expect him to change everything for her. After all, her work commitments were formidable, too. So many evening events and copious reading at weekends.

'You do look fed up, love.' He put down the fork he was holding and drew her into his arms. She closed her eyes, feeling herself melt against him. How right this always was. He pushed back her hair and kissed her eyelids then his mouth found hers. She loved his tender-ness, the way he held her.

'Cheer up, Little Bird,' he said, when they came up for air, and his nickname for her brought a rush of happiness. 'Please cheer up. I know things aren't easy. We're both trying to establish ourselves at the moment, working at what we love. You're doing what you like, right?'

'Yes, of course.' Emily loved her job, had been thrilled when Parchment had headhunted her from another firm.

'We're both very lucky then.'

'Yes,' she sighed, as he released her. 'Sorry, I'm tired, that's all. And hungry. '

'So let's eat,' he said, picking up the plates. 'Can you bring the tea?'

Emily cleared a space on the coffee table and they sat together on the sofa, half-watching a late-night stand-up on the television as they ate. Soon she began to feel better.

'That was delicious,' she said, putting down her plate. 'I did enjoy tonight,' she added.

'It was cool, wasn't it? We sold a few books, too.'

'I've got mine here.' She took it from her handbag and flicked through it. 'I loved your reading, Matt. You were great, you really were.'

'I sounded nervous,' he said, slurping his tea. 'I'm sorry you didn't know many people there.'

'I was fine, honest,' she said vaguely. She'd stopped at a full-page photograph. It was by that girl Lola, the one who'd sold her the book. The picture was effective in a chocolate-boxy way, she had to admit, a soft-focus shot of a rumpled bedsheet, scattered with rose petals. She remembered Lola flirting with Matthew, tactile, vivid, laughing. She closed the book, pushing the memory from her mind. 'I talked to Tobias,' she told him.

'Oh yes? What did he have to say?'

'Only guess what, he's writing a novel. It's hopeless being a publisher at parties. People either ask you to recommend a good book, however you define that, or tell you about one they want to write.'

'I suppose it's better than being an investment banker or a policeman.'

She grinned. 'A doctor's got to be the worst. Everybody telling you about their aches and pains.'

'Seriously, anything Tobias writes is likely to be good.'

'We'll have to see,' she said, yawning.

After they'd made love into the big bed that filled the whole of the tiny bedroom, Matthew fell asleep immediately, but despite being tired Emily was wakeful. The throb of party music came from somewhere down the street. Anxious thoughts spooled through her mind. She felt dissatisfied, but couldn't for the life of her think why. She tried to rationalise her feelings, which her best friend Megan, who was heavily into therapy, was always telling her to do. The new job wasn't going badly, though she ought to prove herself by acquiring one or two promising new authors soon. She was going out with this gorgeous man sleeping beside her, but she had no idea where the whole thing was going, indeed if it was going anywhere. Somewhere there lay the truth of the matter. She sensed that Matthew lived for the moment. He was concentrating on his studies and happy not making plans for the future. He wasn't interested in making money, not that she minded that in itself, but he lived like a student and although she'd at first been enchanted by this unworldliness, now it was beginning to get to her. She had never thought about the business of settling down before, but recently, something within her had begun to change.

The night was chilly and she snuggled up more closely to the slumbering Matthew, breathing in the salty scent of him, but she was still hopelessly wide awake. She thought of all the reading she had to get through that weekend, and wondered whether Matthew had any of Hugh Morton's books on his shelves. She ought to look at *The Silent Tide* again and had forgotten to hunt for a copy in the office. At least she'd got *Coming Home* in her bag, his first novel, it must have been. She wondered where home was for her. Her comfortable Hackney bolthole, perhaps, though that could be lonely sometimes. She loved returning to her childhood home in semi-rural Hertfordshire, but it wasn't home for her any longer, not really, she'd grown beyond it. And Matthew's flat was too chaotic to feel homelike.

The boom boom boom of the party cut off suddenly, and then there was only the distant drone of traffic that in London never ceased.

Chapter 4

Isabel

1948

It was Audrey, the secretary with the gamine looks and the upturned nose, who answered the door of McKinnon & Holt on the morning of Isabel's interview. Her smile was condescending as she led the girl through the shabby room, from which the detritus of the party had been cleared away. Leading off it was a small, book-lined office, where they found Stephen McKinnon reclining in his chair, feet up on the desk, talking on the phone. He removed his feet smartly when the women entered, and waved Isabel to a chair. Audrey departed, leaving the door ajar. Sitting across from him, she listened while he argued furiously with someone at the other end of the line in a mysterious language of profits and percentages, and scribbled figures on a pad. She glanced about the office, noticing the books, the scattered piles of manuscripts, the posters on the wall about book launches and art exhibitions. On the windowsill was propped a photograph in a frame of a fair-haired woman in a wedding dress. It had faded somewhat.

Finally Stephen McKinnon put down the receiver,

scrawled a circle round one of the numbers on his pad, and sighed heavily. He looked up at Isabel and had opened his mouth to speak, when the phone began to ring. 'Get that, Audrey, will you?' he roared. Audrey must have heard for the ringing stopped. He stared at the phone, as though it might burst into flames, then smiled at Isabel and said in a friendly tone, 'Well now.' There was something boyish about him; it was that frank, eager kind of face, and again she thought how much she liked him.

'You look as though you have too much to do,' she said.

'It's always a madhouse, this time of year,' he replied, rumpling his hair. 'The shops want their Christmas orders, and we've the spring list to prepare.' There was a knock and Audrey put her head round the door. 'In heaven's name, what now?'

'It's Harold Chisholm on the phone,' she said. 'He won't tell me what it's about, but apparently it can't wait.'

'Dash it, it'll have to. Tell him I'll ring him later,' he snapped, and she rolled her eyes and disappeared again.

'Chisholm always says it can't wait,' he explained. 'Writers don't have enough to do, you see. They sit in their garrets fretting when they're supposed to be writing. They forget that their publishers have other authors, other things to do. Like selling their damn books. Sorry.' He smiled cheerfully at her again. 'Now, how can I help?'

He seemed to have forgotten their conversation at the party the previous evening, and for a brief moment Isabel's confidence ebbed. Half the night, it seemed, she had lain awake thinking about all she'd seen and heard. She'd gone over and over what she would say to him, this man who couldn't afford to employ her, who said there was no job, but who had still been persuaded to receive her today. She had, she felt, this chance and no other. And now he appeared so sympathetic. Suddenly it all tumbled out.

'I want to do something useful, important, and I think this might be what I'm looking for,' she said, not daring to look at him. 'I'm aware of the power of words. Sometimes I write, oh, bits of stories and poems. I know I'm not very good yet, but here, yes, here, I could help others with their books. Does it matter that I'm very young? I need to be given a chance.'

She saw his expression then and stopped. Somehow these words, which had sounded so clear and reasonable in her head in the cold darkness of her aunt's spare bedroom, sounded silly and plaintive in the hallowed light of a publishing office. McKinnon was watching her intently, a slightly amused look on his face.

'Go on,' he said.

She closed her eyes and took a deep breath.

'I can type – quite fast actually. They taught us at school in case we needed to earn our living, that's what they said. I want a job. I need one. There must be something I can do. And I like all this. Here, I mean.'

'Oh, there's plenty to do here, all right.' She waited, worrying that she was losing him. 'And I'm sure you'd do. It's just I can't afford to pay anyone.'

Just then Audrey interrupted again. 'Your half past eleven's here, Mr McKinnon. And I forgot to say, the man from the *Mail* rang earlier.'

'Damn. I needed to speak to him. Get him back, will you?'

Audrey withdrew and he snatched up a newspaper from a wire tray and pushed it across the desk to Isabel. 'What d'you think of this?' he said, and pointed. It was folded to an advertisement for a female film star's biography, with McKinnon & Holt's colophon beside it. She stared at it. Everything seemed to be neatly designed and correctly spelled.

'It's . . . very nice,' she said politely, wondering if this was the right thing to say.

'And?' he said eagerly.

She looked at it again, then her eye strayed to the article next to it. Suddenly she realised what was wrong.

'Why would they put it on the sports page?' she asked.

'Precisely,' he said. 'This is the kind of rubbish I have to put up with every day. My advice, Miss Barber? You don't want to work for a publisher. The hours can be long and business is precarious. Much work can be expended on books that are ultimately, by anyone's standards, a failure. On the other hand, it can be irksome when books of extreme triviality triumph.'

'I understand that,' she said earnestly, 'but it doesn't put me off.'

'It should do.' He lit a cigarette and contemplated her through a veil of smoke. Finally he sighed and said, 'I can see it's no use. Look, as I say, we are particularly busy at the moment. If you don't mind knuckling down straight away, Miss Foster out there has quite a backlog of correspondence. It'll only be until Christmas. I can't promise anything longer. ' He pushed back his chair and stood up. The interview was over.

'Thank you,' Isabel said, feeling as light as a feather. 'I am so grateful. I'll start tomorrow. Today. I can start now.'

'Tomorrow will do. As for your remuneration. Well . . . three pounds a week.' It was a sum even Isabel knew was modest. He opened the door for her.

Outside, Audrey was typing briskly. Further down the room Mrs Symmonds, the portly over-made-up woman she'd seen at the party, was at her desk making pencil marks on a thick manuscript. On a chair by the door sat the printer's representative, a lugubrious man with a briefcase and a navy raincoat. Seeing Stephen McKinnon, he rose expectantly to his feet, but no one took any notice.

'Oh, Mr McKinnon,' Audrey said. 'I'm sorry, the man from the *Mail* isn't at his desk.'

'Keep trying. Listen, Audrey, you'll need to clear some-where for Miss Barber to sit. She'll be helping you from tomorrow. No buts, please. Goodbye, Miss Barber.' He shook hands with Isabel, then turned his attention to the man with the briefcase. The office door closed behind the two men.

Audrey squared a ream of paper by banging it on the desk as she looked Isabel over. She was clearly not pleased by what she saw.

'Looks like I won my bet, Trudy,' she remarked to Mrs Symmonds. Trudy Symmonds peered over her glasses at Isabel, and her chin sank into her fleshy neck as she gave a deep chuckle.

'What do you mean?' Isabel asked, thinking them very rude.

Audrey shrugged. 'It's just a private joke. Come on, you'd better give me a hand with this lot.' There was a battered desk pushed against a wall from which she started moving boxes onto the floor and Isabel hurried to help.

She was puzzled by Audrey's attitude. She'd thought the young woman would welcome an assistant. Perhaps Audrey believed she would make a hash of it. Well, she wouldn't. She was determined to prove her worth.

She loved it at once. Not the tasks themselves, which were largely menial and often boring. Audrey kept her supplied with anything she herself didn't want to do: copy typing, filing, making tea and running errands. It was Audrey who performed what might be deemed the more glamorous side of being Stephen McKinnon's secretary: greeting visitors, the authors and literary agents, whom she treated with deference. The less glamorous but still interesting selection of sales representatives with their suitcases of samples and their gossip were either flirted with or condescended to, depending on their age and attractiveness.

Isabel quickly learned that there was no Mr Holt. McKinnon & Holt were so called, Trudy explained, because it rolled off the tongue. The business was currently kept afloat by Trudy's husband, Redmayne Symmonds, a shambling bear of a Yorkshireman, who was rumoured to have done very well out of the war making boots for the military. While he'd cleverly switched production to ladies' shoes, he had come to relish the prestige of subsidising books. 'And he likes me to work. He says it keeps me out of mischief,' Trudy would joke with one of her deep laughs. She, too, was from Yorkshire, but you'd only hear it in moments of emotion. It wasn't long before Isabel learned from Berec that the Symmonds's son, their only child, had been killed at Dunkirk.

From the tone of the arguments Isabel could hear on occasion through Stephen McKinnon's office door – Symmonds had a deep booming voice to match his bulk – their backer expected to achieve the same healthy profit margins with books as he did with footwear, and was being rapidly disabused of that idea. It was towards the end of her second week, when nearly everyone had left for the day and she was giving the spider plants a quick watering, that Isabel witnessed Symmonds's frustration first-hand. The doorbell rang long and loud, and when she admitted him, a blast of wintry wind seemed to follow as he forged his way down the office with barely a nod to her, and barged into Stephen's room without announcement.

As she fitted the cover on her typewriter, she saw, through the half-open door, Symmonds write out a cheque and toss it down on Stephen's desk. Stephen was standing, his back turned, peering out into the dark yard as though the dustbins were of particular interest that evening. This tableau was conducted with barely a word on either side, but after Symmonds had marched out and Isabel put a timid head round Stephen's door to say she was off, too, it was to find him sitting at his desk, smoking and staring at the opposite wall, his expression inscrutable. The cheque still lay on the desk, untouched.

'Is there anything you need?' she asked.

'No, thank you,' he said, in a matter-of-fact way. 'There's nothing.' Then he gave one of his boyish smiles and rose to his feet. 'Well, Pockmartin's book will be published,' he said, snatching up the cheque and slotting it into his wallet. His usual air of worry was quite banished. 'We can pay the printer. That's today's achievement.'

Isabel had already gleaned that landing these memoirs was a real coup. Viscount, now Lord, Pockmartin had been a senior attaché to the British Embassy in Berlin in the 1930s and later a prisoner-of-war. His tales of derring-do after his escape in 1943, and his political insights, had 'bestseller' written all over them. If the book worked, it would pay everyone's salaries for a few months.

And so time passed delightfully. Isabel liked the atmosphere in the office, where half a dozen employees, all coming and going at different hours, on mysterious schedules of their own, managed to cut out the noise of each other's conversations and telephones ringing in order to pursue their roles. Despite Berec's disdainful comments about Trudy, Isabel liked her. Trudy combined a no-nonsense approach to the practical business of preparing manuscripts for publication with a motherly tact when persuading writers to accept necessary alterations to their darling prose.

At the desk opposite sat Philip Houghton, an older man with the face of a mediaeval Christ, lugubrious, pale and bearded. He was responsible for the design of the books, both insides and jackets, and received a steady pilgrimage of undernourished visitors bearing portfolios of illustrations, which were commented on, retained or turned away. Any invoices were sent across the hall to a room the size of a broom cupboard, where Mr Greenford, the company accountant, sat two days a week. From the frantic phone calls from suppliers that Isabel sometimes intercepted, it seemed that he was rarely able to get these paid on time.

Next to Mr Greenford's room was the trade counter,

where sales representatives and booksellers' assistants picked up parcels of stock. Downstairs in the basement was a room so cold that the paraffin heater which burned all day made little difference, and between here and the trade counter, wrapped in coat and scarf, operated Mr Jones the packer, sometimes hindered rather than assisted by his son Jimmy, a lolloping fifteen-year-old with no manners. And this was the whole team – oh, apart from Dora, Stephen's sparky bachelor cousin, who would swan in once or twice a week to chatter to Audrey about weekend parties, but was supposed to be working with Philip on an experimental new venture: picture books for children.

It was all a world away from claustrophobic family life on the housing estate, so such so that sometimes she wondered if bright little Miss Isabel Barber, publisher's clerk (temporary), was the same person as the mutinous puss who three weeks ago had snarled at her father and flounced out of the house. Now, she lived life in a fever of ecstasy, from moment to moment, hour to hour. The only trouble was that every day brought her nearer Christmas and after Christmas, despite Lord Pockmartin, Stephen McKinnon might have no money to keep her any longer.

Most of the time she didn't dwell on it. Life outside work was interesting too. She loved living at Penelope's. Her aunt, initially so anxious at the prospect of her niece staying, had said no more about her going, and her sojourn in the house passed with delightful freedom. Penelope Tyler's life seemed to follow no particular schedule, but it was rare that she rose from her bed before Isabel left for work, and the girl found herself creeping downstairs in the early morning darkness to be greeted

by the slap of Gelert's tail on the kitchen lino and his soulful gaze as she made a cup of tea and cut herself a slice of
bread for breakfast. She had been amused to hear that the
dog had been named for the hound in the Welsh legend
who had saved a baby from a wolf. This modern Gelert
was too soppy even to bark at the milkman. On the
evenings when Isabel came straight home from work, the
cleaner, Mrs Pettigrew, would have been and gone and
the store cupboard would be miraculously stocked with
food. Aunt Penelope was usually out, so with Gelert as
her sole companion Isabel would eat a makeshift supper
at the kitchen table, absorbed in some book or other. She
was currently reading her way through McKinnon &
Holt's back catalogue, borrowing office copies from
Trudy on pain of severe punishment for non-return.
Through talk in the office or by reading the reviews files
she learned of new books from rival publishing houses.
She often spent her lunch hours 'devouring' books in the
nearest library, her penchant being for fiction and her
secret vice romance. She'd read all Maisie Briggs's novels,
her eyes widening like saucers at the schmaltzy love
scenes. In *The Stranger Bride* and *Fairytale Wedding*, she'd
immersed herself in the yearnings of young women like
herself, who'd had to make their own way in life but who
found sanctuary in the arms of a strong, true man. She
knew reality didn't offer happy endings – after all, her
parents quarrelled all the time, and then there was Penelope, who seemed perfectly happy living by herself.

Around half past ten or eleven of an evening, her aunt
would arrive home, wrapped in her fur coat, her eyes
gleaming as brightly as the pearls at her ears, her skin
flushed from the warmth of the taxi, and she'd talk

animatedly of the party she'd been to or the play she'd seen. Twice, she'd brought someone back with her, a man she introduced to Isabel merely as Reginald. Reginald was fiftyish, tall and silent with a blandly handsome face and exquisitely tailored clothes. He had politely shaken Isabel's hand with a crushing grip on first meeting, but she sensed no flicker of warmth in its strength so she'd made her excuses and escaped upstairs to bed. That night she lay awake for some time, unable to throw off a sense of unease about the situation. Her room was right above the parlour so she could hear murmurings and movement downstairs. She must finally have fallen into a deep sleep because she wasn't aware of him leaving, but when she passed through the hall the next morning his hat and coat were gone.

It wasn't every evening, of course, that Isabel spent at home. She became quite friendly with Alex Berec, whom she quickly learned to call plain 'Berec' like everyone else did. He had a habit of turning up at the offices unannounced, at least once or twice a week, and was treated as family. Occasionally he'd beg Mr Greenford for 'a little advance payment' and disappear again with a pound or two in his pocket. Sometimes, he just came for the company.

'I was passing,' he'd say, appearing in the doorway, his smile irrepressible. He'd doff his hat and nod charmingly at everyone, though Trudy, who hated being interrupted, would deliver him a stern look in return. 'I promise I won't stop, I can see you're all *verrry* busy. However, I brought a little something for the workers.' And he might produce a box of honey cakes and once, extraordinarily, a bag of oranges – and then, of course, Audrey or

Isabel would have to make him a cup of tea and he'd chat away to whoever would listen.

Stephen might walk through and ask his opinion on a book jacket or the latest Katharine Hepburn film – Berec was a great fan of Hepburn – but if there was a rush on he'd down his tea quickly and depart. Isabel was quickly becoming his clear favourite, and she'd hurry to let him out, even though the street door was kept on the latch during the day. Occasionally he'd ask her to accompany him to a poetry reading or, once, to supper at the home of some refugee friends.

'Myra cannot accompany me – a migraine, the poor lady – but you will like Gregor and Karin, I think.'

The flat she was taken to in a gloomy street off Bloomsbury Square was poor beyond her experience, being a single large room, where the bed was screened off from the living area by two Army-issue blankets on a rail. Karin, a shy middle-aged woman, too thin for her shapeless dress, disappeared and returned soon after bearing a steaming tureen containing an aromatic stew, mostly made of vegetables, which they ate with hunks of greyish bread. The conversation was conducted half in English and half in Czech, which was all Karin could speak. Berec had extracted from his pocket a bottle of sweet-tasting liqueur. This made Isabel's throat burn, but imparted such a deep sense of relaxation she feared she'd fall into a swoon.

She and Karin didn't say much, though Gregor translated any English for Karin, who nodded and smiled, though she never looked happy. Maybe she never would, it occurred to Isabel, who experienced a sense of floating above the table round which they all sat, surprised to be seeing herself here in this place with these people, when such a short time ago her knowledge of the world outside the family home and school had been through books. Of course she knew all about refugees from the newsreels and her father's newspaper, but she'd never actually had a meal with any before, or listened to such passionate conversations about politics or seen such despair in a woman's eyes. Berec had explained to her that in Czechoslovakia, before the war, Gregor had trained as a doctor, but here his qualifications were not recognised and he'd only been able to get manual work. He was well known as a Communist, too, but at home he'd fallen out with his own party and there was no returning for him.

Now Berec was patting her shoulder and saying, 'My poor Isabel, please forgive me. Gregor and I, we would talk all night. It's time to go, yes?' They said their goodbyes and walked arm in arm through the freezing night to the nearest bus stop, where Berec saw her onto the right bus, instructed the conductor to look after her, and kissed his fingertips in farewell.

Dear Berec, she thought, smiling at him as the bus bore her away, what a warm and generous friend. She felt perfectly safe with him. Safe and free to be herself. She thought that, despite his perpetual lack of money, Myra must be a very lucky woman. Sometimes she wondered about him, what exactly had brought him to England early in the war. She'd read his poetry collection, the one dedicated to Penelope, a translation from the Czech, and had been moved by the ones about exile, but some of them were dark, very dark, about violence and death, and she'd skipped over these, not wanting to know. He never spoke to her of these things. Like her, he tried to put the past behind him.

As the days and weeks passed, Audrey, too, was becoming a little friendlier. At first she was sharp with Isabel and disdainful, which puzzled the girl, for she was keen to prove her worth.

She'd discovered from Audrey herself what the bet was that Audrey had had with Trudy that first day.

'Stephen obviously likes you, I could tell it straight away.'

'That's ridiculous.' Isabel pinked up as she caught the insinuation. 'Anyway, he's married.'

'You are such an innocent.' Audrey sat, arms folded, one manicured finger resting against her cheek.

'I'm not, and you're wrong about Stephen.' Isabel stuck her nose in a file to hide her upset. She didn't understand why Audrey put her down all the time.

It was Trudy who took her aside one day and pointed out how irritating it must be for Audrey to have someone like Isabel, younger and more ambitious, foisted on her.

'She thinks you want her daylight. Don't try so hard. Nobody likes a pushy girl.'

Isabel suddenly saw the situation in sharp focus. She thought about it on the bus home. She must tone down her enthusiasm. What was required of her, she decided, was humble obedience. Not, however, subservience. There was a fine line to be drawn, especially with Audrey. She remembered from school how that worked, when she'd wanted a favour from an older girl or been put in charge of younger ones. Fawning was despised. Being spirited but respectful was what brought results. From then on, Isabel made sure that she did everything Audrey asked her, and did it well, but she did not offer to do anything she regarded as being beneath her dignity, such as making tea for young Jimmy Jones. Nor did she openly aspire to tasks that implied she was getting 'above herself'. This meant being furtive about her reading. But with Christmas only a few weeks away, all this effort might be for nothing. Oh, how she longed to be allowed to stay at McKinnon & Holt.

Chapter 5

Emily

The autumn fog rising off the Suffolk marshes was so dense that Emily, glancing up from her novel, couldn't make out the station signs. 'Where are we?' she asked the woman opposite her on the train.

'I reckon it's Ipswich,' came the reply.

'Oh, that's me!' Emily cried, snatching her coat down from the rack.

Hurrying from the train, she followed the crowds across the bridge and through the ticket barrier. Someone from Stone House was supposed to meet her, and she waited by the entrance to the station, uncertain of what to do next, the world being practically invisible in the fog. Minutes passed. The concourse emptied of people and vehicles, and silence fell. She wondered what had gone awry, if she'd got the wrong date or time, or had been forgotten. She was searching her bag for the letter with Jacqueline Morton's phone number when a timid voice said, 'Excuse me, but are you Emily?' Emily turned to see a short woman with pale blue eyes regarding her anxiously. She must have been about Emily's mother's age, or maybe older, it wasn't easy to tell because she was enveloped from head to knee in a dark green cagoule.

'Yes, I'm Emily. You must be . . .'

'Lorna, Jacqueline Morton's daughter,' the woman said in an apologetic tone, putting out her hand. It was a gardener's hand, the skin roughened and callused. Lorna Morton, Emily thought, might once have been pretty in an English rose way, with her round face, pink cheeks and puzzled blue eyes with feathery lashes. Wisps of silvery hair were escaping from her hood. She had a sweet, gentle way about her that matched her soft voice.

'Thank goodness you waited,' Lorna said as they walked across the concourse. 'I'm sorry I was so late, but the fog's even worse out where we are – just awful – and then I couldn't see to park.'

'I should have offered to take a taxi.'

'Oh, it's no trouble, really. The car's here somewhere. I do hate . . . Ah, here it is.'

Lorna, nervous, took some time edging the tiny vehicle into the traffic, then it was nose-to-tail through the town before they finally escaped onto a dual carriageway, where she kept to the slow lane, turning off after a few minutes onto a narrow country road. Here the fog lifted briefly to give glimpses of ploughed fields on either side. They negotiated the twists and turns for several miles, Emily hardly daring to make conversation in case she distracted Lorna from the tortuous business of driving. She learned, however, that the fog had come down in the night, and that Lorna's mother was still fit at eighty-five and liked to get out to see friends as much as possible, but would probably have to miss a concert in Ipswich that evening if conditions didn't improve. Lorna worried that Mother did too much.

'There's been an awful lot to sort out recently,' Lorna said. 'And she's insisted on doing most of it all herself.'

'The will and things?' Emily wondered, never having had to deal with such procedures herself.

'Mother always says being an author is like running a small business. There's so much paperwork. And neither of us is computerish. At least all the filing is in good order. She's always been strict about that.'

'What will happen to the papers? The letters and manuscripts, I mean?'

Lorna eased the car round a tight corner. 'She'll explain everything when you meet. That's probably best.'

Emily thought of the points for their meeting that she'd jotted in her notebook. She'd also brought *Coming Home* with her, which she'd now read and enjoyed. It was a story about a young man taken from the country life that he knew, the prospect of life as an academic, to fly planes in the RAF, and how he returned to find that everything had changed, including the girl he'd loved. She sensed that it had a ring of the autobiographical about it, like many a first novel.

They drove on, as through some shadowy netherworld, London and civilisation worryingly further and further behind. The road descended sharply into thick drifts of fog, so Lorna slowed down to a crawl. 'Not long now,' she remarked, and a few moments later, they passed a village sign, wreathed in mist, then – the air grew momentarily clearer – houses, a village Post Office, the great flint shoulder of a church. Soon after that, Lorna drove between a pair of white posts and along a bumpy drive where delicate winter branches of trees lined the grassy verge on either side. Where the drive dipped, the mist surged in a sinister fashion and the sense of passing into another world intensified. Finally the car lurched to a halt, alarmingly close behind another vehicle, something black and sporty-looking.

'Here we are,' Lorna said with relief. They both got out. The air was chilly, with the scent of bonfires.

Lorna led the way past some outhouses, two with stable doors. 'Are there horses?' Emily asked, shivering.

'Not in our time,' Lorna said, her voice coming across pale and wistful. 'I would have loved to learn to ride, but it wasn't something my parents did. Come on. We'll go via the kitchen, if you don't mind. I must see that lunch is all right.'

She opened a heavy door and led Emily into a square utility room, then on through another door into a farmhouse kitchen. There was a rugged wooden table in the middle, one end of which was piled with clutter – a radio with a broken aerial, cook books, magazines and sewing. Pots and pans hung above a fireplace that was completely filled by a huge old Aga. A crowded wooden dresser of similar vintage to the table took up one wall. Though cramped, the room was homey and warm, and smelled of something savoury and delicious. A grey cat was curled up in a basket by the stove. It stirred for a moment at their entrance, then settled back into sleep. It was wasted with age, its ragged coat barely disguising the ridge of its backbone.

'This won't take a moment,' Lorna said. She'd peeled off her cagoule to reveal an untidy ensemble of cord skirt, flowery blouse and jumper. Taking up a thick cloth, she opened one of the doors of the stove, inspected the contents of a pot and gave it a stir. 'That's all right,' she said, pushing it back. 'Let me have your coat. I'll take you through.'

The kitchen must have been Lorna's domain, for in it she was a different person from the nervous chauffeur, more relaxed, the evidence of domestic interests all around. She changed again, however, as they passed into the main part of the house. She trod softly and wore a furtive look. Emily sensed why. This big light hall belonged to someone else. It was colder than the kitchen and painted white and pale blue.

Lorna tapped on a door at the far end of the hall and waited. At the sound of a voice, they entered a spacious drawing room with book-lined walls.

'Emily's here, Mother,' Lorna Morton announced. Emily walked across an acre of blue carpet to where an old lady was rising with effort from a chair by the fire.

'How do you do?' Jacqueline Morton said.

'Very pleased to meet you.' Emily took the outstretched hand, which felt as light and strong as a bird's wing. She thought how regal and commanding the woman was in her navy-blue suit, the gold buttons of the jacket comple-menting her earrings and necklace, how composed. Her hair, scooped into a pleat behind, gleamed an expensive creamy white. Wide-spaced eyes of faded blue examined Emily. Finally her thin lips curved in a smile.

'Do you know Joel Richards?' she said, indicating the young man who'd stood up from the sofa. He looked oddly familiar, though she couldn't think from where.

'I don't think so,' Emily said brightly, as he came forward. 'Hello.'

Joel Richards was tallish and broad-shouldered. His reddish-brown hair, though long, was neatly trimmed, as was the trace of a beard. Hazel eyes met hers and there was warmth in them. He was smartly dressed in a soft-brown suit and collarless shirt.

'Hi, Emily,' he murmured with an easy charm. His accent had a northern tinge, pleasing to the ear. A firm hand enveloped hers. His eyes said, *Do I know you?*

'Joel,' said Mrs Morton, 'was talking about Duke's College in London. They hold some of Hugh's manuscripts.'

Duke's, that was Matthew's college. And Emily suddenly knew where she'd seen Joel before.

'Weren't you at the poetry launch in Frith Street last Friday?' she asked him. She remembered how he'd stood on his own, surveying the room. How he'd given her that same small, secretive smile.

'That's it. I thought I'd seen you somewhere,' he said, his face lighting up. 'Tobias Berryman is a friend of mine. He took me along as we were having dinner together later.'

'Oh, you know one another – how simply marvellous,' Mrs Morton said with a touch of sarcasm, bringing everyone's attention back to herself.

'And this is Hugh's study.'

Mrs Morton opened the door off the hall with an air of reverence, as though they might be interrupting the great man at his desk. There was, of course, no one there, though the foggy daylight gave the room an eerie atmosphere. A big, leather-topped desk lay before the window, a sheaf of papers splayed across it, a fountain pen lying by the blotter.

'These are all first editions.' Mrs Morton was showing Emily the bookcase. The volumes were in many languages and the majority, Emily gauged, were *The Silent Tide*. She spotted a copy of the novel whose title she'd forgotten, the one her teacher had made her read, about the writers on an island retreat, then noticed one even more familiar. It was an exact copy of the little book she had in her bag: *Coming Home*.

Mrs Morton was now opening the top drawer of one of several large metal filing cabinets at the back of the room to show Joel some of the files. 'The correspondence with Kingsley Amis, yes, here . . . the letters about the honour Hugh really had to refuse . . .' she was saying. Emily would have liked to ask why Hugh Morton refused it, but Mrs Morton had forgotten her.

Emily edged *Coming Home* off the shelf and examined it quickly. There was no inscription in this copy, no mention of any Isabel. She toyed with the idea of showing her own book to Hugh's widow, but something stayed her, the not-knowing who Isabel was. She watched Jacqueline and Joel together, and how Jacqueline seemed to trust him.

Joel had already told Emily how he had introduced himself to Hugh and Jacqueline once at a literary party in London the year before he died. He'd admired all Morton's novels and had felt compelled to meet the great man and tell him so. Jacqueline added that when Joel wrote to her in sympathy after her husband's death, she remembered the young man who'd spoken so charmingly to her husband and who'd impressed her by his knowledge of the books.

Joel had visited Stone House several times since Morton's death, but he didn't seem to mind being made to do the tour with Emily today. So far they'd politely marvelled at the impressionistic oil painting of Hugh Morton in the hall, and the table in the breakfast room where the great man had sometimes worked on sunny mornings, his beloved Persian cats sleeping close by. In the dining room they had studied several photograph albums of awards ceremonies, of the Mortons holidaying in various exotic locations with other distinguished literary figures, Jacqueline cool and elegant in headscarves or shady hats. The number of such pictures had dwindled as the years had gone by.

After they'd finished in the study, Lorna served sherry in the drawing room and Emily took out her notebook to consider her list of questions.

Could Joel tell her a little about what else he'd written? Did he have an agent? Was there an outline for the proposed biography? How long did he think the book would take to complete, and so on? 'I'm sorry to bombard you, but my boss is going to want to know all this,' she told him.

Nervous under this questioning, Joel spilled his sherry while placing his glass on the side table.

'I do have an agent,' he said, wiping his fingers on a tissue Emily gave him. He named someone Emily hadn't heard of at a small, but reputable firm.

Emily knew that Hugh Morton's books were notionally looked after by one of the bigger literary agencies, but that Jacqueline made all the decisions. She wasn't surprised that the agent in question wasn't there today.

'I'm a freelance writer,' Joel was telling her. He mentioned several important commissions he'd had: writing the official history of a big City firm; ghostwriting the bestselling memoirs of a senior business figure. He'd also scripted a

TV series about the 1950s that was in the process of being filmed. 'That's when I became very interested in Hugh Morton. I've always admired his novels.'

He must have been paid reasonable money for some of these, Emily thought. Parchment wasn't going to be able to offer more than a modest advance for this biography, and the thought worried her.

'Joel really understands dear Hugh,' Jacqueline Morton broke in. 'He recognises how central he is as an English writer, don't you, Joel?'

'I certainly feel Hugh's reputation is ripe to be re-evaluated. *The Silent Tide* was actually a very modern book. The character of Nanna, for instance . . .'

'Joel thinks Nanna is a woman for her time,' said Mrs Morton, interrupting once again, 'in the way of Tolstoy with Anna Karenina.'

The pair of them regarded Emily as though daring her to challenge this. Emily hesitated, wondering if they really wanted her opinion. *Anna Karenina* was a favourite novel of hers and nothing to her mind compared with it, but Nanna in *The Silent Tide* was a powerful symbolic figure. She said, 'I do see what you mean. Zara Collins is perfect to play her, isn't she? Have they consulted you about it?' she asked Mrs Morton.

The old woman's expression hardened. 'They had the courtesy to show me the script,' she said, 'but they've not listened to any of my concerns. Too much has been left out, but what can one do?' She sighed. 'I'm sure the series will be very popular, but it's certainly not what Hugh would have envisaged.'

'At least it means a new generation will buy the book,' Emily said.

'I do hope you're right.' Now Jacqueline looked coy. 'There are some, do you know, who used to tell me that I was Hugh's principal inspiration for Nanna.' She gave a light laugh and sat back in her seat. 'Ridiculous, of course, but people will say these silly things.'

Emily and Joel smiled politely. Emily thought the idea most unlikely, but Mrs Morton was clearly charmed by it.

'I can assure you,' Mrs Morton went on confidingly, 'that our marriage was a much happier affair than Nanna's.' She glanced at a large black and white photograph hanging on the wall near her chair. Emily leaned forward to see it better. It was of a family group. Hugh was instantly recognisable. Jacqueline must have been in her prime, a young mother, dressed a bit like Jackie Kennedy. A baby boy sat straight-backed on Jacqueline's knee and another boy of three or four leaned against her. Standing behind the seated grown-ups was an older girl peeping over their shoulders at the camera. From her shy expression, Emily supposed her to be Lorna. What a perfect family they appeared.

Emily looked back at her notebook, where she'd been jotting down Joel's answers. Finally she asked Jacqueline Morton, 'Um, the source material. I mean, you've given Joel full access to the papers, haven't you? '

Mrs Morton appeared irritated by this question. 'It's important to me that a full and accurate record of Hugh's life and work is presented,' she said, emphasising each word, 'and I will be supporting Joel in every way I can. There's something I wanted to ask *you*. I assume he'll be able to look at anything about Hugh's books in Parchment's archive?'

'I don't see why not,' Emily said, making a note of this. 'I don't know what there'll be, but I'll find out.' Being so new, she hadn't had a chance to think about where ancient files might be kept, but there must be a system.

'Brilliant,' Joel said, making a note of his own. 'I'll give you a call about that.'

Lunch, served by Lorna in the austere dining room, was delicious, lamb in a red wine sauce and fluffy mashed potato, comforting and piping hot. It was a stiff occasion, though, with Jacqueline Morton seated at the head of the table, as if at a board meeting. Poor Joel started by eating with his fork only, American fashion, until Jacqueline Morton's frown shamed him into picking up his knife. Emily once had a great-aunt just like Jacqueline, and didn't feel nervous of her exactly, but she was beginning to suspect that the woman needed to be watched. There was something going on about this biography that she didn't trust. However good a writer Joel might be, he'd have to be a strong character to insist on including anything Jacqueline Morton didn't like. Emily resolved to speak to him about this as soon as she could, though she wasn't sure how to frame it.

Mrs Morton turned her steely attentions on Emily. How long had she worked for Parchment? What writers had she worked with? She appeared to be satisfied with the answers. Then came some low-key probing of her family background and her education.

'Dad's a headmaster,' Emily told her, taking a sip of red wine, 'and Mum – well, she used to work in a bank, but then she had us so she left.'

'Us? You have brothers and sisters then?'

'Just an older sister. She was a fashion buyer for a department store, but she's given that up since my niece and nephew were born. They're still only three and eighteen months, you see.'

'No, of course it wouldn't do,' Mrs Morton said, in a tone that brooked no argument. 'Children need their mothers to be at home.' Emily met Joel's eye and he gave an embarrassed shrug.

The old lady talked about her own children, the boys, James and Harry, now middle-aged men. 'Harry has three children, and James one, all grown up now, of course. And all doing *very* well for themselves.'

'Do you see them often?' Joel asked, laying down his knife and fork.

'Not as much as I'd like. They do have such busy lives.' There was a wistfulness in Jacqueline's voice and Emily suddenly glimpsed a chink in her armour. 'I still have Lorna, though, haven't I, dear?' Jacqueline smiled at her daughter, but there was something patronising in the smile.

Lorna stood up. 'Will you have more cabbage, Joel? No?' The top button of her blouse had come undone and as she leaned forward to pick up the vegetable dish, a delicate chain with a gold ring on it swung out. She shoved it back and did up the button, but it was too late, everyone had seen that it was a wedding ring.

Emily helped stack the dishes, though Lorna refused to let her help take them to the kitchen. Whilst Lorna was out of the room, Mrs Morton draped her napkin on the table and said in a low voice, 'Of course, it was simply dreadful for us all when Malcolm left her, so early in their marriage, too, but it was a godsend to have her back home.' Emily was struck by the awful sense that the woman was not really sorry at all about Lorna's heartbreak. Instead she was thinking about her own convenience.

It was at this point that she began seriously to dislike Jacqueline Morton.

After lunch they drifted back to the drawing room. The downstairs bathroom being occupied, Lorna directed Emily to one upstairs. When she emerged onto the landing afterwards, she noticed a door standing open almost opposite and couldn't help peering in.

It was painted in the same cold blue and white as the hall and the drawing room, and in a bedroom the effect was merciless. Everything was meticulously tidy, the curtains folded back and secured by tassels, the bedspread on the double bed perfectly draped, the silver-backed brushes on the dressing table symmetrically arranged. Only a library book on a bedside table next to a spectacle case proclaimed that the room was occupied. It was obviously the master bedroom, and it wasn't hard to guess that Jacqueline slept there. What had it been like when Hugh was alive? Emily wondered, for now it spoke entirely of Jacqueline. Maybe the couple hadn't shared a room. Whatever the explanation, there was something disturbing about this sterile atmosphere. Just then she heard voices in the hall so she stepped back guiltily and hurried downstairs.

Later, Joel offered to drive Emily to the station to get her train. It appeared that he was staying on to take another look at some of Hugh's correspondence.

'Oh, Lorna will take Emily,' Mrs Morton said immediately.

Poor Lorna, Emily thought. Jacqueline's daughter had only just come in to sit down after washing up.

'It's really no trouble,' Joel told Emily, and before their host could draw breath to disagree, Emily accepted.

Outside, the fog had begun to clear, and as she walked with Joel to the sporty black car, Emily turned to view the frontage of the house. She found the grey stone too grim for her liking, but the classical lines were softened by a great wisteria plant, which when it blossomed must be beautiful.

'How old is the place, do you think?' she asked Joel.

'Early Victorian. Most of it, anyway.' There were more modern additions, a newish conservatory to one side, and a flagged terrace in front studded with little flower-beds.

They got into the car, which Joel turned in a single, graceful arc. 'It should only take twenty minutes,' he said.

'This is really kind of you,' Emily said.

'No problem.' He pressed a button and a woman's sultry voice began to croon. For a while they were silent. The drive met the lane on a blind corner and it was a relief once they were clear. When they were through the village, Joel picked up speed, the car clinging to the bends, and Emily sensed his enjoyment. The engine was smooth, the car comfortable with low bucket seats. She felt cocooned from the gloomy world outside.

'I've already started writing the book,' Joel told her, as they gained a straight bit of road. 'I can send you an outline right away.' He glanced round at her. 'I hope you don't mind me asking, but how certain is Parchment to go for this project?'

'I can't say for definite, but it's looking good,' Emily

said. 'Our publisher, Gillian Bradshaw, is keen. And so, of course, am I.'

They came to a narrow bridge and Joel had to concentrate. Afterwards he said, 'I hope I'm not breaking confidences if I say that whilst I would appreciate a decent advance, it's important to me that I have a good publisher like Parchment. Not that my agent won't drive a hard bargain. Mrs Morton will see to that.'

'I can imagine,' Emily replied, laughing, and Joel laughed too.

She wondered how to phrase the question she needed to ask. She didn't want to offend him. 'Given that Mrs Morton has so much control, how do you feel about this project?' she came up with eventually.

'Lucky I'm doing it,' he said. 'Morton is fascinating. So much there in his writing, but so controlled. His early books were stronger, maybe – I think it's the passion in them. I find the later work rather dry, to be honest – as if he became out of touch. I'm so grateful Jacqueline has given me full access to the papers. Sorry – now I sound like a quote from a press release.'

'Not really.' She smiled. 'It's not going to be just about his writing, is it, the biography? I mean, people are going to want to know what kind of a person Hugh Morton was, his life story, what inspired him.'

'The deadly secrets, you mean? The exposures.' He chuckled.

'If you put it like that, yes. Publicity angles. '

'There isn't much. Even the business of how he won the Booker Prize turns out to be in order. It wasn't that he was friendly with the Chair of the judges. It was simply that they thought his was the best book.'

'Why did he turn down an honour, for instance?'

'The official line is he didn't believe in them,' Joel said with the smallest of smiles, 'but I have my suspicions Jacqueline didn't think the one he was offered was grand enough.'

'She fancied being Lady Morton?' Emily giggled. 'She'll hardly let you write that.'

'There are ways of putting it.' Joel tapped his finger on the driving wheel. 'Then there's his war record.'

Emily was immediately interested. 'What did he do in the war? Isn't *Coming Home* based on that?'

'Yes. There's a possibility the rescue for which he got the Distinguished Flying Cross didn't happen quite how he described it, though there's no doubting his bravery. I must talk to a couple of people.' They entered a tunnel under the main road and he fell silent. Emily wondered if he was keeping something back. They turned up the slip road to join the dual carriageway, Joel concentrated on edging in between two lorries. When they were safely in lane, she tried again.

'How is examining Morton's war record going to go down with Jacqueline? Given that she seems to think he's a saint or something.'

Joel shrugged. 'I'm sure she'll be fine,' he said firmly, but something about his tone left Emily feeling uneasy.

The rest of the way they discussed logistics.

'You will let me know about the Parchment archives?' he asked her.

'Of course,' she replied, and put his contact details into her phone.

The car drew up in front of the station, shadowy in the dying afternoon. 'Well, thank you,' Emily said. As she scrabbled in her bag for her tickets, her fingers closed around a book. *Coming Home* – she should have shown him earlier. She pulled it out. 'Look,' she said. 'I found this in the office.'

'Ah, yes.' Joel put out his hand, but before he could take the book, the car shook with a juddering roar from behind; then came a squeal of brakes. She whipped round to see a lorry, pulled up practically on top of them. The driver leaned on the horn.

'What's he on?' Joel muttered, craning in the rear-view mirror. The lorry driver hooted again and revved his engine.

'I'd better let you go,' Emily said, stuffing the book back in her bag and getting out.

'Speak soon,' he called as she closed the door. A wave and he pulled away.

As the train unzipped the darkening landscape to London, she thought about Joel, how impressed she was by him. As well as having the right credentials, he was professional to deal with – straightforward, reasonable. He'd do the job well, she was sure, and deliver on time, most likely. She hoped Parchment did offer for the book. She knew she'd enjoy working with him.

A week went by before she spoke to him again, but a lot happened in that time. His agent emailed her the synopsis for the book and the Introduction, which spoke of Hugh Morton as a key figure in the British post-war literary scene. Joel's approach was suitably scholarly, yet he wrote with style and panache.

At the next editorial meeting those gathered agreed to wait for Gillian's return from Australia before going any

further with the proposal. Emily rang Joel, who was on a
busy street somewhere and, against a background of traffic noise, explained what was going on.

'I've also ordered up those files you wanted,' she told
him. 'They'll take a few days, I think. Apparently they
have to come from Gloucestershire.'

'Gloucestershire?'

'That's where our warehouse is. Shall I call you when
they get here?'

'Yes, please,' he said. Then: 'I must go now, I'm late for
filming.'

A couple of days later, Emily returned to her desk from a
meeting to find that a cardboard box had been left on her
chair. It was stained and dusty and sealed with dozens of
strips of parcel tape. She eyed it with trepidation.

Sarah, her neighbour in the next pod, who edited children's books, peered round the partition. 'I hope it's not a
bomb.'

'Or a three-volume horror story,' Emily groaned.
'Handwritten in blood.' She waved a pair of scissors
dangerously. 'I always get the weird ones.'

But when Emily winched open the flaps, it was to find
three ancient-looking folders, bulky and tied up with
ribbon.

'We're safe,' she told Sarah. 'It's just some stuff I ordered
from the archive.'

In fact, she was rather intrigued. Stuck on the first
folder was a yellowing typed label: THE SILENT TIDE BY
HUGH MORTON, it read. She untied the ends of the ribbon
with an odd sense of excitement, feeling the pull of the
past. The date of a handwritten note from Jacqueline,

acknowledging receipt of a book, suggested this folder was the most recent, though it was full of letters and flimsy carbon copies of memos, going back years, about reprints and new editions. Out of the next folder fell a ragged mass of old press cuttings. The third must be the oldest. Emily turned the whispering dry pages and read with delicious reverence a long typed letter signed *Hugh Morton* in his bold handwriting, familiar from her copy of *Coming Home*. It was only a list of proof corrections addressed to a Mr Richard Snow, who appeared to be Morton's editor, but it was a connection with the famous writer. She smiled when it plaintively mentioned *hoped-for changes to the jacket*. Hugh wasn't the first or the last author to argue with his publisher on that touchy subject.

It was with great reluctance that Emily retied the ribbons and returned all the files to the box to wait for Joel to examine them. She was becoming absorbed in Hugh Morton's life story to an extent that surprised her.

Chapter 6

Isabel

McKinnon & Holt, in common with most other businesses, expected its employees to work Saturday mornings. It was lunchtime one Saturday in December and Isabel had been in London for three weeks. Lately, the weather had turned wet, then icy, so it was with care that she alighted from the bus at Earl's Court and set off towards Aunt Penelope's house, her bag heavy with the weekend's reading. Rounding the final bend, she stopped short in surprise and dismay, for in the porch of number 32 Mimosa Road was parked a pushchair, a very familiar-looking one. It was her sister Lydia's. For a moment she could hardly breathe. Then she turned and started to walk back quickly the way she'd come. And stopped again. There was no shirking it, she'd have to go and face her mother.

For three weeks she'd tried not to think of her family. Most of the time this wasn't difficult; she'd been so busy working, becoming used to a new home, a new way of living. But at times something would catch her off-guard. Twice her pulse had been sent racing, the first time by the sight of a ginger-haired boy ahead of her in the street, a boy with the same rolling walk as the twins'. The other occasion was when a woman in a headscarf identical to her mother's and wearing that same unhappy, wound-up expression, had collided with her in the Underground, and had frightened her by gripping her arm for a moment and staring into her eyes. One night she'd dreamed of her father, her father as he'd been when she was very young, before the war, the gentle, friendly man she'd kept in her heart all those years he'd been away. It was a different person who'd returned and her unhappiness about this was still like a great, tight ball, knotting her insides. There had been no one she could speak to about it. Certainly not her mother, whose own misery was communicated only in her expression and by short, angry movements, dinner plates set down too smartly on the table, the desperate way she'd draw on a cigarette. The twins didn't seem to notice anything. They were bound up in each other, and they'd only been four when their father went away. As for little Lydia, she was the child of the stranger who'd returned. His black moods and his anger were all she'd ever known. Lydia couldn't lose someone she'd never had. Who was luckier, Isabel with her cherished memories, or Lydia with none?

Slowly, wearily, she walked towards the house. Going up the path, the pushchair blurred through unshed tears. Her aunt opened the front door before she could knock and admitted her without a word. Her grim expression said it all. Isabel followed her into the living room.

'Izzy.' Pamela Barber's voice quavered as she rose from the sofa to greet her elder daughter. In her worn navy skirt and jacket she looked even thinner than Isabel remembered, and her brown eyes were dark with worry in her pinched face.

'Hello,' Isabel muttered. She did not go to her, but hovered near the door. Lydia had been playing on the floor, a set of Russian dolls from the mantelpiece strewn about her. When she saw her big sister she struggled to her feet with a shout of joy and toddled across to her, offering up the silly smiling top half of the largest doll. Her nose needed wiping, Isabel saw, ignoring the gift. Lydia gripped Isabel's skirt and burying her face in it, began to wail. Isabel stroked the pale, silky hair and tried to soothe her.

'How very grown up you've become,' her mother said, looking Isabel up and down. 'And I was searching for that cardigan this morning. It really is a dreadful nuisance, you taking it.'

'I'm very well, thank you for asking,' Isabel said. She set about peeling off the cardigan. 'Here, you can have it back. I don't need it.'

'I didn't mean . . .' her mother said, stricken, as Isabel thrust the garment, all warm and inside out, like a shriven skin, into her hands.

Isabel was appalled at her own callousness, yet couldn't stop herself. It was as though she was possessed by some primeval force. Lydia let go of her skirt and Isabel looked down in disgust to see a snail trail from Lydia's cold glistening on the brown wool.

When her mother pulled a handkerchief from a sleeve and bent to wipe it, Isabel let her, but then stepped back beyond her reach.

Mother and daughter stood, eyes locked, the mother clutching the cardigan, the balled handkerchief in her raised hand. Her expression was desperate. Isabel glowered back.

'Oh, for God's sake,' Penelope pronounced, hand on hip. 'The pair of you should be ashamed of yourselves.' She left the room and the door snicked shut.

The rebuke was enough to break the tension. Unable to bear the suffering in her mother's eyes any more, Isabel burst into tears and threw herself into her arms. They clung together for the first time since Isabel could remember. Her mother's suit smelled faintly of mothballs. How light and thin she was, the girl thought, how worn away, yet there was still a wiry strength in her.

'I'm sorry, I'm sorry,' she cried through her sobs. 'I didn't mean to . . . I had to go. Don't you see?'

'I do.' Her mother gave a long, shuddering sigh, like a death rattle to her hopes. She pulled back and studied Isabel's teary face. 'Don't worry, darling, I won't try to make you come back. It would be wrong, I can see that. It was just such a shock, the way you did it.'

Isabel was astounded at her mother's answer. For a moment she felt a sensation of falling. Her mother didn't want her back. *They don't want me, I have no home.* She tasted the selfish little phrases and tried to feel sorry for herself. It didn't work.

'How are the boys? And Daddy?' she asked, her voice uncertain.

Her mother wiped Lydia's nose and tucked the handkerchief back into her sleeve. 'The boys are in bed with the most frightful colds. Charles – well, he doesn't know I'm here,' she mumbled. 'In fact, I'd better go soon. Peter Jones, that's what I told him. Lydia needs a proper winter coat, don't you, poor mite? I've had to cut the feet off her snowsuit, she's got so big.'

Had her father forbidden her mother to see her? Isabel

felt dread, but she didn't need to ask, for the truth was plain in Pamela Barber's face.

'He does care about you, Izzy,' her mother said finally. 'But he finds it very difficult. Everything is black and white to him. He can't help it. Try to understand.'

'Yes,' Isabel said, her voice dull.

'I really must go. Your father has no patience minding the boys. Here, I really don't need this.'

Isabel allowed her mother to help her into the cardigan once more and to straighten the collar of her blouse.

'Would you like the hat back?' she asked reluctantly. Her mother smiled and shook her head.

'No, you keep it. Now, you look very pretty, dear. That new way with your hair.' She turned her face away and set about stuffing a struggling Lydia into the mutilated snowsuit. Isabel collected up bits of Russian doll, her heart suddenly full of things she wanted to say, but couldn't.

Pamela Barber rose to go, with Lydia in her arms. 'It's strange to think,' she told Isabel. 'A long time ago, I ran away from home, but for a different reason. I left to get married. How times have changed.'

Isabel stared as her mother opened the door, wondering exactly what she meant. Had things changed for better or worse? There was no chance to ask.

Out in the hall, Penelope handed the woman her coat and hat. 'Goodbye, Pam,' she said. The two sisters eyed one another. Penelope opened the front door.

'Take care of her, please,' Isabel's mother told her.

'I think Isabel can take care of herself,' Penelope replied.

When her mother and Lydia had gone, Isabel escaped

up to her room and climbed into her bed. There she cried until she fell asleep. When she woke it was twilight, the room felt chilly and she was starving. Going downstairs, she discovered that her aunt had gone out with the dog. There wasn't much in the larder. She opened a can of meat stew and stood wrapped in a coat, spooning it up ravenously. It was here that Penelope found her.

'I walked and walked,' she said. 'Gelert's exhausted, aren't you, poor animal?' The mournful animal lay slumped on his rug.

'Whatever's the matter?' Isabel asked.

'This family – if you can call it that. I suppose my poor mother is to blame.'

Isabel put down her tin, wiped her mouth with the back of her hand and asked, 'Why did we hardly see Granny?'

'Your mother's never explained?' Penelope placed the kettle on the stove. She scraped a match and the gas whooshed into flame.

Isabel shrugged. 'Granny lives a long way away, that's all I know.'

Penelope took a seat at the table. 'Norfolk's not far,' she remarked. 'Drydens is such a lovely old house. I used to think it the most wonderful place in the world.'

'I saw a photograph of it once, with Mummy and you as little girls. Such funny square fringes you had.'

'Oh, those awful hairstyles! We went to the local school because there was no money. Your grandmother was convinced we'd get lice from the other children so she cut our hair short. I never knew such a snob. It was mortifying for her that we went to that school. We were certainly not allowed to bring any of our friends there home. Poor

Mother. Her daughters turned out to be such a disappointment. One divorced, such a disgrace, the other married to ... to ...'

'My father.'

'Yes. A man with no family, an orphan. Pamela would have him, and it was too much for your grandmother. Your mother's actually very like her – they're proud women, both of them, and they'll never admit that they're wrong. Pam is very loyal, but I can tell she's unhappy. She'll never do anything about it, though; she'll see it through. She's that sort. I never was.'

Isabel sat, sipping the tea Penelope gave her, warming her hands on the cup. She'd never heard her aunt say so much before. A lot of things were now clear, but somehow she wished she didn't know them. After a long silence she said, 'Why were you divorced?'

'Because I had the courage to admit my mistake,' Penelope said. 'Life with Jonny was miserable. But I got away.'

'I've got away, too.'

Penelope gave her an odd, sideways look. 'Or you think you have.'

Chapter 7

Isabel

'I'd like your opinion on this,' Stephen McKinnon said the following week, placing a short manuscript on Isabel's desk.

'Me? You want – yes, of course,' she stuttered, hardly believing it.

Audrey turned from the filing cabinet and extracted the pen she was holding between her teeth. 'If you need all those letters typed today, Stephen,' she interrupted, 'you shouldn't ask her.'

'Well, in that case . . .' Stephen looked harassed.

'I can do it this evening,' Isabel said, glaring at Audrey, who rolled her eyes.

The three of them were the only ones in the office. It was Philip's day off and Trudy had been away with flu all week. Just then, Audrey's telephone rang. She reached over her desk and snatched up the receiver. 'McKinnon and Holt? Yes, Mr Watt, how can I help?'

'Would you have time to write a report?' Stephen asked Isabel, with a pleading look. 'I'd be most grateful. The book's about a murder in a girls' school. I'm far from being an expert on female educational establishments, but it seemed rather convincing to me.'

'Mr Watt on the line about our Maisie,' Audrey

announced. She held out the receiver at an angle so she could stare at her new engagement ring.

'Oh good, put him through.' Stephen returned to his office and shut the door. Isabel peeped at the first page of the script, read a line or two, then stowed it in her shopping bag. It was the first time she'd been asked to do something like this, to venture an opinion on a book, and the prospect excited her.

Yours faithfully, Stephen McKinnon Esq., she typed with careful fingers. She wound the paper out of the machine and slipped it into a blotting-paper folder with the other letters for signature. A stack of copy-typing still lay in her tray. It got no smaller because Audrey kept adding to it.

'He won't pay you any more for reading that,' Audrey remarked of the typescript. Nothing escaped her, it seemed.

'I really don't care,' Isabel said. It was vital that she prove herself to Stephen. She was too proud to tell Audrey that she might not be here to bother her after Christmas. There were two weeks to go.

Audrey, however, was one step ahead. 'Has Stephen said anything to you about staying?'

Isabel shook her head.

Audrey let the light sparkle off the tiny gem on her finger, 'Of course, I don't know yet how long I'll be here,' she said, with a little smile, like a cat's. 'Anthony doesn't want me to work once we're married, but that won't be for ages and ages. We're saving for a deposit on a house, you know.'

'What would you do all day if you didn't work?' Isabel asked in disbelief.

'Look after Anthony, of course,' Audrey said in surprise.

'He deserves to be looked after properly, poor love, he works so hard.' Isabel had never met the Honourable Anthony Watkins, but she knew all about him as his name peppered Audrey's conversation. He was a civil servant, currently reporting to a junior minister. Honourable he might be, but his family were as poor as church mice. Audrey went on: 'But I'm sure there'd be time for luncheon with friends. And of course,' she blushed a little, 'a baby might come along. Anthony says we must find somewhere in town with a pretty garden and a room for a nursery.'

Isabel left the manuscript on Stephen's desk the next morning along with a short report that she'd rewritten twice. All day she waited for him to mention it, but he didn't, nor the next day, and she was disappointed. The manuscript disappeared under a pile of others.

One Friday, nine days before Christmas, she arrived early to find him already seated at his desk, surrounded by paperwork and writing furiously. He looked up at her, muttered, 'Good morning,' and though he smiled, his face was tired and greyish, as though he hadn't slept much. She felt a rush of concern.

'I'll make you some tea,' she said. As she withdrew he called her back.

'Isabel, I read that report last night you wrote on the school murder story. I'm glad you liked it. You made some interesting observations, I thought.'

'Oh, thank you,' she said, with a swelling of joy.

'And I agree about that middle section, it does wander about, but Trudy could make him tighten it. I'll get on to his agent this morning, see what he'll take. There's just the space for it in the spring catalogue.'

'That would be marvellous,' Isabel breathed.

Stephen was looking at her with amusement. 'I'm glad you're pleased,' he said. 'I'll give you some more to look at, if you like. It'll have to be in your own time. I can't have reading in the office, there's too much to do.'

'I don't mind,' she said. 'Really. Only . . .' She bit her lip. 'It's nearly Christmas.'

'I had noticed,' he said with heavy irony. His eyes were grave. 'I know I said your job would be until Christmas.'

'Yes,' Isabel said, waiting in desperate hope.

'Well now,' he said, leaning forward on the desk, turning a cigarette packet over and over in his long, sensitive fingers. He extracted a cigarette, lit it and contemplated her through a haze of smoke. Again, she sensed his amusement.

'I know I haven't been here long,' she said, 'but I've done my best and I do like it.'

'You have worked well,' he said, 'and sales have been decent this month. We'll try you a few weeks longer. See how it goes. Keep on the right side of Audrey, though.'

'Oh, I will. Thank you,' she said, jumping up. 'Thank you so much.'

'Good morning.' They both turned to see Audrey framed in the doorway, taking off her coat. She looked from one to the other and Isabel felt uncomfortable at the inscrutable expression in her eyes.

Berec arrived in the office late morning with a box of biscuits tied up in ribbon, but Trudy was still away sick and the phones were ringing off the hook so no one had time to talk to him. 'Go away, Berec, we're busy,' Audrey said.

When Isabel stepped out at lunchtime, intending to visit the library, there he was waving at her from the café across the road. She hurried across to join him, and over a plate of scrambled egg on toast she delivered her news.

'What did I tell you?' Berec pronounced, delighted. 'Stephen is a good man.'

'It's so kind of him. He had been insistent he couldn't pay me.'

'He likes you,' Berec said, looking extremely self-satisfied. 'I knew he would, though Stephen's not a man who shows his heart easily. He had a bad time of it in the war, they say.'

'Oh, the war,' Isabel sighed, thinking of her father. 'Will it never go away?'

'No – at least, not in our lifetimes,' Berec said quietly and this time he did not smile.

'I don't know much about Stephen,' she admitted. 'I've spoken to his wife on the telephone, but she never comes to the office.'

'She wouldn't. She's not interested in his work. I met her once at a dinner, it must be two years ago. Her name is Grace. She's pretty in your pale, English kind of way, but quiet, worryingly quiet. They placed me next to her, perhaps because I talk, but I could hardly get her to say a word to me.'

'How rude of her,' Isabel said, wide-eyed at this peek into her boss's private life.

'I think she did not mean to be,' Berec said. 'Perhaps she did not feel at her ease. The occasion was the publication of a collection of James Milward's poetry. Now there *is* a rude man. So arrogant, so selfish.' He laid down his knife and fork. 'Now, if you've finished your meal . . . some more of this excellent tea, perhaps? No? So what are you doing at Christmas, my dear Isabel?'

Isabel was dreading Christmas. Her mother had written asking her to come home and she wanted to, badly, but it worried her, too. How would her brothers act towards her and, so much worse, her father? Her mother had intimated the Saturday she'd visited that her father was angry and didn't want to see her, yet here was this invitation so it seemed that he'd softened. Still she longed to see them. And after all, the alternative, playing gooseberry at luncheon in Claridge's where Aunt Penelope's boyfriend Reginald seemed to live, wasn't to be endured.

Once she'd written back to say she would go, she felt calmer. On the Monday before Christmas she helped Audrey rig up a small tree and string paper lanterns across the office with all the excitement she'd felt as a child. The days leading up to Christmas were fun, with authors and sales representatives dropping into the office for drinks and a proper party on the Thursday, the night before Christmas Eve. Trudy, still pale under her make-up after her illness, outraged the dignified Philip by catching him under a piece of mistletoe, an act so out of character for both parties that Isabel was rather shocked.

She was even more shocked when Stephen hooked his arm round her on his way out and did the same thing, murmuring, 'A Merry Christmas,' to her. And he was gone.

Late on Friday she joined the great shoal of humanity pouring out of the Underground onto the freezing concourse of Charing Cross station, a suitcase in one hand and a bag of presents in the other. She stepped onto a train, thinking about home.

Except it wasn't home, she quickly saw, and never could be again.

When she arrived, her mother let her in and hurried back upstairs, explaining, 'I've left Lydia in the bath.'

Isabel pushed open the living-room door, to the sound of tinny laughter. At once, her father rose from his chair and stood impassive, his solid bulk dominating the room. He did not come forward to welcome her but reached behind him and switched off the wireless. 'No, Dad!' Ted and Donald, who'd been slumped at the table, a chessboard between them, sat up, indignant, then saw her and looked delighted, whilst glancing uncertainly at their father. His handsome face glowered. He shoved his hands in his pockets.

'Well, we *are* honoured,' he said.

'Hello, Dad,' she said, going to quickly kiss his cheek. She gave the boys a sisterly grimace and handed over the chocolate she'd managed to buy for them.

'Ripping, thanks!' they said in unison.

'It's good of you to turn out and see us,' her father said, sitting down again. 'I hope we'll not be dull company next to your London friends.'

'Don't be silly, Dad,' she said gently, but her fingers clenched into fists.

'Can't we have the wireless on again?' Ted said through a mouthful of chocolate. 'We were listening.'

'To a lot of rubbish,' their father said shortly, but he did as they asked.

'You got yourself work, I hear,' he said, above the comedians' patter.

'Yes, I really—'

'Does it pay you much?'

'No, but it's—'

'You could have saved yourself the trouble. Found a job round here and stayed and helped your mother.'

'There wasn't anything I wanted to do here.' She glimpsed an expression in his face that touched her, before the mask fell again, such an expression of unhappiness. She was free of him now. She'd struggled and got free. Is that what he sensed and resented? Or envied?

He picked up a newspaper and began to read, ignoring her. All was as before. Ted moved a chess piece, Donald gave an impatient whistle. A log settled in the fireplace. On a string above the mantelpiece, half a dozen Christmas cards fluttered pitifully in the heat.

'I'll go and help Mum,' Isabel said feebly and retreated.

Upstairs, she glanced about her old bedroom, disconcerted to find it wasn't hers any more. Lydia's cot had been shoved alongside the bed and a rosy Lydia was in it, dressed in pyjamas, bouncing with excitement as she clutched the rail. The clothes spilling out of the drawers were Lydia's and her teddy bear stared glassy-eyed from the dressing table. Isabel had been away for two months, and she saw no evidence that she'd ever lived here. Then her eye fell on a suitcase standing by the door.

'The rest of your clothes are in there,' her mother said. 'Perhaps you can take them with you. We had to put your books in the shed. There wouldn't have been space for the cot otherwise.' Lydia had previously slept in their parents' room. 'You won't mind sharing when you're here, I'm sure.'

Both the family and the room had adapted to her absence.

The next two days dragged past. She helped her mother in the kitchen and played with her siblings. The atmosphere she found oppressive. Her father was morose and her mother by turns irritable and falsely cheerful. Worse, Isabel felt herself slipping back into her old, mutinous ways. On Boxing Day, only a long, lonely walk across sodden fields saved her from bad temper. Then it was dusk and her brothers walked her to the station, carrying her cases. As the train pulled away, a mixture of relief and loss overwhelmed her. But as it got nearer and nearer to London, the relief won out.

At Earl's Court she staggered up the steps of the Underground, longing for her little room at Aunt Penelope's, and to return to work the next morning, to see Audrey and Stephen and Trudy, and maybe Berec.

It was late by the time she reached her aunt's. The lights were on in the living room, though the curtains were drawn. When she opened the front door and hauled her luggage inside, she heard voices, a woman's laughter, smelled cigar smoke – Reginald's, certainly, but there were others there, too. Gelert pushed his moist nose into her hand. 'Good dog,' she said, stroking his rough hair and wondering if she should announce her presence or creep up to bed. Gelert looked up at her, his eyes shining in the darkness. The living-room door opened in a rush of warm air and there stood her aunt, a vital, glowing presence in a cloud of French scent. She held a glass tumbler in one hand, a cigarette in the other.

'Oh, it's you,' Penelope said, her voice slurred. 'I thought I heard the door, but I wasn't sure. Are you all right? Come in and have a drink. They're just a few friends.' She stood back and Isabel saw past her into the room. Reginald was there, sprawled in an armchair. He nodded in her direction, but did not smile. How unreadable she always found him, though she understood why her aunt might be charmed by his regular good looks. There was another couple there, too, a man of Reginald's age and, sitting in the other armchair, a much younger woman with neatly waved pale hair and an air of fragility, but when Isabel was introduced to them she didn't retain their names, and she soon shyly presented the excuse of having to get up for work next morning and departed for bed.

She tried to settle to sleep, but she was anxious, as though little demons hurled barbed thoughts into her mind. How difficult the last two days had been and how alone she felt. From downstairs came the women's laughter, and the clink of glasses and the men's low voices.

After half an hour of this she gave up, got out of bed, shuffled into slippers and dressing gown and slipped downstairs. Gelert, curled up on his mat in the kitchen, barely raised his head. There was a little milk in a jug in the scullery, and while it warmed in a saucepan on the stove, she noticed an envelope lying on the top of a cabinet, her aunt's reading spectacles weighting it down. The handwriting drew her attention. It was familiar. She poured the foaming milk into a teacup, then glanced at the letter again, frowning. The writing seemed very much like someone's she knew – her boss, Stephen's. But why would Stephen write to Aunt Penelope? She knew they were acquainted – after all, Berec often spoke of Penelope's generosity to him. Perhaps it wasn't Stephen's writing, perhaps she thought it was because she'd been thinking about him just now, and about being back in the office.

She was still puzzling over the matter when she passed back through the hall. And paused as she heard a clear mention of her name. 'Little Isabel.' It was Penelope's voice. The girl couldn't help but listen and she paid the eavesdropper's price. 'I know she's a nuisance, but she's a sweet child, Reginald. I can't throw her out on the street. She wouldn't know the first thing about looking after herself.'

'Oh nonsense,' said the other woman. 'I left home at sixteen and look at me!'

'We know all about you, old thing,' sneered the other man, after which came a squeal of indignation and a burst of general laughter.

Isabel felt her face grow as warm as the milk. Oh, the shame of it, the sudden clear picture of reality. She was a nuisance, she wasn't really wanted here. She'd been so self-absorbed these last couple of months, it had really not occurred to her. But of course, Penelope had her own life, her own friends and Isabel was a little cuckoo in the nest.

Upstairs, she laid the empty cup down and curled up in bed, no longer feeling that the roof that sheltered her was home. She had no idea how she would afford it on the pittance McKinnon paid her, but she'd have to find somewhere of her own.

Chapter 8

Emily

'Quick, she's off the phone now,' Gillian's assistant Becky said, listening at the door of her boss's office. She knocked, announced Joel and Emily, and ushered them inside. It was a pleasant room overlooking Berkeley Square gardens. Being early December, several Christmas cards were already lined up on the windowsill.

'Joel, how wonderful to meet you at last,' Gillian said, coming out from behind her desk and shaking his hand. 'Welcome to Parchment. We're all absolutely thrilled to be publishing you.' She adjusted the long gauzy scarf hanging over her shoulder and indicated the sofa and chairs where they should sit down.

'It's me that's delighted,' Joel said in his warm voice with its soft northern lilt.

'It'll be a marvellous book,' Gillian continued. She leaned forward in her chair, fixing all her attention on him. 'Now do you have a title for it yet? No? Well, we'll have to put on our thinking caps.'

Emily, who'd said nothing yet, secretly admired how Gillian could switch on the charm with authors, shaking hands and making them feel special, all in the space of a few minutes out of her crazily busy schedule. She'd often caught herself studying Gillian, learning from her.

'And how is dear Jacqueline?' Gillian asked, her expression now one of intense concern. 'It must be so difficult for her. They were married for nearly sixty years, weren't they? You will send her my warmest regards? I simply must go down and visit when I have some time.

'I can't say I know her well, but I think she's doing all right,' Joel said with the slightest touch of humour. 'I expect she'd love to see you.'

'And in the meantime is Emily looking after you properly?' She threw Emily one of her keenest stares.

'I'd say so.' Joel said with a laugh. 'No complaints there. She's taking me to lunch later to celebrate, aren't you, Emily?'

'Joel's working up in the boardroom this morning,' Emily told her boss. 'I got some files from the archive for him to look through. The critical reaction to *The Silent Tide* was amazing. I was reading some of the reviews.'

'You've made quite sure no one else wants the boardroom?' Gillian's eyes narrowed.

'I did check with Becky.' Emily was set momentarily off-balance. Gillian didn't like her editors to get above themselves, and booking the boardroom must have sounded a bit grand, but it had been the only suitable room free.

'Well then, I expect it's all right.' Gillian rose to indicate that time was up. 'Joel, it's been utterly delightful. And we'll look forward to reading the finished script. When will that be?'

'I've already drafted a lot of it,' Joel said. 'Most of the research is done, so I'd say another eight or nine months.'

'That means ... let's say September. Marvellous, marvellous. Well, goodbye.' And somehow Joel and Emily found themselves propelled outside and the door closed behind them.

Joel looked relieved. 'Gillian's very nice,' he said, once they were out of Becky's hearing.

'Yes,' Emily said carefully. 'She can be.'

At lunchtime, she went upstairs to the boardroom to find him still surrounded by papers.

'Do you need a few more minutes?' she asked. 'I could let the restaurant know we'll be late.'

'No, I've finished. But come and look at this.'

She sat beside him at the table and he pushed one of the files, opened at a page of faded type, between them. It was a letter from Hugh Morton dated June 1954 to someone he addressed as 'Stephen'.

'Stephen McKinnon was his publisher at the time,' Joel explained. '*The Silent Tide* must just have been published. It's this part that interests me.' He read aloud: '"The response to the novel has been better than anything I could have hoped for after the struggles of the last few years. Little Lorna is well, thank God. Jacqueline is marvellous with her and we live a very peaceful life here. The garden is at its most beautiful at this time of year and I sit in the sun and think that life cannot be more perfect." Now doesn't that sound like a contented man?'

'He does sound happy.' Emily could imagine how lovely that Suffolk garden must be in summer.

'Doesn't he just?' Joel made a final note, then closed the file. 'From what I've read elsewhere, I'd say it's the time he was happiest in his life.'

'What does he mean by his struggles? Writing the book and it being published?'

'Mostly, yes.' For a moment Emily thought Joel was going to add something more, but all he said was, 'Well, I was pleased to find that. And I've cleared up some points of chronology, so this has been really useful, thank you.'

'You're welcome.' It was companionable sitting here with him and she liked seeing him at work. It made her feel a part of what he was doing.

'May I have photocopies of these reviews?' he said, indicating some he'd marked out. 'They're all new to me.'

'Of course.' She gathered up the files. 'We ought to go and bag our table, though. Why don't I do the copying for you later and put them in the post?'

'Actually,' Emily lifted her wine glass in a toast, 'yours is one of the first books I've acquired for Parchment.'

'Well, it's a celebration for both of us, then,' Joel said, smiling as they clinked glasses.

They were sitting at a table in the window of a first-floor restaurant overlooking Green Park, where a few brave souls huddled on the benches, hunched against the sharp wind. The place had only been open for a few months, and given how empty it was, Emily didn't think it would last much longer, though the food was good. The waiter brought Joel a large plate of scallops and Emily a spicy chicken dish. Because it was a special occasion, Emily had broken the firm's stringent rules and ordered a decent bottle of wine.

They argued amiably about what kind of jacket might be put on the book. Jacqueline, Joel told her, would like the portrait hanging in the hall at Stone House, but Emily felt it was too impressionistic and not recognisable as Hugh. She recommended a photographic approach, maybe the studio portrait of him she'd seen in an obituary – was it in the *Guardian*? – looking intense and reflective. Joel said he'd talk to Jacqueline.

Joel talked a great deal too much about Jacqueline, Emily thought. The woman was insisting that Hugh's alleged affair with his publicist be dealt with firmly. According to her, it was just a nasty rumour put about by a gossip column-ist he'd annoyed, a view Joel agreed with, by the way. She'd also been difficult about him interviewing Lorna.

'Jacqueline kept coming into the room,' Joel said, eating a scallop. 'Poor Lorna, she was flustered.'

'I'm a little worried that you're not getting a free hand to write this book.'

'I don't think it's a problem,' he said, clearly wishing he hadn't said so much. 'Why shouldn't she express an opin-ion? She's not telling me what to write. And she has let me see all the papers so far as I know . . . I worry when you look at me like that.'

'What do you mean?'

'That intense expression . . . It's like the way Gillian looks at you. As if you don't believe me.'

'Sorry, I didn't know I was doing it.' She laughed, uncertain whether she liked the comparison. Perhaps she was picking up a few tricks from her boss. 'I do believe you. It's just that this book's very important to me.'

'It is to me, too,' Joel said with feeling.

'Of course. But you must feel free to tell the whole story, not the Jacqueline Morton version.'

'You have to trust me to do that,' he said, and she sensed steel behind the softness of his voice.

'I'm sorry,' she said, and changed the subject. She referred to the letter they had looked at together in the boardroom. 'You said it was the writing of *The Silent Tide* that he meant when he talked about his struggle. It made me think. It's such a powerful and mature work, isn't it? Very different from his quiet first novel. A lot of people haven't even heard of *Coming Home*.'

'I'm sure you're right. He must have put all his energy into writing *The Silent Tide*. It was such an ambitious novel, of course it would have been a struggle to write.'

Emily had an uncomfortable feeling that he was keeping something back.

'What or who inspired him to write it, do you think?' She remembered Jacqueline's coyness. 'Surely not *her*. I don't see it. Jacqueline's a strong person, but she doesn't have the passion and charm of a character like Nanna. Could there have been someone else?'

Joel sighed and reached for the wine bottle.

'Possibly,' he said, filling their glasses. 'Morton was married before, you know.'

'*Was* he? I didn't know that.'

'Briefly, yes. I haven't been able to find out much about her. Certainly not from Jacqueline.'

'What was her name?' Emily was intrigued.

'Her name was Isabel. Isabel Barber.'

'Isabel?' Emily said in surprise.

'Yes. Does the name mean anything to you?'

'Not really. It's just that, you remember outside Ipswich station, I showed you a copy of *Coming Home*?'

'Yes, but I was desperate to get rid of that bloody lorry.'

'I found it in the office. Hugh Morton had inscribed it to an Isabel. I'd been going to ask you about her.'

'Very little is known about her. She wasn't mentioned in most of the obituaries. One said that she left him and died not long afterwards, drowned in the floods of fifty-three.'

'How awful.'

'There isn't anyone much left to ask. I talked to an old family friend of Jacqueline's about the matter, but he'd never met Isabel. He said—'

At this point they were interrupted by the waiter, who cleared away their plates. After they had declined dessert and ordered coffee, Joel moved the conversation swiftly on.

'Where did you work before Parchment, Emily?'

'Artemis,' she told him. 'I'd been desperate to get into publishing, but it was so competitive. I got a temp job first of all, in their Rights department, and then someone needed an assistant in Editorial and amazingly I got it. One of those strokes of luck.'

'So you worked your way up there?'

'Yes – again I was lucky. An editor didn't come back after having a baby and I was given a few of her authors to look after. It went on from there, really.'

'It must have been more than luck,' he teased. 'Not a spark or two of talent?'

She smiled. 'Maybe. Lots of very hard work, certainly. I used to be there all hours.'

'Good for you. It's obviously paid off. And how did you get this job?'

'Gillian was looking for another acquiring editor. I'd had a couple of successes at Artemis. When she called me it seemed a good move. But now I have to prove myself.'

'I'll do my very best for you with this book.' He gave one of his warm smiles and she felt a rush of happiness.

When they'd finished their coffees he said he must hurry; he had another appointment.

'You go,' she said. 'I'll stay and deal with the bill.'

'Thank you for everything,' he said, kissing her on both cheeks. 'I'll call you very soon.'

'And I'll send you those photocopies,' she replied. 'Take care.'

But as she watched him disappear down the stairs, she felt her unease return. It was the evasive way he'd answered her questions about Isabel. Was she wrong to believe he was holding something back?

Chapter 9

Isabel

'No gentlemen friends and the door's locked at midnight.' Mrs Fortinbras, pale, plump and powdered, swollen feet in mid-heeled shoes, had two young daughters of her own upstairs and wasn't the sort to stand any nonsense. Widowhood might mean letting out rooms to strangers, but she still had her standards.

'Of course,' Isabel murmured. Her gaze roved the small ground-floor room, her new home. She noted the cloths stuffed against draughts in the bomb-bowed window, and the ugly utility furniture. It was clear why the rent was so modest. She sniffed a faint smell of gas in the air, presumably from the ugly fire bolted into the old grate. Still, the room was clean and got the afternoon light, and there was a carpet of reasonable quality.

In the end, it had been Audrey who had found it. Audrey, who knew Vivienne, who lived in this shambling house in Highgate, near the cemetery, where a room had become vacant. The previous occupant had been taken seriously ill and removed to hospital, never to return. The thought of this cast a pall over the enterprise for Isabel, but she tried not to dwell on it.

When Vivienne had brought her to see the room a few

evenings previously, Mrs Fortinbras had requested two weeks' rent in cash. This Isabel had just handed over and it had taken up all her funds. That very morning she'd plucked up courage and asked Stephen for a small advance on her wages. He'd said nothing, but had taken out his wallet on the spot, and pressed several notes into her hand. He'd also said that he'd have a word with Mr Greenford the accountant on Monday to see if he 'could do better for her'. Both of them felt intensely embarrassed at the need to discuss money, but she thanked him profusely.

'Not at all, don't mention it. I must say, Berec's a sound chap to have recommended you,' he said, picking up her latest report from the desk and studying it. It was about a novel by a young Englishman who'd been brought up in Kenya. She'd admired the lush descriptions of the African landscape, but found the writer's tone disturbing.

'Yes, this is the crux,' he said, reading from her final paragraph. '"One might call it an old-fashioned approach. The author does not seem truly to understand the people about whom he is writing, nor does he strive to do so. The views bred into him intervene all the time. He has no curiosity." That's exactly it. You've hit upon the problem very succinctly. Let's turn it away.'

As he put down the report, his eyes had alighted on another manuscript on the desk and he brightened. 'This one, however, isn't bad. Have you time to take a look or shall I ask an outside reader?'

'I'll do it,' she said firmly, taking it before he could change his mind. She sensed his eyes on her as she left the room.

She took the keys Mrs Fortinbras held out to her now, and waited till the woman had gone away upstairs. Then she set about unpacking her meagre possessions, lining up her shoes under the rickety bed, hanging her skirts and dresses on the crooked rail set in the alcove, arranging the books on the shelves by the fire. She missed her home with Penelope already, especially Gelert's companionship. Her aunt had been faintly surprised when Isabel announced that she'd found her own place. Isabel was touched when Penelope had tried to make her stay, but she also sensed the woman's relief when she shook her head. 'It's too good an opportunity to miss,' Isabel lied. She turned down suggestions of Reginald's help and transported all her things in a taxi. After all, there wasn't much.

She pushed her empty cases behind the shoes and sank down on the bed, which let out a creak so violent she leaped up and tried again more gingerly. She wondered what to do with herself. Vivienne, who was Jewish, had been spending the day with her family. For the first time in London, Isabel felt truly alone. But not miserable. Before her, the curtains stood open and a golden January twilight began to steal over the room. A blackbird was singing on its perch in an ilex bush and she listened for a moment. How peaceful it all was. Tomorrow being a Sunday, she'd explore. There was Highgate Cemetery to see, which she'd passed on the taxi ride, and a row of interesting-looking shops round the corner.

She was setting her alarm clock on the bedside table, when there came a gentle knock and the door opened. 'Hello, are you decent?' A smiling freckled face with a frizzy halo of fair hair peered round, and a lanky figure slipped into the room.

'Vivienne,' Isabel said joyfully. 'I didn't know you were back. How is your family?'

'Just about endurable today,' Vivienne said, coming to sit next to her on the bed, which squealed in complaint. 'Looks like you've settled in all right, then. Gosh, it's chilly in here. Have you fed the meter? Let me do it.' She slotted in Isabel's last few coins and found matches on the mantelpiece. She crouched by the fire like a spindly insect, then yelped in surprise as the gas caught light. They both knelt down beside the fire, waiting for it to heat up. Soon the room began to feel like home.

'Super. I'll go and make a pot of tea.'

She and Vivienne had taken to each other immediately. The other girl must have been a couple of years her senior, and she, too, had been forced to move away from home to establish her independence. Vivienne was at Duke's College and had recently joined a research team in a laboratory, working towards a further degree whilst earning a little money for setting up equipment. It must be a pittance if she had to live here. Her parents had originally supported her desire to study, but not to pursue a career as a scientist. She and Isabel came from quite different backgrounds. Her parents sounded wealthy, though they tried to control Vivienne by denying her money. The link to Isabel's world was slight. 'I don't know Audrey very well, actually,' she'd told Isabel when they first met. 'My brother works with Anthony, her fiancé. Audrey's awfully stylish, isn't she?' That was something else the girls had in common: nervousness of Audrey.

* * *

Moving to Highgate that winter was only one way in which Isabel began to establish herself and grow in confidence. Lord Pockmartin's book had sold so well over Christmas, along with the film star's biography, that Mr Greenford the accountant agreed with Stephen McKinnon that a small raise for Isabel was indeed possible. The weeks went past and there was no more talk of her having to leave.

Isabel and Audrey had their work cut to a pattern now. There were still hours of typing for Isabel to do, and filing, and showing visitors in and answering phones and making endless cups of tea, but she became quicker at the office tasks and was now reading regularly for Stephen, as did Trudy, and a freelance reader named Percival Morris, who was shy as a moth in person, but devastatingly acerbic in his written reports.

Given that Trudy was back to full strength, Isabel felt she had to be tactful about impinging on her responsibilities, but Trudy was generous and seemed genuinely not to mind. After all, the firm's decision-making lay with Stephen, all aspects of negotiating for new books, indeed any money matter. Trudy's job was to work with the authors and to turn the scruffiest of scripts into rigorously edited and properly proofread books. There was plenty of work for all, and towards the end of January when there was a rush, she asked Isabel to look at some proofs for her and showed her how to mark them up. 'They're a final set, so you're just checking to see that all the corrections have been made properly,' she said. 'It's the Ambrose Fairbrother, and he really has been very naughty with all his last-minute rewriting.'

'I'll can start on it straight away,' Isabel said, glancing at Audrey, who shrugged. 'Stephen's out this afternoon.'

Trudy was pleased with Isabel's careful work and began feeding her other tasks. Before long she was checking rolls of galley proofs and engaging in conversations with writers, typesetters and printers. January turned to February and although she was still anxious that the moment might arrive when Stephen would call her into his office and say sorry, he couldn't afford to pay her any longer, that moment didn't come and she started to relax.

She was enjoying her new life. In the evenings, sometimes, she'd go to a party, the launch of a new novelist, perhaps, or accompany Berec to a poetry reading. If she and Vivienne were both at home, they'd cook a simple meal together in the chilly kitchen at the back of the hall, where occasionally one of the house's other inhabitants might be glimpsed. There was a plain-faced, youngish woman, the secretary for a uniformed church organisation, who once gave them leaflets of Bible verses with her too-bright smile. A fourth tenant was much older, a woman who, Isabel guessed from her manner – rightly, it turned out – was a retired schoolteacher. She wore a perpetual expression of disapproval and kept herself to herself.

On 10 February, Isabel celebrated her twentieth birthday. Despite her general neglect of her nieces and nephews, Penelope had always remembered Isabel's birthday, and this year she sent her five pounds, an unimaginably high sum. Isabel didn't like to question the motive. Perhaps her aunt felt guilty that she'd not been more hospitable. She spent it on clothes, using all her precious ration coupons. After all, she had to be smart for work. And even Audrey gave her approving looks when she wore her new suits. Appearance was everything for a girl on the make.

Chapter 10

Isabel

Isabel sat at her desk, trying to ignore a throbbing headache. She stared at the page in the typewriter in front of her, but the words kept moving in and out of focus. It was a cold day, even for March, but she felt as if she was on fire. A wave of dizziness finally overcame her and she laid her face on the desk. How lovely and cool it was.

'For goodness' sake,' Audrey sighed, 'don't droop about here. Go home. There's no point being a martyr if the rest of us catch it.'

Jimmy Jones, the packer's son, was loitering in the doorway, picking his nose and waiting for Trudy to give him a parcel to take to the Post Office.

'What are *you* staring at?' Audrey snapped. 'Go and find her a taxi.'

'Awright, keep your hair on,' he muttered and slouched off.

'You needn't worry,' she told Isabel, who was trying to finish up. 'Take the fare out of petty cash – spoil yourself.'

Audrey helped Isabel on with her coat. Whilst the older girl's back was turned, Isabel slipped a manuscript that

Stephen had given her inside her shopping bag. If she had to be ill, she'd want something to read.

For the next three days, however, there was no question of reading anything. She slept, cocooned in the extra blankets that Vivienne had dragooned their landlady into giving her so she didn't have to spend precious pennies on gas. Nothing passed her parched lips and burning throat but water. Each evening, when she came home, Vivienne went and sat with her, sponged her face and tidied up the bed. On the fourth day she felt a little better, and on the fifth, well enough to feel absolutely wretched. She missed her home, she missed her old bedroom, above all she missed her mother. She blew her nose until it was swollen and stinging and felt sorry for herself. She must be the loneliest, ugliest girl in the world; everyone had forgotten her and no one would ever love her again. It was in this mood that she cast about for distraction and remembered the manuscript in her bag. She staggered out of bed and fetched it.

An hour later, she had forgotten her aching head and runny nose. She was completely caught up in a young man's voice, as he told her a story of suffering, of love denied. She read until it grew dark and Vivienne knocked on the door to see how she was. She read again when Vivienne left her later. She dreamed about the characters and woke in the night to find pages of the manuscript rustling round her on the bed. The next morning she finished it, actually weeping when the young man and his love, Diana, were finally parted by Diana's death in an air raid when he was on his way to meet her. But when she'd dried her eyes, she gathered up the pages and felt better, much better. She sat up in bed, a coat around her shoulders, and wrote a long and enthusiastic report.

Finally she threw pen and paper aside, tired out. She had to be well enough to go to work the next morning. If she arrived early she could type up the report before tackling the pile of tasks that undoubtedly awaited her return, and eagerly anticipate Stephen's response.

After a week of tense waiting she asked Stephen, 'I don't suppose you've had time to read that report on Hugh Morton's book I left you?'

'Ah, I'm sorry, I forgot to tell you about that,' Stephen replied with a guilty look, and her hopes fell. But then he said, 'The author's coming in next week. I'll make sure the two of you are introduced.'

'We're publishing the book?' she asked, in surprise and not a little anger. She was used to not being told much, to having to pick up information through opening the post or by correspondence she was asked to type, but she was hurt that he hadn't mentioned anything about this project.

'His agent rang accepting our offer this morning, so it certainly looks like it,' Stephen said with a boyish smile. Then, more seriously, 'What I'd like from you is a list of notes. A more detailed version of those changes you suggested in the report.'

'The ones about Diana, you mean?' He was actually allowing her to work creatively with an author. Suddenly, he was forgiven.

'Yes. I'm inclined to agree with you. She does lack spirit. I'll need to speak to him about it.'

'Oh, yes, of course.' She was pleased that he wanted her notes, but disappointed that he would present her ideas for her. Still, it was a start.

* * *

The following Tuesday lunchtime she was absorbed in proofreading when a sonorous voice was heard to ask, 'Where do I find Mr McKinnon?' She looked up. A tall young man with dark springy hair stood at the door. He carried an umbrella, but his coat glistened with rain. She knew immediately who he must be.

'Mr Morton?' Audrey got there first. She slipped out from behind her desk with one of her sinuous movements, introduced herself and showed him into Stephen's office. Hugh Morton did not even glance at Isabel as he passed, and though she typed away furiously, she could not but be aware of him. His presence radiated intensity.

She heard Stephen say, 'A great pleasure to meet you,' to the newcomer, before Audrey closed the door on them and sat down. Five minutes later, the door opened again and Isabel raised her head, half-expecting Stephen to call her in, but instead he took Morton across to Trudy, who congratulated him, and then to Philip. 'The man who'll be responsible for the jacket,' Stephen explained. Finally, they came to Isabel.

'And this is Isabel Barber, who has also read your novel.'

Audrey chose this moment to interrupt. 'Mr McKinnon,' she said, 'would you mind signing this letter before you go out? It's to accompany those urgent contracts.'

Stephen turned away to oblige her. Isabel stood up to take the young man's outstretched hand. 'I'm very pleased to meet you,' she said, suddenly shy.

He replied eagerly, 'The pleasure's mine. So you've read it? I'm rather afraid to ask, but what did you honestly think?' His low voice was husky now, charmingly so, and Isabel felt all his attention upon her.

'Oh, I admired it very much,' she replied, feeling her face colour up. 'I really did.'

'I'm so relieved,' he said, and looked it.

Stephen handed Audrey back her letter. 'We ought to be off, I'm afraid. There's much to discuss over lunch. I should be back for my four o'clock. If that man from the wholesaler rings again, either of you, tell him we'll reprint if he confirms his order.'

Hugh Morton said his goodbyes and Isabel watched them go off together. She could still feel the warmth of his hand and hear the timbre of his voice. It was extraordinary how she felt she recognised him from his book. If she'd been skilled enough to have painted a picture of the hero of *Coming Home*, she'd have painted Hugh, straight-backed, his dark hair springing from his forehead, the bookishly pale complexion and long-lashed brown eyes with their intense, slightly amused expression. He'd look perfect in a pilot's jacket, especially . . .

'Are you all right?' Audrey's voice came from somewhere far off. Isabel glanced up to see that she was putting on her coat. 'You're not going down with something again, are you? You do look peculiar.'

'Perhaps I need some fresh air,' Isabel sighed. 'I might take my lunch now, too, if you'll be here, Trudy?'

'You run along, dear,' Trudy said.

On their way out to the street, Audrey said, 'Well, Hugh Morton's a dish, isn't he?' Seeing Isabel's embarrassment, she laughed. 'You didn't really expect that Stephen would ask you to go with them, did you? You're blushing. You did!'

'Don't be silly,' Isabel said. Sometimes she hated Audrey for her uncanny ability to see the truth, and to portray it in the worst possible light. 'Why don't we buy a sandwich and sit in the park?'

'I'm awfully sorry,' Audrey said, icily polite, 'I'm having lunch with a friend.' And she swept off.

Isabel watched her smart, elegant figure hurry away, and hated her.

Late in the afternoon, after everyone else had gone, she hovered in the doorway of Stephen's office, watching him sort through the papers in one of his overflowing wire trays, an anxious frown on his face.

'I'm off in a moment,' she said, startling him. 'How did your meeting go at lunchtime – with Mr Morton? Did he mind about making the changes?'

'The changes?' The anxiety turned to puzzlement, then his expression cleared. 'Oh, you mean to his book. No, not *per se*,' he said. 'That is, we didn't discuss them in detail. He took the notes away with him, and said he'll give me his opinion.'

'Did you tell him it was I who'd written them?'

'Yes. I don't think he expected . . . Good Lord, well, he said . . .' He stopped and ran his fingers through his hair.

'Did I put something badly?' She was horrified at the idea of offending Hugh Morton. 'Please tell me.'

'No, no, nothing like that. It's just it's important to take matters a step at a time. Isabel, come in and sit down a moment.'

He faced her across the desk, his face serious, but not unsympathetic. 'You must have observed by now that a writer's relationship with an editor is one of trust. A publisher is privileged to work with the creative genius and has to earn that trust. It's important at this early stage that he knows that I, his publisher, care for his work in every way.'

'You mean, he expects any comments to come through you. Even though they're my work. I see.' Her voice was colourless.

'It's not about you. I'm very pleased with your work, it's just one mustn't expect too much of people, and often men don't like . . .' He stopped.

'Men don't like to be told what to do by a woman. Is that what you were going to say?'

'Not at all,' Stephen said mildly. 'You know I don't think like that.'

'But a lot of men do,' she said sadly.

'Isabel, you are still very young and, I have to remind you, very new to all this. Trust me, please.'

Her shoulders sagged. 'I expect you're right,' she said. 'I'm so sorry. I want to do well, though.'

'You are doing well, as you put it,' he replied with a sigh. 'But please try not to take yourself so seriously.'

She stared at him in amazement. How could she not be serious? She so wanted to succeed.

'Confound it, those figures must be somewhere,' he muttered, returning to his search.

She spotted a piece of paper on the floor by his desk and stood up to fetch it. 'Is this what you're looking for?' she asked, handing it to him.

'Ah yes, thank you,' he said, reaching for the telephone. Realising that he'd already forgotten her, she quietly left the room.

Not long after this dispiriting conversation, she was opening Stephen's morning post and found a letter from

Hugh Morton. She read with growing delight. In it he thanked Stephen for lunch and went on to say that he'd done as requested and thought long and hard about the suggestions in the notes that Stephen had given him.

Although I wasn't convinced at first, Morton had written, *I am now of the opinion that they have considerable merit. Since the female psyche is to me, as to most men, something of a mystery, deep, unfathomably so, and mercurial, having a guess at it is like casting a stone into a deep well. I find Miss Barber's notes illuminate the darkness and am most grateful to her for them. I wonder, therefore, if she might find it acceptable to meet me at a mutually convenient date in order to discuss the matter further. Three or four weeks away should do the trick. I will by then have drafted some revisions for you both to consider.*

She took the letter in for Stephen in some excitement and watched him read it.

'I take it that you would be happy to meet Morton?' Stephen said, smiling up at her.

'I'm sure I can spare the time,' she said airily, and smiled back.

This time, when Hugh Morton visited the office, it was to collect Isabel. She'd suggested they repair to a teashop nearby and he said he knew one she might like. The complexities of either trying to use Stephen's office when he was out, or having all her colleagues listening to their conversation, were too embarrassing to be borne. She felt Audrey's disapproving glare boring into her back as they went out, and knew that this time, she had really stepped beyond the pale. She was so happy she didn't care.

Hugh walked faster than she did, as if he was late, and she had to hurry to keep up. She noticed how people couldn't help glancing at them, he purposeful, briefcase under his arm, his coat-tails flying, she a step behind, his humble attendant.

When they entered the smart teashop on Oxford Street it was to find it dark and half-empty, the electricity supply having cut out. A waitress in a black dress and white apron pounced on the new customers gratefully. There was a table free in the window, which Hugh commanded at once. Isabel caught their reflection in a glass panel as they made their way towards it. Her chestnut-red hair and coral lipstick, and his crimson scarf were the only touches of brightness in the place, and when they sat down, the gloom conveyed a thrilling intimacy.

The waitress assured them of the possibility of a pot of tea, and they chose from a selection of cakes on the trolley. When she had gone away, Hugh studied Isabel with amusement. 'Are you all right?' he asked, leaning towards her. 'I don't mean to be rude, but you look . . . well, like Red Riding Hood meeting the wolf!'

It was hard to convey how overwhelmed she felt. Here she was, alone with a young writer whose work she admired and whom she was expected to impress, yet she wasn't sure what to say. Still, his comment roused her. She drew herself up.

'I'm sure I do not,' she said hotly.

He laughed. 'I'm certainly not in the habit of eating women, don't worry.' Suddenly he was serious. 'Thank you for meeting me. I wanted to tell you face-to-face, you see. It was very useful, what you said about my novel. Thank you for taking the trouble. To tell you the truth, I didn't like it at all at first, anyone's interference in my work. But then I thought a good deal about your comments and realised perhaps there was something in what you said.'

'I'm glad if that's the case.' Despite his condescension she felt a massive sense of relief.

'It is.' He reached down for his briefcase. 'I have the script here and I've started work. I should like you to take a look now, if you will. Tell me if you think I've grasped the right end of the stick.'

By the time the waitress returned with a laden tray, the two of them were poring over a pile of typed paper and deep in discussion. They carried on talking whilst the woman laid out cups and plates around them, sniffing loudly.

Isabel hardly noticed. She had completely forgotten her shyness, and was engaging in ways in which Diana might develop as a character on the page. 'You could use the way she dresses,' she told the author. 'She might be dowdy at the beginning, when he meets her, but become more stylish. I do mean stylish, not blowsy.'

'No, she's not that kind of woman at all. I like what you said about the way she speaks,' he went on, turning a page. 'Here, do you think this would work?'

She examined the alterations, which were handwritten, but not at all difficult to read.

'Mmm, I like that,' she said.

'Should I pour your tea before it gets cold?' the waitress broke in.

As they ate and drank, they continued to talk, and Isabel wondered how she could ever have been nervous of Hugh. He was older than she was, thirty, perhaps, and had already seen so much of life – and death, too, she imagined, thinking about the wartime episodes in his novel – but this hadn't thickened his writer's sensibilities. He was intensely defensive of his work, but she respected that. It showed how committed he was. She, for her part, felt she intuitively understood the way that he was working, the paths along which his mind travelled. All she had to do was ask questions, drop the smallest of hints and he picked these up. It was like walking along a balancing bar, being careful never to let him think an idea wasn't his own. 'How clever you are,' was how she merely had to flatter him and he'd brighten. She loved the way his emotions played on his sensitive face.

Eventually she plucked up the courage to ask the question she'd longed to. 'Is the story based on events that happened to you?'

He drew a pack of cigarettes from his inside pocket and when he offered it she felt it natural to take one, though she didn't usually like to smoke.

'To me or to people I know, yes,' he replied. Their hands touched thrillingly as he lit the cigarette for her. 'Schoolfriends, people I grew up with. We'd all grown up having similar experiences and with similar expectations. And then the war came.' He made a gesture of dismissal. 'Now we ask ourselves what it was all for. We can't get ourselves going again as a country, can we? We're stuck in the past, hankering after shabby glories. This government, they think they're reforming everything, but underneath there are the same old rules, and the same men are still in control.'

'Goodness me, you're a radical?' she asked, blinking at the smoke. She'd met several writers of Stephen's acquaintance who had strong left-wing views and thought some of them bitter, angry people, though perhaps they had things to be bitter and angry about. Berec's friend Gregor was like that, always rambling on about social justice. Poor Karin, his wife, on the other hand, hated politics of any sort. 'Trouble,' she'd say, drawing a finger across her throat.

Hugh Morton wasn't one of these firebrands, though. He was passionate, she could see that, but he directed his passion into his writing and seemed sad rather than bitter.

'I'm not a Communist, if that's what you're asking. I'm proud of my country. Just fed up with the same bloody people going on as though they know best. They make a show of asking what ordinary people think but then ignore them. Sorry, I'm preaching. How ill-mannered of me.'

'Not at all,' she said. She had been listening intently, chin in hand, elbow on the table. 'It's interesting. Is that what you want to write about, politics?'

'Don't you think there's a sense in which everything is politics? You and I sitting here, like two different planets, circling one another, that's politics. It's all about human relationships, and that indeed is the territory of the writer.'

He gave one last pull on his cigarette and stubbed it out on the ashtray with a single, savage movement, then looked up into her face, his frown softening.

'What about you? Do you write yourself or just tell other people how to do it?'

She felt the warmth rise to her cheeks. 'Only a little,' she said humbly. 'Scribblings. I'd like to but I'm not very good, I'm afraid. For now, I love working with writers.'

'It's your first job, Stephen tells me. Straight from school?'

'Yes. I had an idea about studying at university, but it

simply wasn't possible. My father . . . well, there's not much spare money and my mother needed me at home.' She told him about her parents, her brothers and her sister and he was interested that her brothers were twins.

'I don't have any siblings, you see, and my parents were often away. When I was four or five I used to imagine I had a brother. He was exactly my age, like my mirror opposite, and I used to speak to him in a language I made up. My father sent me to see a man about it, but it turned out there was nothing much wrong with me. Nothing that school wouldn't sort out. Too much time alone, that was all. It's true. I used to read, endlessly, and now I look back, what was real and the stories I read became muddled up in my mind.'

'That happened to me, too,' Isabel replied with enthusiasm. 'The twins had each other. They didn't take any notice of me. When I was thirteen, I desperately wanted to be Jo March in *Little Women*, but not to marry the dull old professor. I wish she'd married Laurie.' She'd longed to meet a Laurie. She glanced at Hugh's dark shorn curls and the thought popped into her head that he was very like the descriptions of Jo March's rejected beau.

'Ah, so you're a romantic. Very dangerous.'

'Why does talking about love make one a romantic? You said yourself that writing is all about relationships. And what is love but the most intense of relationships. Not,' she added, blushing, 'that I know very much about that yet.'

'Good lord, now I've gone and embarrassed you. Look, it's dangerous to believe in happy endings. Life isn't like that, all nicely tied up in a bow, which you girls seem to think.'

She considered this and said, 'No, but there are moments of pure happiness to be found and we have to believe those will happen, don't we? They keep us going during the bad parts.'

He laughed and said, 'Perhaps you're right.'

She saw he was looking very fondly at her and she found herself liking him more and more.

Chapter 11

Emily

One Friday, a fortnight to Christmas, Emily came home from an evening with friends at a new cocktail bar that had opened up near the office. Megan was her best pal from school, Steffi and Nell they'd got to know when they all found themselves sharing the same flat soon after Emily moved to London. They had become a close four-some, and though they'd all gone their separate ways, they still tried to get together every couple of weeks or so to catch up on news. Emily enjoyed these evenings of chat and laughter and now, closing the door and listening to the silence, she felt a little wistful, remembering the friendly chaos of shared living. This was only moment-ary, however. She loved this high-ceilinged first-floor flat that she'd saved madly to buy, with a bit of help from Dad, and had learned there were advantages to living alone. When she put something down, for instance, it stayed put. It was a shame, she thought, that dealing with people was less certain. She wouldn't be alone tonight – Matthew was due to come over, but what time she didn't know and he hadn't been in touch.

She was starving. The drinks had been expensive so she'd only had a snack in the cocktail bar. She fetched some juice and a pasta salad from the fridge and settled herself on the sofa. She was reaching for a magazine to read when she remembered the video Nell had just given her. It was of the television programme about Hugh Morton that Gillian Bradshaw had recommended, broadcast in 1985 to celebrate the writer's 65th birthday. Nell worked in a film library and had dug out a copy for her. She fetched it from her bag, noticing from the label that the last time anyone had taken it out was 1991.

Setting up her old video recorder was the work of a moment. She knelt in front of the screen and pushed the tape into the slot. It started up at once and there he was, Hugh Morton, close up. She'd never seen footage of him before. She turned up the volume and returned to the sofa to watch it properly. He commanded quite a presence, she had to admit: rangy, masculine, with his handsome, cragged-up face and confident manner. The programme followed the typical format of the time, starting with the writer being interviewed in his study, which she recognised from her visit, though it was summer in the film rather than foggy November, for a flower-filled garden was visible through the window. Morton sat at his desk, informal in shirtsleeves, smoking a cigarette as though he needed it.

'So what if I was friends with the Chairman of the judges. They simply liked the book,' Morton said, in response to the male interviewer's question about his blighted Booker Prize win. 'I'm tired of this argument now. It's a small world, the London literary scene. It's bloody bitchy, it needs more air.'

As the interviewer pointed out, there was plenty of air where Morton lived. Swooping views followed of Stone

House, lovely gardens rolling out towards marshland. The bleak foreshore of the estuary lined the horizon beyond. 'I inherited this house from my father,' the writer explained in a voiceover. 'There have been Mortons here for generations. You might say the river runs in my blood.'

At this point a narrator took over. 'Hugh and his first wife, Isabel, settled here in 1951, but sadly parted less than two years into their marriage. It wasn't long afterwards that he married Jacqueline, a childhood friend. They have a daughter, Lorna, from his first marriage, and two sons, all long grown up.'

Astonished, Emily pressed the pause button. Had she heard correctly? She rewound the tape to listen again. Yes, she had. Lorna wasn't Jacqueline's daughter, but Isabel's. This revelation disturbed her. It seemed so wrong. Poor Lorna, she thought, still living at home, waiting hand and foot on her stepmother while Jacqueline's own children had escaped their parents' reach. She remembered the old woman's wistful expression when she talked about her boys, and the patronising way she'd addressed her middle-aged step-daughter. She wondered whether Lorna remembered her real mother. Joel must surely know, and yet he hadn't breathed a word. Why not? Still troubled by this, she let the film continue.

The camera cut to Jacqueline's matronly figure as she cut flowers in the garden and served tea to her husband at a table in the shade of a copper beech. An arrowhead of wild ducks passed overhead, their harsh cries breaking the stillness.

The rest of the programme focused on the books themselves. Morton spoke interestingly about his influences, the effect of his wartime experience, his fascination with the darker areas of man's soul, defended himself against the feminists who perceived misogyny in his writing.

Near the end, Emily had to get up to buzz Matthew in downstairs. He arrived at the door to the flat to find it open. She was back watching Morton walk by the river, head bowed, presumably deep in creative thought. Then the spell broke as the credits rolled.

'Hello,' Matthew said, leaning to kiss her, 'what's that you've been watching?'

'An old documentary about Hugh Morton.'

'Any good?' he asked, putting down his bag and unwinding his scarf.

'Not bad. A bit deferential. And there was something odd about his first marriage. Do you know anything about it?'

'No, he's not a writer I've come across much. God, I'm hungry. All I've had since breakfast is crisps.'

She offered to make him a ham toastie. 'Thanks. And I could murder a cold beer.' He rubbed his face and yawned. Emily noticed with tenderness that he hadn't shaved. He must have been working hard. She found a can of lager in the fridge. He took a long draught and sank onto the sofa. 'Mind if I catch the news?'

'Sure.'

She listened vaguely to the headlines as she made the sandwich but principally she thought about Isabel. Apart from that brief mention of her name, the first Mrs Morton had been completely missing from the programme. The interviewer hadn't been interested in her at all. And yet

Isabel had been Lorna's mother. What had happened? It was curious.

She carried the sandwich over and curled up beside Matthew as he ate, loving the warmth of him. He seemed a little distant tonight, she thought, self-absorbed. After the news finished she asked, 'How was your day, then?' She remembered he'd been nervous at the prospect of a tutorial with Tobias Berryman.

'Manic,' he replied, swallowing the last mouthful of sandwich. 'I wrote the book review by eleven, then made it by the skin of my teeth to a seminar. After that I hiked across town to interview that PR guru for the magazine, you remember I told you about him? An interesting guy, I thought.'

'And how was Professor Berryman?'

'Feeling emollient, thank God. Liked what I'd done so far. Made some useful suggestions, in fact. Oh, and he said to tell you the novel is nearly ready.'

'I hope he doesn't expect me to read it over Christmas.'

'Probably. Look, I'm still famished. Any chance of another sandwich?'

'Yes, if you make it yourself. I'm feeling too comfortable here.'

After Matthew fell asleep that night, Emily lay awake thinking about him. It occurred to her that he hadn't asked about her day and that was hurtful. He'd been tired, she told herself, that was all it was.

Saturday, however, didn't go much better. Matthew, some time back, had invited Luke and Yvette over to dinner. They were the couple at whose supper party he and Emily had met. It had been decided dinner would be at his flat because it was within walking distance of where they lived. However, since he had to work all day on his assignment, Emily volunteered to cook the meal. She arrived at his flat during the afternoon with two carrier bags of food and took over the kitchen. As she cooked, she glanced from time to time at Matthew, sitting in a pool of light at his desk, oblivious to the activity around him, completely lost in his writing. He always wrote poetry in longhand – he liked to see his crossings out, he said – and she was amused by the way he frowned and pushed his fingers through his hair as he worked. He looked the picture of a poet from several centuries ago, in a garret, writing by candlelight. She smiled to herself as she cooked, treasuring this romantic image of him, but eventually had to interrupt.

'Matthew, we need your desk now or we won't have anywhere to eat.'

When Luke and Yvette arrived they pronounced themselves enchanted by the flat, but all through the meal Emily couldn't help remembering their guests' spacious marital home with its gleaming silver kitchen and designer patio garden. Matthew didn't care about 'stuff', as he disparagingly called it – that was one of the things Emily usually loved him for – but tonight she found herself wishing that he did care just a little bit.

'Em, I think I'd better give lunch with your parents a miss today,' Matthew said from the kitchen the next day as he spooned coffee grounds into the cafetière. 'I won't finish my assignment in time otherwise.'

Emily, eating a croissant on the sofa and flicking through a magazine, was dismayed. 'Oh Matthew, I've told them you're coming.'

'I did say that I hoped to, not that I would.' She had a vague idea that this might be true. 'I am sorry,' he said, coming to sit beside her. 'I'm not much good for you at the moment, am I?' He stroked her hair. She thought he sounded sorry. It was difficult to feel angry with him for long, she loved him so much, but nor could she always tell what he was thinking. What if he simply didn't want to come? The thought of that, he not being interested in her family, was devastating.

'Do you still want me to come to Wales for New Year?' she asked uncertainly. She knew his three brothers slightly and had visited his mother and stepfather near Cardiff for a weekend in September. She found them all warm and friendly. The family were planning a New Year's Eve party and she was looking forward to it. She hoped he didn't regret inviting her.

'Of course I do. And remember, I hand in my assignment next Friday so I'll get a bit of a break. Except for some journalism, that is.'

'It is a shame about today,' she couldn't help saying, but this seemed to irritate him.

'Look, Em, I said I'm sorry. Anyway, it's not just me that cries off things. Sometimes it's you who's busy. Remember last month when you spent all weekend editing and wouldn't meet up at all?'

'That was different. It didn't affect anyone else. Mum and Dad will be disappointed.'

'But the whole clan will be there today, won't they? Your sister's family? They won't notice if I'm absent, not really. Not with the children running about.'

'*I* will notice,' she said firmly. 'I'll tell you something, though – I don't think I'm up to explaining in front of

Mike that you can't come because you're writing poetry.' Matthew and her brother-in-law, bank executive and rugby player, struggled to find subjects to talk about. It was obvious that Mike thought Creative Writing MAs a waste of time and money.

'Yes, tell him,' Matthew said with one of his sudden bouts of passion. 'Poetry is vital, like breathing. It communicates the essence of things.'

She laughed. 'I don't think he'd go for that at all. It would only start an argument.'

'And what's wrong with a good argument? My family is always arguing. It's silence between people we have to worry about.'

'My family's different, you know that.'

Emily considered all this whilst on the train to her parents'. Family arguments were wearing. Silence of the right sort could be wonderful when you felt at ease with someone, like she usually was with Matthew. This weekend, though, she worried that they were losing the connection. Something was different, but she couldn't tell what.

On Monday morning, she found an old cardboard folder on her desk and thought of another kind of silence, the silence of a voice smothered, a secret muffled.

She opened it to find a sheaf of old papers, all neatly clipped together. She knew what it was when she read the typed letter on the top. At the bottom was Hugh Morton's characteristic black signature and the date, October 1949. The letter was addressed to Stephen McKinnon, Hugh's publisher, and it was all about *Coming Home*. It was to thank Stephen for a cutting of a book review, which had clearly been favourable. The whole file was about *Coming Home*!

Joel must see this, she thought excitedly. Had someone found it in the archive? She looked in vain for the official form that had accompanied the other files. Why, anyway, should Parchment possess a file about *Coming Home*? The book was published by a company she didn't know, but obviously owned by Stephen McKinnon.

Emily glanced at her colleague Sarah, who was checking a Twitter feed and frowning. 'Do you know who left this folder?' Emily asked her.

'No, sorry,' Sarah murmured, hardly looking up as she started to type.

'Anyone?' Emily asked, appealing to Liz and Gabby opposite. They said they didn't know either.

'What's in it, something exciting?' Sarah asked, turning from her computer at last.

'It might be, yes,' Emily said. 'But I don't understand. How have I got a file for a book we didn't publish?'

'Who did publish it?' Sarah asked.

Emily consulted again the address at the top of the letter. 'McKinnon and Holt, Percy Street. Any idea who they were?'

Sarah scooted her chair alongside. 'I think I have. Let's see. What book is it the file for?'

'Hugh Morton's first novel, *Coming Home*.'

Sarah inspected the file, flicking the pages. A few were coming adrift from their mooring.

'Interesting,' she said. 'I've no idea about this particular book, but Parchment bought up some smaller publishing companies in the nineties. McKinnon and

Holt came with one of those. Therefore we probably do own the rights to this book.'

Emily looked down at the file in astonishment. So Parchment was now the publisher of *Coming Home*. She wondered if Gillian knew this. But where had this file come from?

Liz's face appeared above her partition. 'Time for the cover meeting, folks,' she called. Sarah slid her chair back to her desk and started gathering up papers.

'Be with you in a sec,' Emily told her. She set about straightening the pages in the file, but more kept coming loose from the old metal binding. One, near the back, simply wouldn't be tidied and she pulled it out to see why. It was older than the letter at the top of the folder, a whole year older, but of course the file was in reverse date order. From it, a name caught her eye. The address typed at the top started *Miss Isabel Barber*. The letter began, *My dear Miss B . . .*

Isabel. She'd found Isabel. She felt almost dizzy with excitement.

Sarah put her head round the door. 'Emily, they want to do your books first,' she said.

'Do they?' Emily said, putting down the file with reluctance. 'All right, coming.'

It wasn't till much later, when the office was quiet, that she had time to inspect the folder once more. Carefully she opened the metal fastenings to free the paper. Then she turned the thick pile over and took up a page from the back. It was from a literary agency, whose name she didn't recognise – another company lost in the mist of history. She read it eagerly.

Dear Mr McKinnon, it began. *I am pleased to send you this novel by a Mr Hugh Morton, whose work I have recently agreed to represent.*

She reached for the next sheet in the pile – no, two, stapled together. It was a reader's report, addressed to Stephen McKinnon and signed with the initials IB. Isabel Barber. Isabel had been meticulous, correcting typing errors in small, neat italics.

Morton paints pictures with words. He writes so tenderly about what it's like to be young, to have hopes and dreams, and then to see them destroyed by war. I have often wondered what it felt like to be in a plane, caught in the open with the enemy shooting at you, how terrifying it must be, and he makes me see and hear and feel it all. This must be the story of so many young men and he tells it with such power. He is a natural writer. The only weakness is his female character, Diana, who seems a little too perfect, passively waiting for him like that. I know I would have been quite exasperated by his behaviour sometimes.

Yes, that is exactly what Emily herself had thought about *Coming Home* – how freshly told it was, how tender. She hadn't minded about Diana though, the hero's long-suffering girlfriend; indeed, Diana's sense of frustration and anger had been most convincing. And then it occurred to Emily that in this report, Isabel had been commenting on an earlier draft. Maybe Morton had made further changes to the script?

Emily turned the fragile pages, noticing letters between Isabel and Hugh Morton. Isabel must have been his editor for this book, she concluded, before the man who worked on *The Silent Tide* – what was his name? Richard something.

As darkness thickened outside, she read on, utterly absorbed.

Chapter 12

Isabel

'You're in a very good mood these days,' Vivienne said, cocking her head to smile at Isabel. They were walking together to the bus stop. It was one of those very clear sunlit days and spring seemed finally to be swinging into action. They would ride the bus together as far as Tottenham Court Road, where Isabel would get off, leaving Vivienne to continue another couple of stops to the great classical portico of the college and the laboratory where she worked.

'Am I?' Isabel said dreamily. 'Must be the weather or something. Isn't it nice not to freeze to death every night?'

'Well, if they bottle your happiness I'd like some.'

Isabel cursed herself for being self-absorbed. Now she came to think of it, Vivienne did look tired and listless.

'Was that your mother again on the telephone last night?' she asked, wondering if something at home might be the cause. On her way to the bathroom she'd passed a long-suffering-looking Vivienne hunched against the wall in the lobby, the receiver pressed to her ear.

'Yes. My cousin's getting married.' Vivienne sighed. 'I'm delighted for Mary, I really am. But . . . it's the third

time I'll have been a bridesmaid and Mummy is finding it
a little hard to bear.'

'Oh, I see.' Vivienne, overtall and awkward, was never
going to be besieged by suitors, but she was such a caring
and interesting person, Isabel felt sure that she'd find someone to love her. They'd reached the bus stop by now and
joined the queue, and couldn't continue the conversation.

Once she thought about it, Isabel began to recall how
quiet Vivienne had been recently. She was still as friendly
as always, and they often cooked together if they were
both in, and sat companionably together in one or other
of their rooms, reading or listening to Vivienne's wireless.
Vivienne would pay attention as Isabel chattered about
her work, the new responsibilities she was being given,
but she confided little in return except once when she'd
complained about an arrogant young man at work called
Frank Something, who kept putting her back up with his
comments, once, failed to invite her to an office do. Isabel
vowed to find out more.

For her own part, as Vivienne had observed, she was
happy.

Since she'd shown something of her abilities by working successfully with Hugh Morton, Trudy seemed to
trust her more and was now showing her how to mark up
manuscripts for design and typesetting. She was an exact-
ing teacher. 'Readers are hawk-eyed. We'll get letters if
we make mistakes,' she told Isabel.

The office was getting busier. There was more and
more to do. Lord Pockmartin's war memoirs were still
selling, and the latest Maisie Briggs had been declared
her best by a romance reading club in the United States
and was going like the clappers. The new children's

picture-book series was also performing well. Stephen looked as harassed as ever, but there were greater intervals between those awful occasions when Mr Greenford shambled through to Stephen's office to complain that they couldn't pay such and such a bill. Audrey, on the other hand, could be heard moaning that since Isabel never had any time to help her now, could she have another clerical assistant, please?

One lunchtime at the end of March 1949, when the office was empty apart from Isabel, who was going through some urgent final proofs, the telephone rang on Audrey's desk. Isabel snatched up the receiver and recited, 'Good afternoon, McKinnon and Holt?'

'Is that Miss Barber?' The cultured voice, warm as honey, was instantly recognisable.

'Oh, it's you,' she replied, sitting down suddenly in Audrey's chair.

'I've finished the final draft,' Hugh said. 'I thought we might meet. How about lunch next week?'

'I've taken a flat in Kensington,' he told her, after the waiter had brought their soup. 'London is where I need to be now.'

'Where in Kensington? Near Hyde Park or the other end?' she asked.

'Very near the park, tucked behind the Albert Hall. I've a bracing new regime. Half an hour's walk through Kensington Gardens before I start work in the morning. It clears the head and it's so lovely there I can almost forgive myself for abandoning Suffolk.' He paused. 'I'm not sure that Mother can, though.' He shrugged and turned his attention to the thin orange-coloured soup.

She picked up her spoon but wasn't really interested in her food. Instead, her eyes were everywhere. No one had brought her to anywhere as grand as this before. She loved the arches and the vaulted ceiling of the restaurant, covered in what surely couldn't be gold leaf. The stiff white linen tablecloth and napkins were an unimaginable luxury and the glass that held the chilled white wine was so fragile she feared she'd break it as she drank.

She glanced at Hugh, who was watching her with an amused smile. 'What is it?' she asked. He was so merry and teasing today, happy probably that he'd completed his book. The precious manuscript lay in a rough brown folder under her chair. She was terrified that she'd leave it behind or that someone might steal it, and kept prodding it with her toe to make sure it was safe.

'There's something that defines you,' he said, watching her finish her soup. 'Nothing bad,' he said, laughing at her wary look. 'It's the way you savour every moment. I'm so glad you're not one of those terrifying modern girls, you know the kind I mean. Stephen McKinnon's secretary, what's her name? Miss Foster. She's one. Knows exactly what she wants and how to get it.'

'Audrey's all right once one gets to know her. Well . . .' With sudden insight she saw what Hugh Morton meant. Audrey had life worked out to a frightening degree. She knew her strengths and limitations, what was acceptable for her to achieve. She read the kinds of magazines that confirmed her prejudices, recognised exactly what she was expected to do and was happy to do it. Audrey was smart, yes, but it was a narrow kind of smartness. Isabel wasn't sure that she liked herself for seeing all this.

'You're different,' Hugh went on. 'Fresh. I like that in a girl.'

'You do say some odd things,' she retorted. 'I'm not sure I'm at all complimented.'

That amused him no end. A waiter appeared and bore away their soup bowls, then dishes of braised steak were laid before them, and a basin of vegetables. Their glasses were refilled and the waiter withdrew.

'It certainly looks like real steak,' Hugh murmured, prodding it with a knife.

'I hope so.' Which meat was on or off the ration was a staple of office small talk. 'Mmm, it's very tender.'

For a while they ate in silence, Isabel never having tasted such delicious food. She cast about for something to say, uncertain what writers liked to talk about. She thought of something her mother had once said, that men liked to be asked about themselves.

'Does your writing take up all your time?' She could only imagine the smallness of the sum McKinnon & Holt were paying him for his novel, but guessed it would pay no rents in Kensington. He must have some other source of income. His family, perhaps.

'Good lord, no,' he said, frowning. 'I only wish it could. Perhaps you don't read *The Times* or you'd have seen my byline. I write book and theatre reviews.'

'Of course,' she said, vowing to pay more attention. 'Just for *The Times*?'

'Mostly. And one or two of the better literary magazines.'

'What will you work on next, now you've finished *Coming Home*?' she asked him, feeling for the manuscript again with her toe. She laid down her knife and fork and he raised his forefinger to summon the waiter.

'I'll start on the next one,' he told her, when their plates had been cleared. He dabbed at his mouth with his napkin and leaned forward with a grave expression on his face. 'In fact I wanted to ask your advice,' he said. 'What's the likelihood of McKinnon coming up with a better advance next time?'

'I . . . You'd need to speak to him about that. I've really no idea how the money side works.' Privately, she thought that it would be most unlikely, but she didn't want to be the one to say.

'No, of course not. I'm sorry if I've embarrassed you.'

'I don't mind. But it's thrilling that you've an idea for another book. What's it to be about?'

'Ah, it's at far too delicate a stage to speak about,' he told her. 'Bad luck. It might vanish like the mist.'

There was an undercurrent of seriousness to his words. She studied him thoughtfully, something of what he meant dawning on her. On occasion she would overhear a few words from a conversation, or be fascinated by a news item and think there was a story in it. It was annoying when a little while later she couldn't recall what exactly it was that had suggested itself. 'Sometimes it's just a feeling, isn't it?' she said to Hugh. 'A sense of something important and truthful.'

'Like a flash of the kingfisher,' he said. 'I will reveal that this one is not unconnected with someone I know.' He watched the effect of his words, smiling as she caught his meaning.

She was astonished. 'Someone?' He smiled more broadly, waiting for her to understand. 'Do you mean me? How could I possibly be involved?'

He laughed and finished his wine. 'I'll tell you sometime, but not yet.'

'Tell me now.' She had a sudden feeling of power
over him.

'No.'

'Hugh Morton!' He threw back his head and laughed.

'You're maddening, absolutely maddening!' She
rapped his hand with the dessert menu. This merely
resulted in the hovering waiter gliding forward to take
their orders. She caught Hugh's eye. He winked and she
managed to stop herself laughing.

'Anything for madam?' the waiter was asking.

'Oh no, I couldn't manage another bite.'

Hugh ordered brandy, and when it came, selected a
cigar from a box the waiter proffered.

'Where do you think of as home?' she asked, thinking
the rings of smoke gave him a glamorous, man-of-the-
world air. 'I know you set part of *Coming Home* in Suffolk.'

'Yes, it's the place I love best, where I belong. It's by a
wild part of the coast, on a river estuary. It can be very
bleak in winter but I think it's beautiful.'

He talked of the family house, which dated back to
the early 1800s. Hugh's grandfather, a successful banker,
had inherited the house from a cousin before the First
War and retired there. It was Hugh's now, his father
having died suddenly several years ago, but his mother
still lived there with a daily housekeeper. There had
been a house in London, too, but that had been sold to
cover the death duties.

She listened carefully when he spoke of his mother.
'She's a survivor – she's had to be. I'm afraid I disappointed her. I didn't go into a profession like my father

did; he read Law and ended up a judge. I would have followed him if I hadn't been called up, but I was – and afterwards, well, I was twenty-six when I was demobbed. I found my interests had changed. I didn't want to continue my studies. I'd started to write when I was at university – short stories, that sort of thing – but when I left the RAF the idea for *Coming Home* possessed me. Once I'd worked it all out, it proved very easy to write.'

'And now it's going to be published, surely your mother is pleased?'

'Yes, she is. Now it feels as though life is finally beginning for me. In fact, I'm having a small gathering next Saturday to celebrate. Nothing very grand, a few friends, that's all. It would be marvellous if you could come.'

'Oh, what a pity.' She'd promised to go to the cinema with Vivienne on Saturday.

'You're doing something already?'

'A girl I share digs with. We often go out together.'

'Why don't you bring her if you think she'd like it?'

'I'll ask her. Thank you.'

Twenty-two Corton Street was a handsome, white-stucco terraced house in a quiet mews amongst the maze of streets behind the Albert Hall. Isabel and Vivienne hesitated beneath the flickering light of an ancient lamp post, arguing about whether it was indeed the right place. It seemed much grander than Isabel had ever imagined. Finally Vivienne, in her matter-of-fact way, took the risk of pushing the upper of the two electric doorbells.

'I'm going, Hugh, don't worry,' trilled a female voice from within. There followed a tripping of high heels down steps and finally the front door flew open.

The woman who stood there was tallish and poised. She had a square face framed by neat, wavy fair hair, with wide-spaced blue eyes. She stared, and something about the two girls seemed to surprise her. 'Hello,' she said finally. 'I suppose one of you is Miss Barber?'

'I am,' Isabel said, relieved that they'd got the right place after all. 'This is my friend Vivienne Stern. Mr Morton mentioned that I might bring her.'

'Yes, of course,' the woman said, standing back to admit them. Once inside they shook hands. 'I'm Jacqueline Wood,' she told them. 'An old friend of Hugh's.'

'I'm so sorry we're late,' Isabel rushed. 'It wasn't easy . . .'

'It's a nightmare to find, the first time,' Jacqueline said. She was older than Isabel, in her late twenties, perhaps. It was difficult to tell. The curves of her full figure were accentuated by the cinched-in waistline of her two-piece costume, which was made of a stiff silk that rustled when she moved. 'Do come on up,' she told them. 'Hugh's tied up with gin and its, poor old thing, or he'd have come down himself.'

She led Isabel and Vivienne upstairs. Isabel, close behind her, thought every movement spoke of calmness, competence and femininity down to her shapely nyloned calves and classic court shoes. Perhaps her own choice of a dress of bright green would be out of place here? Well, it was too late, there was nothing to be done.

'Do you really work at Hugh's publisher?' Jacqueline said, glancing back as they reached the landing. 'I hope you won't be offended, but I expected someone a bit, well, older.' She gave a well-bred little laugh.

'That's Mrs Symmonds you're thinking of,' Isabel said,

intelligence dawning. 'She's the other editor, but it's me who works with Hugh.'

'Please don't think I was implying you weren't up to the job,' Jacqueline said coolly. She raised her hand to push open the door of the apartment and Isabel noticed the glint of a wedding ring. Perhaps Jacqueline really was who she said she was – an old friend.

In the tiny entrance hall of the flat, Jacqueline took their coats before showing them into a charming drawing room, which was sparsely furnished and smelled of fresh paint. A cheerful fire crackled in the grate. Half a dozen people were seated or standing about the room, talking quietly. Heads turned and one or two of the men got up politely. Hugh put down the tray he was holding and hurried over.

'Isabel, how wonderful that you came,' he said, taking her hand in both of his. He swung round and announced. 'Everybody, this is Isabel Barber, my editor. Hell, I love the sound of that word,' he added in a fake American accent. 'And this is Vivienne . . . I'm sorry?'

'Stern,' Vivienne said, 'I'm Vivienne Stern.'

Isabel felt increasingly self-conscious and wrongly dressed as Hugh steered her and Vivienne towards two conservatively suited young men. One was introduced as James Steerforth and the other Victor something she didn't quite catch. They were schoolfriends of Hugh's, it turned out. The girls also shook hands with the wife of one of them and the fiancée of the other. The women both shifted enough for Vivienne to sit between them on the sofa. This group, who occupied the only comfortable seating, sat slightly apart from the other two people in the room, both men, who were standing to one side, more casually dressed. Hugh drew Isabel across to meet them.

One turned out to be the editor of a small literary magazine Hugh wrote for, and the other, whom she guessed to be in his forties, a scruffy-looking individual, was already a little loose with drink. Hugh referred to him as a writer of short stories, immensely talented. The man looked even unhappier at this introduction and took a great gulp of his whisky.

'Everything's still chaotic here, as you can see,' Hugh told her. 'I'm afraid we're short of chairs.'

'Oh, but it all looks lovely,' Isabel said, glancing about. The alcoves either side of the fireplace were lined with bookshelves, as yet half-empty. The sad-happy sound of a jazz trumpet drifted from a gramophone next to the writing desk in the window, across which thick curtains were drawn. In the flattering low light from twin table lamps, Jacqueline looked softer and more graceful as she came up behind Hugh and touched him on the shoulder. He turned.

'Are there more glasses?' she asked in a low voice.

'Oh lord,' he replied. 'In one of the kitchen cupboards, I think.'

'Don't move, I'll look for them,' she said, patting his arm and gliding away.

Isabel wondered again about Jacqueline. She was sure Hugh had never mentioned her as one of his friends, which considering how easy they were with one another, was odd. Or perhaps it wasn't; she had no idea what was normal in these circles.

Hugh was asking the magazine editor whether he knew Stephen McKinnon. The man certainly did, and after lighting a cigarette began to question Isabel about forthcoming books. The doorbell sounded, and Hugh disappeared to answer it.

'You publish Alexander Berec, don't you?' the magazine editor said. 'Now there's a poet with a distinctive voice. I've met him once or twice. What's his background? No idea? Nor have I. Nor has anyone. A man of mystery, Berec.'

'Do you think so? I just find him to be himself,' Isabel said. She always thought of Berec with warm affection, how everybody in the office loved him with his gossip and his little gifts. He was one of the nicest and friendliest people she'd ever had the pleasure of meeting, and she didn't like this man with his vague insinuations. 'He's a good friend of mine,' she said, pressing her lips together.

'I'm sure I didn't mean to offend,' said the man, flicking ash in the direction of an ashtray on the side table so that flakes of it drifted to the carpet. 'Merely to point out that he keeps a great deal to himself. What do you actually know about him?'

'Not very much,' she said. She thought about Myra, Berec's wife, whom she'd never met; no one knew if he was actually married. Then there were Gregor and Karin, and she knew Berec was Czech like them. She had never dared to ask about his war experiences. Berec didn't tend to talk about himself.

'My aunt might know, I suppose,' she wondered aloud. If Penelope gave Berec money, which Isabel believed she did, she might know something about him.

'Your aunt? And who, may I ask, is your aunt?' The magazine editor looked intrigued, and Isabel lost courage, not wanting to tell him about the money.

Instead she leaned across and addressed the miserable-looking writer, who was pulling books off the shelves to examine before slotting them back in the wrong

Rachel Hore

places. He ignored her, but just then Hugh reappeared, ushering another couple into the room, a woman with bright red cheeks and sparkling eyes, who clung onto the younger man she was with, chattering about another party they'd just visited where there had been a dancing monkey that had bitten someone.

What a bizarre lot of people Hugh knows, Isabel thought, accepting another drink from Jacqueline. Apart from the old schoolfriends and Jacqueline, who was acting as hostess for the evening, none of them appeared to be friends of his exactly. They were business contacts, vague acquaintances. Isabel didn't take to any of them particularly, so she eventually sought out Vivienne.

Vivienne, wearing an expression of bored politeness, threw her a thankful glance. One of the men – Isabel remembered he was James Steerforth – was holding court about the difficulty in getting petrol. There was some assertion that the Labour government was to blame, though Victor seemed convinced that the value of the dollar had something to do with it.

'Anyway,' Steerforth's wife, Joan, said, 'it's all most inconvenient. When will things ever get back to normal?'

'I can't even remember what normal is!' put in Victor's fiancée, Constance. She had a high sweet voice like a child's and a nervous way of laughing at the end of every sentence.

There was a silence after this, then Constance politely asked Vivienne, 'Do you work with Miss Barber, dear?'

'No,' Vivienne said soberly. 'I'm a scientist at London University. I'm researching the structures of coal and working for my PhD.' This seemed to cause far more consternation amongst the little group than Isabel being in publishing.

'That seems a funny sort of job for a girl,' Joan Steerforth said. She had an odd way of pronouncing job – 'jorb' – as though it was not a word she came across very often. 'I can't think that we did any science at school, did you, Constance?'

'Not much,' Constance said and smiled. She was by far the nicer of the two, Isabel thought. 'I was a terrible dunce at school, I'm afraid.'

Victor smiled indulgently at her. 'I'll have to be clever enough for both of us,' he said fondly.

'My elder brother's girl is at Oxford,' Steerforth said, looking at the ceiling. 'He thinks it's a waste of his money, but there's no telling her that.'

'She's very clever, mind you, James,' his wife put in.

'No disputing that, old thing. Very pretty girl, too. Makes me wonder how much studying is going on.' He was rocking back and forth now, like some giant-sized toy, a roguish leer on his face.

'James is being naughty,' his wife said to Vivienne. 'He does like a little joke.'

Isabel watched Vivienne trying to smile.

'Coal does sound a dirty thing to work with,' Constance said to Vivienne. 'Why did you choose that?'

'It has an interesting crystalline molecular structure,' Vivienne said, looking more animated. 'It might be eventually that we find there are useful implications for how we use fuel.'

'Yes, I see.' Constance nodded, a serious expression on her face.

'When you look at it under a—'

But Mrs Steerforth's mind had jumped back to domesticity.

'The coalman sent his bill in yesterday, she interrupted.
'Eye-watering, it was.'

'After all the nationalisation fuss you'd have thought
the customer should be better off,' her husband added.
Isabel could see he liked to be at the centre of any
conversation.

'How about we pull clear of politics?' Victor broke in,
going to stand behind his fiancée on the sofa. 'The ladies
find it tedious.' He placed a hand on Constance's shoulder and she covered it with her own, looking up at him
adoringly.

Isabel stared at him, wondering which of the many
phrases forming themselves in her head actually to say
and failing to say any of them. Meanwhile, she was
dismayed to notice Vivienne was starting to shake. It was
a moment before she realised the cause was silent laughter, not weeping.

Fortunately, just at that moment Jacqueline arrived in
their midst holding a plate in an oven-gloved hand.
'Sardines on toast anyone?' she said gaily. 'Girls, would
you mind passing them round for me?'

Afterwards, Isabel took the empty plate into the kitchen
to find Jacqueline in an apron, arranging flakes of cheese
on dry biscuits.

'Oh, thank you,' Jacqueline said, sounding a little flustered. 'Just put it down anywhere really.'

'Can I do anything else?' Isabel asked, eyeing the piles
of dirty crockery with apprehension.

'No, no, really, there's just these. We'll leave the clearing up for Hugh's daily woman tomorrow.'

'Oh goodness, yes,' Hugh said as he sauntered into the
kitchen. 'It's very good of you, Jacks, to do all this.' He

smiled at Isabel. 'She didn't have to, you know. We bach-
elors are not completely incompetent.'

'Your job's the drinks, Hugh,' Jacqueline said briskly,
planting a stray cheese flake on the final biscuit. She
looked tired suddenly, tired and sad. 'And of course I
couldn't leave you in the lurch. It had to be a proper
party,' she said to Isabel. 'He really has something to celebrate, doesn't he? His book and moving in here.'

'He certainly does,' Isabel replied. She was still
gauging the relationship between these two. If Jacqueline's husband was here, then she'd have been introduced
to him by now, surely.

'Jacks is always a good sport, aren't you?' Hugh said.
'We've known each other since I was knee high to a grass-
hopper,' he told Isabel.

Jacqueline brightened. 'Our families live near each
other in Suffolk,' she added.

Hugh said, 'I came in for a cloth, actually. Someone's
knocked over their glass.' He snatched up a tea towel and
hurried back into the living room. Jacqueline turned
towards the sink, but Isabel had already seen her expression and was horrified. The woman was trying not to cry.

'Is there anything I can do to help?' Isabel asked again,
twisting her hands together.

Jacqueline shook her head as she rinsed a dishcloth
and wrung it out. 'Hugh will need this,' was all she said.

'Shall I take it to him?' Isabel said, reaching for the
cloth from Jacqueline, but the look of resentment directed
at her made her feel as though she'd been slapped.

At that moment Hugh reappeared and swapped the
tea towel for the damp cloth. 'Isabel, come along, I must
introduce you to a new arrival. He's finished writing

something rather good, but his publisher's gone broke and can't print it. I was wondering whether Stephen might take a look.'

Isabel went with him gladly. She couldn't think what she'd done to earn Jacqueline's dislike.

Shortly after that, she asked to find the bathroom. When she returned to the drawing room, Vivienne was waiting for her. 'Would you mind if we went soon?' she whispered. 'It's quite late. We might get locked out.'

'Heavens, is that the time?' Isabel said, then seeing Vivienne's glum face said, 'Are you all right?'

'Yes, I'm a little tired, that's all.'

Hugh was most attentive, fetching their coats for them, offering to come out and hail a taxi, but Isabel was firm that they'd find a bus. They said goodbye to everyone.

Jacqueline was nowhere to be seen. 'Will you say good-bye to her and thank you from us?' Isabel asked Hugh.

'Of course,' he said. 'I expect she's powdering her nose somewhere.'

Going down the stairs and out into the night air was a blissful escape. They hurried off towards the main road, where they hoped there'd be a bus.

'Oh, those people,' Isabel said to Vivienne beside her. 'The Steerforths and their ghastly friends. Didn't you think . . . ?' She looked more closely at Vivienne, who'd put up a hand to cover her face, and saw that this time she wasn't laughing, but crying.

'What's the matter?' she said. 'Oh Viv, what's happened?' She put her arm round her friend. This was too much for Vivienne, who began to sob. They were standing in the middle of an empty street, so Isabel took her hand and led her over to a dark building where there was a set of steps. And there they sat until Vivienne recovered herself.

'I'm all right,' she sniffed. 'Shall we go on?'

'If you think you can, yes.'

They walked on in silence for a while, then Vivienne spoke, her voice at first a harsh bark. 'I'm sorry,' she said, then continued more normally. 'It's what those people said. So many of them think it, don't they? That I'm a freak doing what I do. No one will let me be.'

'This isn't to do with your mother again, is it?' Isabel said, feeling her way.

'No, I can manage her now. It's other people. And there's something else. Isabel, I haven't told you this. I thought it was something to do with me – that I wasn't handling the situation properly, that maybe it would go away of its own accord.'

'What are you talking about?' Isabel said.

'I told you about that man on my research team. Well, that's silly, they're nearly all men, aren't they? I mean Frank Williams.'

'I do remember,' Isabel said. This Frank had done something unpleasant. 'Was he the one who didn't invite you to something?'

'Yes, though I suppose I shouldn't have expected otherwise. The men go off to the canteen together every day, and of course they don't let women in there. No, it's worse than that. It's the comments he makes – horrible things, dirty, vile. And a couple of the others are copying him. Anyway, my research supervisor is leaving, and Frank's been given a promotion. He'll be my new supervisor and I don't think I can cope with it.'

'Isn't there anyone you can speak to? Surely if you explained . . .'

'There are one or two who are sympathetic, but I can tell they don't like to interfere. Oh Isabel, this doesn't seem to happen to the other girl in the lab, so I must be doing something wrong.' Her voice turned to a squeak.

'I bet you're not,' Isabel said. They'd reached the main road now. 'Look, there's a bus!' An icy wind was blowing across the park and they wrapped their coats tighter as they ran to reach the bus stop just in time.

Isabel took a while to fall asleep that night. The alcohol rushed in her blood, and the strange conversations she'd had jangled in her head. She worried about Vivienne, but had no idea what to advise. She had no experience of the kind of environment her friend worked in; it was a world away from her own. The situation was difficult given that she was one of only a few women at the university working in her precise specialism. Vivienne told her she would have to endure it until she'd gained her research qualification in two years' time, then look for another job.

Despite the oddness of everything, Isabel had enjoyed the party. It had been interesting, glimpsing Hugh Morton's world. She wasn't sure she liked Jacqueline, who wore a wedding ring yet was clearly very fond of Hugh. She wondered whether it was this that made the woman so unhappy. Then again, perhaps she was a widow, and Hugh wasn't as oblivious to Jacqueline's feelings as he appeared. In which case, what did he think about *her* – Isabel? Oh, it was all such a muddle. And yet she was becoming aware that the answers to these questions were of the gravest importance.

She'd read the new draft of Hugh's novel, read it and

loved it. He'd understood completely what she'd explained and had introduced delicate changes to the book that made the characters more vivid, touching and believable. She'd write to him at once. How should she address him, now that they were becoming friends? Not 'Dear Mr Morton' any more, surely. 'Dear Hugh.'

'Dear Hugh,' she whispered to herself as she slid into sleep. *'My very dear Hugh . . .'*

Chapter 13

Emily

Dear Hugh, began a letter in the old file.

> *Thank you again for lunch last week, and for the most enjoyable party on Saturday. What fascinating people you know. Vivienne enjoyed herself splendidly too.*
>
> *I have now read* Coming Home *in its final form, and it strikes me that you've achieved everything you set out to do. Every note of this book now rings true. Your portrayal of Diana is masterly; she is such a tender, delicate creature, but following your adjustments I exactly appreciate how her claustrophobic upbringing must have damaged her, how frightened she must have been of making any significant decision. I hope you don't mind if I list a few small queries that I made during my reading of the book. You might like to address these before I begin the final mark-up for the typesetter . . .'*

What followed were several pages of detailed commentary, none of it very interesting, so Emily passed on to the next document and struck gold. It was a letter to Isabel signed in thick black ink, *As ever, Hugh.*

My dear Isabel,

Further to your letter of 9 June, I enclose my response to your comments and emendations, together with some replacement pages. I'm sorry that it has taken so long but there were a number of details I needed to check, not least the matter of the dates you raised, which required some delicate tinkering. I think I've solved it now, but am sure you'll advise me if you judge otherwise. I am indebted to you for identifying this problem, which might have caused me significant embarrassment.

You'll see from the postmark that I have returned to Suffolk for the time being. Mother suffers from attacks of asthma and I was briefly worried about her. The doctor assures me that she's well now, but I will be staying on here to enjoy this period of wonderful weather. Please would you let Mr McKinnon know that I look forward to seeing the jacket of Coming Home, *which he mentioned recently was underway . . .'*

On 25 June, Isabel wrote in reply:

My dear Hugh,

I'm relieved to say that Coming Home *is now with the type-setter and that we expect proofs in a few weeks' time. I'm so very glad that you like the picture on the jacket, which I agree is imaginative and well executed, and conveys the tone of the book most effectively. All is well here in the office. Audrey Foster has announced the date of her wedding, so the gossip is all of dresses and guest lists, and it's a miracle that any of us are getting any work done. I am so sorry to hear that your mother has been unwell and hope that the sunnier weather will see her improve . . .*

This letter marked a change. Isabel's voice, previously deferential, was growing more confident. She made wry little jokes. Hugh, on the other hand, took himself a little too seriously, Emily thought, and she loved the way Isabel sometimes dug gently at him for this – only very gently, though.

Letters and memos told the rest of the book's progress. *Coming Home* was published in October 1949. Hugh wrote to Stephen McKinnon to ask about the placing of advertisements. McKinnon's letter in return was evasive. Then, as now, Emily noted ruefully, there was little money for publicity. She read two admiring newspaper reviews. The man in the *Telegraph* called it 'an unusually engaging story about the yearnings of youth' and the *Mail* reviewer looked forward to seeing something else from Morton's pen.

The remaining documents in the file were boringly administrative: a reprint had been considered but rejected, a letter from an Army officer pointed out some error concerning buttons on military uniform.

Isabel's voice, however, fell silent.

Emily, disappointed, tidied up the file. It occurred to her to ring Joel, to tell him about this latest find, but it was late, after seven now, and she thought better of it. She rang Matthew instead, but his phone was turned off so she texted: *Heading home. Speak later? Em xxx*

After supper, she tried to read, but it was difficult to concentrate on anything.

She rang Matthew, but once again there was no answer. It was the first day for ages, she thought, that they hadn't spoken. She texted quickly. *Hello? Worried about you. Is all*

OK? Em xxx and waited, staring at the screen, willing a reply, but there was none. She went to bed, but lay awake for some time, haunted by the thought that something was wrong.

Chapter 14

Isabel

The first signs of trouble came one lunchtime in November 1949 when Isabel was alone in the office, snatching bites from a sandwich and catching up on the filing. The door opened and a smartly dressed blonde walked in. Grace McKinnon was pretty in a pale, demure sort of way, as in the photograph on Stephen's windowsill, but seemed a little agitated. There was something about her, the conventional appearance, the timid way she glanced round the office, that recalled Berec's description. Isabel had never met Stephen's wife before.

'Sorry, I'm looking for Mr McKinnon. Is he here?' she asked Isabel, making no effort to look friendly. 'It's rather important, I'm afraid.'

'He might be in the Fitzroy,' Isabel replied, pointing to the pub beyond the window. 'With William Ford.'

'William Ford?' Stephen's wife asked, looking blank.

'Yes, there's been that awful review in *The Times*. Mr McKinnon thought he needed consoling.'

'I wouldn't know about that. I never read the papers,' Mrs McKinnon said, taking off her gloves. 'There's never anything cheerful in them. Do you mind if I wait?'

'Not at all. Jimmy's about somewhere. I'll send him

across with a message. Would you like some tea or something? It wouldn't be any trouble.'

'Oh no,really,' Mrs McKinnon said.

Isabel dispatched Jimmy, and when she returned to the office it was to find Grace McKinnon examining a wall poster advertising an exhibition of abstract painting as though it were something entirely foreign to her.

'Jimmy's gone to see.'

Mrs McKinnon looked properly at Isabel for the first time. 'You're very kind,' she said. ' I suppose you must be Isabel.'

'Yes.'

'Stephen did mention you. He says you're doing very well – you should feel flattered.' The woman curved her lips in a vague smile and glanced out of the window. They saw Jimmy come out of the Fitzroy Tavern, but instead of coming back to the office he turned right up the street and out of sight.

'I suppose he wasn't there. Do you think he'll be long?'

'I hope not, but Mr Ford can be very . . . time-consuming.'

In the end she settled Mrs McKinnon in Stephen's office with a glass of water, which was all the woman would accept. It was another twenty minutes before Stephen appeared, smelling of the pub.

'Did Jimmy find you? Your wife's here,' Isabel whispered to him.

'No, he didn't,' Stephen replied, looking alarmed. He immediately went into his office and shut the door. Now Grace McKinnon clearly lost her coolness, because the sound of raised voices was audible. Isabel was too curious to absent herself, but to avoid any accusation that she was eavesdropping she started to type loudly as if her life depended on it. A minute or two passed before the door flew open and Stephen stormed out, closely followed by his wife.

'It won't do any good. Stephen. Daddy simply won't have it.'

'I need to go and sort out a misunderstanding,' Stephen told Isabel, snatching up his coat. 'I'll see you tomorrow.'

He left in a hurry, almost bumping into Jimmy on the way. Grace McKinnon and Isabel stared after him.

The next day, Stephen didn't appear in the office at all, but he rang up Audrey and gave her various instructions to pass on to Mr Greenford. Over the next couple of weeks, he was often out and there was a heightened atmosphere of uncertainty. Redmayne Symmonds marched in once and closeted himself with Mr Greenford in Stephen's office, going over ledgers. Everyone else carried on as usual, though Philip looked perpetually worried and Trudy was unusually quiet.

'What's going on?' Isabel asked Audrey when she got her on her own.

'Money,' Audrey said shortly. 'He's looking for new backers. Redmayne Symmonds won't put in any more.'

'No!' Isabel said, horrified. 'But I thought business was going well.'

'So did I, but who knows. Don't worry your pretty head too much. It's happened before. He'll sort it out.'

And that's exactly what did happen. After another week or so, the tense unhappy look Stephen had worn for so long lightened. He even arrived in the office whistling one morning. That was the day he called his small staff into his office, where they gathered in nervous anticipation. Only Trudy was absent.

There was good news, Stephen told them. 'You might have heard rumours about the firm's imminent demise. In fact, it's completely the opposite: we're expanding.' He explained that although Trudy's husband had decided to withdraw as a director, Stephen had secured the investment of two City businessmen. When he mentioned their names, Isabel was surprised. One of the names meant nothing to her, but the other was Reginald Dickson, Penelope's manfriend. From what Isabel could gather, Penelope had introduced Stephen to him.

Stephen went on to assure them that Trudy would continue working with the firm, and to announce that he'd been able to buy up a small publisher of books in a new line: psychology. The editor and his assistant would move into the building. 'We're taking the tenancy of the flat above our heads, all being well. And we're going to recruit a sales manager!'

It was as everyone was trooping back to their desks that Stephen called Isabel back.

'Don't worry,' he said, amused by her anxious face. 'It's nothing terrible. Trudy has made it known to me that she intends to cut down her days. I don't want to lose her. She manages the schedules like nobody's business. But we'll be needing another editor.'

'Another editor? Isabel had a sudden vision of this new editor. A man, probably. But Stephen was continuing.

'You're still very new, but you've been learning fast.

I'd like you to take on the role, if you would. Under Trudy's guidance, of course.'

'Me? Oh yes, thank you.' She was smiling at him stupidly, but he didn't say any more so she thought she was dismissed and she stood to go. At the last moment she remembered. 'I'll need more money,' she told him firmly. 'I can't be expected to manage on what you're giving me.'

Stephen burst out laughing. 'I thought you weren't going to ask at all,' he said. He lit a cigarette and looked at her through narrowed eyes. Her feeling of power began to fail.

'How about another hundred,' he said. 'That'll bring it up to two-fifty.'

Two hundred and fifty pounds a year! She nearly said yes, but something stayed her. She had no idea what other women in the firm earned – no one would have been so ill-bred as to discuss it. But maybe they didn't need money like she did. Trudy was married and Audrey lived in a flat paid for by her father.

'I'd like three hundred, please,' she said, in the same tone in which she'd ask the greengrocer for two pounds of potatoes.

He looked at her in surprise, then thought for a moment.

'Very well, three hundred,' he said finally.

It took Vivienne, that evening, to spell out the maths. 'It's obvious,' she said. 'He's transferring to you the money he's saving from paying Trudy. He's not giving Audrey a new assistant, is he?'

'He hasn't said so.'

'And if he took on a man he'd have to pay him more.'

'That's true.' Still, nothing could stop herself feeling pleased for holding out for the money.

In February 1950, Hugh Morton telephoned her at the office. 'I've tickets for a show on Friday,' he said. 'Tom Eliot's new play. Do you happen to be free?' She pressed the receiver more intently to her ear.

'I imagine that would be acceptable,' she said warily, aware of Audrey earwigging. In truth, she and Hugh had only corresponded on business matters recently and she wasn't expecting an invitation like this. She wasn't sure what it meant and whether she should go. However, she was longing to see *The Cocktail Party*. Berec was always talking about T. S. Eliot.

At the other end of the line, Hugh laughed. 'I'm glad to hear you say so! Shall I come to the office at five? We could perhaps have a drink in the bar there first, a little supper.'

'Oh no,' she said, hunching over the phone. 'How about meeting there?' Coming to the office wouldn't do at all. She'd never mentioned going to Hugh's party – and that, anyway, had been with Vivienne. She wouldn't be able to bear it if they all saw her going off somewhere with Hugh. The embarrassment would be terrible. Going out with Berec was somehow different. For some reason it never seemed to enter anyone's mind that she and Berec were anything but friends. Berec was everyone's friend, as comfortable as toast.

'You'd rather meet me at the theatre?' he said patiently. 'I don't see why not. Shall we say six-thirty?'

When she finished the call, Audrey was looking at her curiously. 'Who was that?' she asked.

'Just a friend.'

'Just a friend, my foot,' was Audrey's drawled reply.

Isabel had rarely been to the theatre, and then only to see productions of Shakespeare or once a J. B. Priestley play. Nothing had prepared her for *The Cocktail Party*. It started in the manner of a drawing-room farce with a married couple quarrelling over the fact that the husband had taken a mistress, and the wife leaving in high dudgeon just as guests were expected for drinks in their London home.

'I must say, I don't see what all the fuss is about,' Hugh confided during the interval. 'All seems very ordinary to me.'

But when the curtain rose once more, the play turned dark and complicated. An uninvited guest brought the wife home again. It turned out he was a psychiatrist and he proceeded not only to reveal the most unpleasant things about the couple's relationship, but to point out how much worse it would be if they were to separate.

'I felt sorry for Celia, the mistress, in the end,' Isabel said afterwards. 'Why did she have to suffer like that? It was dreadful, the way she died.' The discarded mistress had become a missionary, but was killed by the natives she had gone to convert.

'She had to be sacrificed,' Hugh said impatiently. 'It's sad, but symbolic. She nearly broke up the marriage.'

'The husband was as much to blame,' Isabel replied, outraged.

'Quite possibly, but there were more important things at stake here. Celia shouldn't have allowed herself to come between a husband and wife. Of course the institution of marriage had to come first.'

'I still don't see why Mr Eliot let her be killed like that. She didn't deserve it.'

'You don't know anything about Greek tragedy, do you? There are clear references in the play to Euripides. But don't let the play upset you. I should never have brought you.'

'Oh, but I enjoyed it,' she said, her eyes shining.

'Did you?'

'Yes. It made me cross, but I like that.'

'You are a funny girl.' He smiled fondly and the smile started up a little thrill of warmth inside her. 'Funny, but sweet. I like your hair like that,' he said, 'you know, brushed back at the side. Why did you do that?'

She shrugged. 'I don't know. It's just an experiment. Audrey does it.'

'Goodness, don't turn into Audrey, will you?'

She shook her head, rather charmed that he liked her for herself. She knew Audrey won when it came to the beauty stakes and pedigree – and, well, style, she supposed – but perhaps she had her own attractions after all. Hugh didn't seem bothered about silly things like her family background. At the same time she felt a little ashamed for having talked about her grandmother's big house in Norfolk as though it was a part of her life. To think she'd never even seen the place.

She tried for a moment to imagine Hugh greeting her parents in the ugly pebbledash house. The thought was excruciating. Her father would very certainly be wearing his dreadful old cardigan and say something gauche that tried to put Hugh down. But she was running ahead now, into the future. Quickly she reined in her thoughts.

'I rather hoped,' Hugh was saying now, 'that you

wouldn't mind looking at a chapter I've written. I need to be sure about the voice.'

'Of course, if you'd like me to.' She was delighted.

He felt in an inside pocket of his jacket and extracted a folded brown envelope. 'I haven't had a chance to type it up properly yet,' he said, his brow wrinkling in a frown. 'Perhaps you'd forgive me, but I believe my handwriting isn't difficult to read. Do you want to check? Don't read the thing in front of me, I couldn't bear that, but look at the first couple of lines, perhaps.'

He drew some sheets of paper from the envelope and gave them to her. When she glanced at the first line she saw it read, *My darling*. This made her heart beat quickly for a moment, then she saw that, of course, this was one of the characters speaking – the man, she thought, as she read the next line or two.

She felt Hugh's hand over her own, warm and gentle. 'Don't read any more now,' he begged.

For a moment they were still, he holding her hand, she with the papers, caught in his gaze in the soft lights of the bar. Then he released her and she hid her hot face as she stowed the precious pages in her bag.

It was late when she stepped out of the taxi at Highgate – this time he'd insisted on paying for a taxi – and she changed into her nightclothes and climbed into bed, not to sleep, but to read what he'd given her. Once again her heart beat faster to *My darling* . . . It was the opening chapter to a novel.

My darling, I will not see you for a long time now. From what they tell me, I learn that you might never come. But there is much I need to tell you, to explain . . .

She read on, transfixed. It was apparent that the narrator was being held somewhere, but whether it was in a prison of some sort, or a secure hospital, it was impossible to say. But it was definitely a man speaking, an educated, articulate man, and there was some terrible gulf between himself and the woman he was addressing, that by his writing he hoped to bridge. The man went on to describe his reaction on first seeing her. She'd been in WRNS uniform, waiting at a station with a heavy suitcase and there'd been no porter.

How lost you appeared, the narrator went on, *yet when I offered help, how glacial, as disdainful as a goddess. But I expect you'd known a few men like me. Mere mortals, all of us.*

She got out of bed and found a pencil, then marked the paper in the margin: *more physical description for immediacy* was what she wrote. She read on, from time to time scribbling comments or correcting some small detail. *A woman would not have emerged from this with her hair and make-up so intact!* she wrote at one point, after the narrator had ambushed his beloved in a steamed-up kitchen.

She came to the end and lay back against the pillows, thinking. She'd loved the voice of the man, strong, beguiling, yet there was a dangerous edge to it that both thrilled and warned. He was not, she was convinced, a reliable narrator. His would be only one version of the account in this book. But the heart of the story, the girl, Nanna – now *she* was fascinating, if only Hugh would convey her vividly enough. Was the book all to be from the man's point of view, she wondered, or would Nanna have the opportunity to tell her own side? Well, she could ask the author.

She already felt a connection with Nanna, though, and

remembered the conversation she and Hugh had had that first time, in the restaurant with the golden ceiling. No, Nanna wasn't at all like herself. Hugh's heroine was blonde rather than auburn, for a start. He must have been teasing her. A part of her was disappointed.

Chapter 15

Emily

Throughout the next morning Emily kept glancing at her phone, wondering why she hadn't heard from Matthew. All that came through was a long text from her sister about Christmas arrangements: despite having two small children Claire had invited everyone to hers on Christmas Day. Matthew, though, was going home to Wales, where she would join him at New Year.

Something else that arrived was an email from Matthew's tutor, Tobias Berryman. *I've taken you at your word*, it said, *and hope you won't mind reading my draft and telling me what you think.* She sighed, remembering his reference to 'echoes of Marlowe', but clicked quickly on the attachment all the same and scanned the first few paragraphs. To her surprise, what she read was good: dark, thrillerish and sharply written. She wrote him a quick word of acknowledgement then, seeing the file of *Coming Home* on her desk, she rang Joel's mobile number. He answered right away.

'I'm typing Chapter Five as we speak,' he told her. 'Hope you're impressed.'

'I am. Look, I've found another Morton file. Well, it sort of found itself.'

'What do you mean?' Emily explained how it been left on her desk.

'And it's for *Coming Home*? Yes, I ought to look at it.'

'It's all about Isabel. How she and Hugh met. Did you know she was his editor at McKinnon and Holt?'

'Yes, I did.' He paused, then said, 'Of course I'll come in and look at it, but it might not be till the New Year now. What are you up to for Christmas, by the way?' They chatted for a while. He, she gathered, had rather a distant relationship with his parents, and Christmas with them was a bit of a duty. They sounded much older than hers were and he had no brothers or sisters.

She replaced the receiver feeling sorry for him but also a little disappointed by his reaction to her find. Isabel didn't seem to intrigue him nearly as much as she did Emily.

At lunch Emily joined the hordes swarming through Oxford Street, trying to tick some Christmas shopping off her list. She managed to track down a building set for her nephew and chose bath toys for her three-year-old niece, but the men proved impossible as usual, and she couldn't decide what to get for Matthew. She was in the lift going up to her office, wondering whether he'd ever wear the silver cufflinks in the shape of pen nibs that she'd earmarked, when her phone chimed gently and she looked to find a text from him. If she was free, he wanted to meet her after work. Would six-ish suit? Something about the formality of it made her uneasy.

She'd planned to go out with Megan later, but of course she agreed to meet him and he suggested a wine bar just off Bond Street. She knew the place. It was likely to be quiet, even near Christmas. She hoped he wouldn't be late.

When she arrived, however, he was already sitting at one of the round tables, half-hidden behind a screen. She knew by the anxious look on his face that something was on his mind. He kissed her on the mouth, lingeringly, as though the kiss meant something significant. They sat down, their faces close across the little table, and he poured her red wine from the bottle he'd already started. They both drank in silence. The wine was dark and heavy, with an acid taste.

'What's wrong?' She looked straight into his eyes and his gaze faltered. He replaced his glass on the table and brushed his upper lip with the back of his hand.

'I didn't sleep much last night.' He folded his arms on the table, his expression serious. 'I felt bad about the weekend, that I'd upset you. I wanted you to know that.'

'I know some of it was my fault' – she felt a rush of anguish – 'but—'

'It wasn't one of the greats. That's what I wanted to talk to you about. We're both very stressed at the moment. I think . . . I think we need time apart.'

His words fell like a pebble in a deep pool.

'Oh,' she said. She hadn't dreamed that this was what he'd say, but now he'd said it, something settled into place. Her throat swelled.

'We're getting on each other's nerves all the time,' he rushed on. 'You keep wanting me to be different—'

'Matthew, I don't!'

'You do. And I feel I let you down, oh, in all sorts of ways. It's as if . . . you want me to be someone else. Someone I'm not. And it's making me unhappy.'

She picked at a loose thread on the tablecloth and couldn't think what to say. She felt like crying. And now she was crying. She reached in her pocket for a tissue. For a moment she couldn't speak.

'I'm sorry,' he said, when she'd recovered a little. He slid his hand across the tablecloth and touched her fingertips.

How calm and definite he sounded, but when she looked she could see strain in the creases round his eyes, in the warm sympathy of his gaze.

'I don't know why it's got like it has,' she whispered, shaking her head. 'It doesn't feel right, I agree, but surely . . .'

'You're working so hard, and I've got to get this damned course finished. It's the wrong time for us, hey?'

She dabbed her eyes with her tissue and nodded. He'd made his decision, that was obvious, and she wasn't going to beg. She studied him now, trying to fix him in her memory, her Matthew, very dear and gorgeous. But already his demeanour was changing; she sensed his withdrawal.

'Hey,' he said, smiling at her. 'Cheer up, we'll still see each other.'

'Yes,' she said, trying to smile back, then more strongly, 'Yes, of course we will.'

'Will you be all right?' he asked when they reach the Tube station, where he would go off in one direction, she in another.

She nodded, determined not to cry in front of him. They stood together, watching the strings of twinkling snowflakes criss-crossing the shopping street, high above their heads.

'I'm sorry,' he said, 'it being Christmas.'

'We couldn't have gone through Christmas,' she said quickly. 'Or New Year.' It would have been unbearable to have stayed with his family and then for him to have ended things.

'No, we couldn't,' he agreed. 'I got you a present, though.' He lifted the flap of his bag and withdrew a package wrapped in silvery paper. 'It's a book,' he said, with his lopsided grin, 'in case you hadn't guessed.'

She managed a laugh. 'I've almost got you something,' she said. 'I'll put it in the post. Happy Christmas.' And somewhat hesitantly, she leaned forward and kissed his cheek. 'Send my love to your family.'

'You, too,' he said. They hugged each other for a long moment. Then he let her go.

The last time, she thought as she watched him walk into the Tube station. She didn't know if he looked back. She couldn't see for tears.

She was devastated, completely devastated, but it helped to have Christmas somewhere different this year. Her sister Claire lived two miles from their parents and on the day found herself overwhelmed by the preparations for Christmas lunch, so Emily went over early in her mother's car to assist. Claire's husband Mike took the children out to the playground whilst the women cooked, and Emily was able to talk properly to her sister about Matthew. Given Matthew's poor record with Emily's family she'd half-expected Claire to berate him, but instead her sister was surprisingly sympathetic to both of them.

'It's a shame, I liked him,' Claire said as she picked cloves out of the bread sauce. 'Mum and Dad did, too.'

'Yes, so they tell me,' Emily said gloomily, peeling sprouts.

'But you're both so busy with your careers. Perhaps he's right, it's the wrong time.'

Emily remembered with pain the expression on Matthew's face when they parted – friendly, concerned, yes, but no longer loving. 'But he was so special,' she whispered, spilling sprouts over the worktop. The tears started again and she wiped them furiously away. Claire dropped the spoon in the sauce, and came and put her arms round her.

'You know what they say, Em: if it's meant to be, it will be . . . Now let's get that bird out of the oven whilst the kids aren't underfoot. Once they get back and Mum and Dad and Granny come, it'll be chaos.'

Granny, when she arrived, pulled Emily to her soft bosom and stroked her hair as though she were a little girl and not a young woman taller than herself. 'There are plenty more fish in the sea,' she said fondly, as she had done every time Emily or Claire had broken up with someone, but this time there was a tinge of weariness in her voice. 'Don't leave it too long to go fishing again, eh,' she added, releasing her. 'I know what you modern young women are like. You'll wake up one morning and want a baby and find it's too late.'

'I'm only twenty-eight and I don't want a baby at the moment, thanks, Granny,' she said, smiling bravely. 'I'll be fine, don't worry.'

And she would be fine. But that didn't stop her missing Matthew.

Her blood raced when a text arrived from him during Christmas afternoon, but it was merely to say thank you for the cufflinks and to ask if she was OK. She texted him back, ignoring the question, but thanking him for his present.

It had been the first she'd unwrapped that morning when she had awoken in the safety of her childhood room. It was indeed a book: *Poetry for Life. You know I don't believe in the poetry-as-therapy racket*, he had scrawled in the accompanying card, *but I hope you find something you like in here.* He signed it *With love.* It offered poems for life's occasions. She turned the pages, skipping the ones about true love found and gloomily reading one about what happened when love died. It didn't help one bit.

She put the book out of sight in her case. Maybe she'd look at it again when she felt stronger.

On Boxing Day, she met up with her friend Megan, who was spending Christmas with her family, and they walked her mum's dog down by the river. It had been Megan who'd comforted her a week ago, after she'd parted from Matthew. They'd skipped their planned meal out and gone straight back to Megan's, where Emily had spent the night because she hadn't wanted to cry alone.

Megan, a tall and striking-looking girl with long silver-blonde hair, was deputy manager of an online business selling designer furniture. She had lived on her own for the past year, since a painful break-up with the boyfriend she'd moved in with after the flatshare, and Emily knew she was exactly the person to go to, warm, understanding, a listener who didn't apportion blame.

Today they walked together along the muddy towpath where the dark surface of the water shivered in a needle-sharp wind. The little dog darted about in front, occasionally stopping to bark at the river birds wandering about on the opposite bank, their feathers fluffed against the cold.

'That daft animal,' Megan said. 'Hey, it's no good doing that, they know you can't get them.'

Emily's laugh was half-hearted.

Megan asked, 'How are you doing? Have you heard from Matthew?'

'Yes,' Emily said, explaining about the text. 'Do you think it meant anything?'

Megan sighed. 'He might just be concerned. Try not to read too much into it.' She looked keenly at her friend.

'It's the wind,' Emily said, blowing her nose. 'It makes my eyes water.'

Instead of going to Wales for New Year she went to Luke and Yvette's New Year's Eve party in London. It was strange, not being part of a couple.

'At least it was only a few months out of your life,' a schoolfriend of Yvette's said bitterly. She told Emily a long story about her recent separation from someone she had lived with for five years. The implication was that her pain was worse than Emily's. Feeling her own pain belittled, Emily extricated herself as soon as she could.

'That's such a shame, you were so good together,' Luke remarked when he refilled her glass for the fourth time. That made her feel bad in a different way, as though she and Matthew had somehow failed. She stopped counting the glasses after that, and ended up paying an expensive minicab fare back to Hackney rather than risk passing out on public transport. She wondered whether she'd see much of Luke and Yvette in future. All of the people at the party except for herself and Yvette's schoolfriend had been in couples.

January settled in, and although the pain lost its edge she still missed Matthew, kept thinking of things she wanted to tell him, remembered his smile, his enthusiasm about life, the arguments they'd had about, oh, everything from fashion to politics. Matthew had liked to question the truth all the time, which could be exhausting but now she valued it.

Back at work, she'd told Liz about the break-up. And that, of course, was like putting it on the social media networks, and soon all the department knew and gave her sympathetic glances for a couple of days. Even Gillian, who was famously reserved, asked if she was all right. 'Yes,' she insisted hastily, blushing. No one appeared to know anything of Gillian's private life. As far as anyone guessed, she only had her work.

There were other downsides to being single. George, the editor whose voice and manner she disliked, left the office by chance at the same time one evening and suggested a 'friendly drink'. 'I'm sorry,' she said firmly, 'I have to be somewhere,' which was partly true – she was going to try out a samba class, but not until later. Office gossip said that George's sense of boundaries around friendship were vague, to say the least, and the thought of his bearish advances was not appealing.

George, blond and teddy-bear-like, shuffled his big feet. 'What about lunch sometime, then?'

'I'm booked up for the next couple of weeks,' she told him. 'Maybe after that.' She kissed him lightly on the cheek, so as not to give offence.

On the bus home that night an elderly couple were sitting on a seat opposite, holding hands. The old man was smiling at the old lady and it struck Emily that perhaps he saw her still as he'd always seen her, the essence of her beyond the sunken face and the shorn grey hair. This touched Emily so much she had to look away.

Back home, the video about Hugh Morton was still sitting on her table, waiting for the next time she saw Nell to return it. She must remind Joel about the *Coming Home* file. Christmas, and all this business with Matthew, had put Hugh and Isabel right out of her mind, but now she remembered how important it was.

Chapter 16

Isabel

'It's wonderful,' Isabel said, taking the pages from the envelope and smoothing them out. 'You *are* clever.' She and Hugh were sitting at a table in the corner of a tea shop near McKinnon & Holt in Charlotte Street. It was a crisp Friday afternoon in February 1950; the street outside was bathed in wintry sunshine.

Hugh looked extremely pleased. 'I don't usually show anyone my work,' he said, 'but this time it's different. Nanna has to convince.'

'Of course, you're portraying her through a man's eyes,' Isabel said, anxious to be tactful. 'You mean, I take it, that she should still emerge in a true-to-life fashion?'

'Yes, precisely, though there must be a progression from being the woman he wants her to be to how she really is.'

'I see that,' Isabel said. She unfolded the pages and pushed them towards him. He drew his chair nearer so they could both look. 'Perhaps the thing to do later on is to dramatise her a little more so that we learn her side of the relationship. May I make one or two small suggestions? Here, look, and here. Remember she wouldn't be able to "stride" in high heels.'

'Hmmm,' he said, turning the pages and frowning at the pencil marks. 'No, here, "hysterical" was deliberate on my part. That's how a man like him would have viewed her.'

'Even though he knows he's insulted her? Surely her reaction is understandable.' She was aware of his warm closeness as they pored over the paper. He glanced up at her as he thought about what she'd said, and she felt his breath on her cheek. She could see flecks of emerald in his hazel eyes, the shadowy roughness of his jawline. The corners of his moulded lips turned up softly, lending his intense expression vulnerability. He stared down at the pages again, rubbing his wiry dark hair as he puzzled at what he'd written, whispering the words to himself. Finally, he gathered the pages back into the envelope, which he pushed back into his inside breast pocket.

'Thank you, anyway,' he said. 'That's useful.' She started to move her chair away politely, but he stayed her with his hand on her arm. 'What should we do now, do you say?'

'What should we do? I suppose I must go back to the office,' she replied. 'I told Trudy I'd only be a short while.'

'I'm sure she'll understand. I'll explain.'

'There's no need,' she said, more tartly than she intended. She didn't require anybody to stand up for her at work.

'Of course not,' he said, letting go of her arm. 'Well, if you must.'

'I ought to.' She smiled. 'Don't be angry.'

'I'm not,' he said tightly. He felt for his wallet and

summoned the waitress, and for a moment Isabel was worried she'd offended him. But by the time they were outside in the sunshine his mood had improved.

'Are you free on Saturday?' he asked. 'Perhaps we could go somewhere for dinner. I'd like to say thank you properly for your advice.'

'There's no need, but yes, I'd like that,' she said, happiness spreading through her.

He walked her the short distance back to her office and she hurried up the steps, turning briefly to wave. Inside, there was only Jimmy at the trade counter, slitting open a box of books and whistling something unrecognisable. Trudy was away from her desk, though the way a manuscript was spread across it suggested she wouldn't be long. There was no sign of Audrey either. Through the window she could see Hugh as he stopped to light a cigarette, hunched over a cupped hand as he shielded the flame from the breeze. She watched, liking the picture he made, then he strode off in the direction of Oxford Street.

She sensed someone come to stand behind her and turned quickly, thinking it was Audrey – to find it was Stephen.

'That Morton you were with?' he said.

'Yes. He wanted some editorial advice.'

'I see.' Stephen seemed about to say something he couldn't quite frame. Finally, he sighed.

'That was all right?' she said anxiously. 'You don't mind?'

'Do I mind you giving Morton advice about his writing? No, not at all – why should I? This is the next one, is it? What's it looking like?'

'Very promising,' she said, going back to her desk. 'It's early stages though.'

'Well, I can't wait to hear more. I must say, the critical reaction to *Coming Home* has been first-rate. He has something, Morton, we should keep a hold of him. But, Isabel . . .' Stephen was looking at her seriously now. 'I don't like to interfere, but you're still very young and, well, take care of yourself, won't you? It strikes me that he finds you . . . attractive. Not at all surprising, of course, but if you should ever, you know . . .'

'What do you mean?' Isabel asked, a bit taken aback.

'Not that I'm the person to offer advice in that area. But take care of yourself all the same. I shouldn't like to see you hurt.'

'What are you telling the poor girl?' Trudy said, coming into the room with a cup of tea. 'Of course she can look after herself. All the girls do nowadays.' Stephen looked embarrassed and beat a hasty retreat to his office. Trudy took a sip of tea and went on: 'Isabel, dear, I was thinking you should make a start on the new Maisie Briggs. Goodness, I can't believe it's a whole year since the last one arrived.'

Isabel, sitting at her desk, found it difficult to concentrate, so many confused thoughts jostled for position in her mind. She liked Hugh Morton, liked him very much, and looked forward to having dinner with him.

She was surprised and touched by Stephen's concern – that was sweet of him – but what did he mean about not being a good source of advice? He was married, wasn't he, and he must love Grace, she was so pretty and elegant, though she had heard them quarrel that time. She knew they didn't have children and wondered if they minded, but some people just didn't have them, that was all there was to it.

She tried to concentrate on Maisie Briggs's heroine and her eyes of cornflower blue, running her pencil underneath a phrase that was too purple even for Maisie.

When she walked into the bar of the Ritz on Saturday evening, it was to see Hugh waiting for her at the counter; the way his face lit up when he saw her made her feel special. He kissed her tenderly on the cheek and asked her what she'd like to drink. She revelled in his closeness.

'Oh, one of those, please,' she said, pointing to his frosted cocktail glass.

'A margarita for the lady,' he told the barman and looked at Isabel with appreciation. 'That's a very pretty dress,' he said. 'Is it new?'

'It is,' she replied. She'd bought it with money her parents had sent for her twenty-first birthday. Russet and gold with a wide waistband and a little bolero jacket, it perfectly set off the delicate gold wristwatch, Aunt Penelope's present.

'You like brown, don't you?' Hugh said. 'I've noticed that.'

'Brown on its own sounds very dull. In fact, there are so many lovely shades. Apricot and sherry and that warm brick-red.'

'You're right, of course. They all go with your eyes and hair. It's very clever of you.'

'Thank you. Brown is my mother's fault. She didn't think auburn hair went with much. I wasn't allowed to wear red, you know, or pink. And she's got something against green. My grandmother said it was unlucky.'

'I've seen you in green – at my little party. You looked stunning, if you don't mind me saying.'

'Now you're embarrassing me,' Isabel said with a laugh. 'I wear green sometimes to prove my mother wrong. Fortunately, though, brown is fashionable at the moment so I don't really mind it.'

When they'd finished their cocktails they left the Ritz and walked on to a little Italian restaurant in Soho, where Hugh knew the proprietor and exchanged greetings with him in Italian. 'I was in Naples for a while in forty-four,' he explained when she commented, and spoke a little about his experiences there in the wake of the Germans' retreat.

'Of course – you wrote about it in *Coming Home*,' Isabel said, secretly wondering whether the local woman who featured in that particular scene had been based on reality, too. A slight dark girl with huge black-fringed eyes, who had helped the hero escape, then begged to go with him. He'd had to tell her no. Isabel felt an unreasonable stab of jealousy towards this fictional female.

She ate food she'd not tasted before. Wafer-thin slices of spicy ham, then a salty mixture of rice and fish. 'It's delicious,' she said.

'It really needs more butter.'

'Oh, butter,' she sighed. 'There's never enough of it. I can't believe my mother had butter *and* jam on her bread before the war.'

He laughed. 'And cake made with butter and jam and cream, with sugar icing on top. I remember the taste now!' And this brought it home that he was almost ten years older than her. 'I'm sure those days will come again. Now try one of these desserts, I promise you they're delicious.'

'Goodness,' she said as she savoured a sugary pudding, light and creamy, 'I'll never be able to eat powdered-egg custard again after this.'

'There's even proper vanilla in it, I think. God knows where Luigi gets hold of the stuff.'

'Vivienne likes vanilla. She would adore this place.'

'Ah, your boffin friend. I swear the Steerforths and the Robinsons still haven't got over her. How is she?'

'Very well, but maybe not happy. A man she works for treats her abominably,' she explained.

Hugh frowned. 'Some of those fellows aren't used to having women around. It must distract them, I suppose, though they'll have to adapt.'

'I don't know whether it's that. There's another girl there and apparently this man doesn't bully her.'

'Perhaps she's prettier,' Hugh said with a shrug. 'Or knows how to manage him better. She's quite plain-spoken, your friend. Not all men take to that.'

'You mean she has opinions, I suppose.' So what if Vivienne expressed herself honestly? It was one of the things Isabel loved about her.

'Oh, don't say I've offended you. It's only something I've observed.' He took her hand. 'Please forgive me.' They were leaning so close to each other now, their foreheads almost touched.

'Of course,' she said, teasing him. 'But you must behave.'

'I will be as good as gold. You'll make me.' He looked so soulful.

'Will I? Really?'

'Yes, you make me want to behave better. I like that about you. In fact, I like everything about you.'

He caught her other hand now, and bringing them to his lips, kissed her fingers. She held her breath, confused by the feelings of excitement rushing through her. He looked up at her, his expression soft in the candlelight.

'Come on,' he said. 'I'd better get you home before I forget myself.'

In the taxi, he put his arm round her, nothing more, and when they reached Highgate, he kissed her cheek very gently as he leaned across to open the door.

After the cab bore him away she couldn't stop thinking about him. She wasn't sure quite when the line had been crossed in their relationship, but it had. During the evening at the theatre, possibly, but thinking about it there had always been that frisson between them, right from the very first meeting. Tonight had been utterly wonderful.

The Rainbow's End, Maisie Briggs's latest romance, was set in a remote village in the Yorkshire Dales. The heroine had fallen in love with the son of a sheep farmer, but the young man spoke only of abandoning his inheritance and leaving for the city. After various travails he chose to stay, for he realised that going meant losing her.

Isabel, sitting late at her desk a few days later, finished editing it a little misty-eyed, caught in the magical glow that Maisie famously cast over her largely female readers. A writer of romances she might be, but they were superior ones. Her characters were rounded and complex, they made realistic and intelligent decisions. However, they usually learned to put love first, and though one truly wished the happy couples well as they started out on the rest of their lives together, Isabel worried sometimes about the sacrifices they made, men and women both. Would the sheep farmer in *The Rainbow's End* regret abandoning his ambitions and vent his frustration on his new young wife? It was pointless to ponder what would happen after the book ended so she might as well enjoy the romance while it lasted. As she typed up the short list of queries – Maisie was the most meticulous and professional of writers – she found her thoughts drifting deliciously to her own version of a romantic hero. For some years this imaginary paragon had been a changing presence, the features indistinct, but recently it had acquired the very definite dark hair and hazel eyes of Hugh Morton.

She was used to the interested way men looked at her, that could not be denied, and she'd dabbled in one or two relationships, but nothing serious until now, no one like Hugh. She remembered the Polish boy she'd known when she was seventeen, how after the joyful, rackety ride on his bicycle that had so annoyed her father, Jan had waited for her sometimes after school, wheeling his bike to walk alongside her, but although for a while she'd luxuriated in his attentions, and the other girls' envy, in the end she'd not felt tempted to allow it to go further. He was a nice lad, and good-looking, too, but there had been no spark. Since coming to London she'd gone to dinner once or twice with Freddie, a lively, talkative friend of Vivienne's brother. He'd been perfectly gentlemanly on the first occasion, but on the second he'd pounced on her in the taxi home, fondling her breasts roughly and covering her face with slobbery kisses. 'It was almost as though he was desperate,' she told a horrified Vivienne later. 'He only let go when I got him – you know – with my knee.'

Hugh was a completely different proposition. She appreciated the gentle, old-fashioned way he wooed her. He flirted, yes, he paid compliments, but always with courtesy – so different from the gaucheness of her previous admirer. Hugh treated her with respect; he adored her with his eyes. And yet there was something unknowable behind those eyes. Sometimes she wondered what he was really like, deep down. His experience of the world was far beyond hers. He'd been to war, had very likely had to kill, and, if *Coming Home* was based on real life, had also loved deeply and tragically lost. Through all this he must have learned to conceal things. There was the mystery of his relationship with Jacqueline, for instance. All this made her feel uncertain, out of her depth once more. But in this garden of dark bewilderment a fresh young shoot was growing – she knew she was beginning to love Hugh Morton very much.

She sat twisting a lock of her hair, musing on his looks, his profile like that famous portrait of the young Byron. She loved his sensitive face, the way his lustrous hair sprang from his forehead, dark against his white skin, his expressive eyes, the way the corners of his moulded lips turned tenderly upward. She sometimes longed to reach out and touch those lips, to learn the shape of them with her fingers, maybe even to . . .

'Isabel, why on earth are you still here?' She hadn't noticed Stephen walk out of his office. 'Come along, I'm locking up.'

'Golly, you made me jump.'

'You *were* in a daydream,' he said, pulling on his jacket. 'Drooling over Maisie's hero, were you? The book must be good.'

'Our Maisie has certainly pulled it off again,' she replied with a grin. 'I've just finished the edit so I'll send it off to her tomorrow.'

'Good timing on my part then. What do you say to a drink to celebrate? I'm due in Chelsea for dinner at eight, but I was going for a brief sojourn over the road. Unless you have an engagement, of course?'

'No, I'm sad to say that I was going straight home to eat a boiled egg and wash my hair.'

He'd never asked her out on her own before, but she tried to pretend it was an ordinary occurrence and took her time squaring the pages of the manuscript, pulling her notes out of the typewriter and fitting the cover on top. He helped her on with her coat.

The landlord of the Fitzroy Tavern studied her curiously as they entered, but if he wondered what this young woman might be doing in Stephen's company he wisely kept it to himself. He was, she supposed, used to all sorts and combinations here in London's bohemia. She loved the cosy gloom of the pub, where Stephen seemed perfectly at home, greeting one of the regulars, a man who sat alone at a table, making his drink last, writing in an exercise book.

'A double whisky, when you've a moment,' Stephen told the landlord, 'and a gin and it for the lady.'

It was early and the place was still quiet. Stephen showed Isabel to a table by the window. Outside, the street was bathed in lamplight. The landlord brought their drinks.

'And a pint for the gentleman, if you would.' Stephen nodded towards the lone writer and handed the landlord a banknote. The beer was duly delivered and the writer lifted the glass to Stephen in a silent toast.

'That's kind of you,' Isabel whispered to Stephen. 'Do you know him?'

Stephen swallowed a large mouthful of whisky. 'I read a story he wrote once. I've an idea that one day he'll produce something to astonish us all.'

He finished his whisky and immediately ordered another. Isabel didn't remember him drinking like this before. As though he was bolstering himself.

'So Audrey's finally tying the knot,' he said. 'You're going to the wedding on Saturday, I suppose?'

'Yes, of course.' Isabel felt she knew every detail of this eagerly anticipated and likely glamorous affair, which was to take place in a Surrey country parish, where the Foster family had a base. 'Are you?'

'Just to the church, not to the reception. My wife . . . isn't very well at the moment.'

'I'm sorry to hear that,' Isabel said politely.

'She's gone to her mother's in Hampshire and I really ought to visit her this weekend and see that she's all right.'

'I hope it's nothing serious?'

'Nobody quite seems able to tell me,' he said, looking maudlin.

'Oh, I'm sorry,' Isabel repeated.

'It's a sort of distress, I think. We had some disappointing news last year. Apparently we're unlikely to be able to have children. It's terrible to feel one's responsible for another's unhappiness.' He set his glass down very deliberately on the table and stared into the distance.

'That's so sad,' Isabel murmured, a little surprised that he'd told her something so personal.

Stephen seemed to regret it too, for he roused himself and said gruffly, 'I hope you can keep that to yourself.'

'Of course,' she assured him. They were silent for a long moment.

'So,' he said, regarding her thoughtfully, 'when are you next seeing Morton?' There was something about his tone that she didn't like. Was he laughing at her?

'I've no idea,' she replied as coolly as she could. 'I can see you don't approve.'

'I wouldn't dare say whom you should or shouldn't see,' he said. 'Just that if I were your father, I'd advise you not to rush into things.'

The mention of her father immediately incensed her. 'But you're not,' she retorted.

'No, indeed I'm not. But I have seen a little more of life than you.'

She thought about this and decided it was true. 'What do you have against Hugh?' she asked him finally.

'Nothing, really. I can hardly say I know the man. Forget it, please.' He looked at his watch. 'Look, I'm afraid I must get going,' he said. 'Shall I find you a taxi?'

'No, thanks, I'll get the bus.'

They parted at Oxford Street and she watched him stumble off to hail a taxi.

As the bus rattled its way north, she puzzled over their conversation. Under his confident, engaging manner, there was much to suggest that Stephen McKinnon was a deeply unhappy man.

'Tell me about the marriage,' Berec begged as he stirred sugar into his coffee. He and Isabel were sitting in their favourite café in Percy Street one lunchtime the following week. 'Audrey, was she *radiant*, as you English like to say?'

'Very radiant, Berec,' Isabel told him. 'Such a beautiful dress. And the flowers, they came from the Fosters'
garden. Narcissi, spring lilies, the scent was simply
glorious.'

'And the poor Honorable Anthony?'

'Not poor at all. He looked very pleased with himself.
But I don't know how he's going to manage those rela-
tions of Audrey's. There are so many of them.'

'Married alive, is he? Poor man indeed.'

Isabel laughed. She had travelled down with
Vivienne's party on the train, and they'd both enjoyed the
day, but it was an unusually lavish affair for the times
and she was somewhat wistful that she would never be
able to have a wedding like that. Not that, at the moment,
she had marriage in prospect at all, she checked herself.
She sighed. The office had seemed very quiet today with
Audrey away and the excitement over.

'You know, Isabel, I hardly see you these days,' Berec
was complaining. 'And Gregor and Karin, they're asking
for you.'

'How are they both?' Isabel asked. 'I should like to see
them soon.'

'They wish me to bring you to supper one evening.
Karin has been suffering from her old trouble, the rheum-
atic fever, you know, but her spirits are improved, I think.
Especially since Gregor has found a job as porter at a
hospital, which is very good news.'

What a comedown from being a doctor this must be.
But at least it would mean regular money.

'And you, you are enjoying yourself?' Berec asked her.
She could not mistake the twinkle in his eye and smiled
back mischievously.

'Oh, Berec, yes. I must thank you a thousand times for getting me this job.'

He waved the gratitude away as though it were a fly. 'You know I didn't mean the job, but never mind. I saw right from the start that it would suit you.'

'You did, didn't you? It was very clever of you.'

'I wanted to help you, so bright and impetuous you were, arriving like that at your aunt's. I liked that. You'd run away from home to find your fortune. Like in the fairy stories.'

'And you were my fairy godmother.'

The twinkly eyes creased up in laughter. 'Your fairy godfather. That's right. Penelope was the godmother, I think.'

'I suppose she was in a way. I haven't seen her for a long time. Have you?'

'Not very much, no.'

'I will, I must do.' She felt a mixture of guilt and reluctance about this. Guilt because she knew she owed Penelope the courtesy of a visit, and reluctance because Penelope, though generous in Isabel's hour of desperate need, had not adopted the role of affectionate aunt. Reginald Dickson, her aunt's amour, had been discouraging of that. She noted that despite him being McKinnon & Holt's new backer, she hadn't ever seen Reginald. He didn't interfere as Redmayne Symmonds used to do, but seemed entirely happy for Stephen to conduct all business as he deemed best.

'I suppose Penelope is still with Reginald,' she thought to ask now.

'Yes,' Berec said shortly. 'I wish I could say I warm to the fellow.'

'He is a cold fish,' Isabel agreed. 'Do you think she'll marry him?'

'Not while he's married to someone else,' Berec said, crushing his cigarette butt into a small ashtray. 'And even then, I don't know. I remember her telling me one marriage was enough for a lifetime. And Reginald, I believe he likes things exactly as they are.'

'I would hate that,' Isabel said wonderingly. 'If I loved somebody, I would want to be with them all the time.'

Berec began searching for coins in his wallet and she couldn't see his expression. 'It is right that you think like that, Isabel,' he said, 'and I wish above all that you find happiness, but please remember it is not possible for everybody. For some, love is on the ration, for others it is denied altogether. Never allow your own good fortune to blind you to this.'

'You sound so serious, Berec,' she said, hesitant. Indeed it was the most serious thing Berec had ever said to her, and for a moment she couldn't think how to respond. Had something happened to him? Her thoughts flew to Myra, but she had long learned not to ask about Myra; the question appeared to disconcert Berec and she respected his privacy. She'd once wondered if he loved Penelope, but had concluded that if he ever had, he did so no longer. He only ever spoke of her with gratitude and the warmth of friendship.

'I did not mean to frighten you,' he said. 'Especially when I see that you are so happy.' His eyes were dancing with mischief, and she felt her face grow hot. 'No, I am not intruding,' he added hastily. 'But I can see you don't have much time for your old friend Berec now.'

'Berec, don't be silly, I always have time for you. And you must let me pay today, really. I'm the one with the job, remember. Here, take this.' She pushed a note towards him.

'Ah, and I was going to ask you for a book from the office. I can't do that if you pay for me.'

'Yes, of course you can. Was it the Russian poet? Stephen hopes you'll review that somewhere. If you come back to the office now, I'll give you a copy.'

Later that afternoon, she remembered their conversation about Penelope and, on impulse, tried to telephone her. There was nobody at home.

'I've bought a car.' Hugh's voice down the telephone was triumphant.

'We've got a crossed line,' Isabel said. A woman's voice kept shrilling, 'Hello, hello, Bernard?' Then came a click and silence. 'Are you still there, Hugh?' Isabel asked. 'For a moment I thought you said you'd bought a car.'

'I did, and I have. Will you come for a drive, Sunday? I can pick you up around ten.'

'Yes,' she said at once, 'I'd love that.' When he'd rung off she stood for a while in a transport of excitement. She was going out with him for a whole day! Did this mean their relationship was becoming serious? Perhaps she was reading too much into it. Oh blow, if only she was more sophisticated, like Audrey. Audrey would know how to handle things. She sighed and went off to look out something she might wear. The old gold dress with the sweet round collar, perhaps. Audrey had complimented her on that.

* * *

Sunday was blustery, and puffs of greyish cloud charged through a misty sky. She hoped the rain would hold off. The car was a dear, small and painted red, with a detachable roof. It was far from new but it spelled freedom, and once they were through the suburbs and picking up speed, its creaks and vibrations were hardly noticeable above the roar of the engine. Hugh drove fast, but well, and the quaint Surrey villages whipped by. They stopped for an early lunch in a pub in Haslemere, then went on again, reaching Brighton mid-afternoon. He parked the car by the seafront.

Isabel paddled in a freezing sea whilst Hugh, who declined even to remove his shoes, loitered on the stony beach. After she'd dried her feet on his handkerchief they visited the pier, where half a dozen children licking ice creams were watching a desultory Punch and Judy. The spectacle became more interesting when it was heckled by a posse of youths and the puppeteer shambled out of the tent and shouted at them to go away. 'Old 'itler should 'ave seen to the likes of you,' he cried, shaking his fist in a way that bested his efforts with Punch.

Hugh laughed and steered Isabel away. They strolled to the end of the pier and stood for a while watching seagulls circle and dive in the wake of a pleasure boat crossing the bay.

'Why do they do that?' Isabel asked. Her heart ached with the sense of his closeness.

'People throw food, I suppose, or perhaps the propeller turns up fish for them. They're scavengers, aren't they? They live off us, that's why they prosper.'

She thought the birds looked graceful at a distance, but harsh and malevolent up close. A sharp wind had blown up; she shivered and wrapped her coat more tightly around her. 'You're cold,' he said, taking her arm. 'I'm sorry. Let's get some tea.'

They walked back down the pier and found the last free table in the fug of a crowded café where the waitress brought tea and buttered toast and they sat quietly listening to the conversations around them. Once, Hugh smiled at something an old woman said, took out a small notebook and wrote in it, then put it away without a word. He seemed to be brooding on some matter that might have nothing to do with Isabel or the café or the moment, she couldn't tell. Sometimes he would disappear inside himself, or so she fancied. She found herself starting to panic. Perhaps she didn't matter to him particularly. Perhaps she'd read him wrongly, after all.

'Are you all right?' she asked after a time, feeling a little ignored.

'What? Yes, of course,' he replied rather shortly. 'Sorry, I was thinking.'

'I noticed,' she said, trying not to show her hurt. 'I was worried I'd upset you.'

'My dear girl.' He reached out and grasped her hand, interlacing his fingers with hers. 'You mustn't think that. How could you possibly upset me?' His expression was so tender she could hardly speak.

'I don't know,' she managed to say. 'I wasn't sure, that was all.'

And now the moment had come, she didn't know what to do with it. There were things she wanted to ask, but couldn't – not here.

'I feel sometimes,' she murmured, 'just sometimes, that I don't know where I am with you.'

'Isabel, isn't it obvious? Can't you see how I feel? You do trust me, don't you?'

Trust.

And now, surrounded by all these strangers, she was horrified to feel her eyes prickle with tears. She reached for her handbag, but Hugh was already pulling out his handkerchief, showering sand everywhere. He dabbed her cheeks with a clean corner.

'Can we go?' she asked. People were starting to look at her curiously.

'Of course.' He helped her on with her coat and cast a few coins on the table as they left.

Outside on the seafront, there was a sense of doubt about the daylight. Dark clouds had amassed over-head. Sharp raindrops stung their faces. An imposing ochre-plastered building stood opposite, bordered by a covered colonnade, and he hurried her across the road and into its shelter. At one end was a sort of recess where they were protected from public view. There it seemed the most natural thing in the world for him finally to pull her close. Their mouths met in hot, yearning kisses. His lips were soft and tasted of cinnamon.

'My dear girl, I didn't mean to make you cry,' he whispered in her ear, and when she looked into his face she saw deep concern, and for some reason this moved her deeply. How close she felt to him now, and powerful too. She was awed that she could have this effect on him. She did finally what she had longed to do for so long, reached up and traced the shape of his mouth with her fingers, then brushed his rough cheek with her hand, then she kissed him again. And for now, anyway, all the things that had bothered her no longer seemed to matter.

They stood together kissing for a long time whilst the rain fell in earnest, then watched as the buildings around them and the pier turned to silhouettes and the cloud light ripened to deep gold over the sea.

'We ought to go, I suppose,' Hugh murmured eventually. 'Can you manage to run in those shoes?'

'I'll try.'

Arms still round each other, they dashed through the rain, laughing, stumbling over puddles, along the shiny promenade to the car.

Driving back to London, the weather heightened their new closeness. Hugh hunched over the wheel trying to see the road, the windscreen wipers thrashing uselessly against the flood pouring down the glass. With the car heater turned up high, it felt terribly safe and intimate to Isabel.

They had just cleared the summit of the South Downs and were racing for home on an open road when an ominous thudding noise started up and the car began to list.

'The front tyre's gone, dammit,' Hugh groaned, clutching the steering wheel with both hands to steady the vehicle. He slowed down and managed to pull the car into the side of the road, bumping it up onto a grass verge, then got out and examined the wheel on his side.

'Flat as a pancake,' he called to Isabel, looking mournful. 'I'm very sorry, but you're going to have to get out.' She opened her door to find a ditch full of nettles.

'It'll have to be your side,' she said, but he'd already gone to open the bonnet and didn't hear. She climbed across and went to join him.

'Why not stand under those trees while I sort this out,' Hugh told her as he began to unclip the spare wheel.

'No, I'll help.' The rain was already soaking through her coat.

'Don't be ridiculous, you're not strong enough. I don't want you to hurt yourself.'

'I'm sure there's something I can do.'

'You can watch for other vehicles then,' he said, rolling the wheel to where he needed it.

She settled for passing him the jack out of the toolbag and gathering up the bolts when he took the flat wheel off and then substituted it with the other.

'Show me your hands,' she commanded when he'd finished, and with an old rag from the boot scrubbed the worst of the oil off them. They climbed back into the car half-drowned, and at once rich smells of wet wool, earth and leather mingled with the usual stink of petrol and upholstery.

After several tries the engine caught and they smiled delightedly at one another. 'Bingo!' he cried, then turned in his seat and embraced her. 'You're a brick, you darling girl, you know that?' And a feeling of deep joy washed over her.

It was late in the evening when he pulled up outside her house, and both of them were exhausted.

'It's been the most wonderful day,' she said.

'It has, despite everything.' He took her in his arms and kissed her. 'I'd better not risk turning off the engine.' She opened the car door. 'I'll telephone you,' he said. 'Goodbye.'

* * *

She didn't hear anything from him the following day, nor the day after that, though in the office she answered the phone with a little pang of expectation every time it rang. At home in the evening she sat mutinous when any of the other lodgers were on a call in case he was trying to get through. Why didn't he ring? First she was puzzled, then hurt, then despairing. *Trust me*, he had told her. How could she, when he left her hanging on like this?

Her thoughts flew everywhere. Perhaps there was something wrong. Perhaps she'd misjudged him or offended him in some way. And yet he'd made her feel so sure of him. Once or twice she dialled the number of his flat, but nobody answered. Where was he? She whipped herself up into a maelstrom of anger and longing, first one and then the other.

After three days that dragged endlessly, she walked into the office on Thursday morning and picked up her ringing phone.

'Isabel?' It was him. For a moment she couldn't breathe.

'Hello?' he said.

'Hello, Hugh.'

Hearing the dullness in her voice he said, 'You're angry with me.'

'No,' she lied.

'You are angry – I can tell. Look, I'm in Suffolk, but coming back later. Are you free this evening? I'd like you to have dinner with me.'

'I'm busy.' It happened to be true. She was going with Berec to have supper with Gregor and Karin. Part of her wanted to say she'd cancel this, but her dignity would not allow it. He must be made to wait.

'Tomorrow then? Dammit, you are angry. I don't blame you.' She was silent. 'I've been here all week, Isabel. My mother's been in hospital. '

'I'm sorry,' she said, instantly concerned. 'What's been the matter?'

'She had a bad asthma attack. Her housekeeper called me on Monday, very distressed. I got a train immediately. It's been an anxious few days, but she's much better now. I'm sorry I haven't telephoned. I left my address book behind. I tried you at the office yesterday lunchtime, left a message with what's-his-name, that gawky lad?'

'Jimmy?' She'd wring Jimmy's neck for not passing it on.

'That's him. Please, Isabel. May I see you? There's something important I need to say.' He was pleading now and she finally gave in. Besides, she was curious about what he wanted to tell her.

'Tomorrow, then,' she said.

He took her to a restaurant you'd never know existed, tucked away in a side street in the heart of St James's. It was a place of thick carpets, rich furnishings and low lighting, more like an opulent drawing room than a commercial establishment. Here the waiters trod softly and spoke in low voices, and there were no prices on the menu, which was all in French. The head waiter greeted Hugh with enthusiasm, but regarded Isabel curiously as he showed them to their table, tucked in a corner.

'*Le champagne ce soir, m'sieur?*' the man enquired of Hugh.

Hugh hesitated. 'Perhaps not. How about a gin and tonic, Isabel?' She nodded. 'Two doubles, then.'

'And ze light hand wiz ze tonic?' the man said with a crack of a smile.

'That's the ticket.'

'You've been here before?' Isabel asked when they were alone.

'Once or twice,' he said. 'Jacqueline likes it.' He smiled. 'She says it makes her believe the war never happened. The man must have remembered we had champagne.'

'Oh.' With the unexpected mention of Jacqueline's name, all Isabel's feelings of uncertainty returned.

'What is it?' he asked, concerned. 'Are you still angry with me?'

'Hugh, I didn't hear from you and I was worried,' she whispered fiercely. 'And now . . . now you tell me you bring other girls here. To drink *champagne*.'

She was put out when he laughed and said, 'Is champagne so immoral? I didn't know. Anyway, Jacqueline isn't a *girl*, she's a married woman. No, that doesn't sound quite right either, does it? Look, she's hitched up to this chap Michael, who works for Military Intelligence, didn't you know? He's away a very great deal and she gets lonely. I'd be a poor friend if I didn't take her out occasionally to cheer her up.'

The way he explained it made sense and she felt a measure of relief. And yet she remembered the way Jacqueline had been at the party, how she had practically fawned over Hugh. Isabel glanced up at him, wondering if she had the courage to speak of this, but she saw only innocence in his hazel eyes, and warmth, so said nothing.

'You do believe me, my darling?' he begged and she nodded. She believed him.

At that moment their drinks arrived. Next there was

the ordeal of ordering food, French dishes she'd never heard of, but which Hugh decided for her, then the shaking out of napkins, the laying of cutlery. Thick soup was brought in wide-brimmed plates, white rolls in a silver basket. Finally they were left in peace.

Hugh hardly touched his soup. He said gravely, 'I must explain about my mother. The attack was unusually severe. A reaction to dust, the doctors think. From the spring cleaning.'

'Poor lady,' Isabel murmured. 'How is she now?'

'Much better.' He smiled. 'She kept me very busy running errands. I hardly had a moment to telephone.'

Isabel nodded, allowing herself to be pulled round, placated, as she desperately wanted to be. He hadn't neglected her, not really; it was right that he was solicitous of his mother. He'd tried to ring. Jimmy had admitted he'd forgotten to tell her and she'd given him a dressing down for it. Suddenly she began to feel hungry. The soup, when she ate, was warming, delicious.

'I should have tried the office again,' Hugh admitted. 'Somehow when you're down in Suffolk it's easy to let time drift.'

'It didn't drift for me, Hugh,' she told him. 'I thought you'd changed your mind, that you regretted our day together.'

'No, far from it,' he said, putting down his spoon and regarding her earnestly. 'I thought about Brighton all the time, how sweet you were. And then the business with the burst tyre; you were so steadfast, so patient. I told Mother all about it.'

'And what did she say?' Isabel, sensing the importance of Mrs Morton in his life, was anxious.

'She was impressed. She'd like to meet you,' he said lightly. 'Really, though, not every girl would have put up with that situation as cheerfully as you did.'

'Perhaps you underestimate our sex,' she said, her eyes dancing.

'No, it confirmed to me that you're special,' he said. 'I feel I've waited a long time to find you. Since I lost . . . well, you've read about her in *Coming Home.*'

'The girl who was Diana?' Part of her was curious about the girl who'd died, but another part felt that mention of her was an intrusion.

'Her real name was Anne. Anne Sinclair. I've taken girls out since, of course, but I've never met anyone . . . Oh, as bright and pretty and smart as you.'

'Stop it,' she said, laughing. 'I'll have to go through doors sideways, my head will get so big.'

'It's a beautiful head. You're completely beautiful.'

'Shh, people will hear you!'

'I don't care if they do. I love you, Isabel.' He seized her hand and imprisoned it in his, regarding her with an expression of such sincere adoration that the very last trace of doubt was washed away. The previous few days didn't matter. All the times she'd felt confused, unsure of him, the misunderstandings, didn't matter. Everything was all right, after all.

'Oh, Hugh,' she whispered joyfully. 'I love you, too.' She'd never seen him so happy. He kissed her hand, then leaned across and brushed her cheek with his fingers.

'Isabel, my dear girl,' he murmured. 'I know this will come as very sudden. You may think we haven't known one another long enough, but this week I've come to feel sure about it. I've waited so long to find you, and now

here you are. I love you so much. You're so darling and
funny, oh, and passionate about things. I can't bear to risk
you slipping away.'

'I won't slip away, Hugh. Not if you don't want me to.'

'I don't. I want to be with you all the time.' He took a
breath. 'Do you think you could take me on, Isabel?'

Take him on? What did he mean?

'Don't look at me so oddly. I'm asking you to marry
me.'

For a moment she was so surprised her mouth opened
but she couldn't speak. It had all happened so fast. Could
it be only a week ago that he'd first kissed her? She'd
known for a long time that she loved him, of course, but
still . . .

She could hardly think straight. A warning voice in her
head said she should wait to answer, but she ignored it
and instead raised her face to him like a flower and spoke
from the heart.

'Yes,' she said, and watched as his eyes filled with
wonder and delight. They stared, holding hands across
the table, smiling stupidly at each other for what seemed
like an eternity. Never had she felt so perfectly, ecstatically happy.

'Would m'sieur like ze champagne now?' the head
waiter asked when he brought the next course and found
the pretty mademoiselle gazing in wonder at a ring
sparkling on her finger.

They decided that it shouldn't be a long engagement.
Hugh didn't want to wait. There were no real difficulties
about money and his flat was large enough to suit them
both, at least for the moment.

In the end they rejected the idea of a mad dash to a register office. Isabel felt it wouldn't be fair on her parents. Pamela wanted her daughter to have a 'proper' wedding in a church, not that they were a church-going family by any means, but that was the way her family in Norfolk had done things, and Isabel remembered that her mother had missed out.

Caught up in the excitement of it all, Isabel forgot that she'd ever had doubts about Hugh. She was deliriously happy. She'd enjoyed surprising her colleagues, too, who were all delighted for her, even Audrey, who seemed after all to think Isabel had been 'clever' in landing Hugh. Admiration from Audrey was not something she was used to, but then Audrey had softened since the occasion of her own marriage, seemed more mature, and Isabel secretly wanted that for herself, too.

She'd taken Hugh down to meet her parents on the Sunday after their engagement. It had not been an easy meeting. Mr and Mrs Barber had been surprised, of course, and asked Hugh all sorts of questions, which he answered readily enough, but she could tell that her father was on edge. Her mother, coming from a similar section of society to Hugh, was more gracious, but both of them were worried about the idea of a July wedding, not so much because it was all a terrible rush, as because the couple had not known one another long.

'People got married at the drop of a hat during the war,' Hugh reminded them.

'And some came to regret it.' Mrs Barber's retort was gently expressed, but it was still an admonition. Yet Isabel was insistent, passionately so. Her parents could only shrug and give in.

Now she would have to meet his mother. She wondered
nervously how Lavinia Morton would regard her. Hugh
was her only child, after all, and Isabel already had an
inkling of how important mother and son were to one
another.

They drove down to Suffolk the following Saturday.
    Isabel was surprised that he knocked on the door of the
drawing room before entering. 'Mother,' he said, 'this is
Isabel.'
    Mrs Morton rose slowly from her chair by the fire, and
Isabel crossed an interminable acreage of carpet to greet
her future mother-in-law.
    'How do you do.' Hugh's mother spoke in regal tones
as she took Isabel's hand briefly into hers. 'Welcome to
Stone House.'
    'Thank you.' Isabel found herself looking up into a pair
of hazel eyes, Hugh's eyes, in an oval face framed by
lacquered waves of greying hair. Mrs Morton might be
nearly sixty, but she was determined not to let time win.
She was very well made-up, her eyebrows painted arches,
her thickening figure tightly corseted. Her manicured
hand rested elegantly on one hip as her gaze flickered
over her son's choice of wife. Something told Isabel that
she was disappointed by what she saw.
    Hugh didn't seem to notice. He was opening an envel-
ope he'd found addressed to him in the hall. 'Oh blast,' he
said, 'some local society wants me to address them.'
    'I do hope you will, Hugh. I'm afraid it was I who
mentioned your name to them.'
    'I wish you wouldn't, Mother.'
    'But, dear, you must put yourself about to further your

career. Now, will you show Isabel her room? I've given her Magnolia.'

Left by herself in a bedroom at the back of the house whose decor gave off a pinkish-white aura like medicine, Isabel at last felt able to take in her surroundings. She had built up a mental picture of Hugh's beloved childhood home from his descriptions, but Stone House was somehow bigger than she imagined, chilly inside, and alarmingly remote. She went over to the window and found herself looking out across a great apron of lawn edged by a gravel path and flowerbeds. Beyond the garden was a field, and beyond that, as Hugh had told her, the marshes. A line of glittering silver in the distance must be the river. She pushed open the casement, admitting a draught of cold wind. Rich scents of earth and greenery, the desolate cries of seabirds, filled her senses. She leaned over the sill and immediately drew back, shivering. It was a steep drop to the flagstones below.

She did not enjoy the weekend much. Hugh was subdued, not at all his usual self, and she sensed that Mrs Morton was playing some power game with her, the rules of which she did not know, and in which she had no desire to engage. Typical of this was the discussion over dinner of what Isabel should call her.

'I'm thinking it's too familiar for a young person to call me Lavinia,' the woman intoned. 'I would feel most uncomfortable.'

'Isabel can't call you Mrs Morton,' Hugh said. 'That would be impossible. How about "Mother"?'

'But I am not her mother, Hugh, do be sensible.' Sometimes Lavinia spoke to him as though he were still a young boy. 'How about "Mother-in-Law"? Yes, I think that would be best.'

Mother-in-Law? Isabel tried it once or twice but it sounded ridiculous. She decided she would get round it by calling her nothing. Thereafter she thought of her always as just 'Hugh's mother'.

That evening, Mrs Morton insisted on sitting up with the engaged couple so Isabel made her excuses and went to her bed early, hoping that Hugh might not be long. She read her book for a little, then turned out the light and waited in the darkness, listening to the wind outside. It wasn't long before there was a soft knock on the door and Hugh put his head round.

'Are you still awake?' he whispered.

'Yes, of course – come in,' she replied, and he felt his way to the bed.

'Where are you?' he said.

'Here,' she replied, drawing him down towards her. Their mouths found each other in the darkness. She pulled him closer, but he resisted.

'We'd better not,' he said.

'I don't mind, really.'

'No, my temptress, we must wait. It'll be all the nicer then, you'll see.' She wondered vaguely how he knew this, but would never ask.

'I wish you would stay. I won't break.'

'I know, and I want you madly, but you'll see I'm right. Good night, darling,' he murmured, and in a moment he was gone.

She missed him already. When they'd talked about it the previous weekend he'd said the same thing. They shouldn't go to bed together until they were married. It wouldn't be long. She was so young, he told her, and he wanted to protect her. It was the right thing to do.

She thought about this long after he'd gone. She wanted him so much but she could hardly beg him, could she? She imagined that being so much older, he was more experienced. Perhaps she should trust him, even though her body cried out for him? She hugged herself for comfort as she waited to fall asleep.

Chapter 17

Emily

It was Valentine's Day. On the top of the bus to work, Emily watched teenagers in school blazers torment each other. One girl, pretty and flirtatious, waved a card in a pink envelope, which the boys snatched away and threw to one another. The girls all shrieked and giggled as they tried to retrieve it. A young man in a City suit bounded up the stairs carrying a bunch of red roses in cellophane that still bore its price sticker. Emily couldn't help smiling at his self-conscious air, but inside she felt forlorn. There would be nothing for her today. 'It's only stupid commercialisation,' she remembered Matthew telling her once. Even if they'd still been together, he probably wouldn't have sent her anything. He hated following the herd. She tried to remember when she last had a surprise Valentine from anybody. Not since school, that was for sure.

The office, of course, had gone Valentine's crazy. A bestselling romance author sent in a huge box of heart-shaped cupcakes, which did the rounds. Someone strung up pink bunting over the mirrors in the Ladies. Even the sullen girl who administered royalty payments displayed a huge bunch of flora on her desk. Her beatific smile transformed her.

Emily's email box was full of horrors. An overenthu-
siastic marketing assistant had set viral messages to
arrive every hour about a book on internet dating. The
Finance Director picked the day to circulate several
forms about annual budgets. Filling them in would take
Emily hours of meticulous work. And no one seemed to
have told Big Brother, aka the Chief of Operations, that
it was a day of goodwill. For round about midday a very
unloving announcement hit everyone's inbox, ominously
labelled *Maximising Profits*. From around the room came
little sighs and groans as her colleagues opened it. The
management consultants were coming. The words 'cost
savings' were mentioned, which everyone knew meant
redundancies. Suddenly the joy was gone from the
cakes, the bunting and the flowers. Everyone was fear-
ful.

'The bastards,' Liz muttered.

'I don't know what we'll do if I lose my job,' Sarah told
the others, her eyes round and anxious. 'Jules has already
had to take a paycut.'

'You'll be all right,' Emily said, trying to comfort her.
'The Young Adult list is doing brilliantly. I don't see where
they can cut in editorial, anyway. We're already stretched
too thin.'

'That won't stop them,' Liz murmured. 'You watch.
They just don't care.'

Emily spared a moment to worry for herself – last in,
first out being the phrase that rose to mind – and she had
a mortgage to manage. But she'd survived redundancies
at the old firm, and it was Gillian herself who had
recruited her, so she tried to be philosophical. Also, she
was feeling that she'd started to prove herself. Her

marketing colleagues were keen on a historical novel she'd acquired and she'd been allowed to offer for Tobias Berryman's literary thriller. It was set in a sort of dark, alternative Elizabethan world that had resonances of today, very cleverly evoked and spine-chilling, highbrow yet readable at the same time. The Sales Director was crazy about it. Surely they wouldn't get rid of her now. And she genuinely thought they needed Sarah. Everyone relied on her long-term knowledge of the firm.

'They can't possibly let you go, Sarah. No one else can keep Jack Vane in order.' One of the firm's big money-spinning authors, Jack was a notorious complainer.

Sarah rolled her eyes. 'Not having to deal with the Vain One any more. That would be a consolation prize for redundancy.'

She spoke lightly, but Emily saw how jittery she was.

Emily spent a late lunch hour idling the carpeted halls of a huge bookshop on Piccadilly, trying to think how she'd brief the jacket of Tobias's novel. The bookshop was one of her favourite haunts, where she discovered useful hints of what and how to publish. She loved the look and feel of new books, the smell of the paper, the wondrous possibilities that each one suggested.

She picked up a paperback from a table of debut novels, lured by the illustration on the cover, a silhouette of a girl opening a birdcage and a bluebird flying away. *Maybe*, it said to her, *by reading me, you too will escape to a world you've never dreamed of before, and your life will be changed.* She was reading the blurb and wondering whether to buy it, when a woman's voice said, 'Hello, Emily. It is Emily, isn't it?' and when she looked up, she was startled to see Lorna Morton. Maybe she used her married name, not Morton, but Emily still thought of her as Hugh's daughter.

'Lorna, what a surprise!'

'I thought it was you, but I wasn't sure,' Lorna said, beaming. 'It would be typical of me to accost a complete stranger. I'm useless at names and faces.'

Emily found Lorna's self-effacement endearing, but at the same time felt sorry for her. Lorna's country looks were if anything more pronounced today, her face flushed in the warmth of the shop. Instead of her cagoule, she was wearing a jacket of an orangey hue that didn't quite suit the reds and blues of her Liberty-print blouse, and a very unflattering hiker's hat.

'I've just had lunch with Joel Richards,' Lorna confided. 'He wanted to talk to me without Mother hovering about. I feel a bit guilty about it, though.'

'Why? Did it go all right?' Emily asked, the book she'd been looking at forgotten.

'I don't know that I was any help, though he kindly told me I was. He had this awful tape recorder and it put me off a bit. I'm embarrassed to think of him having to listen to my muddle again.'

'What sort of things did he ask you?' Emily wanted to know.

'Oh, you know, my memories of Dad, nothing difficult. I had hoped . . .' she started saying then stopped. 'No, it doesn't matter.'

Emily thought of the *Coming Home* file, which Joel had recently come in to inspect. She was about to mention it when Lorna glanced at her watch and said, 'I must get on and pay for these. I'm due at my god-daughter's, you see.'

Emily was surprised to see that the paperbacks Lorna was clutching were not, as might be expected, about gardening or cookery, nor even romance, but futuristic fantasy. 'They're for her eldest daughter,' Lorna explained. 'Though I have to say I enjoy them myself.'

Emily watched Lorna join the queue, a little flustered, her bag falling off her shoulder as she searched for her money. The choice of fantasy books amused her. Lorna, she decided, might turn out to be the darkest of horses.

When Emily returned to the office it was to find a gorgeous bouquet of roses lying across her keyboard.

'Aren't you the lucky one,' Liz said enviously, her corn-rowed head appearing over the partition.

'Jules only managed a card,' Sarah told them. 'It's years since he gave me flowers.'

Emily gathered up the bouquet to inspect it. The roses were beautiful, proper scented ones, pink and red and white, not those dark forced blooms that you'd find at every street stall. She sniffed their old-fashioned fragrance with closed eyes – wonderful. There was a small envelope stapled to the cellophane, which she opened carefully, savouring the moment.

'Oh,' she said, intrigued and disappointed in the same moment. 'There's no name.' Only the printed care instructions.

'A real surprise Valentine!' Liz's round eyes were saucer-like with excitement. 'Come on, try and guess. Do you think it's from George?'

'I sincerely hope not,' Emily said, the flowers losing some of their lustre at the thought. There weren't many other possibilities, though.

'It is so romantic.' Sarah gave a long sigh.

'No, it's not, it's creepy,' Emily said.

'It could be someone gross.' Liz's eyes now glittered with fun. 'That's the trouble. You might be better not knowing.'

'Thanks for that, Liz,' Emily said. 'Either of you see who brought them?'

They shook their heads.

'Call reception,' Liz said. Emily did, but they couldn't help. There had been so many flowers delivered that day.

There was a vase in one of the cupboards; she brought it out and arranged the flowers, then returned to her desk and shifted a pile of magazines to make room for the vase.

Under the magazines was a slim cardboard box she'd not noticed before. It was quite pretty, decorated in a sort of Orla Kiely pattern and tied with thick green ribbon.

This is a day of surprises, she thought, setting down the vase and picking up the box.

There was no label or anything on it. Gently she pulled the ends of the ribbon and it slid undone with a silken sigh. The lid came off easily. Inside was something flat and rectangular packed in tissue paper.

She took it out, carefully unwrapped it and stared.

'Sarah?' she said, hardly moving.

'Mmm?' Sarah looked up.

'Did you see who left this here?'

'Sorry, no. What is it?'

'Liz?'

'What?' Liz peered over the partition. 'A photograph?' she said, unimpressed. 'No idea. You are popular today. Who's it of ?'

'Extraordinary,' Emily whispered. It was a framed

wedding portrait in black and white. The man was instantly recognisable as Hugh Morton – Hugh when he was young and handsome. But the woman? It wasn't Jacqueline. This woman's hair glinted bright, she had a lively expression in her large dark eyes. They both looked so happy. She knew, she was absolutely sure, that this was Isabel.

'Who keeps sending you this stuff!' Sarah exclaimed, coming to take the photo from Emily. 'It's weird.'

'Isn't it?' Emily replied. Someone was trying to tell her something. Something important, but as to who and what she couldn't guess.

She was about to pack the photo away again when she saw a big envelope at the bottom of the box. She picked it up and read her name on it in printed capitals. She withdrew from it a sheaf of paper, which she unfolded to find it was photocopies of some handwritten documents, letters, perhaps, or a diary, not immediately easy to read. How odd. She turned the envelope over, but there was nothing else written on it, and there was no covering note or anything. Had the whole thing been left by the person who sent the flowers? Again, there was no clue. She sat down and tried to make out the first line of the handwriting. It was a little faint, but she thought the first words read . . . *is writing his book, so I shall write mine*. How peculiar.

She read on: *When his is published, everyone will think it's about our marriage, and they may be right, but it'll be from his point of view. I must tell my side of the story or I'll be erased, made invisible. It feels that this has happened already. Maybe if I write everything down I'll be Isabel once more, not this ragged empty thing that has no life.*

Isabel. This was Isabel's writing, why had she not realised? There had been examples of it in letters in the *Coming Home* file, handwritten alterations to the typing, her signature. But it had been small and neat and flowing there. Here she'd taken less care, though when Emily turned a page, she saw it was tidier, the sentences less rambling, as though the author had been getting into her stride. Emily read the first few lines again. The initial word must be *Hugh*, of course. *Hugh is writing his book, so I shall write mine.* What book was he writing? Of course, it could be any, as there was no date anywhere that Emily could see, but since Isabel died so young it was likely to be *The Silent Tide* she was talking about. So if that book was inspired by Isabel, after all, it seemed that she wasn't a willing accomplice. She had another story to tell, and here it was.

That evening, Emily had a yoga class so she left the flowers on the desk but slipped the photocopied pages into her bag to read. The box with the photograph she locked in a drawer.

Much later, she fetched the pages and started to read. It was a fascinating account. Isabel described how she had left home and found work at McKinnon & Holt, then how she'd met Hugh and fallen in love. Once again Emily heard the voice of this girl she'd never met, but who felt so close as she read her story.

Part II

Chapter 18

Isabel

The parish church where Isabel and Hugh were married was out of its place and time. St Crispin's had once been surrounded by countryside, having been built in the fourteenth century to serve a small feudal community. Now, clutching the skirts of its graveyard close for protection, it towered self-consciously above a sea of red roofs. Which included the Barbers'. Until the occasion of Isabel's wedding, however, no Barber had ever entered St Crispin's through its damp stone porch and wormy oak door. The whole family was there today. Ted and Donald slouched in the front pew, hair ruthlessly trimmed and plastered down, freckles almost scrubbed off. Lydia bounced on the seat beside them, crumpling her dress of pale blue, chosen to offset her fairness. Their mother Pamela, with one hand clutching Lydia's dress to stay her, wore a new suit with a nipped-in waist, and her nerves were ratcheted to snapping point. At the back of the church, Isabel impatiently waited with her father and her bridesmaid, Vivienne, for the service to begin.

Isabel had endured this morning's preparations with a growing sense of hysteria that finally released itself in shrieks of anger after her mother accidentally stabbed her with a hairpin as she tried to fix the veil. Now she stood quietly enough, if pale. She tried to forget the fact that everyone would be staring at her by focusing all her attention on the back view of her darling Hugh, who stood elegantly attired in morning suit at the altar rail with his best man, James Steerforth, beside him. Finally the little vicar found the right page in his book, turned and nodded to the organist. The old pipe organ began to cough out a ragged march tune and the congregation rose to its collective feet. Isabel's father pulled her forward.

When they reached the front, Vivienne helped lift her veil, and her father gave her away with a gruff 'I do,' then she found herself staring into Hugh's bright face, and suddenly nothing else mattered any more.

'I require and charge you both . . .' The vicar's voice was astonishingly deep and resonant. 'Hugh William, wilt thou have this woman, Isabel Mary . . . wilt thou love her, comfort her, honour her, and keep her in sickness and in health, and forsaking all others, keep thee only unto her, so long as ye both shall live?'

If there was a silence, it was probably only the length of the breath Hugh drew to say, 'I will,' but to Isabel it was too long. He sounded anxious, she thought, not himself at all, but when it was her turn to say the words she too could only muster a hoarse whisper. She caught a movement behind Hugh, in the front row: his mother was leaning forward to catch her answer.

Then there was a pause while the best man fumbled with the ring. Finally Hugh had it and pushed it firmly onto her finger. How strange it felt, with Hugh still holding it and his breath warm on her face as he made his vow. And now they knelt together and she was pronounced to be his wife and the atmosphere lightened. Lydia chattered through the prayers and had to be taken outside, an old man at the back had a coughing fit, and soon all were singing 'Praise to the Almighty' and it was over.

Walking back down the aisle, the sea of people – on her side, at least – came at last into familiar focus. Aunt Penelope and Reginald stood alone in the pew behind the Barbers, then came several empty rows before she saw with delight Stephen, Berec, Trudy and Trudy's bearish husband, Redmayne. There was Audrey, chic in navy and white, with slim, aristocratic-looking Anthony beside her. On Hugh's side of the church, though, there were some she'd never seen before. Then she noticed Joan Steerforth standing with the other couple, Victor and Constance. And though she avoided catching the woman's eye, she glimpsed Jacqueline standing with a dark, very correct-looking man of around forty dressed in the uniform of an Army officer. This must be the mysterious Major Michael Wood MC, home on leave. That he really did exist came as something of a relief.

It was Hugh who had suggested the hotel in a nearby town for the reception; Hugh, too, who was apparently paying the greater part of the bill. Her father was furious about this, though, as he acknowledged to Isabel, it would have been a cup of tea and a piece of cake in the church hall for everyone otherwise.

Her parents still seemed a little bewildered by the speed of the marriage, and nervous around Hugh.

He was exactly the sort of man her father disliked: urbane, highly educated, someone who had never really had to worry about money. 'Easy officer material' was how she'd heard him disparage other such men, which Mr Barber, despite his corporal's stripe, had never been. Since Hugh was marrying his daughter, Mr Barber was forced to button his lip, but Isabel guessed his feelings all the same. As for her mother, Pamela Barber could meet Hugh as her social equal, but she was ashamed of the dreary house and the view from their living room of the next-door neighbour's washing. It was no good Isabel telling her that Hugh didn't care about these things. Her mother had seen him noticing, hadn't she?

'He's a writer, Mother, he notices all kinds of things.'

'To put them in his books, no doubt,' her mother murmured. 'And Mrs Morton, I can't possibly receive her here.'

Isabel felt her mother was right on this point, and in the end her parents and Hugh's mother met for drinks the evening before the wedding in the lounge of the hotel where she and Hugh were staying and where the reception was to be held. The occasion did not go badly, exactly, but none of the parties enjoyed it. Isabel was stiff with anxiety – and with good reason. Her father remained silent nearly the entire time. The mothers were as wary as cats, Pamela Barber perched on the edge of her seat, displaying a miserable dignity, Hugh's mother stiff-backed and tight-lipped in the chair opposite.

'I believe my grandfather was a first cousin,' Mrs Barber murmured when Hugh's mother mentioned some genteel East Anglian neighbours, and Hugh's mother raised her eyebrows in reluctant appreciation.

Later, Hugh was to say, 'I think they both relished the battle, don't you?'

On one thing only did the mothers warmly agree.

'Of course,' Hugh's mother said, as though Isabel wasn't present, 'there'll be no need for Isabel to continue working. Hugh will be able to make her perfectly comfortable; we've my husband's family to thank for that.'

'It'll be a relief to see her settled, I must say,' Mrs Barber said. 'She's very spirited, I think you'll find, but a house and, one hopes, children, will do her the world of good.'

Isabel's father made a rare interjection in a growled, 'Spirited, I'll say,' at the same time as Isabel breathed, 'Oh, Mother!'

'I'll order another round,' Hugh said, getting up. 'Same again for everyone?'

Since her job was a subject that she and Hugh were still discussing, Isabel felt more and more agitated, but all she could say to the mothers without seeming rude was a meek, 'I love my work. It would be hard to give it up. And it does enable me to make sure Hugh's books are published well.'

'I'm so proud of him,' Hugh's mother purred, glancing at her son over at the bar, and Isabel tried not to dwell on what Hugh had told her – how disappointed his mother had been that he hadn't taken up the Law like his father, or medicine. 'I'm expecting great things, you know. And it's so important for a man to have a good wife. I always made sure I put my husband's needs before my own, Mrs Barber. And I'm sure he knew and appreciated that.'

Isabel's father made a harrumphing noise, which he turned into a cough.

'You must miss your husband very much,' Isabel's mother said, casting hers an anxious look.

'Every day, Mrs Barber, every day.' Her hooded eyes did indeed look moist. If it was an act it was a very good one.

After the wedding, they returned to the hotel. The reception took place in the shabby grandeur of a large room at the back that opened onto an orchard garden. Isabel swallowed two glasses of sweet sherry in quick succession to bear her up whilst she shook many hands and accepted many compliments on her appearance. Then the photographer ushered them out into the garden. The grass glittered with raindrops from a recent shower. A fresh breeze blew threatening clouds across the sky.

Vivienne secured the bride's flyaway veil and tucked a stray lock of hair back under the headband, then Isabel clutched her husband's arm and smiled and smiled for the camera, until her mouth quivered with the strain. *This is the happiest day of my life*, she told herself. *They've always told me it would be. I must treasure every moment.*

When the rain started up again there was a general move indoors. The table was now spread with a buffet of sandwiches and salad, and everyone bustled up to help themselves, the bride taking only a lettuce leaf and some chicken, being too overwrought to eat. Isabel's mother had made the two-tiered cake in the centre, though she could be heard lamenting its likely awfulness given the shortage of ingredients, which spoiled it for Isabel.

It was overwhelming, she found, being the centre of attention for the first time in her life with everyone telling her how beautiful she looked. An old schoolfriend named

Susan came up and congratulated her with a tone of envy; Susan whom she'd once known well and whom her mother had insisted she at least invite, since Isabel had passed over the poor girl for bridesmaid in favour of Vivienne, whom Isabel had only known 'for five minutes', as Mrs Barber put it. Finally Susan moved on to talk to Mrs Barber, and with Hugh having abandoned her to speak to the Steerforths across the other side of the room, Isabel was briefly on her own. Suddenly she was starving. She snatched up an egg roll that even the twins had missed and ate it hungrily whilst she looked round the room. She was glad of the respite.

Aunt Penelope and Reginald stood alone together by the window, drinking spirits and staring out at the rain-drenched garden. Isabel had spoken to them earlier, of course, and now she hoped that they were enjoying themselves, for they hardly mingled with the other guests. She'd seen her parents speak to them, her father and Reginald managing to stiffly shake hands. As she watched now, Berec went to join them, and Reginald brought out one of his cigars.

She brushed the crumbs from her dress and was wondering where she'd put her drink, when someone touched her elbow and said, 'Isabel.' There was Stephen, smiling at her. His eyes were bright – with alcohol perhaps, or the spirit of the occasion. Usually reserved, he surprised her now by kissing her soundly.

'For the blushing bride. Let's hope the groom doesn't mind,' Stephen said mischievously, meeting Hugh's eye across the room. Hugh merely raised one eyebrow and continued his conversation. He was talking, Isabel saw, to Jacqueline and her husband. She had already been introduced to Major Michael Wood, and wondered if she'd bored him, for he barely spoke to her. She was touched, however, by his solicitous way with Jacqueline, whom he looked for whenever she left his side. She'd thought Jacqueline quiet today, and tired-looking despite her pancaked make-up.

Stephen was regarding her with a most serious expression. 'My dear, I'm so glad it's all worked out for you,' he said. 'My only fear now is that we'll lose you.'

'There's no danger of that,' she said. 'I like my work too much.'

'Hugh doesn't mind then?'

She sighed. 'He knows it makes me happy. What would I do at home all day? Pull my hair out, I should think.'

'I'm very relieved. You should at least have a shorter journey to the office from Kensington.'

'I hope you won't expect me quite so early in the mornings,' she retorted, twinkling at him and he laughed.

'Now that would be too much.'

She and Hugh had made some adjustments to the flat. They'd acquired a big brass bedstead and a mattress, both second-hand. Hugh had told her she could redecorate as soon as paint and wallpaper became more generally available.

'I'm very happy with everything as it is,' she'd told him and when he looked surprised, added, 'Why should we change it all simply for the sake of change? Though perhaps a dressing table would be nice,' she said on further thought. 'I've always wanted one.' The only mirror was in the big double wardrobe and there was nowhere to put what he referred to as her 'potions'.

'What a shame your wife wasn't able to come today,'

she told Stephen. They hadn't spoken again about the matter he had revealed to her in confidence, all those months ago in the Fitzroy, although she knew that Grace had returned to live with him in London.

He contemplated his glass. 'She doesn't always find these occasions easy. Too many people she doesn't know.'

As he said these words, it struck Isabel how one could work closely with someone day after day, and learn all sorts of things about them: how they reacted under pressure, what moved them to laughter or to anger, and yet one might not really know anything at all, not important deep things about their personal lives, their hopes and dreams. Stephen was one such. She felt so fond of him, so grateful, she wanted to hug him.

Instead she said carefully, 'I do understand,' though she thought it very sad for him that he had to come alone. 'I want to thank you, you know. It's all due to you,' she rushed on, 'giving me the job. I know Berec was so clever and kind in introducing us, but you didn't have to employ me. '

'I did, you know. That speech you made in my office. And when I got your aunt's letter—' He stopped suddenly.

'My aunt wrote to you?' That envelope with Stephen's handwriting in Penelope's kitchen.

'You must ask her about it sometime,' he said. 'Look, I think your husband wishes to reclaim you.'

Hugh had disengaged himself from the Woods, and was coming across.

'I feel it's time to move things along,' he said to Isabel as he joined them. 'Do you think your father would be ready to say a few words?'

They cut the cake first, then there were speeches. Isabel

held her breath during her father's, but Charles Barber spoke amusingly, and with affection, about her youthful rebellions and wished Hugh better luck with her than he'd had. Hugh replied with compliments to his bride's beauty and intelligence and made a joke about having married an 'insider' to keep his publisher on his toes. She saw Stephen and Berec laugh at this, but Hugh's mother, standing nearby, rolled her eyes.

At this, Hugh turned to her and said, 'I owe so much to my long-suffering mother,' and invited a special toast for her before he toasted the bride, which for some reason she couldn't fathom made Isabel feel slightly put out.

Finally, James Steerforth gave a speech that Isabel didn't enjoy at all, about cold showers at school, and unpleasant practical jokes. There was a story about a bawdy party, which the men in the room all laughed at whilst the women looked uncomfortable. Then James was gallantly complimenting Vivienne, who blushed and smiled awkwardly.

It was time for Isabel to withdraw and to change into going-away clothes. The plan was that they depart soon for Kensington, where they would spend their wedding night. The following morning they would take a train to Suffolk and spend a few days at a beach house conveniently owned by Penelope's Reginald. Hugh's mother was being driven home that evening by one of Hugh's cousins.

'It's such a beautiful dress,' Vivienne chatted, as she undid the buttons down Isabel's back and helped her peel off first one long sleeve and then the other. 'Such a shame that one only wears it once, though of course you could have it dyed and shortened.'

The dress fell about Isabel's feet with a rustling sound

and she stepped out of it. Vivienne helped her pull the long petticoat off over her head then stooped to pick up the dress. As she gently shook it out, there came a knock on the door and the handle turned. Both girls looked up to see Hugh come into the room. He was still in his morning suit and smoking a cigarette. His eyes were bright.

'What are you doing here?' Vivienne said, in mock admonition.

Hugh ignored her. He seemed transfixed by Isabel, who reached shyly for her petticoat. How odd the smile on his face was. He didn't look his usual self at all. Perhaps he'd drunk more than she knew.

'We'll be down in a moment,' she told Hugh firmly. 'Aren't you going to change?'

'All in good time,' he replied. 'I wanted to come and see my wife.' He stubbed out his cigarette and said to Vivienne, 'I'll help her now. Why don't you go downstairs?'

'Hugh, darling . . .' Isabel started to say, but he held the door open, waiting.

Vivienne glanced at Isabel, who returned a regretful little smile, so she picked up her handbag and hurried out of the room, her face aflame. Hugh closed the door and locked it.

'Darling,' he whispered, and crossed the space between them. His hands were cold on her flesh, but when their lips met, his were warm, his kisses pressing and urgent. He kissed her face and her neck, and pulled her to him so she was almost lifted off the floor. His hands moved over her breasts and back, scrabbling at the straps of her petticoat. The buttons of his jacket scraped painfully on her skin, but she responded passionately to his kisses. They'd waited so long for this.

He released her for a moment in order to take off his jacket and she, somewhat breathless, said, 'We can't, Hugh, not now. People will be waiting.' But he was sitting on the bed and pulling off his shoes.

'Blast them all,' he said, rolling over to her. 'Let them wait. I want my wife and I will have her.' She gasped with pleasure as he seized her again. Gathering her up, he ripped the hooks of her brassiere apart and released her white breasts.

'Ow!' He'd scratched her collarbone with his nail. 'I'm sorry,' he said, as they watched the scratch redden and beads of blood form. He bent his head and licked at it, then his mouth was on her nipples and she cried out. And now he rolled her onto the bed and pinned her there as he loosened his clothing. She felt his hands between her thighs, pulling away her knickers, then he was jabbing at her softest parts. Now his full weight came down and she cried out in pain as he entered her.

'Sorry,' he grunted, but he didn't stop. Instead he began to move violently back and forth, his hipbones grinding over hers and she was fighting against him, on fire with the pain. Tears came to her eyes and poured down her cheeks. She stared at his face above her, but he wasn't looking at her, rather at the bedhead rocking behind her. The bed itself was rocking and creaking as though it would break, and the intensity of his expression turned to an alarming agony. He pushed harder and harder inside her, then gasped and cried out. Finally he collapsed on top of her, his heart pounding into her chest, his breath coming in sobs.

'God,' he whispered after a moment, breathing hotly into her neck, 'my God, I needed that. I'm sorry.'

She lay trapped under him, aware of him still inside her. The pain was still hot, but there was a warm tender feeling, too, not unpleasant.

Carefully he withdrew, patted her rump, then got off the bed, reaching for a towel from the rail.

The pain still burned, so she lay for a moment, her face turned to the window, watching rainclouds scud across a late-afternoon sky. She was shivering, she realised, though her body was burning. She started to sit up. At once she felt a little gushing between her thighs. She put down her hand to explore and when she looked at her fingers, they were red with blood. She sat up and saw her thighs were bright with it.

'Hugh,' she cried.

'What is it?' he said.

She cried out again, for a great red stain was spreading across the candlewick bedspread.

'Oh God, lie down,' he said urgently, and helped her spread a towel beneath her hips. She heard the rush of water in the basin and then felt a plug of cold wet cloth. 'Christ!' he said, when he took it away. 'What do I do?'

She was sobbing now.

'Shh, shh,' he said, hugging her clumsily. 'Shall I get your mother?'

'No!' She shook her head furiously. The minutes passed. Eventually, the flow of blood stopped, and he helped her clean up. Her going-away clothes lay on the floor where he'd cast them. He did his best to shake out the creases and helped her to get dressed. They regarded the parlous state of the bedclothes doubtfully. Hugh balled them up to hide the damage.

* * *

Isabel felt tired and shaky by the time they made it down-stairs with their cases. Cold water and thick make-up could not disguise the puffiness of her face, and she moved care-fully, nervous of setting off the bleeding once more.

The guests were clearly tired of waiting. Stephen and Berec had already had to leave. James looked pointedly at his watch, and gave Hugh a lascivious wink, which Hugh ignored.

Someone had brought their car round. It was time to go. 'Where's your bouquet?' her mother called and she realised to her horror she'd left it upstairs on the window-sill. Before she could intervene, her mother sent Vivienne up to fetch it. When the girl came down again with the flowers, her face was unreadable. She didn't say a word as she passed the flowers to Isabel, standing by the car. Isabel looked down at the wilting blooms.

'Goodbye!' everyone cried.

'Throw it, then!' Joan Steerforth called. Isabel looked around the assembled guests and her eye fell on Vivienne. Swinging her arm she tossed the bouquet lightly back to her bridesmaid, who lifted her hands auto-matically and caught it. Then stood there holding it, a look of bleak despair crossing her face.

'No,' she said, taking it back to Isabel. 'It's not for me. Someone else must have it.'

The guests murmured in disapproval and a man's voice said, 'Shame.'

Profoundly embarrassed, Isabel looked about again and seeing Susan's eager face at one end of the line, threw it to her instead. And was touched by the look of joy that spread across the girl's pinched features as she caught it and held it close.

'Well, someone will probably marry Susan,' she told Hugh as they drove away. 'And no doubt be very happy.'

'Funny girl, your friend Vivienne, though,' Hugh said. 'I don't understand her at all.'

Isabel said nothing to that. She understood perfectly.

Chapter 19

Emily

Isabel's account finished abruptly after twenty pages, in the middle of a line, when she was saying something about Vivienne. It was puzzling and frustrating. Had there been more? There was no way to find out, since Emily had no idea who had sent this missive from the past. She sat and thought about this. Surely she'd only received all these mysterious packages because of her involvement in Hugh's biography. There must be someone who wanted Isabel's story to be told, but she'd not the slightest idea who.

She wondered what she ought to do, whether to talk to Jacqueline about it, or Joel. Not her boss, Gillian, she was too busy at the moment. In the end she decided on Joel. He was, after all, the author and, anyway, she wasn't sure what Jacqueline's response would be. No, Joel would be the best person, then he could talk to Jacqueline if necessary and follow up the line of enquiry himself.

The next day she rang his mobile and listened to his warm brown tones inviting her to leave a message.

When he rang back she explained about Isabel's writings and he seemed interested. 'I'm a bit busy this week, though,' he said. 'Would it be all right for you to put them in the post?'

'Yes, of course. I'd better take copies.'

There was a brief pause before he said, 'I don't suppose you'd like to come and hear me at the South Bank Thursday next? I'm "in conversation", as they say, about the Angry Young Men of the fifties. I did a documentary about them last year.'

'I think I'm free, so yes. Perhaps we can talk about Isabel's writing then.'

The following Thursday, Emily followed the crowds out of Embankment station and up onto the pedestrian bridge from which she watched the river sparkling in the early evening sunlight, the trains rumbling across the rail bridge that ran alongside. The esplanade on the opposite bank was busy with people sitting at café tables, despite the cold, or rummaging through second-hand books on the stalls or simply passing through on their way home from work.

Emily's destination was one of the concert halls. She weaved her way between the loitering tourists, then went through a set of glass doors into a large foyer and followed the signs to a small lecture theatre.

She was a little early and the room was still filling up, so she found a seat a few rows from the front, happy to wait. She loved events like this; there was often such a mix of people and she enjoyed watching them and imagining what their lives were like, and marvel how books could bring them together. Though, she had to admit that in this case, it might be because Joel had appeared in their homes on a TV screen.

And now Joel himself came in, chatting to a trendily dressed young man, who stepped up on the stage ahead of him, clutching a notebook. They sat down at either end of a low table and clipped on microphones. 'Good afternoon,' the interviewer's voice boomed out. Someone adjusted the volume, and everyone quietened. 'My name's Lucan O'Brien,' the young man said, 'and I'm going to be talking to Joel Richards here about writers who the media called the Angry Young Men. Joel has written a book which ties into the recent series that he presented and I produced. Between us, we hope to give you further insight into some of these fascinating writers.'

Emily had been staring at Joel, thinking how nice he looked in his crisp white shirt and chinos, how composed. All of a sudden he looked directly at her and gave her a discreet smile, which she returned.

The talk was informative and very funny at times, and the audience loved it. Joel spoke briefly and without notes about his book, then answered the interviewer's questions with eloquence. Emily hadn't seen this side of him before. It was good news for her professionally, of course, since he would obviously be in demand for publicity when the Morton book was published, but his assuredness made her consider him differently as a person, too. It gave him a dusting of glamour. She listened particularly closely when he described the masculine nature of the writers, and she wondered about the wives and girlfriends behind the scenes, what they had thought of their men's views of sexual politics and what their own opinions had been.

She was envious of anyone who could stand up and entertain an audience. She still felt a little clammy whenever she was asked to speak at sales conferences or launch parties. She was bursting to ask about the women, however, so when questions were invited from the audience, she put up her hand.

'Yes, the girl with the green headband,' Lucan said, pointing at Emily.

'Were there,' Emily asked, 'any Angry Young Women in the fifties?' From the fact that several other women murmured agreement, she gauged that she'd asked the burning question.

Joel smiled, but didn't embarrass her by giving away that he knew her. 'I've been waiting for someone to raise that,' he said. 'I'm sure that there were behind the scenes, but hardly any of them made it into print or onto the stage. There was one in 1958, Shelagh Delaney. Anyone heard of her play *A Taste of Honey*?' Emily saw several people nod. 'She tried to write it as a novel first, but couldn't make it work.'

'Time for one more question,' said the interviewer, who was glancing impatiently at his watch. Emily would have liked to have asked Joel *why* there weren't more women, but it was someone else's turn.

After the event had finished, Joel was led outside to sign books at a table in the foyer, and although the vast majority of the audience drifted off, happy to have been entertained for an hour, a few lingered, buying books and asking him questions. Emily waited nearby, reading.

'Emily?' She looked up to see Joel was ready. 'Lucan's invited us out to supper. Pippa Hartnell's coming too. She's the one who's producing *The Silent Tide* for BBC. Would it be an awful bore?'

'It certainly would not,' she replied, gathering up her

things. 'I'd love to meet her.' Finding out about the *Silent Tide* adaptation was an opportunity not to be missed.

They went to a Thai restaurant behind Waterloo station, not a grand place at all, but cosy and welcoming. Everybody was paying their own way and the atmosphere was informal and friendly. She sat with Joel on one side of the table with Joel's interviewer, Lucan, and Pippa on the other. She secretly found Lucan a little self-absorbed, for he hogged the conversation, showing off about his ambitions, ideas he had for books and television dramas, about plans to move to New York or perhaps Berlin, which was really cool right now. She must remember to give him her business card later, though. Just as with Tobias Berryman, you never knew where the next wonderful book might come from.

The food arrived in a delicious scented cloud of lemongrass and coriander. They shared it round and ate with gusto.

Emily watched Joel covertly. He was very at home with the television people, while she didn't feel so sure-footed. He knew his way about, remembered the names of those who mattered, spoke the jargon. He even listened politely to Lucan, whom she sensed Pippa didn't like very much either – though she too was courteous and professional, and they all argued quite good-naturedly about the latest Scandi thriller and whether the audience had had enough of the genre. Lucan was well-informed and made some good points about audience bases. Emily managed to feel a little sorry for him, a young man on the make in difficult times.

It was eleven by the time they left the restaurant. Lucan and Pippa said goodbye at Waterloo station and went off separately.

Joel and Emily walked together to the river and back over the pedestrian bridge to Embankment. They paused halfway across the bridge to gaze at the view, St Paul's Cathedral glowing creamy silver in the distance. The walk had been the first chance they'd had to talk alone all evening.

'How is the book coming along?' she asked. 'The TV adaptation will be a great preparation for it.'

'Won't it. I still hope to deliver to you by September. I've reached nineteen ninety now. That's when he tried writing crime fiction. It was a bit of a disaster, unfortunately. He couldn't really do plot, could our Hugh.'

She laughed. 'What did you think about the photocopies I sent you?'

'Lord, I did read those. Where did you say you got them?'

'They were left on my desk. On Valentine's Day, of all days. Joel, I don't know who's doing it. They left a photograph, too, taken at their wedding – Hugh and Isabel's, I mean.'

'I've seen one or two of those in albums at Stone House.'

'This one's in a frame.'

'Interesting. I don't remember seeing one about the house.'

'Nor me. It's all most mysterious.'

He was quiet for a moment. 'I'm not sure,' he went on, 'what to make of what you sent me. Whoever it's by . . .'

'Isabel,' Emily said firmly.

'How can we know for certain it's Isabel? The handwriting is all over the place.'

'Joel, I'm sure it's hers.'

'Whoever it is, she sounds a bit mad. All that ranting about Hugh's book.'

'That would be *The Silent Tide*.'

He sighed. 'Perhaps I should simply show it to Jacqueline.'

'Maybe you should. What else has she given you about Isabel?'

'Precious little. She says it's not something she wants opened up again. It distresses Lorna, apparently.'

Emily hadn't thought of that. 'That's difficult,' she admitted. 'But you can't ignore Isabel. She was Hugh's wife and the mother of his eldest child.'

'I promise you that I am not going to ignore her,' he said shortly, and she saw that she was irritating him.

They watched a motor-launch power towards them and disappear under the bridge. A cold draught rose in its wake and Emily shivered in her short jacket and flippy skirt.

'Shall we go on?' Joel said. Emily nodded. She was thinking about the photograph of Hugh and Isabel, how bright and alive the bride had looked, the dark eyes in her heart-shaped face sparkling with intelligence. She believed Isabel to have been the more likely inspiration for Nanna in *The Silent Tide* than the more placid-looking Jacqueline.

As they came to the steps that led down to Embankment, she caught her high heel in a crevice and stumbled. Joel gripped her arm to save her.

'Thank you,' she said. When he released her she still felt the warmth of his touch.

At the Tube station they passed through the ticket barrier and stood together awkwardly for a moment.

'You go down there, don't you?' he said. 'And I go this way.'

'It's been a lovely evening, thank you,' she told him. They solemnly kissed each other's cheeks.

'It has been good,' he said, standing close, his eyes steady on hers. 'We must do it again sometime.'

She watched his tall figure disappear round the corner and tried not to think of Matthew.

A week passed, then one morning Emily came into the office to find another of the mysterious envelopes in her pigeonhole. She opened it carefully and held her breath as she withdrew another thick wad of pages covered in Isabel's handwriting.

It started halfway through a sentence, she saw, the sentence that had been left broken off at the end of the previous tranche. She took it back to her desk with a burning sense of excitement. There was no time to read it now, so she stowed it safely in her bag to read at home. Every now and then, as she went through the day, she thought about it there, waiting for her.

Chapter 20

Isabel

The autumn of 1950 was a time of deep happiness for Isabel, but so busy was she that she moved through the days with the constant feeling that she'd forgotten something. From the moment when the alarm clock went off at half past six, even in November, when it was still so dark that her body told her it was the middle of the night, she had to be up and active. Sometimes, though, it was a few minutes before Hugh would allow her to leave the bed.

Since Hugh would usually fall asleep again, it was she who put the kettle on, hurriedly washed and dressed whilst it boiled, then drank a lonely cup of tea at the kitchen window, looking out on the frost-dusted roofs of the houses behind as the sky lightened and the cats of the neighbourhood made their way home for breakfast after a night's hunting. Then she'd make breakfast – eggs and bacon for Hugh, if she could get it, and toast for herself – before setting out for work.

Life at the office was as frenetic as it had ever been. Indeed, for large parts of her day she didn't think about being Mrs Hugh Morton at all, for she was concentrating on being Isabel, editing manuscripts, reading proofs, typing lists of queries for authors, or writing copy for book jackets. Sometimes, though, she would be reminded, for Hugh would ring up to tell her that he was stuck between paragraphs, and simply wanted to hear her voice. She'd have to patiently talk to him for a minute or two before gently finishing the call.

Audrey had finally given up her job for a life of domestic bliss, though she occasionally swanned into the office during a shopping trip to say hello. Stephen had a new secretary, Cat, short for Catherine, who had some connection with the literary editor at the *Herald*, looking to get into publishing. Cat was silky-haired with long-fringed eyes, like an appealing bushbaby. Stephen was beginning to get quite impatient with her, for though her easy manner made her an asset when working with people, she responded tearfully to brisk orders and demanding work schedules. Isabel, too, was getting fed up with digging her out of various messes. Trudy regarded Cat's tribulations as 'silly nonsense' and wouldn't help at all. Unfortunately, the *Herald*'s literary editor was not a man to cross lightly, so the weeks passed and Stephen did not quite muster up the courage to sack her. There was talk of passing her on to the psychology editor upstairs, who could do with another assistant, but the psychology editor wasn't altogether happy about this, and a low-level if good-humoured warfare ensued, the nature of which Cat, bless her, seemed unaware, so that in the end everyone got used to her and she stayed.

These days, Isabel had her coat on and was out of the door on the dot of five-thirty, a bag of scripts to read in one hand and her shopping in the other, and her life as

Mrs Hugh Morton resumed. Their daily came only twice a week and it couldn't be guaranteed that Hugh would have seen about supper. There was, after all, a handy butcher near the office where the queues weren't too long, so it was sensible for her to shop there during her lunch break rather than Hugh having to stop what he was doing and go out. It all meant that there were so many things to think about and there never seemed time to relax when she ate her lunchtime sandwich, or to idle in the library as she used to.

But she loved getting home to their little flat and to have him waiting for her. She didn't miss her bedsit days one bit, although she wished she saw more of Vivienne. Her room had been taken by an austere older lady, so she feared Vivienne might be even lonelier than before. Every time she saw her friend she berated herself for not doing so more often, but married life was proving terribly absorbing.

Was there anything nicer, Isabel asked herself, than preparing a little supper for your husband and sitting down with him to eat it and to talk about one another's day? Of course, she made plenty of mistakes to start with, serving up a chicken that was practically raw inside, and a Victoria sponge that flopped. Poor Hugh always tried to laugh and not to mind, though it wasn't really fair on him.

She knew Hugh's working life wasn't easy. He was on his own a good deal of the day – unless he'd had lunch with someone from a newspaper who was commissioning him to write something, or was visiting a library or the offices of a literary magazine – and her homecoming was much looked for.

'I wrote a thousand words this morning,' he might say as soon as she walked through the door. 'I'll type them up this evening and let you have a look,' and after she'd flown about the kitchen washing the dishes, cleaning, rinsing out a few clothes she might need between laundry trips, they'd work companionably in the drawing room until bedtime, she reading, he typing or sighing over some book he'd been given to review, a tumbler of whisky at his elbow, the wireless playing softly in the background.

Some evenings there would be a cocktail party to go to, or dinner out with friends, and more often than not the theatre, and then there'd be little time for anything when they got home but to fall into bed. And there they might not sleep at once. That first disastrous occasion had cast a pall over their short honeymoon by the sea, for the bleeding she'd experienced at the hotel continued for a day or two, but lighter. She visited the doctor on their return to London and he was able to reassure her. Perhaps, he told her, with some concern, her husband should not treat her quite so enthusiastically. She'd sustained a small tear, although it had quickly healed.

There came times when Isabel arrived home and knew as soon as she opened the door of the flat that the day had not gone well for Hugh. He'd be morose or sardonic, and she'd feel an awful lump in her throat, fearing that in some way she'd annoyed him, that his mood was her responsibility.

'What is the matter?' she would ask repeatedly, but it might just be that his mind was wrestling with some dilemma in his writing, or the muse had failed him that day. In time she became used to these occasions, though they still upset her.

Then there'd follow a delicious making up when she'd
weep and he'd apologise for being monstrous, and somehow they'd end up in each other's arms. There were other
times again, when the writing went so superlatively well,
that he might rise in the night and switch the light on in
the drawing room and write until dawn. Then both of
them would be tired and crotchety in the morning and so
she tried to forbid these episodes. But if he didn't get up,
the sounds of him lying awake beside her, restless and
tormented, stopped her sleeping anyway. Such were the
proud marks of being married to a writer.

Autumn became winter, and winter turned to spring. In
May 1951 the Festival of Britain opened to much fanfare.

'It's just hanging in thin air, isn't it?' Isabel whispered.
'Extraordinary. It's like they say, a giant icicle.' She and
Hugh, sheltering from the heavy rain, were staring up at
the Skylon, trying to make sense of its strangeness, the
way it appeared to be suspended from the sky.

'Or a flying saucer tipped on end,' Hugh said. 'It's
certainly much bigger now one sees it close up.'

'Isn't it a shame about the weather, though.'

It was the opening day of the exhibition. They'd come
through the turnstiles amazed by the alien landscape
spread out before them. Acres of bombed-out buildings
south of the river near Waterloo station had been transformed into a designers' playground. There was the new
Festival Hall, all bleak modernist concrete, the Skylon, a
sculpture like a mock cathedral spire apparently floating
in the sky, though actually held up by cables. Most
extraordinary of all was the curved white roof of the
Dome of Discovery.

'Heavens, won't it blow away in this?' Isabel said, pointing in alarm. Sure enough, the huge circular canopy, like a big top without walls, was shivering and lifting in the gusting rain, straining at its tethers.

'A triumph of illusion over practicality,' Hugh murmured, getting out his notebook and writing the phrase down. He'd been commissioned by a newspaper to write his impressions of the day.

Isabel struggled to open her umbrella, but the wind took hold of it and swung her round, so she gave up and tightened her rainhood. To one side of the exhibition area, masking the ugly lines of the railway bridge, was a display of giant coloured balls, like a child's abacus. 'Oh, I like those,' she said. 'And the fountains.' The water-spouts gushed every which way in the gale so that anyone near them was at risk of a soaking.

This is the new Britain, she thought. We're finally leaving the dowdiness behind. She tried not to think of the ugly old London hinterland, the brooding hulk of Waterloo station visible between gaps in the bright festival buildings, the acres of sooty houses with their villainous smoking chimneys beyond.

'Where shall we begin?' Hugh asked, offering her his arm. 'Why don't we visit the Dome first of all, before the shenanigans begin. At least we'll be dry under there.'

Despite her pleasure at being there, Isabel was tired. It had been a difficult week at the office and she'd not been sleeping well. Now she clung to Hugh to avoid slipping as they crossed the vast expanse of concrete, shiny with rain.

The weather was a terrible shame for the opening day and its ceremonies. Great walls of rain blew across the concourse, the sort of rain that wets right through, dulling the bright plastic seaside colours of the striped pavilions, the automatons and the merry-go-rounds. They passed a tribe of half-drowned donkeys, waiting for custom with all the endurance of their breed. 'Look at them!' Isabel exclaimed. 'Surely no one would hire one in this weather.'

'A display of British stoicism too far,' Hugh agreed as they reached the shelter of the Dome of Discovery.

'Are the poor troops really going to parade about in this? We're not all as long-suffering as the donkeys.'

They wandered about under the wind-tossed marquee for an hour or so, looking at displays about British discoveries, famous people and their achievements. It felt like being in the bowels of a great ship, the roof shifting and sighing overhead as though with the movement of wind and sea, and this compounded Isabel's feeling of light-headedness. After a while, Florence Nightingale seemed to blur with Sir Isaac Newton and Charles Darwin and she couldn't care less about any of them. She found herself staring blankly at an empty showcase, its shelves covered modestly with coloured paper.

'They haven't finished putting everything up, have they? Darling, you look cold,' Hugh said. 'Why don't we get you something hot to eat?' They hurried over to a large tent that housed a café. Here she ate soup and an omelette and was able to recover a bit.

'You are a bit pale, you poor old thing. We won't stay too much longer, but I really ought to walk round quickly and get a sense of everything. Shall I leave you here and come back later?'

'No, I'll come. I do feel a little better now.'

The weather was clearing slightly and the place was beginning to feel crowded. As Hugh and Isabel trailed round the sights, the sun even made a brief appearance, so that all the bright colours gleamed and the shiny ground threw up iridescent reflections of the buildings and sideshows. The layout was very eccentric, Isabel thought, not grand at all. In fact, there was something intimate about the jumbled way the different structures were juxtaposed. She and Hugh might leave a building through an inconspicuous doorway to find it opened onto a series of courtyards cheerful with murals. It was a voyage of continual discovery.

She loved watching the people. Groups of schoolboys would push past, intent on secret business of their own, to them the whole thing being like a giant playground. In one room Isabel admired a group of women fashionably dressed in jackets with wide shoulders and matching narrow skirts, finding them more interesting than the textiles machine being demonstrated. In another building, spectators tried samples of party pastries which a chef whisked piping hot from the very latest in modern ovens.

People had come from all over the world. On the escalator travelling back down into the Dome, Isabel watched eight members of an Indian family from father down to youngest child pass on the upgoing escalator, their dark eyes round with wonder. She smiled at them, but was alarmed that their bright figures were coming in and out of focus, the children's shrill voices ringing round her head. She experienced the sensation of floating like a balloon, up towards the roof of the Dome and looking down on everything and everybody spread out below.

'Isabel!' she heard her husband cry, as though from very far away. 'Isabel!' And after that she knew nothing at all.

'Isabel!' When she came to consciousness, it was to a cacophony of sound and a throbbing pain in her side. Someone was calling her name. Hugh, it was Hugh. Her eyes fluttered open, but she couldn't focus.

'Lie still, Mrs Morton.' It was a woman speaking, soothing, but at the same time firm. 'The doctor will be here in a minute. He must check that we've not broken anything.'

'I don't think I have,' she said, concentrating on a pair of shrewd blue eyes. She tried to sit up. She felt a little sick, and her hip hurt, but she thought she'd only bruised it.

'Isabel, thank God.' Hugh's face appeared before her and she fell into his arms.

'Did I faint?' she asked him.

'Yes, on the escalator,' he said, kissing her face. 'If it hadn't been so crowded I dread to imagine how far . . .'

'It's not very helpful to think that, sir.' It was the nurse again, brisk now that it was apparent her patient was perfectly all right. 'It was only a tiny little faint. Once the doctor's here and has had a look at your wife, I suggest you take her straight home. Fainting is something that often happens to women in her condition.'

'My condition?' Isabel stared at the woman, who looked rather disconcerted.

'I'm sorry. It was only a guess, but you have that look about you.'

Her meaning was becoming clear in Isabel's mind.

'I can't be,' she said, almost fainting again with surprise. 'It's impossible.'

'My congratulations, Mrs Morton,' said the young doctor in his Kensington surgery, ten days later. 'The test results have come back and I can confirm the good news. It'll be the end of December, if we've got your dates right. A Christmas baby. What could be more special?'

Isabel's face was a mask of misery. She didn't want a baby. Not now, it would ruin everything.

'Now come, come,' he said, patting her knee. 'I know you're feeling unwell, but I can assure you that everything should proceed normally. Thousands of women every day have babies with very little trouble at all.' He stopped, aware that he wasn't carrying his audience.

'I don't know how it happened,' she said, bewildered, and seeing his man-of-the-world smile, rushed on: 'No, no, I understand the process, but you see, my husband was very careful. He uses French letters.'

The doctor started to look a little uneasy, now that he saw his patient really was unhappy.

'They are not, unfortunately, infallible,' he said gently. 'Cheer up. It might have happened a little sooner than you'd have liked, but children would have come along at some point, eh? You'll get used to it, I promise. Or is it your husband who's nervous? He can always call in to see me. That's the ticket.'

She remembered Hugh's face when they'd got home from the festival and they'd discussed what the on-site nurse had implied. He'd been as surprised as she was, but then, she supposed the only word to have described his expression was proud – yes, he'd looked proud, and as the days passed and her pregnancy was confirmed, he frequently told her how delighted he was. It was only she who was sunk in gloom, and it wasn't just due to the onset of nausea and the episodes of light-headedness, which continued to plague her for the next fortnight. It was the idea of a baby itself. It would get in the way of everything, especially her work. She had vaguely imagined that they'd have children sometime, but not for years and years. She'd not chosen this baby. It had insinuated itself into her body without permission, and when it was born it would take over her life as she'd seen Lydia, whose birth had also been unplanned, take over her mother's.

The dawn light coming through the curtains would find her sleepless, her mind alert and anxious, as it grappled with this new reality. Her body felt different; it wasn't hers any more. It had abandoned its usual secret harmonies and was singing a new song, one which she'd given it no permission to sing. Her body was at odds with her mind: her breasts tingled uncomfortably all the time, her nerves thrummed with electricity.

Pregnancy revolted her in various ways. The tang of metal was constant in her mouth. The next time she arose early and made a cup of tea, hoping to dispel the nausea, she spat out the first mouthful. It tasted of fish. At a launch party Berec took her to, she sipped a glass of wine and screwed up her face. After that she stuck to gin. The tiredness was the worst thing, though. She dragged herself through the days, and any glimpse of her face, oatmeal-grey, in a mirror would send her hunting for her powder puff. Nothing, of course, was said to anyone yet, but she knew that Trudy, at least, had her suspicions. The older woman was too reserved to say anything, but sometimes Isabel caught her curious glances.

It was a couple of weeks after the doctor's confirmation that she was indeed two months' pregnant that she and Hugh paid a visit to her family. They were on the way back from lunch with the Steerforths, who had recently moved house down to Kent. Constance and Victor, whose wedding the Mortons had attended shortly after their own, were also there, and Constance announced at lunch that she and Victor were expecting a happy event. Her obvious happiness, her ethereal glow, the protective way Victor reached for her hand as she delivered the news, so touched and at the same time horrified Isabel because it contrasted with her own feelings, that she could barely get out her congratulations. The men smoked cigars on the terrace while the Steerforths' four-year-old girl Sally ran about in the garden, drowning flowers with a toy watering can, and the women drank China tea in the drawing room, the French windows standing open. Joan Steerforth gave Constance a liturgy of advice about everything from vitamins to layettes, and Isabel listened, a fixed smile on her face.

'I hope we aren't boring you, Isabel,' Joan said, noticing. She and Constance were still nervous with Hugh's independent-minded new wife. They never knew what to say to her, though they felt they were doing their best. 'I'm sure a baby will happen for you soon.' Isabel nodded and said nothing rather than say something she'd later regret.

When the men came in from the garden, Hugh stood behind her chair and massaged Isabel's neck. Though finding this public show of affection irritating, she forced herself not to pull away.

She'd seen the pain in his eyes about the way she'd withdrawn into herself over the last few weeks and felt awful that she'd caused it, yet couldn't help herself. She'd try to go to bed before him, no hardship given how tired she was, and curl up, pretending to fall asleep straight away if he came to join her, but after he fell asleep her tears would silently soak the pillow. Last night, though, she'd allowed him to roll her over and had buried her face in his neck as he made gentle love to her. The tenderness helped, but it did not allay the tide of anger and frustration about the coming child.

When they reached her parents' house, she helped her mother in the kitchen to cut sandwiches and arrange buns on a plate. Pamela kept shooting her concerned glances.

'Are you all right? You're not sickening, are you?'

Isabel stared down at the fishpaste she was spreading, grey and awful-smelling, and her stomach gave a lurch.

'You can guess what it is,' she said.

Her mother put down her knife and came to her, took her by the shoulders and looked into her face. 'My dear girl,' she said. She started to smile, but Isabel's miserable expression stopped her. She pressed her daughter to her as the tears flooded forth.

'I don't want it,' Isabel sobbed on her mother's shoulder. 'It's spoiling everything. I'll have to give up my job to look after it. I'm too young. I haven't lived yet.'

Her mother lightly rubbed her back. 'Don't be silly now, it'll be all right. I was caught out with Lydia, as you know, but she arrived and it was wonderful. It hasn't been easy having a young one so long after the rest of you – I thought I'd finished with all that after the twins – but she's a sweet child and very loving. Yours will be a splendid little person, you'll see.'

Isabel had tried that line of thought already. *It's a baby in there, a person,* she'd said to herself as she lay sleepless during those early mornings, her fingers pressing her abdomen, trying to feel where it might be but sensing nothing very different at all. She couldn't picture what was growing there as a baby. The doctor had said it was still very small and had shown her a diagram. It didn't look like a baby in the book, more like a shrimp. There was a shrimp growing inside her, with staring lidless eyes, and her mind refused to connect it to the plump pink-skinned babies with wide blue eyes on the posters in the surgery waiting room.

For a week or two she sleepwalked through life, exhausted because of her anxious nights, trying to deny the truth of what was happening to her.

'Ridiculous,' she said aloud when she put down the phone to a printer she'd been arguing with for the past half-hour. 'Utterly ridiculous.'

'What is?' enquired a familiar female voice, and she glanced up to see her aunt, looking very soignée in a soft, dove-coloured jacket and matching felt hat. A brooch of pink gems, in the shape of a flower, sparkled on one lapel.

'What a lovely surprise,' Isabel said, standing up to greet her. When she kissed her, she caught a whiff of that scent that always made her think longingly of glamorous nights out.

'I'm having lunch with Stephen,' Penelope said, and Isabel immediately wondered why.

'Oh, I'm sorry, Mrs Tyler,' Cat piped up, 'but that's in his diary for tomorrow.'

'I'm sure it was today,' Penelope told her, frowning. 'I have another long-standing appointment for tomorrow.'

Cat appealed to the rest of the room. 'I wrote it down for tomorrow. I'm sure that's what we agreed.'

Isabel bit her lip and said nothing. It wouldn't be the first time that Cat had made such a mistake.

'Never mind,' she told Penelope. 'Stephen's out all day today, but I'm free. Shall we? We could try the café opposite.'

'So gorgeous to have some sun at last,' Penelope said as they stepped outside. 'You haven't told me who it was you were calling ridiculous?'

'Oh, that,' Isabel replied with a laugh. 'Dear old Harold Chisholm wanted to use, shall we say, an *impolite* word in his novel and the printer was refusing to set it. Chisholm's stubborn and wouldn't offer a suitable substitute so I took matters into my own hands and told them to put in a blank. At least it'll get the book printed.'

She held open the door of the café and Penelope followed her inside. The waitress was glad to seat two beautifully dressed women at a table in a patch of sunlight right by the window.

'Dear me. What happens if your Mr Chisholm complains?'

'Then Stephen will tell him we can't publish and I expect he'll throw one of his spectacular rages about being censored.' Isabel sighed. 'Frankly, I think Stephen would be relieved if Chisholm jumped ship, but since no one else is likely to take him on, as he's such a nuisance, I imagine that we're stuck with him.'

Penelope laughed. 'My goodness,' she said, laying her gloves in her handbag, 'the things you have to deal with. I can hardly believe you were once that innocent little thing I found on my doorstep.'

They ordered toasted sandwiches, but Isabel could do no more than nibble at the crusts. When she fussed that her tea should be poured without milk, Penelope studied her thoughtfully.

'Yes, is the answer. Don't say *anything*,' Isabel murmured, seeing this scrutiny.

'My dear girl,' Penelope said, putting her hand over Isabel's.

Isabel was touched by the sympathy in her aunt's face. She noticed that beneath the perfect mask of Penelope's make-up, the signs of ageing were clearly visible. Her aunt was fighting a battle she'd eventually lose.

'How is Reginald?' Isabel asked, to change the subject. Penelope withdrew her hand.

'He is very well, thank you,' she said, sipping her tea.

'Stephen is very grateful for his investment in the business. It must be thanks to you, for persuading him.'

Her aunt gave a little smile. 'Reginald likes to please me, but I assure you he would only place his resources where he saw a good return.'

Something about this made Isabel feel uncomfortable. Did Penelope also cast herself in this category? What return did her aunt give her lover?

'Well then, I hope McKinnon and Holt do well enough,' Isabel said smoothly. 'May I ask why you were having lunch with Stephen?'

Penelope shrugged. 'We are old friends. Why shouldn't we have lunch?'

'No reason.' She was thinking about what Stephen had said once, hinting that Penelope had been involved in her recruitment. What did that matter now? It was so long ago.

'Does your mother know about – you know?' Penelope said, her tone unusually urgent.

Isabel nodded and looked down at the ravaged sandwich on her plate. Tears welled unbidden, as they often did these days. More evidence of her treacherous body.

'My dear.' Penelope tipped Isabel's chin up with her finger. 'Look at me. How far along?'

'It'll be Christmas,' Isabel managed to say. The tears spilled out like dew from a flower.

Penelope read her mind in her face. 'Mmm,' she said, releasing her. She looked round quickly to check that no one was listening, then leaned forward and said in a low voice, 'You don't have to have it, you know.'

Isabel stared at her, at first in incomprehension, then astonishment.

'There are ways. I know a doctor who's very discreet.'

Still, Isabel could not speak.

'I suppose Hugh knows?'

'Yes.'

'That needn't be a problem, of course. Things sometimes do go wrong with babies.'

'Aunt . . .' The shock was fading, to be replaced by a horrifying sense of possibility.

'If you need me to help, you only have to ask,' Penelope said, sitting back. 'Think about it, but don't leave it too long.'

Isabel was left stupefied by this conversation, which she could hardly believe she'd had. She was partly shocked that she'd listened to it at all. As she went mechanically through her tasks that afternoon, part of her mind dwelled on that sense of possibility. Freedom. She could return everything to how it had been.

But as she lay awake that night it came to her that she couldn't do it. Things could never return to how they'd been. She had already been changed, changed for ever. She knew she could not deliberately destroy what was growing inside her. She was a happily married woman with the resources to bring up a child. Everywhere, as the doctor said, women were having babies and devoting their lives to them. That's what one did and it was selfish and unnatural to think otherwise.

She was hazy about what she expected out of life, but she had imagined children would come along for her sooner or later. It was unfortunate that she was still so young, only twenty-two, and there was so much else she wanted to do. But get rid of it? No, she couldn't. And as for doing it and telling Hugh that she'd 'lost' the baby, that was out of the question. She wouldn't be able to look him in the face. It would destroy all integrity between them, ruin their marriage.

Her thoughts drifted on to Penelope. The fact that her aunt knew all about what to do made her consider her in a new light. Perhaps Penelope had done it herself, visited this doctor, while she was married or . . . perhaps since. Maybe it had been the reason for the failure of her marriage. Isabel's mind ran on uselessly. There was so much she didn't know.

Eventually, resolving to keep the baby, she was able to fall into a deep slumber.

In the morning, when she visited the bathroom, she

was shocked to find she was bleeding. Hugh sent her back to bed and telephoned the doctor, who arrived shortly after lunch and examined her.

'It might be nothing at all,' he said as he packed his stethoscope away, 'but only time will tell. You must stay in bed and rest, Mrs Morton. Your husband tells me you go out to work.' His tone was disapproving. 'I think they'll have to do without you for the present.'

'I have tried arguing that before,' Hugh said from the doorway. Seeing his wife's annoyed expression, he shrugged.

'Please don't worry,' she told them both. 'I will rest.' She was surprised to find that now she might be losing the baby, she desperately wanted it. She'd had no power in determining its beginning, but she'd do everything she could to help it survive.

As it turned out, there was no more bleeding and, after a week in bed, the doctor reluctantly agreed that she could get up. A few days after that, she was back doing half-days in the office. Her colleagues gave no indication that they knew what was going on, and for this she was grateful. She realised, though, that it was impossible now that they hadn't guessed.

Chapter 21

Isabel

A few weeks later, halfway through June, Hugh asked if they should start telling people their news.

'No,' Isabel said, panicking. 'Surely it's too early.' She'd been a little brighter recently. The nausea had begun to recede and her skin had lost its blotchy porridge look.

'You're blooming,' he told her as he watched her dress, 'all round and soft, my precious. Can't we at least tell Mother?'

Least of all your mother, Isabel thought but did not say. 'Perhaps our having a baby would make her like me better,' she said cautiously, and seeing his exasperated expression, 'No, honestly, Hugh, I'm sure she feels I've stolen you.' She'd lately decided that Lavinia Morton didn't only disapprove of her, but that she'd disapprove of any woman Hugh might have decided to marry.

'That's nonsense. The two of you need to get to know one another better. This will be the opportunity.' He said this with an air of finality, and reached for the notebook he always kept by his bed and scribbled something in it.

'What are you putting down now?' Isabel said,

examining a tiny hole in one of the stockings she'd just put on. 'Oh, blow,' she muttered.

'Nothing to worry you,' he said absently.

She got soap from the washstand and rubbed it on the hole to stop it running. 'If you're writing down something I've said, then don't, it's disconcerting.'

'It's not about you, my sweet. It's about life. Everything in the world around is a writer's raw material.'

'I don't like being your research.'

'That's ridiculous. I can't help it if something you say gives me an idea. That's how the creative process works.'

She glared at him as she tugged at the zip of her skirt, which was getting tight, but decided to say no more. Hugh seemed in a very happy mood these days. He was delighted about the baby and his writing was going well. It would be a mistake to spoil that. Besides, she was in danger of being late for work.

A week later, she stammered out her news at the office and was pleasantly surprised by the reaction.

'Congratulations!' Stephen gently kissed her, and stood back to look at her. 'You are positively glowing, I must say.'

She laughed, feeling very tenderly towards him. It must be so difficult when he and his wife couldn't have children, to rejoice for other people, but there genuinely seemed to be nothing but happiness for her in his eyes.

There was, however, an assumption.

'We'll be sorry to lose you,' Trudy said.

'Yes, indeed,' Philip said, coming forward to solemnly shake Isabel's hand.

'At least you'll look after Hugh for us,' Stephen said. 'We shall have to be thankful for that.'

'Who said I was going anywhere?' Isabel asked them, drawing herself up to her full five feet two.

Trudy raised her eyebrows, but said nothing.

Only Cat did not congratulate her, though she looked thoughtful. Later, when Isabel came across her alone, making a muddle of the filing, Cat said shyly, 'I'm really pleased for you about the baby.'

'Thank you,' Isabel replied.

'Do you feel different? I mean, when you get married and start having babies, do you stop wanting other things?' Some pages of the file she was handling slipped out and floated down to the floor.

'What things do you mean?' Isabel asked, troubled by the girl's perception. She bent too quickly to pick up the papers and felt dizzy.

'Thanks. It's just I can't ever imagine wanting to do anything but work with books,' Cat said. 'I know I make mistakes, and Audrey used to be so efficient, but it is what I want to do – you know, be a success. How can you bear to leave?'

'You won't know until it happens to you,' Isabel said, and turned away.

She wanted to tell Berec herself, before somebody else did, but nobody had seen him for several weeks, which was not only unusual but unprecedented.

'Did he say he was going anywhere?' Isabel asked Trudy, who had been the last one to speak to him.

He had drifted in from the street one afternoon the previous month and asked Mr Greenford for a small advance on his next poetry collection, Trudy said, but had been forced to leave empty-handed.

'I hope he's all right,' she added.

Nobody had a telephone number for him.

'There is a number, but it's of a public house in the East End,' Trudy said. 'I remember I tried to get in touch with him once before and the barmaid said she'd pass on the message. Philip, do you remember, it was when that odd character came in asking for him?'

'Now *he* was a most extraordinary individual,' Philip said, looking up from his spyglass. He'd been examining some photographic negatives laid on a lightbox.

'Who do you mean?' Isabel asked.

Trudy leaned forward a little dramatically. 'Well, I'm used to pansies, but this one was dressed most outrageously. Like an actor, all made-up. At ten o'clock in the morning.'

Philip coughed, said, 'Quite so,' and bent once more to his spyglass.

'He wouldn't say what his business was with Berec, so I didn't tell him anything. And when I told Berec about it soon afterwards, he seemed upset. Said he owed the man money and would I keep mum about the matter. So I did and we heard no more about it.'

'How intriguing,' Isabel said. 'Do we have Berec's address? Surely, we do.'

Trudy flipped through the cards on her Rolodex. 'Here we are,' she said, scribbling it down. It was an address in Bethnal Green, somewhere Isabel didn't know at all. She bit her lip, wondering whether she should go round to see him, but decided no, he was very private about himself and he might not like it.

'I'll write to him,' she decided. 'And we can always try the pub.'

She remembered the conversation she'd had with the editor of the literary magazine at Hugh's housewarming party all that time ago. How little she knew about Berec, even now. He was not a man who wasted time mourning the past. His interests were life around him, literature and gossip about poets and publishing. She'd never found out how he'd got to know her aunt, either – except it was turning out that her mercurial aunt had her fingers in more than a few pies. Reginald, it seemed, was a man of wide business interests so it might even have been through him.

She hadn't seen her aunt since that conversation in the café. Somehow she couldn't bear to telephone her and expect her congratulations about the baby after what had passed between them.

She wrote a short letter to Berec, enquiring after his health, and that of Gregor and Karin, and conveying her news, begging him to be in touch with her soon as she didn't know how long she'd continue to be in the office. She put the letter in the post and waited for a reply.

Since she was feeling brighter about the baby, Isabel invited Vivienne round to supper. She'd hardly seen her friend for their paths didn't cross naturally any more, and they had to make that much more of an effort. When she rang Vivienne's digs it was the retired schoolteacher who answered.

When Isabel identified herself, the woman's tone became breathy with indignation.

'This place has changed immeasurably since you left, Isabel. I really can't see how I can continue to stay.'

'Why? What is it?' she asked the teacher, but the woman

was talking to someone else at her end and then Vivienne came onto the line. In the background there came the distinct sound of a door slamming.

'What on earth's the matter with her?' she asked Vivienne after issuing her invitation.

'I'll tell you when I see you. Isabel,' she went on, 'would you mind very much if I brought someone with me?'

The 'someone' was called Theo. He was tall and slim and graceful, with hair that shone black and thick as night, and a flawless olive skin. He and Vivienne were clearly enchanted with one another, and the lustre of love made her beautiful.

'Theo's from Kashmir,' she explained to Isabel as Hugh poured the drinks.

'I am studying medicine at Vivienne's college,' Theo said. 'She has been very kind to show me everything.'

Isabel liked his lilting voice, which was soft and clear. He refused the offer of gin, but accepted some cordial. Not only was he meticulously polite, but he'd taken the trouble to buy a copy of *Coming Home* and was in the process of reading it. Whilst he was enthusiastically praising Hugh and asking questions about his writing, Isabel went out to the kitchen to see how the stew was progressing. Vivienne followed her, holding the oven door as she drew out the pot and laid it on the stove.

'I'm so sorry about all that unpleasantness with Miss Milliband when you telephoned. The wretched woman has got herself into a state. Theo came to the house to meet me the other day, and it upset her for some reason.'

Isabel said, 'He seems very nice. Do you . . . are you . . . ?'

Vivienne's eyes danced mischievously. 'We do seem rather to like one another, if that's what you mean.'

'But . . .' Isabel made a helpless gesture. 'What does your family think? Isn't he – I mean, Kashmir – he's probably . . . what are they there? Hindus?'

Vivienne nodded, hunching her thin shoulders in a hopeless gesture. 'My parents don't know yet. I'll tell them when I'm ready. Whatever they say, he's not Jewish so it'll be awful.'

'Oh Viv,' Isabel said, throwing down the oven gloves and regarding her friend with dismay. 'Is he very special to you?'

'Yes,' Vivienne said, the colour flooding her eager face. 'Yes, he is. Isabel, I never thought I'd have the chance to be this happy. Please tell me we'll still be friends, whatever happens?'

'Of course,' Isabel said, going to hug her. 'We'll always be friends, always.'

The Sunday after this little supper party, Hugh and Isabel drove down to Suffolk early to have lunch with Hugh's mother. It was June and the house and garden were lush after the recent rain. Lunch was a cold collation, eaten in the cool of the dining room, for Sunday was Mrs Catchpole the cook-housekeeper's day off. Today Hugh and Isabel couldn't do anything right. Mrs Morton complained about having to manage for herself, but turned down Hugh's offer to take her out to lunch.

'I don't feel like going out today,' she said irritably, and indeed she did appear a little pale and out of sorts.

After the pressed meats and salad from the garden, Isabel brought in the raspberries that her mother-in-law had asked her to pick before lunch. Mrs Morton turned to Hugh and said, 'I suppose you've heard Jacqueline's news? Her husband's being sent to Korea. He's in Intelligence, isn't he?'

'Something like that,' Hugh said, pouring cream on his fruit.

'It's a terrible shame for her. So dangerous out there. Remember the Japanese?'

'It's not as though he'll be in the front line, Mother.'

'I so hope you're right. I happen to know that she's very keen to start a family, and that can't happen, can it, if her husband's away.'

'I suppose not.' Hugh winked at Isabel, who did not react. She spooned a raspberry into her mouth. It tasted woody and bitter.

'I hope you two won't be waiting too long to make me a grandmother.' Hugh's mother gave a silvery laugh that grated.

'Well . . .' Hugh started to say, but Isabel had had enough. She rose sharply to her feet, threw down her napkin and swept out of the room.

It felt a long, long time, but was probably only quarter of an hour before Hugh found her out in the further reaches of the garden where, over the fence, was a field with two donkeys. She was stroking the animals' noses and crying gently.

Hugh was petulant. 'Isabel, what the hell's the matter? My mother's terribly upset.'

'*She's* upset,' Isabel managed to say. One of the donkeys pulled at her cardigan with its teeth, but she distangled herself and stepped out of its reach.

'Oh, darling, you know she means well,' he said,

putting an arm round her shoulder. Drawing her to him, he kissed the top of her head. 'I've told her about the baby and she's thrilled. You must come in and apologise.'

She jerked away from him. '*Me* apologise?' she said, her eyes wild. 'What about her? She tries to run your life.'

Hugh sighed. 'I know women feel very up and down when they're expecting, but you mustn't rush out like that. If you'd explained . . . Mother can be irritating, I see that, but I must insist that she's treated with respect.'

She noticed a tension about him, how straight he stood, what passion there was in his eyes, and all the fight went out of her. He loved his mother, she saw that, and now she had a sudden vision of herself through his eyes – an hysterical, self-centred little girl. She turned back to the fence. One of the donkeys had drifted away, but she stroked the rough back of the other as it tugged up grass and thistles.

Finally she said in a low voice, 'You're right, I'm sorry. I'll come and apologise at once. I don't know what came over me.'

Hugh smiled delightedly. 'You are a good girl,' he said, and led her by the hand back to the house.

Behind them the donkeys bowed their heads and continued to eat.

Although Hugh spoke to his mother on the telephone every Sunday after this, they did not go down to visit her again. The episode was not referred to, but Hugh seemed to recognise that his wife was under strain enough with the pregnancy and the busy life she was leading. She knew he worried about her. Besides, he had a concrete excuse for staying in London. He was getting into the stride of writing his new book and trying to devote as much time as possible to it.

So she continued to go into the office most days and tried not to think of the future at all, about what might happen when the baby came.

Some time had passed and she'd heard nothing from Alex Berec. One day, she tried dialling the number of the public house Trudy had unearthed for her, but the woman who answered the phone knew nothing about him. Isabel felt strongly that there was something wrong. It was no good, she would have to go and find out for herself. She chose a day when the office was quiet and set off at lunchtime.

Having seen the poor conditions in which Gregor and Karin were forced to live, she hadn't been expecting anything much, but the dark brick tenement building in Bethnal Green where the pub landlord directed her was still a shock. The children who played in the streets around were silent and undernourished, most of them filthy. She stopped a young woman who staggered along with a sack spilling over with dirty washing, and asked her where she might find number 52. Inside the block that the girl indicated, she followed a gloomy concrete staircase that stank of urine up to the second floor. How could this be the right place? she asked herself, as she walked along the row of doors. Number 52 proved to be the last one along. She took a deep breath and knocked.

For a long time there was no answer, and she was just debating whether to give up when she heard a noise from within. She pressed her ear to the door. There it was again. Shuffling footsteps, then silence. Someone was just inside, waiting. She knocked once more and this time there came a familiar voice. 'All right, I hear you. Who is it, please?'

'Is that you, Berec?' she replied, then the door was opened and she found herself face-to-face with someone she almost didn't recognise.

'Berec,' she said, recoiling – for it was Alex Berec, but not the cheerful, urbane character that she knew and loved. This man looked wretched. He was unwashed, his hair was greasy, he wore a ragged dressing-gown over pyjamas. One sleeve hung empty, for his arm was in a sling. Around one of his bloodshot eyes he sported fading evidence of the worst bruise she'd ever seen.

'Isabel. I thought it was— You can't . . .' He started to shut the door again, then changed his mind. He laid his forehead against the frame in a dejected movement, eyes closed.

'Berec,' she breathed. 'What's happened to you?'

He raised his head and sighed, 'No matter, it's getting better now. Some men did this to me.'

'Some men? What men? Why?'

'They were drunk, that's all,' he mumbled. 'Wrong place, wrong time.'

His breath reached her, sharp and sour, and she knew he'd been drinking too.

'Can I come in?' she asked.

'No, better not.' And by his weak smile she caught a glimpse of the Berec she knew. 'It would shock you. '

She hesitated, then said, 'Is there anything I can do to help, then? Some shopping for you maybe.'

'No, really,' he said. 'There is a woman nearby, a neighbour, who brings me food. Though it is very kind of you.'

She stepped back, sensing strongly now that he wanted her to go, but it didn't feel right to just leave him like this.

'Have the police caught them – the men who did this to you?'

'I don't know,' he replied, and she was suddenly certain that he hadn't reported it to the police. 'Thank you for coming, my dear Isabel,' he said. 'I do not forget this. But please keep it to yourself. I should be ashamed for everyone to know. This must be private, do you promise? I prefer you tell no one, not even your husband.'

After a moment she nodded. Something occurred to her. Swiftly, she opened her handbag and took out her purse. 'Here,' she said, extracting several notes. 'I won't go unless you accept this. Please, I can afford it.' She pushed the money into his hand.

'Ach,' he said, 'thank you,' with a quiet dignity, and she felt her face colour up.

She started to walk back down the corridor, but he called out, 'Isabel,' and she paused.

'My regards to your aunt. Perhaps you might tell her I've been . . . unwell. Just that.'

'Yes,' she said with relief, sensing that her aunt would know what to do. 'Of course.'

She hardly noticed the bus journey back to Oxford Street, she was so absorbed in her thoughts about Berec. The idea that there were people who would do that to someone, beat them up, because they were different, from another country, when everyone knew how much some of these refugees had suffered . . . it cut across everything she ever knew and valued. Poor Berec. She wished there was something else she could do for him. Then she remembered that there was.

When she arrived home from the office that evening, she was surprised to find that her husband was out.

Whilst she waited for him, she wrote the letter she'd worked out in her head. It was to her aunt, and in it she quoted Berec's words exactly, that he was 'unwell' and she included the address. She must trust that her aunt would know what that meant and act accordingly. She went out straight away to put the letter in the post.

Hugh rang later that evening. 'I'm in Suffolk. Didn't that daffy girl give you my message?' he asked in puzzlement.

'Which girl – Cat? She might have tried, but I've hardly been in today.'

'It's Mother, she's been taken ill. Mrs Catchpole rang me at lunchtime.'

'Oh Hugh. Is it another asthma attack?'

'The doctor wasn't sure so he arranged for her to be taken into hospital. That's where I am now. She has a very high temperature. There's a possibility it's pneumonia.'

'Hugh!' She had heard the anxiety in his voice. 'What shall I do? Do you want me there?'

'Stay put for the time being, I think. We'll see how things are in the morning.'

With all this going on, the matter of Berec slipped to the back of her mind.

'I can't see any way round it,' Hugh said, a fortnight later. 'It's very hard on you. I'm sorry.'

They were standing in Hugh's old bedroom at Stone House. Isabel, arms folded, a cardigan draped on her shoulders, was staring out of the window across the garden, to the field with the donkeys and the wild marshes beyond. She was trying to take in what he'd just told her, though she'd known in her heart of hearts it was the only sensible decision and she must accept it.

She and Hugh would be moving here in order to look after his mother, who was now out of hospital and in bed in her room down the corridor. It *had* been pneumonia. Lavinia Morton had been left very weak and confused, though, and the doctor was unable to say how quickly she'd get well. Hugh's mother was just sixty, but being asthmatic she was not as robust as some women her age so it might be a slow process.

They'd keep the London flat on for the moment, Hugh said. It was on a long lease and he would need to be in London occasionally. So might she, she tried to tell herself, so might she.

'Couldn't we afford to have a companion for her?' she said, turning to him, already knowing his answer.

'I've thought of that. I can't do it to her, Isabel.' Hugh sat down on the bed and studied his hands: strong hands they were, but smooth-skinned, sensitive. 'She is my mother, after all. I owe it to her.'

But I don't, Isabel wanted to say, and didn't.

'There's every likelihood that she'll recover very well, but I still don't want to leave her on her own. And since you'll be stopping work shortly anyway, it seems the obvious solution.'

'I was hoping to continue going to the office for a while yet, Hugh. It's five months till Christmas. I'm not ill, after all, only having a baby.'

'You know I'm not happy with the idea of you doing that. You'll exhaust yourself. And there's no need, we've plenty of money. Surely McKinnon can send you some work here. Reading and so forth?'

She thought about this and finally nodded. 'I suppose so,' she said, for the moment defeated.

That night, waiting to fall asleep, she lay listening to the owls, the sough of the wind from the river, and considered how pleasant it might be here. One had, after all, to make the best of things. And as if in response, she felt for the very first time a tiny movement deep inside her, like the brushing of a butterfly's wings. She held her breath. There it was again.

'Hugh,' she said, and he answered sleepily. She reached for his hand and placed it on her abdomen. 'Feel there,' she commanded. It was the baby, moving inside.

Chapter 22

Emily

Sitting in her flat, Emily put down the pages she was reading. There was so much to take in: the rich variety of Isabel's life in London, her happiness at being married to Hugh. Emily thought how content they seemed together, though it struck her that Isabel did two jobs, her publishing work and looking after Hugh when she came home in the evenings. And then other things crowding in: the discovery that a baby was growing inside her, the need to look after Hugh's mother. Isabel's life was changing in ways that she couldn't control. Most women would have been happy about the baby, but there was bitterness and desperation in the tone of Isabel's account. She clearly felt that her young life was closing down. There was still quite a bit of the account to read.

Emily got up and poured herself a glass of fruit juice from the fridge, then settled down again to find out what happened next.

Isabel

The summer of 1951 should have been one of the most idyllic of Isabel's life. She was in the middle trimester of her pregnancy, the nausea of the early months entirely gone, and some of her former energy returned. She had exchanged London with its views of bombed-out buildings for a large and beautiful house in the depths of the lush Suffolk countryside. The weather was often warm and sunny. Since it wasn't long since she'd been a schoolgirl, she still felt it natural for July and August to pass in idleness. Not that she was idle now exactly, but nor did she have to leave the house at an early hour to get to the office in Percy Street.

True to their promise, Stephen and Trudy were supplying her with plenty of reading and editing. At least once a week the postman would bring some well-wrapped manuscript accompanied by a neatly typed instruction from Trudy or a hastily scrawled comment from Cat. These notes Isabel scanned greedily, hoping for some snippet of gossip from the literary world to make her feel she still belonged. During the first weeks, Cat would sometimes telephone in a panic, wanting information concerning some author's foibles or to put Stephen on the line with a query. She strained for the inference that she was missed. Though at first she welcomed these conversations, they left her longing to be back in the office and she was almost glad when the gaps between them lengthened. It was only a matter of getting used to her new life, she told herself, then her restlessness might cease.

Whilst she struggled to adapt, Hugh seemed sated

with happiness that summer, for he'd found a rhythm
that suited him. Once a week he'd spend a night or two in
their London flat, which enabled him to visit the men
who gave him commissions, men who were becoming his
friends, to see plays or exhibitions and go to parties,
though summer offered thin pickings for parties. When
in Suffolk he would shut himself in his study, away from
the busyness of the house, and write.

And Isabel would be left to attend to Hugh's sick
mother in the house that, though technically Hugh's, was
Lavinia Morton's home.

'Don't!'

Isabel let fall the curtain as though it burned her. 'Sorry,'
she whispered, trying to make out the face of the woman
in the bed. She rubbed her hands together nervously. 'It's
so dark in here.'

'Good,' her mother-in-law mumbled.

'I–I came to see if I could fetch you anything. Or read to
you, perhaps.'

'There's nothing. That nurse woman – what d'you call
her – where's she gone now?'

'Nurse Carbide. I don't know. I'm sure that she'll be
back in a moment.' Isabel sat down on the chair by the
bed. Her eyes were getting used to the gloom and she
thought Hugh's mother looked horribly old, hanks of
pewter-coloured hair spread wild on the pillow, her skin
with a yellowish tinge. Isabel felt sorry for her. No wonder
Lavinia Morton liked the darkness.

The woman was still complaining about the nurse.
'Fusses about, not at all gentle, then never there when
you want her.'

'Are you sure I can't help?'

'The nurse, get the nurse. I need the article, you silly girl.'

'Yes, of course,' Isabel said, getting up quickly. She found Nurse Carbide and fled the scene, relieved that someone else would have to deal with the matter of the commode. Hugh's mother was far from an easy patient and Isabel did not have the temperament to care for her.

For the first few weeks she didn't have to, for after she was discharged from hospital, the sick woman was bedridden, and Hugh employed the retired nurse, who arrived on her creaking bicycle every weekday and saw to her medicines and her most personal needs. Mrs Catchpole, the matronly cook and housekeeper, would walk up as usual from the village after breakfast. She cleaned, prepared meals, and sent out the laundry. After she pointed out the extra work generated by Hugh and Isabel's arrival, her cheerful sixteen-year-old daughter Lily was engaged to help.

These arrangements still left Hugh's mother in her daughter-in-law's care first thing in the morning, during the evening, and for part of the weekend. There was breakfast to assemble and take up on a tray, pills to count out and administer. There was the settlement of a dozen little tasks. After the first week, Hugh's mother could get herself out to the bathroom, though once in the night she misjudged the uneven floor, fell, and had to be rescued. She grew stronger and got rid of the despised nurse. Although she would get up for part of the day, the doctor still recommended bedrest.

A large brass handbell now lived on the bedside table: it could be heard anywhere in the house. 'Would you mind just . . .' Lavinia would say when Isabel appeared in response, but if her words were more polite than they had been, the tone still meant an order. The task might be anything: rearranging pillows, finding a particular pair of spectacles, clearing up a spill, adjusting a curtain against the sun, finding one of the myriad medicines she used to relieve wheeziness, making a telephone call.

Isabel carried out these instructions as readily as she could and tried not to show resentment. It must be awful to be ill, she upbraided herself, and to feel so helpless, and Hugh's mother, once so capable, must hate it. She herself could be moody and complaining, and she remembered with shame how she'd ordered Hugh around during her own period of being confined to bed after the threat of miscarriage two months before.

What they'd expected to be a short-term difficulty – helping Hugh's mother to recover from an acute illness – became a long-term problem almost without anyone noticing.

July turned to August. The doctor now advised that the patient get up in the mornings, and he prescribed a programme of light activity. If the day was warm, Isabel was to settle her mother-in-law outside with books and a newspaper. The patient was given a walking-frame and encouraged to amble about the garden with someone to assist her. She was to take a nap in the afternoon and later to enjoy some stimulating activity such as a visit from a friend. Hugh's mother had many acquaintances but few close friends. There were one or two good souls who came faithfully. The Rector's wife was one, a plain-faced but sunny-natured woman. She didn't seem to notice how Hugh's mother patronised her.

Isabel's aim after breakfast, Hugh's mother allowing, was to settle at the dining-room table, sharpen her pencil and begin editing a manuscript or writing a reader's report. It was always only a matter of time, though, before she'd be interrupted by the jangling of the handbell. If Isabel was lucky, Mrs Catchpole might call out, 'Don't you worry yourself, dear, I'll see to her,' but even then Isabel would wait, tense, in case she was needed after all, before she could relax and resume her work.

Sometimes, however, Mrs Catchpole might be out or immersed in some task, so Isabel would sigh angrily, push back her chair and go to find out what was needed. Then it might be five minutes or half the morning before she could return to her work.

By the end of August, Hugh's mother was almost back to her normal competent self. Oddly, this didn't stop her from interrupting Isabel. During her illness she had gradually gained the upper hand. Now that Isabel felt it fair to fight back, they were locked in bitter silent warfare.

She'd hear Lavinia Morton's wheezy breathing long before the woman herself entered the dining room – *her* dining room, as she saw it. 'I'm so sorry to disturb you,' she would say very deliberately, 'but would you mind removing your books from the drawing room. The Rector will be calling and I do like things to look straight.'

Or, 'Do you have the newspaper or has Hugh got it?' The implication was that Isabel should locate it. Strangely, Hugh's mother never disturbed her son with these questions.

Hugh was always easy with his mother, solicitous of her comfort. When Isabel complained to him in the seclusion of their bedroom, his brow would wrinkle in a frown.

'I'm sure she doesn't mean to interrupt,' he'd say. 'It's a bit difficult when it is her home.' Or, 'I'm sure she's only trying to help.'

'You take her side all the time,' Isabel cried once.

'I don't think it's a question of sides,' he said. 'There are no sides. I hardly believe she's being deliberately offensive.'

His mother was no longer exactly rude, but she expected her views to prevail. For Hugh, this was normal life.

Sometimes, his mother would watch Isabel tidy up the books or locate the newspaper and say something like, 'You are working very hard at the moment, dear, do you honestly think it's good for you?' Or she'd try to distract her with some local task, which needed volunteers. There were, it seemed, endless hassocks to be embroidered for the church, or cakes baked for a charity sale. 'I suggested to the Rector that you might like to help. It would introduce you to some other ladies, you know.'

Isabel wondered if she ought to want to do this, but the fact remained that she didn't. She attended church one Sunday, but none of the younger women who spoke to her seemed her sort at all. When Hugh asked her, with some exasperation, why they weren't, she couldn't give an answer that satisfied him. 'They aren't interested in anything,' she said. 'Not the things that I'm interested in, anyway.'

She missed Vivienne badly, and her friends at the office. Vivienne went away with her family for a fortnight and sent a postcard of a Cornish beach. *I'll write again with news*, it said, but no further letter came and when Isabel rang the house in Highgate on a whim one evening, nobody answered. She wondered how matters stood with Theo. She hoped nothing was wrong. She was extremely anxious about Berec, too, and wrote to him, but there was no reply.

'Perhaps you ought to help prepare for the autumn bazaar,' Hugh said doubtfully. 'It'll get you out a little.'

Isabel resisted. She took to walking across the marshes to the estuary, where she'd contemplate the wild landscape and listen to the cries of the birds. It reflected her melancholy mood.

One Wednesday morning, she finished editing a manuscript for Trudy and packed it up, eager to make the short walk to the Post Office before half-day closing. When she arrived, she was annoyed to find a queue. The postmaster, whose bad temper everyone put up with because he hadn't been the same since having a metal plate put in his skull after being blown up in Normandy, had a habit of closing the counter at twelve-thirty on the dot on Wednesdays, and anyone he'd still not served could lump it.

Fortunately, the people in front of her were familiar with this and conducted their business efficiently. The morose postmaster had just dropped Isabel's parcel in the sack, and she turned to go, when a woman further back in the queue said, 'Hello.' She looked up to see a familiar pair of wide-spaced blue eyes.

'Jacqueline,' she said in surprise, then hushed her voice because the whole queue was now listening eagerly. 'What are *you* doing here?'

'Next,' barked the postmaster, stabbing his bell with the rubber thimble he wore on his forefinger to count banknotes, and everybody shuffled forward.

'Buying stamps, of course,' Jacqueline replied, showing the envelope in her gloved hand. She was overdressed
for a country Post Office, in a suit with a narrow skirt that
emphasised her generous hips, a small hat that clung to
her perfect curls and a toffee-coloured bag and shoes.
Isabel, conscious of her dusty walking shoes, felt dowdy
in comparison.

'I meant I didn't know you were in Suffolk,' she said
gently.

'Twelve-thirteeee,' the postmaster called as the person
in front of Jacqueline moved away. He started packing
everything into the drawer behind the counter.

'I say, can't you sell me . . . ?' Jacqueline bent forward,
waving her envelope in a manner that Isabel knew would
annoy the man.

'Sorry, madam,' he said, pointing to an officious little
notice about opening hours on the wall behind. He came
out from his seat, pushed past several people still waiting
and held open the door. Everyone filed out obediently.
The door shut firmly behind them and the lock clicked
into place. As Isabel and Jacqueline watched, a hand, still
wearing a thimble, flipped over the sign to read CLOSED.

'Well, he really is the limit,' Jacqueline sighed. 'I say, I
don't suppose you can sell me a stamp?'

'There are some at home,' Isabel said, remembering a
strip of them in the writing bureau. 'Is that yours?' she
asked, seeing a smart little open-top car. 'If you drop me
back, I'll find you one.'

She wanted the lift. It was one of those warm and
drowsy days of late summer, and the walk down had
been a little tiring. Her centre of gravity had changed and
a nagging pain had started up in her lower back.

'You didn't walk, did you?' Jacqueline said, with an alarmed glance at Isabel's swelling girth. 'I don't know how you can. But let me take you home. If I miss Aunt Hilda's birthday, I'll never hear the last of it.'

'I wish Hugh would teach me to drive,' Isabel told Jacqueline as they got into the car, 'but he refuses.'

'Very sensible of him,' Jacqueline said as they pulled away. 'You have to think of Baby.'

Isabel smiled grimly in reply. She closed her eyes, enjoying the breeze on her face, the scent of cut grass.

Jacqueline was the sort who gave women drivers a bad name. She drove along the middle of the road, and swung the car almost too wide when she turned up the drive. As she raised one arm from the wheel to shield her eyes against the dazzling sun, the car swerved alarmingly and Isabel had to clutch the door. Inside, she felt the baby leap in alarm.

As they drew up safely outside the stables, Isabel asked, 'Are you in Suffolk for long?'

'I'm not sure,' Jacqueline replied. 'I hate it in London when Michael is away. I wish we could settle down here, but he says he has to be in Town.' She smiled at Isabel wistfully. 'I do think you're lucky. This place is paradise to raise a family.'

'I suppose so,' Isabel said, pushing the car door open and heaving herself out. 'But I still prefer London.' She laughed. 'Perhaps we should change places.'

Jacqueline bit her lip. 'Don't say things like that.' She lifted her handbag from the back seat. As she shut the car door she stared up at the house. Her expression could only be described as yearning.

Inside, the house was shadowy and cool. From the kitchen came the tranquil sounds of lunch being prepared.

'Mother-in-law?' Isabel called out. There was no answer. 'Perhaps she's in the garden,' she told Jacqueline, who was adjusting her hat in the hallstand mirror. 'Wait, I'll fetch you that stamp before I forget.'

While in the drawing room, lowering the hinged lid of the old writing bureau, she heard Hugh's voice in the hall. 'Jacqueline, my dear girl. What a wonderful surprise.'

She heard Jacqueline answer, but not what she said. She tore off a stamp from the strip and went to join them.

'Oh, I say, that's marvellous,' Jacqueline said, counting out coins despite Isabel's protest.

'It's clever of you to find Jacqueline,' Hugh told Isabel. He stood behind his wife and placed his hands on her shoulders in a possessive gesture. Jacqueline concentrated on licking the stamp and pressing it down on the envelope.

'I'm sure you'd like something to drink,' Isabel said, then they all turned as they were interrupted.

'Jacqueline, how splendid. I'll tell Mrs Catchpole to put back lunch.' Hugh's mother, a little out of breath, had entered the hall from the garden. 'How are you, dear?' she asked with a warmth Isabel hadn't seen before.

'Mrs Morton, you do look well.' Jacqueline stepped forward, and the two women clasped hands. 'I was so concerned when I heard about your illness.'

'How kind of you to write that sweet little note,' Hugh's mother replied. 'And Hugh said you telephoned. I felt so fussed over.'

'The least I could do,' Jacqueline said. 'And Hugh has been so reassuring.'

'Mother must have the constitution of an ox,' Hugh

said. 'The doctor was very worried at first. I could tell he thought we'd have a funeral on our hands.'

'Oh, Hugh,' his mother said, 'don't joke about such things.'

Still, everyone laughed.

Isabel didn't recall Jacqueline ringing up, but she did remember Hugh's mother exclaiming over a card with flowers on it.

'Isabel, do take Jacqueline into the garden. It's so beautiful out there. I'll just have a word with Mrs Catchpole. Have you had luncheon yet, dear?'

'Not yet, Mrs Morton,' said Jacqueline, 'but there's some waiting for me at home. If a glass of water wouldn't put you out . . .'

'Oh, I think we can manage something a little stronger than that,' Hugh broke in and went off to mix cocktails.

A table and chairs lay in the shadow of the cherry tree, and here they sat. Isabel always became ravenously hungry by this time, and the unaccustomed Martini went straight to her head. Bees buzzed around the wild flowers in the grass and the sun slanted through the dark-green leaves. Ice clinked against glass and she let the conversation drift around her, wondering when she'd ever get lunch.

'He's still in Korea,' Jacqueline replied to Lavinia Morton's question about her husband. 'The fighting's terribly fierce, they say, but I don't listen to the news and try my best not to worry. Do you think he'll be all right, Hugh?'

'Military Intelligence operates behind the lines, doesn't it? I'm sure he knows how to look after himself.'

'I'm sure you're right,' she said. 'He's not allowed to say anything in his letters, of course.'

'You're being very brave,' Hugh said, placing his hand over hers.

Isabel closed her eyes against this picture and saw two tiny suns swirl on the inside of her eyelids. She opened them again. Hugh had removed his hand.

'I met your father at the Brigadier's the other evening,' Mrs Morton told Jacqueline. 'I'm glad he still plays bridge.'

'Yes,' Jacqueline said, a little sadly. 'Poor Daddy. It's been two years now, but he still misses Mummy like mad.'

'I'm sure you do too,' Mrs Morton said gently. 'Dear Dorothy, she was always such a good friend. Especially when I lost Hugh's father.'

'I do remember,' Jacqueline said, her voice quivery. 'It was while Hugh was away, wasn't it, Hugh? We were so sad for you, Mrs Morton, coping with it on your own.'

'You all rallied round marvellously for Mother,' Hugh said, taking out a pipe and a wallet of tobacco.

Isabel frowned. The pipe was a recent affectation and when he lit it indoors she hated how the smoke burned the back of her throat. It didn't matter so much out here, though it spoiled all the other smells, the flowers and the earth itself, that she experienced so intensely.

'. . . in her condition.' Hugh was talking about her now.

'What?' she asked.

'You're wool-gathering, darling. I was saying how glad I am that Jacqueline is down here for a while. She'll be able to keep you company.'

'Are you?' She turned to Jacqueline. 'How nice.'

'I'm sure Jacqueline will help you with a layette for the baby,' Hugh's mother said. 'Of course, I have a few things left over from when Hughie was small. You remember that dear little sailor suit, Hugh?'

'Oh really, Mother, you haven't kept that, have you?' Hugh puffed out smoke as he laughed. 'Anyway, it's only any good if it's a boy.'

'I'm sure it'll be a boy,' Lavinia said, clasping her hands together. 'Mortons always have boys. Your father, your grandfather, your great-grandfather. Not a single daughter amongst them. A son and heir, that's what it'll be.'

'There's that trick you can do with a wedding ring,' Jacqueline said, opening her eyes very wide. 'It might be a lot of rubbish, but it worked for a friend of mine. Anyway, it's fun to try.'

'No point,' Isabel said. 'My mother-in-law is always right. It'll be a boy. It certainly kicks like one.' She shifted slightly to get comfortable.

'I am not always right, Isabel,' came the response. 'Jacqueline, Isabel is still working herself much too hard. It would be marvellous if you came to see us often. It would take her out of herself, and you know how I always love our little chats.' She smiled.

Isabel tried not to snap. 'I am perfectly happy, I assure you both. Not that it wouldn't be delightful to see you, Jacqueline.' Whether it was hunger or hormones, or a sense of injustice, a terrible rage was surging up in her that she struggled to contain. Because she was having a baby the world was treating her differently. Not as competent editor Isabel Barber, but as an infirm imbecile.

'Once Baby comes you'll wish that you'd rested more, dear,' Hugh's mother said to her, swatting at a wasp.

The figure of Mrs Catchpole could be seen at the door to the garden.

'What I need most,' Isabel said, pushing herself up, 'is lunch. I'm simply dying of starvation.'

Towards the end of September, a letter finally arrived from Vivienne. It contained the news that Isabel had half-expected – that her courtship with Theo had ended, not just because of opposition by Vivienne's family, but by Theo's, too.

Vivienne's story was heartbreaking, but she was obviously trying to be very brave.

I knew I'd have difficulties with Mummy and Daddy, but I was sure that once they'd met Theo and got to know him as I did, they'd see how wonderful he really was, but the meeting did not go well and Theo wasn't at all at ease. They're always telling me how they want me to be happy, but when I chose someone I know I can be happy with, they wouldn't accept him. I suppose I do understand. So many of our kind of people are quite narrow-minded and, of course, there's been so much awfulness with Mummy's family in the concentration camps that I don't want to upset them any more, but I still hoped that with time they'd come round. But we weren't given that time.

Theo wrote to his family about me, you see. We had such plans – that now I've finished studying I would accompany him to India to meet them, but I know now that this was naïve. Two weeks ago, Theo came to see me, very sweet and shame-faced, and confessed that he was forced to break things off. He loved me, he said, he'd always love me, and I believed him, but his father had issued all kinds of threats about cutting him off and not sending him the money for his studies. I could see that there was no alternative, so I let him go. But now, my dear Isabel, I feel dreadfully hurt and sorry for myself.

Mummy's sent me away to stay with Aunt Rosa in Bath, which is so beautiful and restoring that I'm sure I shall be back to my old self soon. And then I must decide what to do with my life. Well now, that's all far too much about me, and I should be asking after you and hoping that you're getting plenty of rest and fresh air. Suffolk must be marvellous at this time of year . . .

She folded the letter and put it with some others she must answer. Poor, poor Vivienne. It seemed so unfair that she, Isabel, should be settled here, when Vivienne's life was so fraught with difficulty. It made her own troubles momentarily fade in comparison.

Chapter 23

Isabel

'Are you sure this won't hurt the baby?' Hugh said.

'Never mind the baby,' Isabel gasped. 'It feels marvellous. Go on doing that. Oh . . .'

Afterwards, they lay spooned together in the darkness of the bedroom, his hand cupped around her belly.

'I must say, I can hardly keep my hands off you at the moment,' he growled, nuzzling her neck. 'There's something so gorgeous about all this, this *fecundity*.'

'I'm sure it is all right,' Isabel wondered. 'It's not exactly something one likes to ask Doctor Bridges. He might be rather shocked.'

The local doctor was youngish and unmarried. He had pale freckled skin, which coloured up easily, and any appointment with him about her pregnancy rendered him permanently red-faced. Fortunately, she mostly saw the midwives.

She disliked the fact that she and her mother-in-law had the same family doctor. She didn't really believe that he'd discuss her health with Hugh's mother, but just the idea that he had seen intimate parts of both their bodies, and knew their weaknesses, was a distasteful one.

She was falling into sleep when Hugh said in her ear, 'I wonder if you'd do something for me while I'm away in London.'

'Mmm,' she said drowsily. 'What?'

'I've got to a tricky part in my novel. Could I show it to you?'

'Yes, of course,' she said, waking up a bit.

He hadn't told her anything about his writing for a while, had brushed questions about it away, and she'd been hurt. After all, it was the thing that had brought them together in the first place. She'd worried that he thought less of her professional opinion now that she was his wife. Did he view her differently? It wasn't a topic she felt she could explore with him so she'd stayed silent. In one sense it was perfectly natural that their relationship had evolved into something else. She'd told herself he wanted emotional support from her now, not criticism.

'Are you sure you want me to, though?' she asked.

'Yes, I do,' he said. 'I need to know I've got certain things right.'

She found the stack of typed pages left for her on the breakfast table the next day, after he'd gone. Since there was nothing else urgent she had to do for McKinnon & Holt, she said firmly to Hugh's mother that she had promised to do something Very Important for Hugh, and shut herself away in their bedroom all morning, where she sat in bed, ate apples and read.

As before, the writing engaged her at once. He'd given the novel a title, *The Silent Tide*, and redrafted the early chapters according to her suggestions all those months ago before their marriage. Nanna emerged now, through the male narrator's eyes, as a vividly drawn character, strong, passionate and individual, but unselfconscious, too, not concerned by others' expectations of her. Isabel read, enthralled, how she forged a career as a newspaper journalist, keen to report hard news, while encountering resistance from her male colleagues. And then – Isabel turned a page – she fell in love with one of them, the narrator.

Soon after this, Isabel read something that tugged at her memory, a phrase: 'I feel as if I'm two people,' Nanna was saying. 'One is the real me, and the other is the person men expect me to be. Why can't I just be myself?'

She remembered saying something like that to Hugh once, soon after discovering she was pregnant. Never mind, it was hardly of great originality. She read on.

Every now and then she'd stop, arrested by something Nanna said or did, some detail of her life that seemed faintly familiar, though the actual words were changed, had become part of the seamless voice of the fiction. Yet they were about her, about Isabel herself, she began to realise. Hugh was writing something utterly magnificent and important *but he had used her as his model.*

She reached a description of Nanna getting up in the morning to go to work, and Isabel remembered with clarity that time in early pregnancy when she'd been doing that exact same thing, examining her stockings for holes, complaining about her mother-in-law, and she'd noticed Hugh scribbling some notes.

A variety of emotions passed through her at this realisation, but above all, shock. She hadn't asked to become part of his book – indeed, he hadn't asked her permission to do this – but now it was clear that all the time he must be observing her, secretly recording his impressions. She couldn't quite take it all in.

Unable for the moment to go on, she laid the pages in two piles on the counterpane, the bigger pile that she'd read and the smaller one she hadn't, and eased herself off the bed. She roamed about the room, picking items up and placing them down again, then sat on the stool in front of the dressing table and stared at her reflection.

She hadn't troubled to look at herself closely for a while, not generally liking what pregnancy was doing to her body, but now she did, imagining how Hugh saw her, how he'd describe her now. Fat and pasty, she thought. Her hair badly needed cutting and the auburn waves were difficult to tame. She picked up a brush and began to tidy it as best she could. Probably Jacqueline would be able to recommend a hairdresser, she thought, as she gazed at the result with dismay. She threw down the brush, unable to stop thinking about Hugh's novel.

If he'd taken notes then they must be somewhere. He was never without a small black notebook, and would have the latest with him today, but he must keep the old ones in his study. She got up and hastened downstairs, almost tripping in her hurry.

In the study she felt she was intruding, then it struck home that he had been intruding on her by writing about her. She went straight to the desk. There were three drawers on each side and one long one across the middle where he kept blotting paper and other stationery. In one of the deep bottom drawers was a bottle of brandy, half-empty. A smaller drawer was stuffed with various letters and receipts. These weren't what she was after, though, so she scooped them out to check underneath, then shoved them all back, hoping he wouldn't spot that they'd been moved. In another drawer she smiled when she found a box of liquorice sweets, one of his weaknesses, but nothing of real interest. She turned and looked about the room. There was a big filing cabinet behind the door. It was locked, but she remembered seeing the key and recovered it from the desk.

In the top drawer of the cabinet was a stack of bank statements and, at last, a pile of his old notebooks. She picked up the first one and flicked through the pages. The shorthand wasn't always easy to decipher, but in between jottings about conversations overheard, and descriptions of strangers, were sections about 'N'. 'N' was described variously as having 'bright coral lips, slightly parted, plumply beguiling', as 'throwing herself into a tantrum when she burned some fried chicken'. That was unfair, it hadn't been a tantrum, she'd merely cursed a bit. She read on with increasing horror. There were comments on episode after episode of their life together, and not all of them were flattering.

Finishing that notebook, she dropped it back in the drawer and picked up another. The first page fell open at a stinging little comment about Alex Berec being 'old womanish'. Hugh had drawn a little cartoon of Berec, too, which exaggerated his beaky nose. It was perceptive but cruel, she thought, remembering how she'd last seen poor Berec.

Two notebooks in, she suddenly couldn't bear it any longer. She replaced everything in the drawer as it had been, locked it and returned the key to its hiding place. She sank down into the baggy leather armchair, where she hugged a cushion for comfort and wondered what she should do next. The discovery had shifted her view of their marriage. Hugh had been observing her, like a creature in a bell jar. She remembered how she used to joke with him sometimes when they went to some stuffy party, or if something unplanned happened like being stuck on a bus in traffic, that even if they didn't enjoy it there might be some 'good material' in it. All human relationships might be for a writer as shiny loot to a magpie. She knew this, but the irony was that now she herself was loot, she didn't like it at all. How could she be natural, her husband's other half, if he offered her up in this way to the public view, in a book to be discussed, as universal modern woman? It made her feel grubby.

She had just determined that she'd return upstairs and finish the manuscript when there came a knock, then the door opened a crack and her mother-in-law's head appeared. Lavinia didn't see Isabel at first, but when she did she came in, a look of suspicion on her face. 'Oh, what are you doing in here?' she said.

Isabel couldn't help feeling guilty. 'I was checking something for Hugh and felt tired,' she explained. This was more or less true. Her mother-in-law's face softened.

'And no wonder. I was going to ask if you'd like to come and look at some things for the baby, but perhaps you should go back to bed. Mrs Catchpole could take you a cup of tea.'

'I'm better now. What did you want me to see?'

'Come,' Hugh's mother said, and Isabel edged herself out of the chair and followed.

Mrs Morton walked stiffly ahead of her up the stairs and along the landing, and opened a door at the end to a room Isabel hadn't been in before, but which she knew

was full of junk. She gazed about. There was an old stand-
ard lamp with a heavy tasselled shade, several odd chairs
with broken arms or unravelling seats, a couple of ancient
trunks. She shivered. It was noticeably colder in this
room. Hugh's mother picked her way through the jumble
to get to a huge built-in cupboard on the back wall.

'There are one or two things in here that might be suitable,' she said, pulling open the double doors. 'Ah, Hugh's
old cot. He can take that out for us.' The pieces of it had
been neatly stacked against the back of the cupboard. A
set of shelves ran down one side and Hugh's mother
began exploring the contents of a cardboard box.

'Can I help?' Isabel offered. Her mother-in-law was
coughing at the dust.

'No, no,' the woman replied. 'I'm seeing what's here.'

Behind them, something started buzzing at the
window and Isabel turned round to see a bumblebee.
Poor thing. She went over and managed to get the
window open to let it out. On her way back she glanced
at a large painted fire screen propped against the wall
opposite the door they'd come through. From this angle
Isabel saw that it half-covered a second door. A door
presumably to an inner room. She stepped across to
look more closely.

'What's in here?' she asked and her hand went to the
door knob.

'You'll find it's locked. It's private.' Hugh's mother
sounded so fierce that Isabel snatched her hand away.

The woman was holding what looked like a dress box
in her arms. 'Now,' she said, lifting the lid. 'There are
some cot sheets in here. And that case up there,' she
nodded towards the top shelf of the cupboard. 'I'm sure

there are some matinée sets in it. One hopes that the moth hasn't got to them. Can you reach?'

Isabel pulled down the small suitcase indicated. The little costumes, wrapped in paper, were intact, though they smelled unpleasantly of mothballs.

'I can't think what I did with that sailor suit Hugh hates so much. He looked perfectly sweet in it when he was two.'

'The baby won't need it at once,' Isabel said. She knew she ought to feel grateful for all this, but instead she felt depressed. None of this old stuff felt anything to do with her or any baby she might have.

The dust and the smell of naphthalene was making both of them cough.

'That'll do for now,' Hugh's mother managed to say.

As they left the room, Isabel's eyes rested on the locked door. What was beyond it that her mother-in-law didn't want her to know about?

She spent the rest of the morning washing the little woollen jackets and matching leggings in soapy warm water, gently squeezing out the excess. As she pegged them up to dry outside she glanced up at the house. A thought occurred to her. She started counting the windows on the upper floor. Hers and Hugh's room looked out to the front. At the back there were two bedrooms with a bathroom in between then a blank wall stretching under the eaves to the right. The window of the box room was to the front. She fiddled with the sleeve of the last matinée jacket, and pinned it with the peg she took from between her teeth. It was strangely satisfying to see the little costumes dancing on the line. The matter of the secret room still bothered her. She scanned the downstairs windows to make sure her mother-in-law wasn't spying on her, then left the wicker washing basket and strolled round to the front of the house to scrutinise the windows on that side.

Yes, next to Lavinia Morton's room was the window to the box room. So where was the window to the room beyond the locked door?

An ancient wisteria grew up the side of the house there, snaking around the box-room window. The flowers had long blown, but the leaves were lush, and in between them she glimpsed something she hadn't seen before, a small round window like a porthole. The glass glinted, opaque. From that moment on, Isabel's curiosity as to what lay in the room behind it began to grow.

After lunch, she retired to her bedroom and took up Hugh's manuscript once more, finding a stub of pencil to write notes. It was again disturbing to read about herself. Like her, Nanna had become pregnant soon after her marriage and struggled to maintain her normal work patterns, though in Nanna's case she received no sympathy from her male colleagues. The narrator, Nanna's husband, had got himself involved in some political intrigue that involved Russian spies, a plot line which Isabel thought worked well, and so skipped over. Instead she found herself marking again and again infelicities in his observations about Nanna. The script ended quite abruptly at a point where Nanna had to all intents and purposes been fired from her job. Isabel lay back and considered this scene, thinking how Hugh could make it more convincing. Then she turned back to the beginning and started to read again, making more detailed notes for Hugh. She was still angry with him, but at the same time she was caught up in Nanna's story and desperately wanted the character to emerge sympathetically. She worked all afternoon.

Hugh returned from London the following evening somewhat out of sorts. When they sat down to a dinner of roast mutton, he brushed off enquiries with, 'Nothing's wrong.'

'Come now, Hugh,' his mother said, unrolling her napkin. 'I can always tell with you.'

'Oh, it's simply . . . You remember my story about the ageing impresario? Well, at the last moment the magazine wants alterations or they won't put it in. It's bad form, if you ask me.'

'I think you should stick to your guns, dear,' Hugh's mother told him. 'More potatoes, Isabel? You are eating for two, you know.'

Isabel, who already had three potatoes on her plate, shook her head. 'But it's a shame if it means they won't print it,' she told her mother-in-law. 'What exactly does the editor want you to do, Hugh?'

'That's the trouble. It's not the same editor, it's a new man. He thinks the ending should be more decisive. Says the readers won't understand it as it is.'

'I should just insist,' Hugh's mother said, liberally piling salt on the edge of her plate.

'Mother,' Hugh said, 'it doesn't work like that.'

'What do you really think about the ending?' Isabel persisted.

'It follows the integrity of the story,' he replied, shrugging. 'Life doesn't have tidy endings.'

'Perhaps you should think about it. Negotiate with

him,' Isabel said patiently. 'I'm sure there's an answer you'd both be happy with, if you look for it.'

'Ridiculous,' Hugh's mother snapped. 'Hugh should write what he wants to write and they should be grateful to have it.'

'Oh, Mother,' Hugh said crisply, 'if only you ran everything.'

'I think we do, as wives and mothers,' she said, coquettish. 'The women behind the men, aren't we, Isabel?'

Isabel was eating a mouthful of potatoes and could not speak.

After dinner, they sat in the drawing room, Hugh's mother playing patience whilst listening to the wireless and Isabel altering an old dress to fit her expanding shape. Soon Hugh took himself off to his study to write a review and she, tired and fed up, went to bed early.

She was reading a library book when Hugh came upstairs. The baby was active tonight and she stroked her bump to soothe it, watching her husband potter about the bedroom, getting ready for bed.

'I read your script today,' she said.

He looked up eagerly. 'Did you? Thank you. And what did you make of it?'

'It's wonderful, Hugh.'

'You really think so?'

'I do. Of course, there are parts that need further attention.'

'Oh?' Less eager.

'Very, very minor points,' she said.

'I'm most grateful to you,' he replied. Did she imagine the sharpness in his voice?

'I'm sorry,' she said. 'I assumed that's why you wanted me to read it. To help you.'

'Yes – yes, of course. As long as you like it generally,' he said. He still sounded defensive and this bewildered her. He'd always taken note before of what she'd said about his work. This had changed. It came to her now. He only wanted her to say it was wonderful, not to criticise.

'There was something important that I didn't like,' she said, stung by this realisation. 'You've put me in there.'

'You? No, I haven't.'

'You have, Hugh. Things I've said, things I've done. I—' She almost mentioned snooping for the notebooks, but knew that would be disastrous.

'A writer has to have material, my darling one, but that doesn't mean I've put you in there. Nanna is a certain kind of modern woman. I know several women like her, in fact. I've read about others. I assure you, I don't need to put real people in my books. You of anyone should understand how a writer works.'

'I do. But, Hugh . . .' Something about the look on his face warned her to stop. If she argued, he might become really angry – angry like her father could be. She was frightened about that.

'Never mind,' she said. She took up her book and tried to read, but the print swam in front of her eyes. There was a lump in her throat and she swallowed.

'I've upset you now,' he said, coming swiftly over to kneel on the bed beside her. 'I don't mean to.'

'I'm sorry,' she said, trying hard not to cry. She cried so easily these days.

'My poor love,' he said, settling beside her and

drawing her to him. 'You mustn't get so worked up about things. I shouldn't have given you the book, it's made you upset.'

'No, it hasn't, Hugh,' she said. 'I wanted to read it. It's that . . .' Her voice fell to a whisper. 'It's that you don't listen to me any more.'

There was a pause, then he said, 'I don't mean to do that. Perhaps we shouldn't try to talk about my work.'

'Hugh! Of course we must.'

'Shh,' he said. 'Now I wanted to tell you. I went to McKinnon and Holt on my way through today. To pick up a book Trudy had for me.'

'Oh, how are they all?' Isabel said, cheering up somewhat.

'All very interested to hear how you were,' he said. 'I was introduced to Mr Snow, who's taken your place.'

'Taken my place?' she echoed, hurt. She imagined this shadowy man sitting at her desk, using her typewriter.

'Why yes, of course, silly. They do need another editor. I imagine we'll get on – he seemed a decent cove.'

Richard would be Hugh's editor. This second wave of realisation was painful. Like Nanna, she had lost her job.

Chapter 24

Isabel

Towards the end of September 1951, as the apples in the orchard were ripening and the nights were growing chilly, a letter arrived from Isabel's father. This was an event in itself – she'd never had one from him before – and when Hugh brought it to her in bed, Isabel opened the envelope with a sense of premonition. She scanned the single sheet that it contained.

'What is it?' Hugh asked, seeing her hand go to her mouth.

She read it again and passed it to him, wordlessly.

Charles Barber's message was brief and to the point.

My dear Isabel,

Your mother doesn't know I'm writing to you, being a proud woman who doesn't like fuss or anyone's pity. The fact remains that she's not been well recently and requires a short stay in hospital. I thought you should know this. The operation's to be next Tuesday and Mrs Fanshawe from across the road will be taking Lydia for a few days. The boys and I will manage perfectly well and there's no need to trouble yourself

*at all. I don't expect you should be travelling much in your
condition anyway.*

I hope this finds you well and you're not to worry.

Sincere best wishes,
Your Dad

Hugh looked up from the letter.

'I'm sorry,' he said, and sat down near Isabel on the
bed. 'Your poor mother. I wonder what's wrong?'

'I must go to help,' Isabel said miserably, shuffling off
the bedclothes.

'I can see why you'd want to,' Hugh said carefully, 'but
your father said—'

'I don't care what he said,' Isabel interrupted, tying on
her dressing-gown. 'Tuesday is tomorrow. Will you drive
me or shall I take the train?'

'What – now? Today?'

She saw a range of conflicting emotions struggle in
Hugh's face. Finally, decency won. He said smoothly,
'Yes, of course I'll drive you. Do you mind if I don't stay?
I do have an awful lot to do at the moment.'

'No. No, I'm sure that would be all right,' Isabel replied,
but she couldn't help feeling a pang of disappointment.

The week she spent at the family home was fraught with
misery, but was most memorable in the end for a conversation she had with her mother.

Charles Barber was in one of his difficult moods, obviously terrified about his wife's illness. The boys were
jittery and skulked about, and she had to order them to
help. Being nearly seven months' pregnant, she found the

cooking and cleaning exhausting. The hospital was five miles away and because her father went to work as usual and couldn't drive her, it was only accessible by bus for visiting hours in the afternoon.

She saw her mother briefly the evening before the operation, which she gauged from her father was to remove a lump from one of her breasts. Mrs Barber's bed was at the end of the ward, behind a pillar on its own, which gave her a modicum of privacy. Isabel, approaching unseen, was shocked to see the change in her. Her mother, always thin, had lost weight and her face wore a strained look, though she managed to smile when she saw her daughter. 'My dear, I had no idea you were coming!'

Isabel sat by her and took her hand. 'Dad told me,' she said. 'I could hardly stay away.'

Pamela Barber was frightened, though she tried not to show it. She'd noticed the lump some weeks ago when she was bathing, she told her daughter. Initial tests had been inconclusive, so this was to be on the safe side. She sounded as though she was trying convince herself.

At that moment, a nurse interrupted them. 'I appreciate that you've come a long way, but visiting hours have ended,' she said, thereby curtailing the visit.

Isabel's father came with her the following evening, after the operation. The curtains were drawn round the bed and her mother was drifting in and out of consciousness. All the tubes and machinery unnerved Charles dreadfully, and after ten minutes he couldn't bear it any more and stood up, saying they ought to get back to the boys.

Ted and Donald, catching their father's fear, had

refused to come, and five-year-old Lydia was of course far too young, even though she kept asking for her mother, so the burden of the visiting fell on Isabel. She didn't consider it a burden exactly, but the journey was undeniably tiring and she hated the way other women on the bus stared at her and made intrusive comments about her condition, when normally they'd not have noticed her at all.

On the Friday afternoon, she found her mother sitting up in bed with her hair brushed and more colour in her face, the drips and machines all gone. There was no one in the next bed, so it felt quite private. Isabel sat close and asked how she was, told her how the boys sent their love and reassured her that Lydia was happy staying with Mrs Fanshawe.

'It's good of you to take the trouble to come,' her mother said. 'I was a little cross with your father. I didn't think he should worry you.'

'That's silly, of course I should have known.'

'He hates all this, you know. Illness, hospitals. It's not that he doesn't care.' She smiled. 'I must say, you're looking very bonny,' she told Isabel. 'Marriage, a baby, it's suiting you.'

Isabel hesitated, then said, 'It's not as I expected.'

Her mother considered this. 'There's a lot to get used to,' she said finally. 'Men need different things from us. It's best to accept that.'

'Is it?' Isabel whispered. 'But what about me? Are my needs of no importance?'

Her mother sighed, then reached out and touched Isabel's hand.

'Of course they are. It's not always easy,' she said, 'but

you have to get on with it.' She was quiet for a moment, searching for the right words. 'Your father . . . he can't help what happened to him. At least he came home alive. I remind myself I'm one of the lucky ones.'

Isabel thought about this, the way her father swung from periods of black depression to latent anger. She knew deep down that he loved her mother. She'd glimpsed this the other day after her mother's operation, the tenderness and vulnerability beneath his dour surface. Perhaps that was why he'd disobeyed his wife and written to Isabel. It was he who'd needed her to come, as well as her mother. Isabel could say the things to her that he couldn't.

'We were so very happy together,' her mother murmured, her thoughts far away. She smiled. 'He had a sweet way about him, so charming.'

'How did you meet? You've never told me.' Isabel had not asked before, but then her mother had never been like this, a frightened patient in a hospital bed with time to talk.

'We met in Norfolk on a jetty in the rain.' Her face lit up, remembering. 'Your Aunt Penelope and I had a cousin with a sailing dinghy and he used to take us out on the Broad in it sometimes. Well, one day when I was nineteen, another boat tied up next to ours with four young men on it. They'd come for a week's holiday, up from London. One of them was your father.' She gave a little laugh. 'I knew straight away he liked me. Whenever he looked . . . he couldn't help blushing.'

'But he managed to ask you to go out with him?'

'We met up with them again the following afternoon, hung about in a group together, talking. One of Charles's pals took pity on him and we went out to a film together, with poor Penelope dragged along as a fourth. After that I'd slip out to meet your father on my own, not that we did anything we shouldn't' – at this, Isabel smiled at her mother – 'but he wasn't shy at all. Oh, we did have fun. After that, he wrote to me from London. Mummy found one of his letters and there was the most terrific row. He had no money or connections or anything. I didn't mind that, of course, but Mummy did dreadfully and tried to stop it. That was silly of her, because it made me want to be with him even more. I'm not saying I would have changed my mind about your father,' she assured Isabel, 'but at least if she'd been more reasonable it would have prevented the family rift. Your generation is lucky. Class isn't so important any more, but it mattered very much back then.'

'What about Penelope? Granny didn't approve of Uncle Jonny, either, did she?'

'Oh, Penelope didn't meet him till much later. After I left home she must have been so lonely. I felt a little guilty abandoning her.' Pamela looked at her daughter. 'Penelope was always secretive, you never knew what she was plotting, but if I'd still been there, perhaps she wouldn't have taken so many wrong turnings.'

Her mother looked so anguished now that Isabel regretted making her talk about past troubles. At the same time there were still many questions she wanted to ask. What had her mother and Penelope then quarrelled about? What had gone wrong with Penelope's marriage?

It was at that point that a young nurse with a gentle demeanour appeared at the bedside. 'You don't have to go,' she said to Isabel, 'but I must ask you to wait outside a moment while I look at the wound.' She started to pull the curtains round the bed.

'I will go, I think,' Isabel said, seeing that her mother was tired, 'but I'll come with Dad to pick you up tomorrow.'

She hardly noticed the journey home. Her mind was full of her mother's story. How had she never known these things before? *You never asked*, she told herself. *You've always been too caught up in your own concerns.*

'I think things are getting back to normal,' Isabel told her husband at breakfast one morning two weeks later, putting down a letter from her mother.

'Oh, good, so you won't have to be galloping off to Kent again,' was Hugh's response as he folded his newspaper and got up from the table, his mind clearly on the morning's work.

When he opened the door, Lavinia Morton could be heard out in the hall, talking on the telephone.

Isabel returned to the letter. *I am slowly recovering*, her mother had written, *but still feel very tired. Dear Joyce Fanshawe has been a marvellous neighbour, coming in every day to do the heavy work.* There was little other news. Lydia would be starting school after Christmas, the twins finishing their education in the summer, or maybe staying on at school, no one seemed quite sure yet. Isabel slotted the letter back in its envelope. Perhaps her mother would manage without her, though she felt guilty. She swallowed her last mouthful of toast and started to ease the string off a parcel bearing Cat's handwriting. She would find somewhere warm after breakfast to settle down and read the contents.

Just then, Hugh's mother came in. 'I don't know whether you have any plans today,' she said, 'but that was Jacqueline. She's coming for morning coffee. I thought we should make a start on preparations for Baby.'

'That's very kind of you both,' Isabel said dolefully. She was clutching the manuscript to her chest like something precious. Hugh's mother's gaze did not waver. After a moment, Isabel reluctantly laid the script back down on the table. She would have to deal with it another time.

'I thought Isabel would like the Rose Room as the nursery,' Lavinia Morton said, pushing open the door to the smaller of the spare bedrooms.

Isabel walked over to the window with its rose-patterned curtains and looked out across the sodden lawn. The half-dressed trees were dripping with rain and the marshes beyond were veiled in mist. She shivered and turned to see Mrs Morton and Jacqueline watching her.

'Yes . . .' she said tentatively. 'I'm sure it will do. Anywhere really.'

'We must ask Cooper in to redecorate, if we can find anywhere that has wallpaper,' Hugh's mother said.

'A friend of mine knows a man who found her quite a pretty design,' Jacqueline said, glancing round the room. 'Shall I make enquiries?'

'He must be a magician,' Hugh's mother replied. 'Would you, dear?'

'Of course. I made a note of his name – just in case, you know.' She sounded a bit wistful, which moved Isabel to thank her.

'Nice to see the two of you getting along,' Lavinia murmured.

Isabel changed the subject. 'Was this bedroom Hugh's nursery when he was little?'

'No,' her mother-in-law said. 'That was the one you and Hugh are in now. This was always a guest bedroom. Really, a proper washstand would be desirable.' She was contemplating the cracked handbasin. 'I suppose there's no chance of finding one of those?'

'At least the bathroom's next door,' Jacqueline said. 'Did I see a little tin bath in the big shed a while back?' Of course, Isabel thought, she knew the house so well since playing here as a child.

She wished she could warm to Jacqueline more, but found she couldn't; her dislike was an almost physical thing. The woman's staidness, the dull perfection of her hair and dress, even her talcum-powdery smell, repelled her. On all sorts of levels Isabel resented her. Jacqueline never passed up an opportunity to imply that she knew Hugh so much better than Isabel did. Hugh's mother was clearly fond of her, too, and Jacqueline played on this affection. As for Hugh, he behaved only with gentle gallantry to Jacqueline, oblivious to the way the young woman's eyes followed him and seemingly unaware of the stiff relationship between his childhood friend and his wife.

'What is that book like?' Isabel asked Hugh after dinner that evening as they were sitting before the fire in the drawing room. Lavinia had gone out to play bridge. It was unusual for Isabel and Hugh to have an evening alone together.

Hugh took his pipe out of his mouth and looked up. He'd been reading a novel he'd been asked to review, from time to time stopping to pencil a note in the margin.

'Better than your knitting,' he murmured, rescuing a runaway ball of wool. Mrs Catchpole had given Isabel a magazine with knitting patterns in it and she was trying now to make a pair of bootees for the baby with wool from an old cardigan.

'You may well be right,' she said, frowning at her misshapen efforts, 'but I want to know what you think of your book.'

'What? Yes, yes,' he said, and turned another page.

'What is it about?'

Hugh looked up and sighed. 'Party politics. The chap's got something, I have to say. It'll annoy a few of the Socialists though. They'll think he's laughing at them.'

'And is he?'

'Probably, yes.' He returned to his reading. The Socialists. Hugh rarely mentioned politics these days. She remembered the spirited discussions they used to have. Now he sounded disparaging.

'Drat,' she said, dropping another stitch. She laid down her knitting. She was simply no good at it. The manuscript she'd received that morning was lying beside her. She hadn't found time to start it today, and now she wasn't in the mood.

'What about your own writing, Hugh? How did that go today?'

'Oh fine, fine,' he said absently. He pencilled a margin note.

'Was what I said any use to you?' she persisted. He had, in the end, read her comments.

'Mmm, oh most certainly.'

'I'll look at the novel again sometime if you like.'

'That's most kind.' He smiled at her. 'You know, you are looking pretty tonight. That's a new dress, isn't it?'

'Thank you, but no, it's not,' she said sadly. 'It's an old one I altered. Hugh?'

'Mmm?'

'Now that your mother's so much better,' she said carefully, 'could we move back up to Town? I mean, some of the time. Perhaps we could come here at weekends.'

He closed the book, but kept his finger in the place.

'Are you not happy here?' he asked. 'I know Mother loves having you. And you seem to be making friends with Jacqueline.'

'I'm not sure that I agree with you about any of that,' she said slowly. 'Hugh, I don't think she likes me very much – Jacqueline, I mean.'

'I'm sure she does, why?'

'Oh . . . she can be quite stiff with me.'

'I'm sure she likes you. Why shouldn't she?'

'I don't know. Now I feel a little silly that I mentioned it.'

'No, not silly, but I do think you're imagining it. Doesn't like you . . .' He frowned and shook his head. 'Jacqueline's a good sort. I should be sad if you didn't try to get along.'

'I do try. But what about Kensington? Can't we move back?'

Hugh put down his book and eased himself forward in his chair. He smiled at her lovingly and she thought how dear he was with those lively eyes and his turned-up mouth. He came and knelt before her, and rested his head against her belly. She stroked his hair, then leaned over and kissed it, breathing in the smoky maleness of him.

'I thought you were happy here,' he said. 'It certainly makes me happy, having you in this house all to myself.

And it feels the right thing to be here, looking after Mother. It's part of the reason she's recovered so well actually. The doctor says she's in much better spirits.'

'Oh,' Isabel said, considering this. 'Of course, she must like having her son back.'

'And I don't think you'd be so delighted with Kensington when the baby comes. Think of those stairs for a start.'

'I suppose so,' she said doubtfully. 'I miss my friends, that's some of it. I haven't seen Vivienne for months. Or Berec.'

'I know. But they'd be at work all day even if you were up there. Maybe not Berec, but, well, somehow I don't see Berec with a baby.'

They smiled at each other at the thought.

'I think here would be best, Isabel.' And there was something very definite about the way he said it. 'When the baby's born you'll thank me. Try it and see. I think there's no better place in all the world.'

She thought about this, bringing up a child in the country, the benefits of the nursery upstairs. It should look very nice once it had been brightened up and the cot brought out of the box room.

'Hugh?' He'd returned to his book.

'Mmm?'

'You know the box room at the end of the landing.'

'What about it?'

'What's in the one beyond, the one your mother keeps locked?'

'Old things of hers, I don't know. I've never looked.' He returned to reading his book.

Jacqueline brought round some precious wallpaper samples and Lavinia Morton picked out a new design: a little girl with big eyes curtseying to a boy who was doffing his hat. Isabel secretly liked one with giraffes better, but her mother-in-law pronounced them 'daft-looking', and she was paying, so that was that.

The rolls of paper miraculously arrived late in November, and Cooper, the local handyman, was summoned. A big man who didn't say much, he seemed to be used to Mrs Morton's constant interference, for he would simply nod and carry on regardless. After he'd hung the paper and touched up the paintwork, a big rug in surprisingly good condition was brought out of the box room, as well as the cot. Finally Jacqueline appeared one day with a wicker bassinet she'd borrowed. 'You'll need this for Baby when he's tiny,' she explained to a puzzled Hugh. 'He can't go in the cot straight away, he'd roll between the bars.'

Isabel had not been allowed to assist much, but one afternoon when she climbed the stairs to fetch a book, she went to the door of the new nursery and peeped inside. It really looked very pleasant in the afternoon light, though it would be too chilly for a baby, she feared. An electric fire stood ready by the grate, but she wondered if this would be enough. She was finding the house very cold in winter after London. It must be its closeness to the estuary and, beyond, the great expanse of the North Sea.

The question began to bother her. Next to a chest of drawers, the bassinet stood ready on its stand. Where were the blankets Hugh's mother had found in the box room? She pulled open the drawers one by one, but there were only the piles of little clothes. Perhaps they were in the airing cupboard on the landing?

She pushed the last drawer shut and went out to the

bathroom, where she opened the big doors of the airing cupboard and stared at the shelves of neatly pressed linen. On a shelf above her head she thought she could see the blankets. If she stood on the bathroom chair she would reach them easily.

It was her scream as she fell that brought the household running.

The murmur of distant voices. 'She's coming round,' someone said loudly and she opened her eyes to see a woman's face – Jacqueline's – close to hers. It was dark and something heavy lay across her forehead. She reached up a hand and touched wet cloth.

'Leave it,' Jacqueline commanded, adjusting the flannel. Liquid trickled in Isabel's eyes and she blinked it away.

'Is she all right?' Here was Hugh's face looming into view and there was his mother peering past him. Isabel was lying on their bed and the curtains were drawn. Her head hurt. She tried to change position but Jacqueline ordered her to lie still.

'The baby,' Isabel said, her hands going to her belly.

'Darling, we're waiting for the doctor,' Hugh told her. He was sitting beside her on the bed. 'You must have hit your head.' He bent and kissed her cheek. 'What were you doing, climbing on chairs?'

She started to sob quietly. Her head ached and she was anxious about the baby. She stroked her belly and prayed for a movement. There was none.

The doctor arrived and examined her, the stethoscope cold against her skin. There was a swelling on one temple, which he prodded gently. When he left her alone in the room, she could hear the murmur of voices out on the landing, but not what they said. Soon afterwards Jacqueline entered with a glass of water and an aspirin. 'Lie still, everything's all right,' she said and went out again. Isabel wondered vaguely when Jacqueline had arrived. She felt so confused, and desperate. Why didn't the baby move, and what had they been talking about outside? She tried to sit up, but this set her head throbbing horribly and she sank back onto the pillow.

'You've given yourself quite a bump on the head, my dear, and you're concussed,' the doctor said when he'd returned. 'However, I don't see any point in moving you.'

'But the baby?'

'A nice little heartbeat there. A bit fast, but then he's had a shock, too.'

'Why doesn't he move?'

'I expect he will soon, you mustn't worry. But no more climbing for you, young lady.'

Only later, when she began to feel the child stirring inside, did she allow herself to cry with relief.

Everything changed after that. It was as though they united against her. Jacqueline came every morning for the three days the doctor recommended that Isabel stayed in bed. Apparently, she'd trained as a nurse towards the end of the war and certainly she knew exactly what to do, helping her out to the bathroom and keeping the room orderly and cheerful. Gradually the headache eased, but Isabel still felt tired and slept a great deal. On the third morning she felt much better and decided to get up.

Jacqueline chose some clothes for her.

'I can manage by myself now, thank you,' Isabel protested.

'Of course you can,' Jacqueline said and withdrew. Isabel tried to hook a stocking over her foot and wished she hadn't sent her away.

Downstairs, she discovered Hugh to be shut in his study and her mother-in-law out somewhere. She remembered that McKinnon & Holt had sent her some editing she ought to finish, but it wasn't in the dining room where she'd left it. She looked for it in the drawing room, Jacqueline trailing around after her, asking her how she could help. Finally, she knocked on the study door and went in.

'Isabel, my darling,' Hugh said, rising from the desk. 'Should you really be up?'

'I feel quite tired, still,' she said, pushing her hair back from her face, 'but I can't lie in bed for ever.'

'God, that bruise!' he exclaimed, examining her forehead.

'It doesn't hurt so much,' she told him. 'Only looks bad. Have you seen that script I'm supposed to be working on?'

Jacqueline had appeared at the open doorway and Hugh threw her a glance of appeal. He said, 'You're not to worry about that. We've sorted everything out.'

'What have you sorted out?' Isabel asked him. He was talking in riddles.

'I spoke to Stephen on the telephone yesterday morning,' Hugh said. 'I told him you couldn't possibly do the work.'

'I sent it back to his secretary,' Jacqueline said. 'That was right, wasn't it, Hugh?'

'Perfectly right,' Hugh said.

'But it's mine,' Isabel said. 'You didn't ask me.'

At this, Hugh became impatient. 'Really, Isabel, I don't see how you could have carried on. It's only someone's book. I had a quick look myself. It had no merit in it. I found it rather ponderous.'

'But I was working with the author on it. Hugh . . .' She glanced towards Jacqueline. She felt she could hardly speak freely whilst the other woman stood there.

'I ought to go and do some shopping,' Jacqueline said, and left, shutting the door.

'Hugh, it's my work – I wanted to do it.'

'I know, I know,' he said, hands raised in a mock gesture of surrender. Then: 'Listen to me. You are in no fit state to work,' he told her quietly. 'And as your husband I have decided you need to rest. Stephen was perfectly reasonable. He sees the sense of it. When the baby comes you won't have time, anyway.'

'What did you tell Stephen?' she said angrily.

'We simply agreed that it was sensible for them not to send you any more work. My dear, you must take care of yourself and rest, like the doctor says. It's only another month to wait.' He came and put his arms round her. 'Our own little baby, just think.'

Chapter 25

Emily

When she was swimming, Emily felt ecstatically free. The pool was streaked with light from the curved glass roof and she, too, felt made of light as she slipped with ease through the dazzling water. Lost in the rhythm of her stroke, she only registered the other swimmers as passing shapes. She forged on, length after length, turning as she needed to with a slow twist of her body. Her thoughts no longer raced anxiously, but quietly drifted.

She needed this brief respite. The next day, according to the rumour machine, a restructuring of the company was to be announced. The atmosphere in the office was horrible. All the talking and worrying wouldn't make much difference, Emily believed. She coped best by staying away. Swimming was blissful.

She pondered with pleasure the coming evening – a party with Joel Richards after work. He was always doing something interesting – going to a talk or a launch event or the latest movie – and she found his company stimulating. He had a great many friends, and a whole black book of media contacts, so she told herself it probably meant nothing special when he asked her to go with him. He was always relaxed on social occasions, good at the small talk, but she sensed a more intense side that intrigued and excited her. He watched people as though he was measuring himself against them. It was ambition, she supposed, but a quite different sort of ambition to Matthew's. No, it was pointless to think about Matthew, she told herself fiercely as, her forty lengths done, she ducked under the ropes and swam to the steps. Matthew had not been in touch and she must try to forget him.

'You're my plus one,' Joel told her, smiling, when he presented his invitation at the Guildhall that evening. They were ushered down yards of marbled corridor into a vast, high-ceilinged hall already packed with people, talking, drinking champagne and eating canapés. The occasion was a big anniversary for a magazine Joel wrote for, and this had to be the most glamorous party of the summer. *Everyone* was here, Emily thought, spotting George, who waved back cheerily before continuing to chat up a slim blonde woman he had virtually pinned to a wall. Not that she was acting as though she wanted rescuing.

The speeches started up and went on and on. Emily didn't know any of the names from the past that were mentioned or the magazine's in-jokes, and it wasn't getting any cooler, so she slipped through the crowd to the back, where there was more room and chatted quietly with a young woman trying to soothe a tiny baby in a sling. As she jiggled him up and down, there was a strange, desperate look in her eyes.

It was here that Joel found Emily after the speeches finished in a smattering of exhausted applause and people started to drift off.

He smiled vaguely at the young mother when Emily introduced him to her. 'Shall we go?' he asked, and Emily told her goodbye.

'Why on earth would someone bring a baby here?' Joel remarked as they headed for the cloakroom. 'It's too hot for the poor thing.'

'She didn't think it would be that bad,' Emily said. 'She told me she'd just gone freelance from the magazine, but didn't want to miss the party. I felt sorry for her.'

'They certainly didn't look like they were enjoying it.'

'No,' Emily agreed, 'but I'd feel the same as her. I'd go bananas at home on my own. I don't know how my sister does it.' She glanced sideways at him, wondering whether he was interested, but he didn't respond.

Outside in the cool night air, Joel said, 'Would you like something to eat?'

'I'd love that,' Emily replied. 'It'll take my mind off tomorrow. It's likely to be a bit nerve-wracking.'

As they sipped wine and waited for pasta and salad, she explained about the expected redundancies. All the time she was aware of his warm gaze as he listened.

'You'll be all right, I'm sure,' he said, touching her arm. 'I don't suppose it would help if I rang up your boss. "Don't sack my editor or I'll leave with the book I haven't finished yet!" Shall I say that?'

'Don't you dare ring anyone,' she told him, laughing. 'I'd be so embarrassed.'

'They won't let you go, Emily,' he said, 'you're too good at your job.'

'That's sweet of you. I'm not sure they take account of that in the boardroom. We're just worker ants, statistics.'

In her heart of hearts she didn't believe the decision-making was that basic, but these days she found herself veering from optimism to worst scenario in the space of a minute.

'Anyway, there's no point dwelling on it. How is the book you haven't yet finished?'

'Ah, the great oeuvre. I've cleared some time over the next month to get to the end. Then there'll be revision and a bit of fiddly fact checking. After that, Jacqueline will have to read it.' From the face he made, she saw he wasn't looking forward to that bit.

'Have you shown her Isabel's memoir yet?' she asked.

'Not yet,' he sighed. 'That's one item on my very long list.'

'Quite a big item, though.'

'You are a very demanding editor,' he said, waving a finger at her.

'Isn't that a good thing?' she smiled.

'Probably. Hey, that looks like our food coming. I don't know about you, but I'm starving.'

Later he walked her to the bus stop where there was a long queue of people waiting. The bus came almost immediately and everyone surged forward.

'I'd better go. Thanks for a lovely evening,' she said, looking up at him. He was standing very close, and when she leaned to brush her lips against his cheek he pulled her towards him and kissed her firmly on the lips.

'Ring me tomorrow when you know what's happening,' he murmured, narrowing his eyes, and she smiled and nodded, a pleasant burning feeling spreading up inside. 'Don't spend the night worrying. I'm sure you'll be fine.'

'Thanks,' she said, making a face. 'I hope you're right.'

When she climbed onto the bus she hardly noticed where she sat as the doors shut and the bus moved off and she caught a last glimpse of Joel walking away. Tonight was the start of something, she thought. She leaned her forehead on the cold window and remembered the touch of his lips, warm and deliberate; no hesitation there – he knew exactly what he wanted, judged the moment and took it. And she wanted it too; there was no denying that she found him immensely attractive. But she couldn't help remembering when Matthew first kissed her, a shy, clumsy affair on the evening they'd first met, after he walked her to the Tube station.

Chapter 26

Isabel

There was nothing to slow down time like waiting for a baby. Christmas, the doctor had said, but 1951 turned to 1952 and each day dragged. The child had dropped in the womb, and now Isabel felt like an overripe fruit waiting to burst. Outside it rained perpetually and the dark sky and the dankness of the garden through the window compounded the feeling that her world had boiled down to this little existence.

There came a day when she awoke feeling not herself. The baby wasn't moving again and this, combined with the frequent tightenings of her belly, made her peevish. There was a stickiness between her thighs, which she was too embarrassed to mention to Hugh, although it worried her.

After breakfast, her husband shut himself in the study as usual. His mother sent word downstairs that she had a cold and was staying in bed. All morning, Mrs Catchpole was out of breath from going up and downstairs to answer her commands. Restless, uneasy, Isabel prowled the gloomy house. Once she went to look at the nursery where everything lay ready now, the bassinet on its stand, three soft blankets folded inside. The room was gloomy.

Even when she switched on the ceiling light the weak bulb made little difference to the feeling of oppression. She switched it off and withdrew. As she raised her arm to close the door, her belly tightened again, more sharply this time, and she gasped with the discomfort, then cried out as the discomfort intensified to pain. Finally the contraction faded and she managed to get herself downstairs before the tightening began again.

'Hugh,' she gasped, falling against the study door. He opened the door to find his wife on all fours, crying out like an animal.

'Bloody hell, what do I do?' he cried. 'Mrs Catchpole, Mrs Catchpole. Get out here, will you?'

Mrs Catchpole had been quartering a freshly killed chicken, and later Isabel was to remember her running from the kitchen wiping blood from her hands. Under the woman's instructions, Hugh somehow scooped up his wife and hauled her upstairs to her bedroom, where she had to stand waiting whilst Mrs Catchpole spread old sheets and towels across the bed. Hugh was dispatched to fetch the midwife. It was the last time she was to see him for many hours.

She lay down the bed, tensed against the next pain to grip her, her breathing shallow with panic. She'd known it would hurt, but was it supposed to be as bad as this? As the pain gripped her once more, she tried to roll over on her front, but Mrs Catchpole held her on her back and pushed a wad of towelling between her teeth. 'Here, bite down on that, it'll help.'

At last, one of the midwives – a short portly woman in uniform and with a battered Gladstone bag – arrived and took charge. Her orders, delivered in a soft country accent, brooked no argument and Isabel gave into her gladly.

The contractions were coming with increasing speed and intensity, and now she entered a long tunnel of pain from which she could sense no way out. The midwife's commanding voice became something to cling to in the nightmare. She breathed when she was told to, dumbly spread her legs to be poked and prodded in her most tender parts. Daylight faded and she sank into a kind of delirium as exhaustion took hold. Worse was to come.

'She's pushing,' came the midwife's voice. Who was she talking to? 'Maybe it won't be long now.' But it was. The electric light flickered. The contractions went on uselessly. The midwife inspected her again, then went to the door.

'Best telephone the doctor, tell him to hurry,' she heard her say to someone outside. She was dimly aware that the door kept opening and the bedroom seemed to fill with staring faces. She didn't care, just wanted the pain to stop. The youngish doctor arrived, pushed her knees apart and jabbed her painfully. Shreds of conversation flew about with increasing urgency. She heard the click of the doctor's bag, the splash of water, and the scrape of metal passing over metal, then the doctor laid hands on her once more. There followed a sharp, hot sensation, then she shrieked aloud at the most unimaginable agony as the forceps entered her. 'Push, my dear,' the midwife insisted, squeezing her hand. 'Hard as you can.' Isabel took a great breath and pushed.

She must have passed out briefly, because the next thing she knew was a sharp smell searing her nostrils. 'Mrs Morton, dear,' the midwife was saying, 'the head's out but you must push again when I tell you – not before, there's a good girl,' and she tried to obey, though she had no more strength. *Again. Ah.* There was a twisting feeling as the baby passed out of her.

She lay, too exhausted to speak, hearing murmured conversation, and finally the thin wail of a baby. Time passed. She was wondering vaguely what was happening when her belly was gripped by another contraction. And now the midwife's anxious face appeared and her warm hand pressed down on her abdomen. Someone kept calling her name, but she felt so relaxed and woozy that she couldn't answer. All she wanted to do was sleep.

When she came back into consciousness it was dark and the air smelled different. There were voices murmuring in the distance, but she couldn't hear what they said. She moved her lips to call out but no sound came. Once more she slipped back into darkness.

The next time, she woke to a pain throbbing low in her body. She opened her eyes. Daylight filtered through a grey curtain. A high white ceiling. Was she awake or dreaming? Awake, she decided finally, realising she was in a hospital bed. And now she started to remember. The baby . . . She wanted to move, but something was holding her left hand down. She tried to lift her other arm, but it was a moment before the limb obeyed. She felt clumsily for her belly through the sheet. The familiar hard roundness had gone; there was only a mound of her own soft flesh, and the throbbing pain. She groaned and tried shifting to get more comfortable.

The curtain twitched open and a young woman's face

appeared. 'Mrs Morton? Oh good, you're awake. I'll get Sister.' She withdrew and the curtain fell back into place.

An older nurse appeared now and gave orders to the younger one. Isabel was fussed over, her temperature taken and, to her embarrassment, the sheet pulled back and her gown lifted briefly. The sheet was tucked back in, pinning her down.

'Is my baby all right?' she asked, her voice hoarse.

'Doctor will be along later,' was all the young nurse said. 'Now swallow this down, there's a good girl. It'll help with the pain.'

'Is my husband here?'

'He was, but Sister sent him home. The poor man was exhausted.'

'Oh dear,' she said, feeling guilty that she'd caused his tiredness.

'There now. Try not to move at all. I'll be back shortly.'

She lay for what seemed like a long time, the pain dulling now, drifting in and out of sleep. She knew she ought to be worried about what was wrong with her, worried about the baby, but somehow it was easier not to. As the medication got to work, she felt only a blissful peace.

She was woken again by the violent swish of metal curtain rings and blinked in the sudden harsh light. When she raised her head, she was horrified to see a group of men in white coats staring down at her.

'How are we, Mrs Morton?' The most senior and grizzled of them wore a lugubrious expression. 'You don't mind my students, do you?' The three younger men stared as though she was some peculiar specimen in a jar. One had an awful crop of acne. Another kept pulling at

his collar and clearing his throat. The third was ghostly
pale with red-rimmed eyes and the slight tremor of the
hungover. Her fingers plucked at the sheet.

'What's the matter with me?' she asked the senior
doctor. 'Where's my baby?'

'There's no need to be anxious.' The doctor sat on the
bed and felt her pulse. 'Your daughter's doing very well
now, though we were worried for a while, I must say.'

'A . . . girl?'

'Yes,' he said, surprised. 'Didn't anyone tell you?'

She shook her head. A girl, she'd never imagined a girl.
Her mother-in-law had said the Mortons only had boys.

'I suppose I should ask to see her.'

'Of course you should,' he said, squeezing her thigh
through the bedclothes. 'All in good time. She's been very
poorly, but has rallied splendidly. How are you feeling?
You have been in the wars. Forceps, haemorrhaging.
What a lot of trouble you've given everybody.' The
students all tittered.

'I didn't mean to,' she said, not sure if he was serious.
'I'd like very much to see my husband, please. And I am
rather hungry.'

Hugh was allowed in to see her during the afternoon.
He'd brought some early daffodils from the garden,
which a nurse whisked away to arrange in a vase.

'Oh Hugh,' she said, when he bent to kiss her, holding
his face against her cheek. She was so relieved to see him
that she started to cry. Everything hurt and she felt so
weak, and sort of empty, too.

'My dear, dear girl,' he whispered into her hair. 'I
thought I'd lost you.'

'I don't remember what happened,' she said in anguish and so he told her.

The baby had taken a little while to breathe after the birth, and after she came to life at last, the midwife experienced difficulty delivering the placenta. Rather than wait for the ambulance to come from Ipswich, the doctor had taken mother and baby to the hospital in his car, she laid out on Hugh's lap in the back seat, the midwife in front holding the child.

'It was the worst moment of my life. I really thought you were going to die,' he said quietly, hugging her.

'All I remember is wanting to sleep,' she said, stroking his hair.

During the afternoon she was allowed out of bed and Hugh pushed her in a wheelchair to a room down the corridor which was full of small cots. A nurse brought the little girl swaddled in a sheet for them to see. Isabel was appalled. The baby's head with its twist of black hair had been squeezed into an odd shape and there were dark bruises on her temples where the forceps must have gripped it. She put her hand out to touch the small red face, but the nurse stayed her.

'It's because of germs,' she explained. 'It won't be long. She's doing very well, drinks plenty of milk, don't you, my precious?' The baby gave a lopsided yawn. Its eyes rolled unfocused. Isabel thought she'd never seen such an ugly creature.

'She does look a little strange,' Hugh said doubtfully.

'That's not unusual with forceps, the poor little pet,' said the nurse, and bore the baby away.

As Hugh wheeled Isabel back to the ward she tried to shut out an awful thought. That it was difficult to see how the misshapen scrap of humanity she'd just seen had anything to do with her.

'Hugh, are you sure there isn't anything wrong with it?'

'You mean with her,' Hugh said, looking at her curiously. 'No, they say probably not.'

The following morning when Isabel awoke, she was upset to find her breasts were bursting with milk, and after some consultation amongst the staff the baby was brought to her. One of the nurses showed her what to do, but Isabel hated clamping this small alien creature to her tender breast, and although the baby made feverish attempts at sucking it didn't seem to get any milk and cried, and the whole thing was painful and somehow disgusting.

'Never mind,' the nurse soothed. 'I've a nice bottle of warm milk here.'

Isabel handed the baby back with relief.

They bound her breasts to make her comfortable, but it was several days before the engorgement went away. Meanwhile the baby was brought to her at regular intervals so she could give it the bottle, and she watched its greedy gulping with alarm.

Hugh wanted to call her Lorna, a character from one of his favourite novels, *Lorna Doone*. Isabel agreed, liking the sound of the word – Lorn. It sounded like forlorn, which was how she felt.

The weather on the day Hugh fetched his wife and daughter home was the grimmest Isabel could remember for a long time. The short January day was dark and stormy. Rain beat down so hard the windscreen wipers were useless. The baby in her lap cried weakly the whole journey and Isabel was terrified that the car would crash and kept telling Hugh to go slower. 'We're already going at the pace of a funeral procession,' he snapped back.

Hugh's mother was waiting in the hall with Mrs Catchpole and her daughter Lily to greet them. They all stood around as though uncertain what to do next.

'She's a funny little thing,' Mrs Catchpole said doubtfully as she peeped into the bundle of blankets. The baby's cries were no longer weak, but growing in volume and urgency.

'She's hungry,' Isabel said despairingly. 'But she's not allowed anything more for two hours.'

'Poor little mite,' Mrs Catchpole said. 'Now if you don't mind, I ought to get on with lunch.'

'Why don't you take her upstairs?' Hugh's mother suggested. 'Put her in her cradle. She'll soon settle if you leave her. Babies need to learn who's boss.'

But Lorna didn't settle.

An hour of crying later, Mrs Catchpole was asked to warm a bottle of milk. Lorna drank it down quickly but still she cried. As the daylight faded, she cried more and louder. Isabel fed her again and winded her, changed her nappy, and put her down to sleep. She cried. Isabel picked up her again. She still cried. Mrs Catchpole filled the baby bath. Perhaps warm water would soothe her.

Naked, little Lorna looked sinister – like a witch's manikin was Isabel's unpleasant thought, her skin the colour of uncooked sausage. She wasn't plump like the pictures of the blond babies in the doctor's surgery in London. Her eyes were navy, not clear blue. When Isabel had first bathed her in hospital, there had been a crop of fine dark hair over her back, and although thankfully most of this had fallen off, patches of it remained, giving the impression of mange. The bruises were healing and the squeezed length of her head wasn't so pronounced, though it was still an odd shape. Looking at her now, Isabel felt a swell of pity for this little creature. She waited for a rush of love. Nothing.

This was her secret, the secret she'd had to keep for the two weeks since Lorna had been born. She did not love her child. She didn't know what was wrong with her, what to do about it. She couldn't even tell anyone. During that fortnight she'd been cosseted at every turn. Nurses had helped her feed Lorna. They'd taught Isabel how to wind her after the feed, how to bath her and dress her. They'd packed Lorna away in her cot to sleep in another room so that Mother could rest or chat to the other women and generally bask in the wonderful aura of new motherhood. Life had passed very pleasantly, and yet she'd felt completely numb about the whole experience.

During visiting hours she'd received Hugh, and once or twice her mother-in-law who, on the second occasion, brought Jacqueline, whose London couture drew the interested eyes of the other new mothers. Once her own mother had come, travelling all the way from Kent by train, staying the night at the Mortons' and returning the following day. Isabel had thought she looked grey and drawn, and didn't dare speak of her own miserable secret. After her mother said goodbye, Isabel felt so completely alone that she cried for an hour.

The truth was, she felt that there was something missing. She couldn't be a proper woman, could she, if she didn't love her child.

She looked around at the other mothers, nursing their babies or cradling them to show older brothers and sisters. She'd seen some who were anxious about whether they were doing things right, or weepy with hormones and tiredness, but what she hadn't seen was indifference. Why did she, Isabel, feel no reaction at all to her child except pity?

'Why were you unlucky enough to get me?' she whispered now to the infant on the towel on the bathroom floor. The baby stared up at her, puzzled. She was a child with a perpetually puzzled expression.

Oh dear, she'd get cold. Isabel wrapped her carefully in her towel and picked her up to take into the other room and dress. She was halfway through doing so when she discovered that Lorna's nappy needed changing again and had to take her back into the bathroom.

Never mind, she told herself dully. *It's not the baby's fault. It'll just have to be done.*

Finally, Lorna was clothed in nappy, gown and jacket and laid in the bassinet to sleep. Isabel withdrew, closing the door, then went to her own room and lay down on the bed. She wasn't tired exactly, just lacking in energy. She lay staring at the ceiling for some moments, thinking of nothing.

There came a short cry from the other room, but she hardly noticed it. Anyway, the nurses had told her crying was healthy. There came another cry, longer this time, and soon the baby was complaining lustily, then yelling at full volume. Still Isabel lay there.

Hugh opened the door and put his head round. 'The baby's crying,' he said.

'We're to leave her,' she replied. 'That's what they said at the hospital.'

His brow wrinkled. 'How long for?' he asked.

'I don't know.'

'Oh,' he said, and withdrew. The baby cried on. Isabel stopped hearing it and slipped into sleep.

'For God's sake.' Hugh had come in again. 'I'm trying to read, Isabel, this noise is terrible.'

Isabel raised her head sleepily. She had no idea how much time had passed, but the baby was still crying.

'I can't do anything about it,' she said. 'Maybe your mother can help.'

'My mother says she doesn't remember about babies,' he said, ruffling his hair. 'I'm afraid it's up to you.'

'I suppose I'll go then,' she said, swinging her feet onto the floor.

'Right. Thanks,' he said. He held the door open for her, and while she went across the landing to the nursery he hurried away downstairs.

She opened the door. The noise immediately doubled in volume. She stared into the cradle. Lorna had kicked off her bedclothes and lay, fists clenched aside her head, her screaming mouth a great chasm in a purple face. Her whole body was convulsed.

Isabel stood watching, her arms crossed, feeling completely detached. It was how Hugh's mother found her a few minutes later.

'For pity's sake,' Lavinia said. She picked Lorna up, laid her against her shoulder and rubbed her back. Lorna gave a great belch, mewed a little and fell asleep.

Chapter 27

Emily

The day of the redundancies was horrible, as though an Angel of Death passed overhead. No one knew who would be chosen. Everybody sat at their desks pretending to be busy. All appointments had been cancelled. The office was abuzz with rumour. Two of the sales reps had lost their jobs, it was being whispered. There were fewer bookshops to visit these days. In Emily's office, four pairs of frightened eyes looked up when Gillian's assistant Becky came in, her small young face pale with shock; it was not to summon any of them to Gillian's office, however, but to inform them that George had been made redundant.

'Oh no – poor George!' Emily was puzzled, and genuinely sorry. George had been the golden boy, the charming one. She wondered who he'd annoyed, or perhaps that wasn't the way things worked. It was pointless speculating, but if George was gone it might be herself next.

But it wasn't. As she stood with the rest of the department in the boardroom later, she felt a delirious relief, yes, but also anger and survivor's guilt. They studied a chart on the plasma screen, full of boxes with people's names, the company's new reporting structure. Reference Books downstairs had suffered the worst. Emily didn't know the people there. At one level it all made sense, as readers had moved online, but it must be awful for the staff and she wondered where they would find new jobs.

George, when she went to see him in his office – how he'd managed to get his own office had always been a mystery – tried to be philosophical. He lounged in his chair, feet on the desk, talking with his usual bluff about new opportunities and irons in the fire, but then the bluster petered to a halt.

'I'm glad you're all right,' he told her, ruffling his blond curls. 'You seem to be making your mark.'

'Do I?' she said, cautious, not sure if there was sarcasm in his tone, but she was surprised, too. She hadn't for a single moment seen things this way.

'You've brought in some good authors. People like you.' He did sound sincere. Then he spoiled it by adding, 'I guess they couldn't afford me any more.'

Typical George. Why did he need to bolster himself in this way? Still, it was probably true. They'd been doing a similar job, she and George, but she'd long suspected that he was paid more than her. Not that she had proof. She'd always felt she'd break some unspoken rule at Parchment if she discussed her salary with others. The company was quite old-fashioned in many ways. But other people dropped hints. Still, out of the two of them it was she who had a job.

'How much longer will you be here?' she asked.

'End of the month,' he said, starting to play with an annoying clicking-ball toy he kept on his desk.

'Well, I am sorry. I hope they have given you a good package.'

'Not at all bad,' he said. 'Once I'd mentioned the magic word "lawyer". I'll be all right for a while. Take a bit of a holiday, perhaps.' The balls clicked slower and she saw past his bravura to the fear underneath. He didn't want her sympathy, however. 'I'll hook up with you later,' he said, picking up his mobile, and she nodded and opened the door.

Something stayed her. 'By the way,' she said, 'it wasn't you who sent me flowers on Valentine's, was it?'

He smiled at her as he put the phone to his ear. 'That would be telling, wouldn't it?'

Back in her office she found that several of her authors had telephoned. She rang them back to assure them her job was safe, and then spoke to Joel.

'Phew!' he said, when she imparted the news. 'I told you you'd be all right, but it's a relief, isn't it, to have it confirmed.' They talked about meeting up, but both of them were busy for the next couple of days and Joel was going away on Friday for what he called a 'writing week'.

'A friend of mine has a cottage in Gloucestershire. They've got a cat that's allergic to catteries, so the deal is I stay there while they're away and feed the mog. There's no Wi-Fi and the mobile signal's pathetic so I can just concentrate on my writing.' He told her he aimed to write two chapters and draft the final two in the time, which struck Emily as an impressive feat.

'I'll be home Sunday week,' he went on. 'Would you like to come over for supper when I'm back? Tuesday perhaps?'

'Tuesday would be great,' she said.

'You have my address, don't you? I'll give you directions. It's very easy.'

Emily had plenty to keep her mind off waiting for Joel's return. Tobias delivered some revisions to his novel. There was an auction for a brilliant new memoir by a Korean-American writer which involved a great deal of discussion and rejigging of balance sheets, and which in the end she acquired for Parchment in a rush of terrific excitement. Concentrating on this meant that more routine work stacked up and she had to work late to clear it.

For the moment there were no more mysterious packages.

Emily gazed about the huge open-plan loft, Joel's home, admiring the high Victorian windows, the soaring peaked ceiling.

'Unicorn House used to be a printworks,' Joel explained as he splashed white wine into big goblets and handed her one. The wine was chilled, fruity and delicious, the glass so fine it rang when she knocked it accidentally with her nail. 'It closed down a few years ago and they turned it into flats.'

'That makes sense of the decorations on the staircase!' she exclaimed. Bits of old metal font had been set in patterns on the walls of the entrance hall and all the way up the stairs to the second floor. 'I wondered if it spelled out anything.' She'd tried to make out words as she climbed, but decided it was random.

'I suppose it would have been too complicated,' he said, 'but some quote about the passing of time might have been appropriate, don't you think?'

'Mmm,' she said, sipping her wine. They were standing in the kitchen area, which took up half one end of the flat. Halogen light reflected off grey metal and granite. A narrow dining table and six high-backed chairs in pale ash filled the other half, then there was a lounge area delineated by a long L-shaped sofa. The walls were lined with bookshelves, rows and rows of them, filled with books, floor to ceiling. In a corner, against a partition wall, a workstation was built in.

'And here's my bedroom,' he said, showing her a neat spartan room with a large geometric painting over a low white bed. For a moment his hand brushed her shoulder in a way that might or might not have been an accident. 'Next door's the bathroom,' he said, moving on swiftly, 'and this bedroom's the spare.'

'It's all really beautiful,' she sighed, as they returned to the kitchen. She loved the skylights with their sunscreen glass. As he stood at the stove, frying chicken, she perched on a bar stool, drinking her wine and watching the changing patterns of the evening light.

'So how was Gloucestershire? Did the cat behave itself?' She liked the way he looked tonight, in a soft linen shirt, half-covered by a butcher's apron, his sleeves rolled up to reveal tanned arms. He couldn't have been inside the cottage working all the time then.

'I hardly saw the blessed thing,' he said. 'It ate the food I put out, unless it was some other beast that came through the cat flap every night. The writing went really well. I started work at eight every morning, kept going till lunch, walked a mile to the shop and back, then got in another couple of hours' work after tea.'

'So you did your chapters?'

'I did,' he said with a satisfied grin. 'I'm on the home straight.'

'Wow!' She was genuinely impressed.

Just then, the doorbell rang and they both looked up. 'Who's that?' Joel said as he went to open the door. A young woman with a swathe of glossy blonde hair caught up in a pretty comb stepped inside.

'Hi, I'm Anna.' Her light voice had a transatlantic twang. 'Oh my God, you guys are cooking dinner. I'm so sorry but I need help really badly,' she said to Joel, tweaking a stray piece of hair back into the comb. 'I've just moved in and there's something wrong with the faucet in the kitchen. It won't turn off and there's going to be a flood any moment.'

'I can have a go,' Joel said. 'Do you mind, Emily?'

'No, of course not,' Emily replied. 'Poor you, I hope he can fix it,' she told Anna.

'That's so kind,' Anna said. 'But can you please hurry?'

'Back in a minute,' Joel told Emily, pulling the door to behind him.

Alone in the flat, Emily checked the chicken, which looked nearly done, and measured rice into water simmering in a saucepan. A green salad waited ready on the side. She took it across to the table, already laid. Then she wandered around the room, touching the books and examining some prints of contemporary architecture on the partition wall. It was odd that there were no photographs of family or friends, she thought, looking about, just one of Joel by himself in a graduation gown.

On a shelf near Joel's workstation was a row of books with *Joel Richards* printed on the spines. She hadn't known he'd written so many: there was the one about the Angry Young Men, several histories of big companies, one copy leather-bound. She recognised a tie-in book of a television series about Britain in wartime from a couple of years ago. There was no author's name on this one so she picked it up and found *Joel Richards* on the title page inside. All this confirmed to her that Hugh Morton's book was an important one for his career, definitely a step up from all these others. She felt she understood him more as a result. He was further ahead in his ambitions than Matthew. All Matthew had so far were some poems in anthologies. She knew he longed to have a collection published, but this would be a while off for him. She put the book back on the shelf. Joel was being a long time, she thought. Perhaps the flood was quite bad.

She came to his desk and leaned across it to read the labels of some box-files on a shelf above. MORTON, each one said in neat capitals, giving dates or a subject: CHILD-HOOD, CORRESPONDENCE WITH K. AMIS, PHOTOGRAPHS, JAPAN. When did Morton go to Japan? On the desk was an open laptop and a pile of notes in Joel's neat handwriting. She was unable to stop herself reaching for them, but in so doing she accidentally jogged the laptop, causing the dark screen to brighten. She hadn't known it was still switched on.

Amongst the array of icons on the computer's desktop, one labelled *Morton Biography First Draft* caught her eye. It was very tempting to take a peek.

Just as she was moving the cursor towards it the flat door clicked open and she turned, caught in the act. But it must have been a draught, for there was no one there. Her relief was short-lived, for she heard voices on the stairwell, Joel's low one and Anna's high American drawl, and then approaching footsteps.

Quick as a wink she left the desk and by the time Joel walked in she was back at the stove, draining the rice.

'Everything's ready,' she told him calmly.

'Thanks,' he said, slightly out of breath. 'Mission accomplished. I'm sorry about the wait.'

She prodded the bits of chicken and said nothing.

'The tap was just stiff, so I easily sorted that out, but Anna's removal men had parked a chest of drawers in a stupid place so I had to shift that for her.'

'I bet she was grateful.' She suspected that it wouldn't be the last time Anna would ask for help.

He came up close behind her now, so she felt the warmth of him – and her body was suddenly light, electric. There was a brief moment when she was sure he was going to touch her, and she was disappointed when he merely switched off the extractor fan, then moved past, opened a cupboard and reached for plates.

They sat opposite one another at the table and helped themselves to salad. He poured more wine and the tension she'd felt eased. Perhaps she'd imagined it. Joel talked about a new TV script he was being invited to write and Emily filled him in about the situation at work, and soon they began to play a game of looks and touches and gestures that needed no words. Beneath the table his foot brushed against her ankle. The food was delicious, though she didn't eat much of it. There was something spicy in the chicken that made her lips feel hot and tender.

Part of her wasn't sure about Joel; he didn't reveal much about himself, but she did find him madly attractive, so perhaps everything would work out. She had to get over Matthew, she couldn't stay on her own for ever. And no one at work need know about it. The thought of secrecy was exciting.

'Shall we have pud later?' he said, clearing the plates. 'It's just something from the chill counter.'

'You mean you haven't been slaving away to make it from scratch?'

'No, should I have done?' He came back to the table, his brow wrinkled.

'It was only a joke, really,' she said hastily. 'Later would be lovely.'

'Sorry,' he said. 'I've been focusing on other things. All the writing and not speaking to anyone for a week, it does your head in.' He rubbed his face. 'Shall we go and sit more comfortably? I've got some photographs to show you for the book.'

They took the wine over to the sofa. Joel switched on a lamp and fetched a box-file from the shelf above the workstation. Sitting beside her, he set it on the coffee table in front of them and opened it. It was half-full of photographs, some loose, others in plastic wallets or envelopes.

'These are the ones I'd really like to use,' he said, drawing out a plastic wallet. 'A lot are Jacqueline's, but not all. You know this one, of course.'

He was sitting very close now and their fingers touched as she took the photograph from him. It was a smaller version of the family portrait that was on the wall of Jacqueline's drawing room.

'They look like a perfect family, don't they?' she said, studying it once again.

'Textbook,' Joel agreed. 'Here's the war hero.' It was

one of Hugh Morton as a very young man in a pilot's jacket. Others included a snapshot of a baby in a huge old-fashioned pram – Hugh again – then a few of him in middle age. In one he wore a corduroy jacket and a shirt with wide lapels and was giving a speech at a micro-phone. 'The British Council trip to Japan in seventy-five,' Joel explained. Another was a still from an interview on a well-known chat show in the 1980s. There were several prints featuring Jacqueline: one in an evening dress, one in headscarf and dark glasses on a café terrace, snow-capped mountains rising behind. Emily examined for some moments a studio portrait of Jacqueline as a girl of about twenty. She was pleasant in appearance, but her clothes were staid, and there was something stiff and undeveloped about her. Who would have predicted that she would turn into the blooming wife and mother of the family group portrait?

'That's it, really, I think,' Joel said, checking the other packets in the box.

'None of Isabel?' Emily asked. 'You will use the wedding photo, won't you?'

'If I can persuade Jacqueline. I did mean to show you this other one.' From a small brown envelope he brought out a black and white print. He turned it over to check the writing on the back, then held it between them. 'An office party, I reckon.' He pointed to a very young woman at the edge of the photograph. Emily took it from him and angled it towards the light.

It must have been from around 1950, judging by the clothes and the hair. Isabel's mouth was partly obscured by the glass she held, but the eyes were large and lively. She was quite small in stature, Emily saw, and very stylish, with fine features. Her hair waved vibrantly around her heart-shaped face. Next to her, unmistakably, was Hugh, saturnine, smiling secretly. On her other side was a man with fair hair and an intelligent, boyish face. 'That's Hugh's publisher, Stephen McKinnon,' Joel told her. 'This here . . .'. The third man in the picture had a clever, foreign-looking face, Eastern European, possibly. He was speaking in an animated fashion to an older woman with a double chin. 'Alexander Berec. He was a poet. And that, I believe, is Trudy Symmonds, who worked for McKinnon.'

It was amazing to see all these people she'd read about. Emily stared again at Isabel. She thought how pretty she looked, interested and vivacious. Here was a young woman confident about who she was and what she did. She looked completely at home amidst these literary people.

'It's the only photograph of Isabel that Jacqueline has given me, so we'd better put it in. And apart from that wedding photo you found, it's all I have.'

'What about Isabel's birth family? Would they have some?'

'Of the twin brothers, one is dead and I haven't been able to trace the other,' Joel said. 'Her sister, Lydia, would have been too young to remember her, so I haven't tried to find her.' He set about replacing the photographs in the box and shut the lid. 'Don't forget there was a shortage of film then, and it would have been expensive.'

'It's strange, though,' Emily said. 'You'd think that someone would have something.'

'Don't let's worry about that now,' Joel said softly.

She found herself looking into his eyes, which were

warm and passionate. Gently he took her wine glass, then leaned in and kissed her mouth. She closed her eyes, and as they kissed more deeply, all her doubts went tumbling.

Chapter 28

Isabel

It was March, though Isabel hardly cared. After lunch, she stood at the nursery window watching the trees sway in the wind. The garden was patched with spring flowers, gold, indigo and white. In the field beyond the fence the donkeys stood resolute, facing into the breeze. Behind her, after much grizzling, the baby had fallen asleep, and this meant for Isabel a brief respite from the grim exhaustion of looking after her, the constant pretence. She turned from the window and stooped to gather up a discarded garment. The movement was enough to cause little Lorna to stir, and Isabel froze, anxiously waiting, until the child sank deeper into sleep.

She was two months old now, Lorna. Her head was a normal shape, the black hair had fallen out and a blonde fluff had replaced it. Her body, too, was smooth and hairless, and though plumper, she remained pale, long and wiry. The navy eyes had lightened to forget-me-not blue.

'She's a Morton in every respect,' Hugh's mother would say proudly, cradling her granddaughter, and Isabel could not disagree. She was surprised to see how Mrs Morton's expression softened as she gazed at the baby and wished she too could summon that warmth. But when she looked at Lorna, the lump she felt in her throat was not motherly tenderness but a deep sadness.

She tried her best. She spoke lovingly to the child, she returned Lorna's rapturous smiles. She was always gentle with her, but increasingly, the sadness she felt was so heavy that everything was too much effort and her movements were clumsy. When Lorna woke crying from her nap, sometimes Isabel's feet rooted to the spot, and it would be a moment before she could force herself to go to her. She'd read in a Maisie Briggs novel once of a mother consumed with longing to see her child asleep in the next room, and wondered why she never felt that about Lorna. She still dared not speak of it to anyone, especially the young doctor, who was a bachelor, for fear of being seen as unnatural, a monster. Perhaps they'd take Lorna away, and she didn't want that either.

A monster. Twice, maybe three times, there had been moments that frightened her most of all, when despair turned to rage at the baby. Once, exhausted, she snatched up the crying child, intending to shake her, but some inner voice stayed her. No, that had terrified her.

At least now all was peaceful. She slipped past the sleeping Lorna and out of the room, towards the stairs. A sound made her glance back down the landing, where she saw something odd. The door at the far end, the door to the box room, was open, and it creaked as it moved in some draught. And through the doorway could be seen the back view of Hugh's mother, shutting and locking the door of the inner room, the room that Isabel had never seen.

Isabel ducked into the open doorway of her bedroom

and peered round, only drawing back when Hugh's mother came out of the box room. She heard the woman go into her room, then the sound of a drawer opening and closing within, before she emerged once more. Isabel heard her wheezing breath as she walked past Isabel's hiding place and made her way downstairs. Isabel waited a moment or two before closing her bedroom door. Then she lay on the bed for some time, thinking. Her curiosity about the little room was piqued, and this time she knew where to look for the key.

She did not have long to wait for an opportunity to present itself. Hugh was away, and the following day, Hugh's mother announced that she was going out to visit some friends. A taxi duly arrived mid-afternoon and bore her away. Lorna was asleep and Isabel finished helping young Lily Catchpole hang up a load of baby washing on the line. Lily was always cheerful and a tireless worker. Quite how they'd all have managed without her, as Hugh's mother was wont to say with a meaningful look at Isabel, nobody knew. The job done, it was easy for Isabel to gather up a pile of ironed sheets for the airing cupboard as an excuse to steal away upstairs.

Since Hugh's mother had recovered from her illness of the previous summer, Isabel rarely entered her room. All was familiar: the chilly pale blue of the walls and hangings, the room so orderly, the old silk bedspread so perfectly draped that it was difficult to imagine that anyone slept there. A window had been left open and she shivered in the cold air. If ever a room reflected the personality of its owner it was this one, she thought as she glanced round, rubbing her arms for comfort as much as warmth.

Despite Lavinia Morton's pious sentiments about her dead husband, there was no sign here that he had ever existed. Both wardrobes, when she peeped in, contained only the widow's clothes. On a lace mat on the dressing-table were arranged two silver-backed brushes and a matching hand mirror, but no photographs. There was only one on the mahogany chest of drawers, but that was of Hugh in RAF uniform.

She looked about, nervous with guilt, wondering in which drawer the key might be kept. The dressing table first. Two deep drawers, one either side of the mirror, contained her mother-in-law's vast collection of asthma remedies and other medicine. There was no sign of a key. The small top drawers of the mahogany chest contained gloves and jewellery cases, neatly stacked. She slipped her fingers down to explore the base, but could feel only the bottom of the drawer. A couple of the bigger drawers she tried were full of clothes of an intimate nature and she closed them quickly, starting to lose her courage. She was about to abandon her quest when she saw something she'd missed. Set under the bevelled top of the dressing table was an extremely shallow drawer, of the sort that had no handles. She gripped its underlip and pulled. It moved with a low squeaking noise, exactly the sound she'd heard the day before.

Within was a tray divided into compartments. In some were strands of costume beads, coiled like sleeping snakes, others held items of make-up, hairpins or similar. And in one long narrow compartment at the front was a large key. Her fingers closed over it. It was heavy and cold, but as she held it, it warmed quickly in her hand. She pushed the drawer shut with a strange feeling of excitement.

The box room itself was not kept locked so she let herself in and closed the door behind her. The door to the hidden room stood before her. The key turned easily enough. The door opened inward. With a terrible feeling of trepidation she pushed it, heard a sigh as it scraped over carpet.

Up until that moment she hadn't really thought about what might be inside. She didn't think it could be anything really horrible, but maybe something valuable that couldn't be left about, unguarded. Or a secret store of something that one might have got in trouble for having during the war – black-market goods, perhaps. But there was nothing like that. The room was dark inside, a curtain drawn across the little window, and there was a smell of musty cloth mixed with a faint fragrance of flowers. It was empty but for cupboards, a large chest under the window, and an upright chair with arms. She stood for a moment feeling the ambience. Perhaps it had been the sigh of the door over the rug that made her think of whispering voices.

She stepped forward and unlatched the nearest cupboard. Immediately the door burst open and something rustling billowed out. Cloth, light and lacy, floated wide. The cupboard was full of dresses, gorgeous dancing dresses, she saw, reaching for the hangers and bringing them out one by one. Tulle and silk, satin and organza, all redolent of waltzes and orchestras and handsome young men in elegant suits. And again that flowery fragrance – the simple scent that might be worn by a young girl to her first ball. She opened another cupboard. Clothes again, but this time more exotic: fancy-dress costumes. A Spanish flamenco dress in cobalt blue; a long

straight garment made up of strips of colour like a rainbow, with a netting cape stitched with pearl-beads shaped
like raindrops; a long low-waisted dress with a girdle like
a lady's on a mediaeval tapestry. She pulled them out one
by one, poring over the beauty of them, the exquisite
embroidery of one, the thousands of sequins on what
looked like a mermaid's tail on another. They were
gorgeous. Greedy now, she opened more cupboards of
more clothes, then her eye fell on the trunk beneath the
window. She loosed the catch and opened the lid.

Inside were more secrets: a pile of letters tied in red
ribbon addressed to a Miss L. Osbourne – her mother-in-
law's maiden name, Lavinia Osbourne. She peeped at
one. It was signed *All my love, Arthur*. Photographs in
frames of a shy young woman with large doe-like eyes,
not classically beautiful, but with all the loveliness and
hope of youth. Could Hugh's mother really ever have
looked like that, so tender, so radiant? There were pictures
of the young man, too, boyish with a light-coloured
moustache. In one he wore the uniform of an Army
officer. Underneath these, at the bottom of the trunk,
Isabel found a shoebox, and its contents told the rest of
the story. Another collection of letters, this time black-
edged. A pressed flower, the photograph of a plain
wooden cross stuck in a heap of earth amidst other such
crosses. Its poignancy struck Isabel with such force that
she clamped her hand over her mouth to prevent herself
crying out.

This, then, was her mother-in-law's secret: that she'd
been young once and happy, had loved and been loved,
and she'd lost. Here, perhaps in this chair that Isabel sank
into, was where Lavinia Morton, née Osbourne, would sit

and remember the past. Isabel wondered about Arthur, who'd been killed in the Great War, but something stopped her reading the letters. And now coming out of her reverie, she felt deeply ashamed of herself, being here, intruding. What right did she have to pry into an older woman's girlhood secrets?

Quickly but carefully she replaced everything in the trunk, then set about tidying the clothes into the cupboards. Finished, she made sure everything was as before, except . . . She tucked a scrap of indigo velvet back into its cupboard, then backed out of the room, closing the door.

At once the baby's cry came to her ears, and when she let herself out of the box room, she met Mrs Catchpole carrying a screaming Lorna.

'Oh, there you are,' Mrs Catchpole said, worried. 'I can't quiet her. She's been crying and crying.' She thrust Lorna into Isabel's arms. Lorna's crying stopped abruptly and she snuffled into Isabel's shoulder.

'What are you doing, anyway?' Mrs Catchpole asked, seeing the key in her hand. 'The mistress wouldn't like you going in there.'

'You won't tell her?' Isabel asked anxiously, but Mrs Catchpole pressed her lips together in a firm line. 'Mrs Catchpole,' Isabel said, 'please. I – I didn't mean any harm.'

The woman looked her straight in the eye. 'You may not mean any harm,' she said softly, 'but nothing's been the same in this house since you came into it. You need to pull yourself together, Miss, if you ask me. Now let me get on, will you?' And she swept away downstairs.

Shocked and shaken, Isabel, still carrying Lorna,

entered Hugh's mother's bedroom and replaced the key
in its hiding place. The drawer creaked shut, but not quite
flush, she saw with irritation. However, it wasn't possible
to correct it without putting Lorna down, so she gave it
up as a bad job.

Much later, in bed as she prepared herself for sleep, she
mulled over the secrets of the inner box room. She
wondered if Hugh knew about the young soldier who
had died, and speculated about the circumstances of his
mother meeting his father, a London barrister, soon after
the war, when many women who'd lost fiancés had no
chance of finding another. Had her mother-in-law truly
loved her husband, or had he simply filled a gap? She
didn't feel she could ask him: 'Did your mother love your
father?' And how could she frame it anyway without
drawing suspicion as to why she thought to ask it? But
she was haunted now by the young Lavinia Osbourne,
her parties and balls, the true love she had lost. There
seemed no connection between this girl and the hard-
faced, correct woman who presided over this house that
Isabel could not bring herself to call home. No, young
Lavinia Osbourne was no more, a memory to be taken
out and looked at and regretted. How tragic, Isabel
thought, how absolutely tragic, to lose all one's hopes and
dreams in a second's blast of a shell or the thrust of a
bayonet blade.

For most of the previous six weeks, very soon after the
baby's birth, in fact, Jacqueline had been gone, back to
London to live with her husband, who had returned from
Korea, for the time being at least. At first she had travelled back and forth to Suffolk, because Hugh had begged

her to help. Isabel, in the early days after being discharged from hospital, was aware of hushed conversations and anxious looks about her health and whether she was managing, but she couldn't care if Jacqueline was there or not. The other woman was helpful in practical ways, but Isabel could sense her sympathy running out to be replaced first by puzzlement at Isabel's behaviour, then downright frustration.

'Do try to make an effort,' she burst out one day when Isabel wouldn't leave her bed to rescue the crying baby, and although Isabel's response to this was to force herself to get up, she threw Jacqueline such a mutinous look as she passed that the other woman seized her arm and said, 'What is the matter with you?' But Isabel threw her off and went to the nursery. Jacqueline didn't visit for a week after that, until Hugh persuaded her to come back.

The evening after the incident with the box room, Hugh returned from two nights in London to say he'd been to dinner with Jacqueline and her husband. 'Poor Jacqueline,' he told Isabel, as he poured himself a whisky, 'Michael's going out there again any day now. She's dreadfully cut up. I said she should come and stay for a while. I expect you would like the company.'

'I don't need any company,' she told him. She was sitting on the sofa where she'd been trying to read a book, but somehow these days she couldn't take any of it in. She'd get to the bottom of a page and realise she'd have to start all over again.

He was silent for a moment, watching her. 'I think you do,' he said. 'Isabel, you don't seem yourself at the moment. Look at you – I mean . . .' He made a gesture of helplessness.

'What?' she said fretfully.

'Well, I don't mean to be unkind, but your hair. And you used to take such care with your clothes.'

She closed the book and threw it down beside her. 'Hugh, I have a baby. I don't have time for hairdressers and fussing about. Anyway, who is there to look at me?'

'Me?' he said mildly. He put down his drink and came to sit next to her. He took her hand and pulled her gently to him. She buried her head in his shoulder and began to weep.

'I don't know what's wrong with me,' she managed to say between sobs. 'I didn't think it would be like this.'

'We definitely need Jacks,' he murmured.

Chapter 29

Isabel

Jacqueline arrived two weeks later on one of those hot days that trick the world into believing that summer has arrived. Hugh fetched her from the station, and Isabel watched sullenly from the bedroom window as she stepped out of the car, a squarish figure dressed today in a full-skirted yellow dress and a small felt hat. Like a daffodil, Isabel thought uncharitably, turning away. And caught her own puffy-eyed complexion three times reflected in the triptych mirror of her dressing table. She bit her lip, picked up a brush and began to drag it through her hair, then gave up and went to lie on the bed.

One of the windows was open and from the courtyard below she heard Hugh's mother say clearly, 'She's asleep in the garden, the little dear,' then the voices receded as presumably they all trooped through the house into the back garden to view Lorna in her pram. Isabel rolled over and lost herself in the safe warm country of the bedclothes. During the last six or seven days she'd felt mugged by sleep, hardly able to get up at all. The doctor had visited and pronounced her 'run down', but the pills he prescribed only made her feel worse. Hugh insisted she continue to take them, to give them a chance to work. The anxiety of his expression was enough to make her agree. There was something wrong with her, she knew deep down, a spreading darkness that numbed energy and feeling.

Jacqueline, Hugh explained to her, would be living here for the time being, sleeping in Magnolia, which Mrs Catchpole had made ready. It would be easier than her staying with her father. She wouldn't need to make the journey every day. 'Why does she need to come every day?' Isabel had asked Hugh crossly, but this was before she felt so unwell, and now she accepted the situation. Someone was needed to help with Lorna, and Hugh had begged Jacqueline. 'It'll give you a chance to get better,' he told Isabel. Lily Catchpole would help, too, but he and his mother couldn't be expected to get up at night if Lorna cried.

As the spring days passed, the household settled into a new kind of rhythm. Jacqueline managed Lorna beautifully, with set hours for her feeding and sleeping, although Mrs Catchpole, possibly out of some sort of skewed loyalty to Isabel, remarked that babies sorted themselves out by this age anyway. While pleased to have Jacqueline's help, the woman was suspicious about her appearance in the household and her pity swung to Isabel, who only a few weeks before had been the object of her disapproval.

Isabel sensed that Jacqueline was trying to be tactful. She'd bring Lorna to her sometimes and say, 'Why don't you play with her?' and Isabel would dutifully hold her and wonder at her huge blue eyes and her smiles, but when the baby became restless, she'd panic and hand her back. 'What's the matter with her?' she asked Jacqueline once as they stood in the nursery. 'What have I done to make her grizzly?'

'She's probably teething, poor lamb.' Jacqueline's eyes had a soft glow as she took the fretting child from its mother, then her nose wrinkled. 'Oh, I think it's her little derrière.'

The way she knelt to lay Lorna down to change her, then slotted her limbs back into her clothes, was deft and tender. I can't do that, Isabel thought, with a sharp pang of jealousy and, what was worse, I don't want to do that.

'You are marvellous with her,' she said bitterly, watching Jacqueline's busy fingers.

'She's a good little baby,' Jacqueline said, stroking the child's hair. 'Aren't you, darling?'

'I suppose it's practice for when you have your own.' That came out without thinking and she was ashamed, for Jacqueline's hands stilled momentarily.

'Yes, well,' Jacqueline replied. 'That's not likely to happen soon, with a husband who's always away.' Her voice shook slightly and Isabel understood that there was something deep there, unspoken. 'You're so lucky, having Hugh at home most of the time.'

'Yes, I suppose,' Isabel said, going across to the window to look out. She thought of Hugh, shut in the study downstairs. With Jacqueline's arrival he wore a great air of relief. He could retire again to write without worrying about what might be happening in the house.

She sometimes wondered how the novel was going, for he no longer spoke of it to her. Perhaps he thought she wouldn't want to know, or that she wouldn't have anything useful to say. She knew she hadn't shown any interest recently. She felt a little better today, but some days she lay in bed, unwilling to get up, feeling as though she was at the far end of a long dark tunnel. The rest of the world might not exist. She wasn't even curious about whether Hugh took notes about her any more. They'd be very boring, if he did. There wasn't really anything for him to write about.

'I'll take her downstairs, shall I?' Jacqueline was scooping Lorna up and rising to her feet. 'Perhaps we could walk down to the village with the pram. We need some more disinfectant.'

'I suppose so.'

'Oh come on, getting out will pep you up a bit. It's an awfully nice morning.'

This was the height of her days now, Isabel thought as she went to fetch a cardigan. Walking a pram down to the village shops. She rarely thought about her life in London. That was only a colourful dream that had vanished with the reality of marriage and motherhood. She was Mrs Hugh Morton now, not Miss Isabel Barber, and she had different responsibilities. Probably there would be more babies. Maybe sometime she would throw off this feeling of despair and learn the trick of happiness. Other women seemed to. She was lucky, she knew she was lucky. Poor Jacqueline had no child and wanted one. Jacqueline effectively had no husband much of the time, either, and was lonely. Only once in the past few weeks had Isabel known a letter to come from Michael. Jacqueline had taken it away to read in private. Isabel had not thought to ask her about it.

* * *

It was around this time that a letter arrived for Isabel with a French stamp on it. The handwriting was familiar, but she knew no one in France, so she didn't realise until she opened it that it was from Vivienne. She read it with complete amazement.

It began *Ma chère Isabelle* and went on cheerfully:

That's about as much French as I'm capable of writing at the moment, but I imagine that I'll soon learn. You'll be so surprised, but I'm living in Paris now. It all happened so fast that I've had no time to tell you. As you know, I got a job at King's College, London, hoping that I'd get on better there than at the college where I did my PhD, but I hated it, Isabel. The work was interesting, much more so than at the previous place, but the men weren't what you'd call friendly and I was terribly worried that the same thing would happen all over again and that I'd end up with some sort of breakdown. Anyway, I had to give a paper on X-ray developments at the Royal Institution, and there were two Frenchmen in the audience who were crystallographers at a French government laboratory. A woman friend of mine from Cambridge introduced us and we had such an inspiring conversation about our work! The next thing I knew, they wrote and offered me a job in Paris, and so here I am! I only have temporary digs at the moment, but I'll send you my permanent address when I have one. In the meantime, it might be best if you wrote to me at the laboratory, address above. Isabel, they're so kind to me here, it's a completely different atmosphere. I'm sure that I'll be happy. You must come and stay with me . . .

Isabel was both amazed and delighted to read this. Poor old Vivienne, unappreciated here in England but with so much to offer, seemed at last to have found her feet. But how sad that she'd had to go so far. Isabel wondered when she'd ever see her again. Paris at this moment seemed to her the other side of the world. Despite her happiness for her friend, she felt a stab of envy.

One Friday morning at the beginning of July, Hugh Morton burst into the kitchen to be greeted by what he muttered was 'a scene from hell'. Through swirling steam and smoke he could make out his wife at the stove, dressed in an apron and a most unbecoming mob cap, stirring a great vat of – he wrinkled up his nose – boiling nappies. Young Lily Catchpole was plucking a duck, its feathers flying everywhere. At that moment, Lily's mother entered bearing a box of vegetables pulled from the garden, a great streak of earth down her face. Outside, Lorna started to screech in her pram.

'Baby's awake,' Mrs Catchpole said to Isabel unnecessarily. 'And Miss Jacqueline's gone out.'

'I'll go.' Isabel laid the washing tongs across the pot and hefted a bucket of freshly boiled and rinsed nappies.

Hugh stood in the doorway, completely ignored, which he wasn't used to.

'Hello?' he said loudly. Three heads turned and three pairs of eyes blinked at the strange sight of a man in the kitchen.

'Sorry to interrupt. I came to tell you I've finished,' Hugh said to Isabel. He looked triumphant.

'Finished what?' called Isabel, halfway to the back door with the bucket.

'My novel, of course.'

She stared at him, a blank look on her face. 'Well, that's

simply marvellous,' she said finally, and disappeared out of the door.

Outside, the crying immediately rose in volume and intensity. Isabel dumped the dripping bucket on the flagstones by the mangle, wiped her hands on her dress, then went over to the pram. She flicked up the muslin canopy and undid the pram cover. Lorna had kicked off her sheet and her long thin body was stiff with rage.

'Shut up,' Isabel said through clenched teeth. 'Just shut up.' She gripped the pram by its handle and had to force herself not to shake it. Anger ripped through her. Anger at what? She didn't know. It had been simmering all morning, since she woke and remembered that Jacqueline was going up to Town to meet some friends. Friends! When could Isabel see friends? The pressure intensified as she dealt with the nappies. The smell was revolting and nothing she used, the Milton's, the laundry blue, ever seemed to get them really clean. And lastly there was Hugh, who with his appearance in the kitchen, had summarised in a few words how wide the gap between the two of them lay.

'What on earth's the matter?' Hugh's voice came from behind her, disapproving, annoyed. 'All I said was—'

'I know what you said.'

Lorna stopped screeching, then took a long breath and started once more.

'Oh, do pick up that child.'

She leaned into the pram, unclipped the harness and lifted Lorna out. The screeching ceased, but the baby continued to sob, sitting up in her mother's arms and looking about. Seeing her father, her mouth widened in a gummy smile.

'Shh, shh,' Isabel said, resting her cheek on the child's hair.

'Well, I thought you'd be pleased.' Hugh was speaking. 'Of course, I say the book's finished, but I mean the draft. It's all typed up but I need to go over it, make little adjustments. Still,' he started pacing about, 'I can't tell you the relief to have mastered the body of it. It's lived with me for, I don't know how long.'

'I'm glad you've finished it,' Isabel said. She forced her anger down. 'You've worked hard, I've seen that.' It's my book too, she thought. He wouldn't have written it without me. All those notes he'd made about Nanna, the suggestions that she had put to him about it. Not that she could say any of this, of course. He'd deny it, say he didn't understand what she meant.

'*The Silent Tide*. D'you like the title?' he said, and she nodded. 'I've put my all into writing this. Every last drop of blood. I don't know what Stephen will say, of course, but if he doesn't like it I'll take it to another publishing house.'

The mention of her old boss was enough to make Isabel's spirits plummet deeper. She knew the book was good. At least, the parts she'd seen were extraordinarily so. McKinnon & Holt would take it, they'd be mad not to. But it wouldn't be Isabel herself who would edit it. It would be Trudy or that new man, what was his name, Richard someone. And she would be here washing nappies.

'Of course he'll like it,' she said. 'Would you like me to read it?'

'Mmm? Oh, I expect you can. Not yet, though. I'll be working on it.' And so he brushed her off with a few casual words. He, who had always trusted her advice. She was only his wife now, he didn't want her to be anything else. These were her thoughts, and she was plunged into misery.

Chapter 30

Emily

Emily was pleasantly surprised by the growing excitement at Parchment about Tobias Berryman's novel. When she'd finished going over his rewrites she suggested she pop in to see him at Duke's College to deliver them as she'd be passing near Bloomsbury after lunch. She could have sent them in an email, of course, but she was curious to see Tobias on his home territory, and anyway there was something else. A small, secret part of her that she tried and failed to ignore hoped to catch a glimpse of Matthew.

She climbed the marble steps of the college to a scrolled Corinthian portico where a pair of glass doors swung inward to admit her. The reception area was familiar: she used to meet Matthew there occasionally and memory brought a sharp pang of regret. She didn't know where Tobias's office was so she asked the young woman in a hijab who sat behind the counter. Following her directions, Emily turned down a long corridor and went through a door into a cloister that bordered a grassy quadrangle. Entering the building at the far end, she followed the signs to the English department.

Tobias's office was a scholar's haven, smelling delightfully of old books and brewing coffee. They arranged themselves on comfortable chairs with the manuscript on a low table in front of them. The novel was finished now, but Emily thought it needed a final polish.

'Usually it's the other way round, me advising other people how to write,' Tobias quipped as he poured coffee. She was surprised to see he was nervous, though he was trying not to show it.

'Don't worry,' she told him. 'The book is already wonderful but there are a few things you could consider doing to make it perfect.'

As they discussed her notes she was impressed by his responses. He was protective of his work, yes, even a little arrogant about its merits, but that was all right, she could respect that. She approved of the fact that he was used to the hard toil of writing, the discipline of rewriting. He understood the need to beguile the reader and to make the language sing.

'I'd love to be a fly on the wall at one of your creative writing workshops,' she sighed when they'd finished and she gave him the script and her notes. 'It would be really interesting.'

'Do you write at all yourself?' he asked, and she shook her head.

'I don't think I could. Anyway, I never have the time.'

'No excuses. Real writers make time,' he said. Again, she glimpsed that passion in him, the same passion Matthew had. She had a feeling in her bones about Tobias's book, and about him, too, and was relieved that others in the office agreed with her. Nobody could guarantee anything in publishing, whether critics and readers would like a book, whether it would win prizes, whether it would hit some lucky streak – or sink without trace. All she could say was that this one deserved to do well.

She was still thinking about this after they said goodbye: making time for what you felt passionate about. Matthew's face came to mind, and as she walked back the way she came, through the door out into the cloister, part of her was looking for him. So she was hardly surprised when, in one of those odd coincidences, she glanced across the grassy sward and saw him.

He was strolling in her direction, his old messenger bag hooked over one shoulder. She stopped, unable to move. There was something so dear and familiar about him. She loved that rolling walk, the casual way he tucked his thumb in his jeans front pockets, his intent expression, as though he was exercised by some deep philosophical problem – which, she smiled at the thought – he probably was. She waited in the cloister, knowing he'd see her in a moment, if only he'd look up.

Then someone shouted, 'Matthew!' and he turned, alert to the girl dashing across the grass to him. She was dressed in a green floaty tunic over jeans. Her long dark hair flew out behind. It was Lola, the girl who had been selling the poetry books at the party where she first set eyes on Joel. Matthew waited for her. Emily couldn't see his face but she imagined him smiling. Lola reached his side, panting, her face alive. She threw her arms about him and kissed him, then they linked arms and went off together, back in the direction from which she came. Neither of them saw Emily. She might just as well have been a ghost.

She felt at first shock and confusion, and then an appalling sense of loss washed over her. She hardly knew how she got herself out of the building and onto the street. Travelling back to the office, anonymous amongst the crowds on the tube train as it roared through the dark tunnels, she was grateful to feel a numbing oblivion.

That evening, at home in Hackney, she tried to rationalise her feelings. What was she doing, seeing Joel when she obviously hadn't recovered from Matthew? She didn't quite know, only that life had to gone on and she was very much attracted to Joel. She'd told him about Matthew, of course, it seemed only fair, and he'd said, 'Poor you. These things take time to get over,' so she'd thought he understood.

They'd been together several weeks now, but he'd only been here to her flat once. It was partly that it felt very small and poky after his, but partly that it still felt strange having another man here. She hadn't slept with Joel, but if and when she did, she couldn't envisage it being here with its memories of Matthew. She was always comparing them to one another and decided they were as different as chalk and cheese.

Their attitude to their writing was a case in point. Matthew was a romantic in the sense that he had to write, it was as natural to him as breathing. He'd die if it was forbidden him, she sometimes used to think. Joel's attitude was much more pragmatic. He earned his living by his pen and was good at it. But it was what the writing brought him that he liked most of all: the kudos, the lifestyle, the people he mixed with. He had a shiny gloss, sophistication, she felt good being with him. He appreciated nice restaurants, fine wines. He liked to know what was going on in the world and to be sure of his place in it.

And here she was moving along with him, meeting interesting people and learning the media gossip, his gloss
rubbing off on her. With Joel she lived for the present,
and the present was where she was happy at the moment.
She was sensible enough to know that this state of things
couldn't last for ever. It never did. But for now it would
do. She hadn't mentioned the relationship at work. The
news would go round like wildfire. No, it was best to
keep it quiet.

   She thought of Isabel long ago, a lifetime ago, marrying her author, imagining that her life would broaden
out. Instead, how small and sequestered it had become.
She still hadn't sent Joel the latest tranche of Isabel's writing, which was lying on her coffee table. She'd hardly had
time to read it herself and then she'd been so upset about
Matthew that she hadn't been able to concentrate. She
reached for it now, and despite her fears was quickly
caught up again in Isabel's story.

Chapter 31

Isabel

For three weeks in July 1952 no rain fell. The days wore on, hot and humid, the nights giving little relief. Each morning Isabel had to drag herself from sleep to plough through the day's routine. Lorna developed heat rash from her plastic pants and was fretful. The whole household was bad-tempered. Hugh's mother sneezed all the time and the hay fever somehow set off her asthma. Hugh stayed in his study all day with the household's only electric fan, revising his novel. On several occasions Mrs Catchpole packed picnics and Jacqueline drove Isabel and the baby to the east coast, once to the small seaside town where Isabel and Hugh had spent their short honeymoon in the wood-framed beach house belonging to Aunt Penelope's Reginald.

Isabel always looked forward to these days out. Not only were the offshore breezes a relief from the heavy heat and the claustrophobia of Stone House, but she was shameless about leaving Lorna with Jacqueline and walking off along the shore by herself, where the dramatic pounding of the waves and the desolate cries of seabirds lulled her thoughts. It was as though the sea scooped all thought and care out of her, the *shh* of the water across the shale scraping her mind as clean and empty as one of the scallop shells she'd pick up and rub smooth inside with her thumb. She'd wade knee-deep into the freezing cold sea and welcome the numbness it brought, not minding if the waves soaked her skirt, so that Jacqueline, for whom a day on the beach involved protective headscarves, windbreaks, rugs and sunglasses, would scold her on her return for ruining her clothes, as though she were a child.

On one of these days, she walked further than usual until she came to where a narrow river ran into the sea. She stood looking down at the water where it swirled fast and deep. On the far shore, more beach stretched away invitingly, but there was no obvious way to reach it. She turned to go back, then paused. Somewhere up beyond the dunes must be a sandy lane running parallel to the beach. If she followed it back in the direction of where she'd left Jacqueline and Lorna, she'd find the house where she and Hugh had honeymooned. Curious to see it again and remember their happy time together, she walked up the beach carrying her shoes and waded across hillocks of loose white sand, avoiding the wiry seagrass that hurt her feet.

Eventually she came to it, a white wooden bungalow set in a square of scrubby garden, behind a paling fence. The house was as pretty as she remembered it – prettier, in fact, for it had acquired a new coat of white paint since she'd seen it last. The door of the glass porch was open. Perhaps Penelope was staying there now, she thought. She stopped in the lane to fasten her sandals, her hair blowing in her eyes.

When she looked up again, it was to see a man

standing in the porch watching her, one arm resting on the open door. He waved and called her name and she stared in puzzlement. Then she recognised him.

For a moment she was transfixed in amazement and then, 'Stephen!' she cried happily and walked quickly to meet him.

'Isabel, by all that's wonderful, what on earth are you doing here?' he asked, laughing as he shook her hand.

'I could ask you the same question,' she said, pushing back her wild hair. As his gaze passed over her, she was conscious suddenly of her bare legs, scrubbed face, the splashes of seawater on her old cotton dress. He, on the other hand, might just have returned from strolling round the town, for he was dressed in flannel trousers and a white shirt with a loosely tied cravat. His boyish features were so much more tranquil than in London, his normally pale complexion browned by the sun. The expression on his face was not disapproval of her looks, however, but admiration.

'Come in, won't you? Your aunt's lent me the place for a couple of weeks. Or rather, Reginald has.'

'You, on holiday?' she said, stepping inside. She remembered him as always too busy for holidays.

'I've left Philip in charge. Doubtless there'll be a disaster, but I imagine the business will survive.'

'Isn't Grace with you?' she asked him. 'I should like to say hello.'

'No, she isn't,' he said shortly. He showed her into the little sitting room. It was as pleasant as she remembered it, with a picture window looking out across the dunes and an alcove stuffed with books; on a shelf over the fireplace were scattered shells and lucky stones – ones with holes through them. A manuscript lay strewn on the sofa. Even in a gale this house had felt cosy.

'I oughtn't to be long,' she said suddenly, recalling Lorna and Jacqueline.

'Is Hugh here?' he asked. 'You must both come and have tea, or a drink, perhaps.'

She shook her head and explained that she'd left Lorna with a friend on the beach. He said, 'In that case I'll walk along with you. I should like to take a look at your daughter.' In the hall, he took up a jacket and hat from a row of hooks and opened the door for her. They walked together along the lane in the lee of the dunes towards the promenade, below which she'd left Jacqueline.

'How is everything?' she asked. 'I often think about you all.'

'We wondered how you'd been. None of us have set eyes on you for so long. Maisie Briggs keeps asking after you and no one ever knows where anything is. As for Cat . . .' He frowned. 'One can't tell her a thing without her bursting into tears.' He glanced at her and smiled. 'You've been busy with the baby, though, and we were sorry to hear you'd been so unwell.'

'Unwell – is that what Hugh has told you?'

'Why, yes. Reading between the lines, he's been quite worried about you.'

'What does he say is wrong with me?'

Stephen appeared rather embarrassed. 'Oh, I don't know,' he said. 'I've obviously got the wrong end of the stick. I've only seen him occasionally, when we get invited to the same do's. I expect that'll change once the book is finished. It's most eagerly anticipated, you know. Your husband is spoken of as quite an upcoming talent.'

'Is he?' she said, pleased. 'That's marvellous. I didn't know.'

'You've read the book already, I imagine. What's it like?'

'I've read some of it,' she said cautiously. 'I know I would say this, but I genuinely think it's very good.'

'I'm delighted.' Stephen thrust his hands in his pockets and began to look about at the glory of the day, whistling tunelessly. Then he broke off, saying, 'And how are you really? I must say, you don't look at all ill. Motherhood must be suiting you.'

'It's kind of you to say so,' she said dully, 'but it isn't really. You don't have to be gallant. I look an absolute mess.' They were walking up a concrete slope onto the promenade now and there were the steps down to the beach. She stopped, suddenly lacking the will to go on. And felt his hand on her arm.

'Not a mess, my dear,' he said gently, looking into her face. 'But you do appear – well, different, if you don't mind me saying. A little forlorn, if that doesn't sound rude.'

'Yes, that's it, forlorn,' she sighed, covering her face with her hands. She remembered how close the word sounded to the sound of Lorna's name.

There was an old bench nearby, and he drew her across to sit beside him. For a moment her thoughts were too tangled to allow her to speak again. Forlorn was exactly how she felt, but angry, too. Angry and restless.

Finally, she said, 'Don't let us speak of things like that. Tell me what's happening in London, Stephen. Cheer me

up. I'm such a country bumpkin now, I hear nothing.
How's Aunt Penelope? I'm always meaning to write to her
or telephone . . .' To tell the truth she hadn't even thought
of Penelope for ages. Until today, seeing the house once
more. She had only really known her aunt for that short
stretch of time she lived with her. It had always been
patently obvious that the woman had her own life and
wasn't suddenly going to turn into the ideal of a generous
aunt. That opportunity, if it had ever existed, must have
been lost when Isabel was still very small.

Stephen said, 'Your aunt, as always, has been most
generous. And she manages Reginald superbly. He hardly
tries to interfere with the business at all.'

'Do you think he'll ever divorce his wife and marry my
aunt?' Isabel said.

'He has two children. It doesn't suit his wife to be
divorced. But there's more to it than that. From what I've
learned of Penelope, she's perfectly happy with it being
that way.'

'Is she?' Isabel asked, interested.

'You look surprised. Perhaps you don't know the story
of her first marriage. It's not a deadly secret.'

'No one's ever told me,' Isabel said. 'I know my parents
believe her divorce to be scandalous, that's all.'

Stephen said quietly, 'She married young. Jonny Tyler
was a drunk and a bully. Your aunt didn't discover this
until it was too late.'

'She defied her mother to marry him. I know that
much.'

'I think the reason why was very complicated. And in
matters of love, we always think we know best. I'm afraid
I was the same.' He suddenly looked immensely sad and

Isabel didn't know what to say, but he immediately went on, 'I only came to know Penelope well after the marriage had ended. But Jonny, I knew. He was an editor at Ward and Atkins, where I got my first sales job, just before the war, and the stories one heard. He was a mess by then, old Jonny. Missing the mark all over the place. They had to let him go.'

Stephen took a packet of cigarettes from his pocket, extracted one and lit it. The match fell flaming to the ground. Isabel watched it char a stalk of dry grass and go out.

'I hardly remember him, I'm afraid,' she said. 'Aunt Penelope and my mother had little to do with one another even before the divorce.'

'So I gather,' he said. 'I first met Penelope at a literary party. She was seeing one of Jonny's writers by then, which was the last straw for her and Jonny. And then the man died – the writer, I mean – and left her the house in Earl's Court and a very tidy sum of money. The best thing that ever happened to her, she told me once. It meant she could be independent. So you see, she's quite happy not to marry Reginald. Nor does she have to be alone. She has the best of all worlds.'

'Oh.' This was all new to Isabel, and answered a number of questions that she hadn't known to ask. It explained something of her aunt's aloofness, the background of Penelope's friendship with Stephen and how she came to be connected to the world of literary bohemia. None of this, of course, would make a ha'porth of sense to Isabel's parents. Close they might have been when young, the abyss that separated Penelope and Pamela now was deep, possibly uncrossable.

'She's a very wonderful person, your aunt. She's helped me so much in a number of ways and, well, all this business with poor Berec . . .'

'Berec!' Isabel said at once. 'Has something happened?'

Stephen wore an odd expression on his face. 'I'm sorry, I imagined that you'd have heard, that Hugh might have told you.' He seemed uncertain how to go on. 'Look, it's best if you ask Hugh about it. You shouldn't hear it from me.'

'Hear what? Stephen, you can't do this. Tell me. I'll have to know sometime.' She remembered the last time she'd seen Berec, after he'd been assaulted. Was it related to that?

'Perhaps it slipped Hugh's mind,' Stephen went on, frowning. 'Surely not, though. Isabel, Berec has gone to prison.'

She was silent, shocked, trying to absorb this. 'Why?' she gasped. 'Was it to do with money?'

'No, I wish it were. We might have been able to help him better. I hope this doesn't shock you, my dear, but it's for gross indecency. With another man. Apparently Berec and this man were living together and some nosy blighter thought to make something of it. The police raided the flat one night and, well, both of them have been locked up.'

Isabel put her hand to her face. 'Poor Berec,' she murmured. 'I'd simply no idea.' Then she said, 'Myra. I had my doubts that Myra existed. We never met her, did we?'

'Oh, Myra existed all right. Still exists, I mean. It's just it turned out that she is really a he. Mikhail, the man's name is. He worked as a waiter in one of the big Hyde

Park hotels, I forget which one. They lived on very little, by all accounts. Penelope knew, or rather, she guessed. Penelope never asks questions, you know that.'

'She's the only person he allowed to help him,' she said, and explained to Stephen about visiting the flat in Bethnal Green.

'I heard about that,' Stephen said. 'Penelope said she couldn't get out of him who was responsible. In my darkest moments I think it might have been Mikhail himself. He's quite a troubled character from what I hear.'

'That's appalling,' Isabel whispered, hardly able to take all this in. Penelope, Berec. Who else was there? What else had her upbringing sheltered her from? Berec had been such a friend to her, had helped her in so many ways out of pure generosity of spirit. She'd never thought of him as anything but a friend, nor he of her, she acknowledged now, her thoughts racing on. What did men do together? she wondered, and felt her face grow hot, as though Stephen might be able to read her mind. She knew some men were called pansies, but had never given the matter further consideration. Others were obviously not pansies, but didn't like women or were frightened of them. Like William Ford, the ageing writer, or that man, whatever his name was, at her friend Vivienne's laboratory, who persecuted her. Vivienne. Someone else she'd neglected. How useless she was to everyone, so wrapped up in her own petty troubles.

'ISABEL!' The angry voice cut through her misery. She looked up to see Jacqueline labouring along the promenade towards them, Lorna clamped to her hip, wide-eyed, hair in a fluffy halo, like a baby ape. As they approached,

Jacqueline panting heavily, Isabel saw that the make-up on her agitated face was streaked with perspiration.

'How could you?' Jacqueline cried as she reached them and Isabel took Lorna from her. The older woman fumbled in a pocket for a handkerchief and dabbed her forehead. 'You can't imagine how worried I've been. I've been looking everywhere. Sent complete strangers up the beach to search for you.' She barely glanced at Stephen. 'Poor Lorna was quite beside herself, weren't you, precious? Isabel, you are simply so selfish.'

The baby didn't look at all upset and just laid a sleepy head on her mother's shoulder. 'This is Mr McKinnon,' Isabel told Jacqueline. 'Mrs Wood, Stephen. You probably met at our wedding. Jacqueline, I'm very sorry but—'

'And this must be Lorna.' Stephen was smiling at the baby. 'She's very sweet, and very like you, Isabel.' He then looked straight at Jacqueline. 'I think we do know one another already, don't we?' he told her in a soft, dangerous voice. 'We've certainly met in London.'

Jacqueline examined him more closely, an expression of puzzlement on her face and then recognition. And Isabel, astonished, saw the woman's face colour up.

'We might have been to the same party once,' she said in a dull voice. 'I don't properly recall.'

Stephen opened his mouth to speak again, but Jacqueline ignored him and spoke to Isabel instead. 'Come along, I've left everything on the beach and the tide's coming in. Good afternoon, Mr McKinnon.' She turned and walked away.

'Goodbye, Stephen,' Isabel said. 'Come and see us. Please do come.'

Stephen merely nodded. He seems sad, Isabel thought

as she followed Jacqueline's angry figure. When she looked over her shoulder for one last sight of him, he was still standing watching her, turning his cigarette packet in his hands.

'Did you enjoy yourselves?' Hugh asked later, coming into the breakfast room where afternoon tea was laid out.

'Yes, we did,' Isabel said firmly, glancing at Jacqueline, who was making goldfish faces at Lorna in the high chair as she fed her gloop from a bowl.

'Lorna had a lovely paddle, didn't you, precious?' was all Jacqueline said.

'Jolly good.' Hugh smiled at Lorna, sat down and started to pile up a tea plate with sandwiches and cake.

'We saw Stephen McKinnon,' Isabel said, sipping her tea. Jacqueline shot her a look of dislike, which gave Isabel a sense of satisfaction. They'd hardly spoken on the drive home. Jacqueline was furious at Isabel's disappearance and Isabel was cross at being humiliated in front of Stephen. There was something else swirling around, too, something darker that neither of them could even begin to broach.

'Did you now?' Hugh said mildly, taking a bite out of a scone. He could be impossible to read, Isabel thought with annoyance.

'He was staying in Reginald's chalet,' she said.

'Oh really? Did you tell him I'd finished the book?'

'No.' She felt angry with him, for reasons too numerous to mention.

Hugh looked surprised. 'Well, what did you talk about then?'

'Just general matters.' She didn't want Jacqueline to

hear about Penelope and Berec and everyone. On a wicked impulse she added, 'I didn't know you knew Stephen, Jacqueline. Apart from meeting him at the wedding, I mean.'

'I don't know what he was implying . . .' Jacqueline started to say.

The door opened and Hugh's mother came in.

'Ah,' she said, 'the travellers return. Jacqueline, dear, I think you've caught a touch of the sun.'

'Why didn't you tell me about Berec?' Isabel asked Hugh later, viewing him in the dressing-table mirror as she brushed her hair. He was already in bed, reading. 'He's in prison. That's simply dreadful.'

'Oh, Stephen let that cat out of the bag, I suppose,' Hugh said, pencilling a note in the margin of his book. 'I wish he hadn't.'

'Hugh, I needed to know,' she said, putting down the brush. She studied her reflection, her face drawn and thin, the dark shadows under her eyes exacerbated by the poor light. 'He was my friend. Is my friend,' she amended.

'It's all exceptionally sordid. I don't like the idea of you knowing about that sort of thing.'

'I shouldn't worry, I'm pretty ignorant. What I do know is that Berec is a good person. He helped me and I want to help him.'

'Well, you can't. He's beyond anyone's help. That type have to face the consequences of their actions.'

Isabel was astonished. She hadn't known he held such strong views on the subject. 'That's harsh, don't you think?' she gasped.

'I don't feel it is. Now can we leave this unpleasant

subject.' He sounded quite angry, and Isabel's eyes prickled with tears. She hadn't stopped thinking about Berec since she heard the news of his arrest, and Hugh was dismissing him as if he didn't matter. She wondered where he was in prison and whether it was possible to visit him, but she had no concept of how to find out. The whole thing was like another world to her. Anyway, if she did try to visit Berec, Hugh, obviously, would be furious. Probably try to stop her. What should she do?

In the end she pursued the obvious path and telephoned Penelope, to discover that Berec was in Wormwood Scrubs prison in West London. Penelope told her that she had been to see him and found him outwardly cheerful, but thin and hollow-eyed, which worried her. After thinking about it for a day or two, Isabel packed up a parcel of essentials and sent it to him with a newsy letter. She hoped he received it safely for she didn't hear back.

By the end of October 1952, Hugh had finished the revisions to his novel and typed it up. The top copy he sent to his agent, Digby Lane, the carbon he kept.

Isabel again offered to read it.

'All in good time,' Hugh replied. 'I want to know what Lane and McKinnon think about it first.' He did not sound enthusiastic and for a while Isabel did not ask again.

He went up to London for a few days and when he came back he brought with him a bottle of particularly good wine and wore an expression of such smugness, Isabel knew before he said anything that the news was good.

'Lane is worried that one of the saucier scenes will

attract the attention of the Lord Chancellor's Office, but more importantly, the words "work of genius" have been mentioned,' he told them all proudly when his mother enquired at dinner if there had been a response. 'If only in Stephen McKinnon's reader's report. We must wait and see what McKinnon has in his company piggy bank. I've told Lane he mustn't take less than five hundred for it, but he doesn't seem to think the money's there. "Five hundred," I said, "or you can take it to another publisher."'

Isabel thought this was an extraordinarily ambitious sum of money but didn't like to puncture the exuberant atmosphere by saying so. She drank a large mouthful of the very fine wine and looked down at her food, suddenly unable to eat.

After dinner she took one of her lonely walks in the dusk, past the donkeys and through the marshes to the estuary where she stood for a long time, watching the light disappear from the sky and listening to the cries of the birds. The tide was running now and the river swirled silently past, on to the sea as it always had.

And when she returned home and no one asked her where she'd been, she found some paper in Hugh's study and crept upstairs like a ghost. There she sat on the bed and started to write. Her thoughts tumbled out on the page.

I feel that I'm fading, becoming transparent – that soon I'll disappear altogether. In the circle of light from her bedside lamp, her hand moved across the paper. Once she began, she found it impossible to stop. She covered one page then another and another. Only when she heard someone coming up the stairs did she put down her pen and hide the pages in the bedside drawer. Across the landing, she heard the distinctive creak of the nursery door. It must only be Jacqueline looking in on Lorna.

She felt sleepy now. It seemed too much effort to get out of bed to go downstairs and say goodnight to the others. Too much effort even to get up and close the curtains. She took off most of her clothes in bed and snuggled down under the bedclothes, curling up in the warm space she'd made. And there she fell asleep.

She woke briefly when Hugh came to bed, and was aware of the odd disparate noises he made, moving about the room, but the next time she wakened, the room was dark and she was cold without her nightdress. She shuffled herself towards Hugh, for warmth, and realised with surprise that he wasn't there. She gathered the bedclothes about herself and waited, but it was a long time before he returned.

'Are you all right?' she whispered when he got into bed. His heart was racing away and he seemed a little agitated.

'Yes,' he said. 'I went to the bathroom, then I heard Mother call out. Her breathing was a bit laboured so I fetched her a glass of water.'

'Is she better now?'

'Yes, she took something. I'm sorry to wake you.'

'As long as she's all right.'

'Yes. Go to sleep now.'

He settled down and turning his back on her, seemed to fall asleep at once, but she lay there for some time, staring into the darkness, unable to dispel the sense that something was wrong.

The following morning, Hugh's mother sent down word that she'd like her breakfast delivered on a tray. Isabel told Mrs Catchpole that she'd take it up.

When she entered it was to find the old lady sitting up in bed, breathing strenuously. Later the doctor came and prescribed ephedrine. Her condition improved over the next few days and everyone relaxed once more.

As Isabel suspected, Stephen McKinnon could not or would not raise an advance of anywhere near £500 for Hugh's novel, no matter how highly he rated it. But the sum promised, £200, was twice as much as for *Coming Home*, and McKinnon wrote him such a complimentary letter that Hugh seemed to forget his threat to go else-where. Or perhaps the rival publisher had seen the book and not liked it, or not liked the price, Hugh didn't choose to explain. Three weeks later, he returned from London one day to announce that McKinnon & Holt would publish *The Silent Tide* in the spring.

'The new man, Richard Snow, wants me to make a few adjustments,' he told Isabel, when she ventured that she hoped she could read it soon. 'Very small things. Let me do those first.'

During November, he shut himself in his study and worked on the manuscript every day.

Unknown to him, upstairs, Isabel wrote too. Page after page she stowed in her bedside drawer. She wrote about everything – her family, her move to London, the people she'd met. All of it poured out of her with freshness and passion.

Chapter 32

Emily

She'd reached the final page now and Isabel's voice, which had seemed to fill the room, fell silent. Again the story had stopped abruptly and Emily felt disappointment that there was no more. She shuffled the delicate pages together and laid them with the others, some still in their envelopes, on the dishevelled pile on the coffee table.

Arms round her knees, she sat in the pool of light from her table lamp, absorbed in the world of a woman sixty years ago. How fresh and full of hope Isabel had once been, a life of promise spread out before her, and how her bright flame had dwindled. Emily was still not sure what exactly had happened to Isabel in the end, nor how to find out. If she could only discover where these fragments of manuscript came from, then perhaps the mystery would be solved. She'd thought about this a lot. It was probable that they were from some source within the Parchment building, but where? Someone employed at the archives, perhaps, in Gloucestershire? But who there could possibly have an interest in Hugh Morton or even have known that Emily was the editor responsible for the biography? Perhaps the very fact she'd asked for

the files had alerted someone. She mulled over that idea.
No, the copy of *Coming Home* had been left in her pigeonhole *before* her request to the archives. There had to be a
different answer.

She considered ways she could advertise for the
mysterious person to get in touch, but all the ones she
could think of – emails to the whole office, or notices in
the lift – had drawbacks. They'd have everyone thinking
she was odd, paranoid. Perhaps the thing to do was to
play along and see what happened next. Surely at some
point the person would reveal themselves.

She picked up her mobile, smiled briefly at a cheerful
text message from Megan, and switched off the table
lamp. The rest of her living room came drearily into focus.
Dirty supper plate on the table. Her office bag, still
containing unread scripts, lying by the door. Tomorrow's
problems. She sighed, and taking the plate to the sink,
dropped it into the washing-up water and watched it sink
to the bottom. She was still in this thoughtful mood when
she climbed into bed. She dreamed of diving into deep
black water and trying to fight her way to the surface
again, her lungs bursting for breath.

Days passed and there were no more mysterious packages. On Sunday, she gave Joel a copy of the latest
instalment when they went back to his after lunch with
friends in a local restaurant.

'Thanks, I'll have a look,' he said, putting it down on
his desk with hardly a glance. He brought mugs of tea
across and sat next to her on the sofa.

'Thanks. So what did you think of the last part I gave
you? Did you read it?' she enquired.

'Of course I did. It backs up my own discoveries,' he told her. 'Isabel was unstable mentally. That must be why the marriage ultimately went wrong.'

This puzzled Emily. 'Unstable? I don't see that. She was probably depressed. It happened to my sister after Harry. Everyone was worried until the doctor got on to it.'

'All those hormones sloshing around,' Joel said, his eyes twinkling. 'Poor Hugh must have felt at his wits' end.'

'Don't be contemptuous,' she said. 'Anyway, in Isabel's case I think it was more than that. She found herself in a role she couldn't play.'

He considered this carefully. 'That role thing must have happened to lots of women then. It was part of the culture. Don't you think most just made the best of it?'

'That doesn't sound very sympathetic.'

'I'm totally sympathetic. I suppose as his biographer I'm trying to look at the matter from Hugh's point of view. He must have felt trapped in a situation way beyond his experience. The doctor didn't seem much use. Jacqueline and Hugh's mother seemed fairly helpless, too. What could he have done? That's how things were then.'

'I see what you mean.' Emily was thinking how alone Isabel must have felt. She'd been so young, so lacking in advice or any perspective, her own mother struggling with health problems, her mother-in-law rigid and judge-mental. 'So you wouldn't examine the marriage more – shall we say objectively – in your book?'

She sensed Joel's discomfort. He got up and started to pace around. 'I feel I have done,' he said. 'I don't think that you're being unbiased yourself, Emily. You seem set on turning Hugh into the villain of the piece.'

'No, really. I understand that Hugh was a man of his times.'

'Exactly – that's how people like him thought then. You can't blame them for that, can you?'

'He was quite selfish.'

'Perhaps we should blame his mother for that.' Joel smiled.

'She was awful, wasn't she? No, what I meant was that you can still tell Isabel's story.'

He sighed. 'Where it's relevant, yes, and where I've got sufficient evidence. That ragbag of a memoir is not reliable, especially since it was written when Isabel was depressed. And I'm certainly not going to run some present-day feminist viewpoint on the matter.'

'Joel, you know that's not what I mean.' Emily stood up and went to the window, trying to hide her frustration. There was an injustice to be righted here. Isabel's story was not generally known and it had become increasingly obvious to her that Jacqueline Morton and Joel were happy to keep it that way.

Joel said, 'Of course I'll read all the new stuff you've given me. And take a judgement. But it's me writing this book and I've got to follow the way I think best.' There was a sharpness to his tone and she sensed she was offending his pride.

'Of course,' she said wearily, turning to face him. 'I don't mean to interfere, but . . .'

'But what?'

'I don't know.' He was right about it being his book, but she was his editor. She felt justified in giving him advice and she did genuinely feel that Isabel deserved a prominent part in Joel's biography. But it was more than that.

The quest for Isabel had become a personal mission of hers and Joel seemed to be standing in her way; their whole relationship was becoming a battleground in this struggle. What was she to do? She looked out of the window. In the street below, a young man was crouching to soothe a screaming toddler, struggling to get out of its pushchair.

She felt Joel move behind her, his arms enfolding her waist, drawing her back into the room. He nuzzled her neck and she shivered with desire. 'Let's not quarrel any more,' he whispered in her ear. 'It's not worth it.'

'I'm not quarrelling,' she murmured, turning in his arms and raising her face to his. 'I'm arguing. That's different. Arguing can be good.' *It's silence that is bad.* Who had said that to her? As Joel bent to kiss her mouth, she gave herself up to the very delicious feelings running through her body, but when his hands began to move over her breasts through her delicate cashmere top, arousing her, she suddenly remembered. It was Matthew.

'Shall we . . . ?' Joel's breath was hot in her ear.

'Mmm . . .' she said, closing her eyes, her body arching towards him. Their mouths met in a deep searching kiss that banished all thought but of the here and now as he lifted her up and carried her to the bedroom.

On the bus home that evening she wondered why, despite the thrill of their love-making, she felt so at odds with herself. It was months since she'd broken up with Matthew and here was Joel, who she was so attracted to, was free to be with and wanted to be with. And yet memories kept getting in the way. Matthew. What if she never got over him, could never love anyone else as much ever again? It didn't bear thinking about.

The argument that she'd had with Joel about Isabel bothered her, too. She didn't know Joel very well, yet couldn't feel sure of him. She wondered what his feelings were for her, apart from the obvious physical attraction, that is. He seemed so self-contained, even in his love-making, never whispered her name . . . Oh, it was all so confusing.

She was still distracted by all this when she arrived at work the following day, but when she found another tranche of Isabel's story lying in her pigeonhole she snatched it up eagerly. At lunchtime, with the office quiet, she read it as she ate her sandwich, quickly absorbed by Isabel's world.

Chapter 33

Isabel

One morning at the beginning of December 1952, Hugh left for London, giving Jacqueline a lift. He was going for professional reasons he said, and would stay several nights in Kensington. Jacqueline would stay one night only, to check on her house and do some Christmas shopping. Later the same day, Isabel opened the front door to a young man with a telegram for Jacqueline.

'Mrs Wood isn't here at the moment, but I'll let her know,' she told him. She telephoned Jacqueline's London house several times during the course of the day, but there was never any answer.

By evening, the telegram still sat ominous and unopened on the hall table, and Hugh's mother fretted about what it might contain. 'Suppose it's news about Major Wood? One feels so *responsible*,' she kept saying.

Finally, Lavinia Morton tried ringing Hugh to ask what might be done. It wasn't until late in the evening that he answered the phone. Isabel, who was passing through the hall on her way up to bed, heard her say, 'Oh, do you? Yes, it might be as well.' She replaced the receiver and told Isabel, 'Hugh's going round there straight away to try and find her.'

The telephone rang only a short while later. Hugh's mother answered. 'Jacqueline, thank heavens you've called.' From the drawing room, Isabel heard the clunk of the receiver being placed on the table and the older woman's hoarse breathing as she fumbled the envelope open.

'Oh!' she said in tones of relief, then picked up the phone and told Jacqueline, 'Thank God. He's coming home, dear. I'm so glad. *Extended leave stop.* That's all it is. Your husband is on his way back to England.'

As Isabel lay in bed, waiting for sleep to come, the relief she'd heard in Lavinia's voice echoed in her own mind. With her husband coming home, Jacqueline would presumably move back to London properly. The oppression Isabel felt with her presence would be gone. They could all get on with their own lives again.

During the night, she surfaced from sleep to hear Lorna wailing softly. She waited a minute or two, but the crying subsided. As she lay trying to sleep again, she found her thoughts take a darker turn. It was as though a formless shadow of a nightmare swept over her, stifling all hope and happiness. For a while she could hardly breathe, but finally the shadow passed and she fell once more into a troubled sleep. When she was dragged out of it by her child's more urgent cries, it was dawn, a pale and cold one.

During the day, Jacqueline telephoned again to say that instead of returning that evening as planned, she was staying in London to wait for her husband.

Hugh wasn't due home for another two days and he, too, rang that evening. He had a meeting with his editor, he told Isabel, some contacts to look up and a couple of Christmas parties to attend, if he could. 'The fog's getting very bad here,' he went on. 'The traffic's at a standstill. It's very difficult to get anywhere.'

It was early the following morning before everyone was up that Isabel was awakened by the ringing telephone. She grabbed the receiver, fuddled with sleep. It was Hugh.

'Jacqueline's just called,' he said. 'I'm afraid I have bad news. There's been an accident.'

He went on to explain that Major Wood's plane had landed at a military base in Norfolk late the night before, but that instead of waiting until morning, Michael Wood had insisted on being driven to London straight away. The car had run into thick fog in Central London and had driven off the road at Piccadilly and overturned. Major Wood was gravely injured and in hospital. The driver had died at the scene.

Emily

Sixty years later, Emily looked up from Isabel's account and gazed out of the window. The accident must have happened just down the road from her offices. She glanced back at the pages. There weren't many more but, as she read, she sensed she was coming closer to the dark heart of Isabel's marriage. Isabel's voice resounded in her head, passionate, urgent. She had written:

Our little household was thrown into a subdued mood, not helped by the shroud of fog. Hugh telephoned again later and

announced that he'd be staying up in London to be of assist-
ance to Jacqueline, and although I knew he was right to do
this, at the same time something in me cried to him to come
home. The day inched past in freezing gloom. No one went
out. We lit the fire in the living room, but the damp fog must
have come down the chimney, for the flames were desultory
and the fire smoked. Lorna played happily enough in her pen.
Even Hugh's mother agreed that the weather was too bad to
put a baby outside.

I tidied a bit upstairs and laid the table for lunch, all
the time weighed down by this awful knowledge that there
was nothing to be done but to sit with Hugh's mother and
Lorna, waiting for news. We tried not to mind a disgust-
ing smell of burned chicken bones. All the upset had put
Mrs Catchpole's mind right off the soup and when it came
it was only vegetable.

At six o'clock that evening, I was pouring Hugh's mother
a glass of sherry when he telephoned at last. There was,
however, little to say. Michael Wood had taken a serious blow
to the head and the doctors were doing all they could.

After Lorna had been put to bed, we sat down to the frugal
supper Mrs Catchpole had left us and when I'd washed up we
listened to a comedy on the wireless, but neither of us felt like
laughing and the evening seemed never-ending. Hugh's
mother brooded, and I noticed her breathing, clearly audible in
the silence. I sensed her frustration at our situation, the wait-
ing and the worrying about poor Jacqueline, but we weren't
used to discussing feelings with each other, the two of us. I
regret that I had never had an easy relationship with her, but
her disapproval of me had always been strong. We can't always
help our feelings, but she wasn't fair not to hide the fact that
she cared more about Jacqueline than about me.

'I'm sure it would be all right if you went to bed,' I told her. 'I don't suppose we'll hear any more news till the morning. Poor Jacqueline.'

I might not have liked Jacqueline, but one would have to be a very hard person not to feel pity for her now.

'Yes, indeed, poor Jacqueline,' Hugh's mother said in a strange low voice. 'It ought to be her sitting here now, not you.'

I was so shocked that for a time I was deprived of the power of speech, but a response didn't seem required, for she continued, 'They were made for one another, she and my son. You know, when they were quite small, when he was eight and she was only four, he told her he'd marry her.' She chuckled at what she clearly thought was an endearing memory. 'They saw a great deal of one another later, when Hugh was home for the holidays. There was a very nice group of young people here. But the war came and of course it spoiled everything – everything. I suppose I should hardly have been surprised when he met someone else. Hugh told you, I suppose, about Anne, the girl he loved who was killed in an air raid.'

'Yes, of course,' I said. I didn't know anything more than those bare facts, but I wasn't going to let her know that. Though because I'd read Coming Home, in a sort of way I did know – Anne, of course, being Diana in the novel.

'He was very taken with Anne, who was a sweet girl in her way. But then, of course, poor Jacqueline was left out in the cold. After Anne was killed, Hugh had to return to his squadron, and in the meantime Jacqueline met Michael. I was never of the impression that she was very much in love with him, but he was undoubtedly suitable . . . And Michael was always fond of her, very fond.' Hugh's mother, I noticed, was already speaking of the poor man in the past tense.

'*So you see there was never a right time for Hugh and Jacqueline – and then, of course, he met you.*'

She said this with such a tone of accusation, it was like a cold blade passing through me. She was breathing very heavily now and I was frightened.

'*How can you say these things?*' I whispered.

'*You,*' she went on. '*With your selfish ideas, your dereliction of duty.*'

'*Stop it!*' I said. We glared at one another and her breath became more laboured.

Eventually she said in a tight voice, quite choked, '*Get me some water . . . and . . . my pills.*'

I was glad of the opportunity to leave the room, for I couldn't bear her to see how terribly upset she'd made me. As I filled a glass at the kitchen tap, my hands shaking, I tried to make sense of all she'd told me, but it didn't make sense, not quite. It was as though I saw a blurred picture that refused to come into focus.

I remembered the evening I'd first met Jacqueline, at that party at the London flat, soon after Hugh had moved in there. Michael had been away then, and I'd been struck by how dedicated Jacqueline had been to making the party a success, but also by how lightly Hugh had treated her. If Jacqueline did indeed adore my husband, as his mother seemed to be saying, then he had seemed completely unaware of the fact – or uncaring. A childhood promise. Surely no one would ever make anything of that? Could Jacqueline really have nursed a calf love all those years? It seemed unlikely, for she was a mature woman now, and yet there was no doubting her steady loyalty to him. And he, what did he feel about her? It was difficult to think straight.

I returned to Hugh's mother with the glass and realised that *in my upset I'd forgotten the pills. 'Where are they?' I asked. She took a gulp of water and said, 'Dressing table.' I ran upstairs.*

At first I couldn't see which ones she wanted, as there were so many powders and potions in the dressing-table drawers. There was, however, a small brown bottle standing on the table by her bed, and when I picked it up and unscrewed the top, I found it contained the yellowish tablets I'd often seen her take. These must be the ones.

I returned to the drawing room to find her in quite some discomfort, and when I shook out the pills, she took two quickly and swallowed them, without looking closely at them. After that, she leaned back in the chair and closed her eyes. When I asked her how she felt, she gestured that I should be silent.

'Shall I call the doctor?' I asked, but she shook her head.

We sat together for quite some time until, to my relief, her breathing became calmer. Eventually I persuaded her to turn in for the night. In the bedroom, I placed the pills once again by her bed. She wouldn't allow me to help her change into her nightgown, so I left her to manage as best she could and went downstairs to damp down the fire and lock the back door. Then I looked in on Lorna, who was sleeping peacefully. All this while, though, I was thinking over and over everything my mother-in-law had said. I wanted to dismiss it as the ramblings of a bitter woman with deluded ideas, but too much about her account struck me as plausible. I was beginning to see Jacqueline as a threat to my marriage.

It was late now, but I was too agitated to sleep. So instead of going to my own room, I did something I'd never done before. I opened the door of Jacqueline's room and switched on the light.

The Magnolia room, which had been mine when I stayed

here before our marriage, would have been more pleasant without the cold pink aura imparted by the wallpaper and the hangings, a colour delightful in the garden against the fresh green leaves and dark twisted wood of the tree in late spring, but less so in a bedroom, especially in the yellow glow of the ceiling light. The bed was neatly made up, and although Jacqueline had departed to London with a suitcase and a vanity case, she'd left behind copious marks of her presence: a lacy shawl around the back of a chair, a pile of her favourite ladies' magazines under the bedside table.

There was a dusting of talcum powder on the dressing table. I ran my finger through it and stirred up its faint, sweet aroma, Jacqueline's scent. On the chest of drawers was a photograph of her and Michael on their wedding day. I picked it up and tilted it towards the light. She was looking directly at the camera with a slight smile on her face, a smile that, with the knowledge I now had, was sad. I should feel sorry for Jacqueline, I told myself. Life hadn't turned out quite the way it should have done for her. A husband who was her second choice, and who, after several years of marriage, had given her no child of her own. And yet I couldn't.

She might not have meant it, but her presence here in this house, making up for my many failings, looking after my child, cast a pall over everything. And yet my husband and my mother-in-law seemed to collude in all this, couldn't understand why I resented it. On the one hand I knew that this past year or so I wouldn't have managed without Jacqueline, but I couldn't find it in me to be grateful.

As I made to leave the room, there came a noise from the landing, the sound of a door opening. Fearing I'd be found in the wrong room, I switched off the light and stood motionless, waiting. I could hear Hugh's mother shuffling past, then the bathroom door opening and the mysterious sounds of water in the pipes. I dared not move in case she walked out suddenly and caught me, so I stayed, breathing in the scents of talc and old wood, and something else – an oily chemical smell, not unpleasant, in fact very familiar. My hand brushed against cloth; there was a dressing gown hung on the back of the door. The other scent was coming from this, but I couldn't think what it was.

After Hugh's mother returned to her bedroom, I escaped to bed myself where I lay exhausted, trying to calm myself by cuddling Hugh's pillow. There was that familiar aroma again. As I fell into sleep I realised what it was – the scent of my husband's hair cream.

It was after seven and still dark when Lorna woke me by calling out. I changed her nappy and took her downstairs while I warmed her milk, but as I passed the telephone it began to ring. It was Hugh, with the news that Jacqueline's husband had survived the night.

When at half past eight there was still silence from upstairs, I ventured up with a cup of tea to convey the news to Hugh's mother.

When I opened the door, I was shocked to find her lying on the floor in her nightgown, staring sightlessly, her body as cold and unyielding as marble.

Shocked by this tragedy, sixty years later, Emily read on.

Hugh had returned to Suffolk immediately, leaving Jacqueline to watch at her husband's bedside. Just after lunch, hearing his car, Isabel went out to greet him, Lorna in her arms. She was shaken at the sight of his face, bloodless and exhausted, shocked. He put his hand briefly on her arm and ruffled Lorna's fluffy head, but otherwise hardly registered either of them at all.

'Where is she?' he asked, looking up at the house, as though his mother's face might be seen at one of the windows.

'Oh Hugh, they've taken her already,' Isabel whispered. An ambulance had visited a short while before and Hugh's mother had been removed on a stretcher covered by a sheet. 'Doctor Bridges is away and it was a new man who came. I'm afraid he wouldn't sign the certificate. Hugh, there's to be a post-mortem.'

He closed his eyes briefly as he registered this news. 'Tell me – tell me exactly what happened,' he said, his gaze now focused on her, penetrating, urgent. Lorna moaned and wriggled in Isabel's arms, and Isabel hushed her.

'Let's go in first. She's due for her nap.' They went into the house to be met by a tearful Mrs Catchpole, murmuring words of sympathy. Isabel got rid of her by passing her the baby.

In the drawing room, Hugh paced the carpet as Isabel, as calmly as she could, narrated the events of the previous night: Hugh's mother's struggle with asthma, the giving of the pills, how she'd found the woman that morning. She carefully left out all mention of the subject of their conversation, of where she'd been when she heard her mother-in-law visiting the bathroom.

'The other doctor asked to see the pill bottle and I gave it to him. They were her usual ones, I think – the ephedrine.' She explained about the cautious way the man had reacted, the questions that had followed. 'He asked if she was known to have heart problems and, Hugh, I didn't know. She never said anything.'

'You gave her some pills and you weren't sure what they were?'

'I was. It's just the label on the bottle was blurred.' She was surprised at his sudden anger and the way he twisted her words.

'Why didn't you ring the doctor last night or try to get her to hospital?'

'Hugh, don't be like that. Her condition improved after she'd taken them and she didn't want the doctor. There seemed no need. Obviously I was wrong.'

'She took all sorts of rubbish. Are you absolutely sure you gave her the right ones?'

'I think so, yes. The doctor didn't say. Anyway, the pills might not have anything to do with it. Oh, Hugh, you don't think they might?' She was horrified by the brusqueness of his tone, the accusation in his face, unable to find any sign of the familiar Hugh who loved her.

It was several days before the results of the post-mortem were known. Lavinia Morton had died of a heart attack possibly brought on by prolonged use or misuse of her asthma treatment, small amounts of which had been found in her body. During her life an underlying heart condition had remained undiagnosed.

A police detective came to interview Isabel, but her obvious distress, her narrative of what had happened and Hugh's insistence that his wife shouldn't be cross-examined in this way, meant that her version of events was accepted. At the inquest, a week after her death, the coroner questioned her and judged that Hugh's mother had died of natural causes, possibly exacerbated by her medication. The doctor who had attended her after death suggested that more research was needed into the possible side-effects of long-term use of ephedrine. Publically, at least, Isabel was exonerated of all blame. In private, she knew that Hugh was impatient with her muddled account about his mother's medicine and angry at her failure to summon medical assistance. In short, deep inside, he believed that she was responsible for, or at least might have prevented, his mother's death.

Major Michael Wood lingered on for many days in the grey lands between life and death, but the brain damage he'd sustained from his head injury was severe and he never regained consciousness. On the very day that Hugh's mother was buried next to her husband in the graveyard of the parish church came the news that Jacqueline was now a widow.

Chapter 34

Isabel

Christmas Day 1952 dawned in a doleful manner.

It didn't even feel like Christmas, Isabel thought, turning from the window. Outside, a squally wind blew off the estuary and the sky was gunmetal grey. Hugh, to keep up his mother's tradition, had gone to morning service, but Lorna was fretful and full of cold, so Isabel stayed behind with her. Having got the child off to sleep again, she was glad of the time alone in the house.

Jacqueline and her father, a retired country solicitor, whom Isabel had only met for the first time at the funeral, were expected to lunch. Fortunately, Mrs Catchpole and Lily had worked efficiently during the preceding days, preparing a brace of pheasants and several pans of vegetables as well as laying the dining-room table, so there wasn't very much Isabel had to do. She had a moment ago placed the birds in the oven, as Mrs Catchpole had shown her, and parboiled the potatoes ready to roast. She needn't rescue the pudding from the steamer for another hour. She could use this brief respite to open a parcel that had arrived from her mother.

She went to fetch it from where she'd left it, under the

big Christmas tree in the drawing room amongst a small number of other packages – mostly presents for Lorna. She wanted to open it alone because she had some premonition about it. A bigger parcel had already arrived from the Barbers addressed to Hugh, Lorna and Isabel, so there must be something special about this extra one. She had to fetch her scissors to cut the old bits of knotted string.

The brown paper fell away and she found herself holding a square shallow box covered in black velvet. There was an envelope too, addressed merely to 'Isabel' in rather untidy italics. She opened the box and stared at the pearl necklace that lay there, its three strands shimmering in the winter light. It was beautiful, but dismay overcame her at what it meant. Her mother was giving her the most precious object she possessed, the only valuable thing that she had ever had from her own mother. Why was she giving it to Isabel? Why now, when it meant so much to her? Isabel remembered Pamela wearing it on only a very few occasions, her wedding to Hugh being the most recent. She took it out of the box and lifted it to the light, remembering how it had glowed around her mother's neck. The fastening was lovely too, intricately wrought and inlaid with tiny diamonds. On an impulse she clipped it round her neck where it lay warm and heavy. Then she turned her attention to the letter.

There were several pages, written in pencil on cheap paper, and the address at the top was a surprise. It was a hospital ward – the same hospital where Pamela Barber had been admitted more than a year before, and where Isabel had visited her. She had a sudden picture of her mother lying in the bed, grey-faced and worn through.

Her first instinct was to refold the pages, so frightened was she to read what they contained, but then she steeled herself and started to decipher the straggling handwriting, so unlike her mother's usual tidy italics.

My darling Izzy,

I expect you'll be surprised to learn that I'm back in hospital again. I'm sorry not to have sent warning. I thought I wouldn't need to come yet, but then it all happened quickly, you must ask your father about it. I'm afraid that the trouble I had last year returned in the summer, and I'm here for a few days for tests.

Forgive me if I'm not making much sense, darling, the medication they give me makes me stupid. I hope that you can read this. Your father is taking it and will post it with the necklace. I'm sure I will be with you for a long while yet, but I want you to have it now with all the love I have for you. You have always been very special to me, and are my eldest, and it seems right.

Penelope came to see me yesterday. It is the first time that we have talked properly for many years and we had so much to say to one another, I can't tell you. Penelope is very fond of you, darling, and I've asked her to speak to you about a matter very close to both our hearts.

It's very Christmassy in here. The nurses have seen to that with decorations and carol singing and the sweetest little Christmas tree. Your father is coming on Christmas Day with Lydia and the boys, and I'm sure we'll have a very jolly time. We'll think of you and Hugh and little Lorna with love. I hope that our parcel has arrived. There's no need to rush to my

*bedside, I'm doing perfectly well, but when I get home after
Christmas it would be lovely if you'd telephone.*

*With my deepest love, darling,
Your mother*

Isabel sat for a long time after finishing this, trying to
accommodate herself to all it contained. Her mother had
not actually said as much, but the subtext was clear. She
was very ill. Isabel's first reaction was fury, fury at her
parents for telling her nothing. She got up, went into the
hall and dialled the number of their house. It rang and
rang, but no one answered. Perhaps they were out at the
hospital. She slowly replaced the receiver, then went
upstairs to find her address book. She dialled Aunt
Penelope's number in London, but again there was no
one.

When Hugh returned from church he found her lying
on the sofa, clutching the letter and weeping. Upstairs,
Lorna had awoken and begun to cry.

Jacqueline, when she arrived with her father, had to
rescue the pheasants from burning. As might be imagined,
Christmas dinner was a subdued affair. Little Lorna
grumbled her way through, refusing all food, her eyes
unnaturally bright.

'Hadn't you better put her back to bed?' Hugh asked.

Isabel felt Lorna's face. 'She's running a temperature,'
she replied.

'Poor little mite,' Jacqueline said. 'You finish your meal,
I'll take her up.' And she hefted the child out of her high
chair. 'Oh, she's not at all well.'

'Let me take her,' Isabel said, 'please.'

'No, really, I've finished,' Jacqueline said and swept off with Lorna. Isabel didn't like to argue in front of the men so sat down again, but her appetite was gone.

When Jacqueline came downstairs again, having left Lorna to sleep, they put off the washing-up to listen to the new Queen's first Christmas broadcast on the wireless. Isabel tried telephoning her father again, but still there was no answer. She grew increasingly agitated. Stealing upstairs, she watched Lorna fret in her sleep and wondered if they should call the doctor.

When she returned to the drawing room and asked Hugh, he said not to bother the poor man on Christmas Day. 'I think it is only a bad cold,' Jacqueline assured her. Not long afterwards, Lorna woke up once more.

After Isabel fetched her downstairs, Hugh handed out the presents from around the tree. For Lorna, they'd bought a wooden trolley to push, filled with bricks. Although she was, at nearly a year old, unable to walk unaided, she tried her best to haul herself up and teetered briefly, clutching the handle, until the trolley shot forward and she fell with a wail. This did not deter her from trying again, each time becoming more tired and more tearful.

Jacqueline had bought gloves for Isabel, a tie for Hugh. Isabel handed over the gift from her and Hugh, some more of the favourite talcum powder. She was privately furious over Hugh's present to herself, which was a pretty apron. Since she'd gone to some lengths to procure him four ounces of expensive tobacco, she was hurt that he'd made so little effort. A small package from her friend Vivienne cheered her up though: a little bar of creamy soap with an exotic smell. The note that accompanied it was full of happiness and she put it in her handbag to read again later.

Twilight was already stealing across the room, and Hugh was stoking up the fire against the evening chill, when the sound of a car was heard on the drive.

'Who on earth can that be?' Isabel wondered, going to the window. She did not recognise the blue-black car with its flowing lines and silver piping, nor did she immediately know the driver, a broad-shouldered man in a thick overcoat and with hat pulled down low, who walked round to open the passenger door. The elegant lady in a fashionable cloak who stepped out, however, was immediately familiar. Penelope's brimmed hat lifted in a gust of wind and went sailing across the courtyard. Isabel laughed for the first time that day as the man she now saw was Reginald set off in dignified pursuit.

'It's Penelope!' she dashed to open the front door. 'Aunt Penelope,' she cried out, hurrying to meet her. Her aunt greeted her with a graceful wave, and opened the car's rear door. Out bounced Gelert and galloped, leash flying, across the flagstones towards Isabel.

'We were staying at the beach house,' Penelope explained as she gave Hugh her cape. 'It's delightfully cosy with the wind howling outside.'

'We've had quite a decent meal at The Boar,' Reginald said. 'Do you know it?' He was unusually talkative today.

'Reg simply bullied the poor man there until he found us ham and potatoes.'

'Nonsense, Pen, he was glad of our custom.'

It was as though a blast of fresh air had blown through the house, Isabel thought, as she introduced them to

Jacqueline and her father. The old man tried to get up, but Reginald stayed him then sat by him and started up a hearty conversation on the subject of gun dogs, about which astonishingly he seemed to know a great deal. Hugh stood nearby, packing his pipe with the new tobacco as he listened. Penelope paid polite attention to Lorna, whom Jacqueline was amusing on the floor with the building bricks. Isabel sat next to her aunt on the sofa, and stroked Gelert.

'I had no idea that you were down this way,' Isabel said. 'It's a lovely surprise.'

'We came the night before last,' Penelope said.

'You've been to see my mother,' Isabel said in a low voice. 'She wrote to me. Tell me, how is she?'

It was as though a shadow fell across Penelope's face. 'We will speak about that,' she whispered, 'but not now, not here,' and Isabel felt a kind of dread.

'Extraordinary how that child looks like her,' Penelope went on, staring at Lorna.

'Does she?' Isabel replied. 'Sometimes I think she looks like pictures of Hugh as a baby, but I can't see our side of the family in her at all.'

'Oh, she does look like Pam. So strange.'

'I suppose it's not really.' Penelope was cast in a mood Isabel had seen her in before – sad, less dégagée – She thought, surprised how glad she was to see her aunt.

She glanced round the room. How bright the house seemed suddenly. With the fire leaping in the grate the atmosphere was quite cheerful. They'd all been so dreary of late. Jacqueline had retreated to a chair by the fire, cuddling a sleepy Lorna. Hugh stood to one side, at the chimney piece, quietly smoking.

'Shall I make some tea?' she turned and asked Penelope, and saw her aunt surveying Hugh and Jacqueline with a concentrated sort of frown. 'There's a Christmas cake of sorts.' And now Isabel saw it too. Hugh, Jacqueline, Lorna. In the halo of light cast by the old table lamp on the mantelpiece, they formed a tableau like a little family. A sense of desolation stole over her.

Out in the kitchen she concentrated on taking up the kettle and filling it. She placed it on the hob, then stood wiping her hands on a towel. The teapot, she told herself. She opened the tea caddy and the musty fragrance of the tea was soothing. Everything was tumbling into place now. How could it be that she hadn't seen it before?

The sound of tripping footsteps. She glanced up to see her aunt, her still-lovely face wearing an air of concern she'd never seen before. Penelope regarded her for a moment, then murmured, 'You poor child,' and came and stroked Isabel's cheek.

Isabel grasped the hand and gave a great quivering sob. They stood there together for a moment, then Penelope gently withdrew and said, 'We must stay calm and try to think.'

'I can't.'

'You can. I feel I must tell you. Stephen has often seen them together in London,' Penelope said. Seeing slow tears course down Isabel's cheeks, she produced a lace handkerchief from her handbag.

'I don't know what to do,' Isabel said, wiping her eyes.

'You must confront him.'

'He's been so cold to me lately. It's as though he blames me.'

'What does he blame you for?' Penelope remained cool,

aloof, but her voice was gentle and her expression sympathetic. Isabel found she could think more clearly.

'I never got on well with his mother, you see. And he thinks her death was my fault, I know he does.'

'But that's ridiculous.'

'I should have realised how ill she was. I should. But it's more than that. I've never been the kind of wife he wanted. I should have been more like *her*. It was Jacqueline whom *she* wanted for him.'

'Surely that's nonsense.'

'It's not. She told me. Then there's Lorna. I didn't know it would be like that, having a baby. How it takes you over. I'm very fond of Lorna . . .'

'Of course you are,' Penelope said. Her long, manicured fingers made a silky sound as she ran them together.

Isabel remembered the conversation she'd had with Penelope in the café in Percy Street. Penelope had never wanted a child. She wondered again if it was something to do with that which had darkened irreparably the relationship between the two sisters.

'How is my mother?' she asked.

'It's hard to say. There has to be another operation.'

'Oh.'

The kettle was boiling away now and as she swirled water round the teapot to warm it, she told her aunt about the letter and the pearls. Penelope laid cups and saucers on a tray as she listened.

'They might have gone to the neighbour's house for Christmas,' she said when Isabel explained about them not answering the telephone.

'The Fanshawes?' Isabel asked as she fetched the cake from the pantry and loaded up the tea trolley.

'That portly woman who looks after your sister.' Penelope was looking intently at her now. 'Isabel, my dear,' she said. 'We have to talk. Reginald and I are on our way back, but I'll arrange something soon. Why don't I come down again and fetch you out for lunch one day?'

'I'd love that,' Isabel said. 'When Lorna's a little better.'

'Bring the child with you, if you like. Sea air is good, I suppose? I'll telephone you.'

'Thank you,' Isabel said, wondering what on earth her aunt wanted to tell her. 'Did Stephen mention that we saw him there in the summer?'

'He did, poor dear man,' she said.

'Why poor?'

'His wife has left him. Her father wants the marriage annulled on the basis there are no children. Quite how that's to be achieved I don't know.'

Isabel thought about this and how kind Stephen had always been to her. It must be her low mood, but there seemed so much unhappiness in the world.

'Berec was very pleased to receive your parcel. I visit him from time to time. Dear Berec. He's entirely selfless. His greatest worry is for his friends, Gregor and Karin.'

'Has something happened to them?'

Penelope leaned forward conspiratorially. 'Gregor's name has appeared on some list of political undesirables. He's to be deported, and Karin will go with him. Berec has asked me to write to the Home Office. I will, but it won't do any good, of course.'

Isabel remembered Gregor, his passion for justice. Surely he wasn't dangerous, and Karin was the most gentle of women. How was it that no one was as they seemed.

Gelert had followed Penelope out to the kitchen. He nosed open the door to the pantry.

'Oh lor, the ham,' Isabel said, leaping up to rescue it. 'Won't you both stay for supper? There's an awful lot of food.'

Penelope shook her head. 'Reginald wants to get back to London.' She stood up. 'Isabel,' she said, 'you're a Lewis. And our mother used to tell Pamela and me that Lewis women do not lie down and give up. You must find a way, but I can't tell you what that way is. It's for you to find out.'

Isabel felt at that moment that lying down and giving up was all that she could manage, but she nodded.

'One more cup of tea,' Penelope said, 'and then I really think we must be going.'

That night, Lorna became very ill. Her temperature shot right up, and her eyes glittered with fever. Worst of all she began to cough, a strange tight little cough like a seal's bark, and she couldn't quite catch her breath. The doctor was summoned and pronounced it to be croup. A steam kettle was unearthed and Isabel spent an anxious night with Lorna in a bathroom filled with steam to ease her breathing. By the morning the worst was over, but several days and nights of careful nursing were required before the baby was declared completely out of danger. Isabel was exhausted. By the time mother and child were strong enough to travel to Kent, her mother was out of hospital – for the time being, at least. Isabel took Lorna with her, which pleased her family, but she was shocked by her mother's appearance; Pamela was so thin and pale it seemed that light shone through her.

It was soon after her return that she plucked up courage to speak to Hugh about the matter that was upmost in her mind.

'I don't like her coming here, Hugh.'

'Jacqueline? Why not?'

'I – she tries to come between us.'

'That's a very unkind thing to say. I think she's been a tremendous help. Look how much she's done for you with Lorna, especially when you've been . . . unwell.'

'She has helped, I see that, but I'm much better now and she doesn't need to keep coming to the house.'

'Isabel, she's a friend, and she's recently lost her husband. You're surely not suggesting we drop her when it's her turn to need us?'

'And I'm sorry for her. But don't you think it rather odd, that she latches on to us the way she does?'

'That's rubbish, Isabel.'

'It isn't, I'm sure it isn't. Your mother said—' She stopped.

Hugh folded his arms. 'And what did my mother say? Wait, I think I can guess. She's always had a thing about Jacqueline. Absolute nonsense, of course.'

'But is it? I can't feel settled about the whole thing. And I know that you've been seeing her in London.'

'Seeing her? Now what can you possibly mean by that? If you mean that she's accompanied me out to dinner occasionally, or to a party, why, yes, I've been seeing her. But we're both married, or rather she was then. Someone would have to have a particularly nasty mind to make anything of it. Who is it? Tell me.'

'It doesn't matter. That's not the point.'

'It's your aunt, isn't it? She pretends to be so aloof, but she enjoys giving the pot a stir.'

'That's a horrid thing to say. She's not like that at all.'

'Nor is Jacqueline the person you seem to think she is. She's always been a friend to my family, right since we were small. She's loyal and kind and helpful, and now you're hitting her when she's down. It's not very Christian of you.'

'Hugh! I didn't say she wasn't any of those things. Oh, you don't see it at all, do you? I can't be myself when she's here. She takes over. It makes me feel useless – useless, don't you see? And people are talking about it. It must stop.'

'You're being irrational. Why does everything have to be a big drama with you? Accusing people of this and that, with not a shred of evidence. It's wild.'

'It is *not* wild, Hugh. Or irrational. It's a feeling I have.'

'If we all followed our feelings we'd be like animals. Listen to me. Jacqueline is closer to me than any of my relatives now that Mother's gone. She looked after Mother, too. Such a comfort to her after my father died.'

'Any of your relatives? What about me – don't I matter?'

'Of course you matter, you silly thing. But I'm not going to blank my friends because you have feelings about them. It's balderdash.'

She looked at him steadily. 'Hugh, I'm sorry that you think so little of my feelings. I am your wife, after all. And I have to ask you something. Are you having an affair with Jacqueline?'

'How can you even ask that? Don't you trust me at all?'

'Just answer the question. Please, I need to know.'

'I don't feel I have to. That's a monstrous accusation.'

'Does that mean the answer's no? Please, Hugh, it's important.'

He opened his mouth then closed it again and looked wildly about the room. 'I can't see that there's any point in continuing this conversation,' he said. He walked about, randomly picking up clothes, his brush and comb, and putting them down again. Then he threw aside the pillow and grabbed the pyjamas lying underneath.

'I'll sleep in Mother's old room tonight. It'll give you the chance to calm down.'

'Hugh, please.'

But he was out of the door without another word. She went after him. 'Hugh,' she called, 'the bed's not made up.' But he ignored her, swept into his mother's bedroom and shut the door. She went and stood outside, and was about to grasp the handle, when she heard the key turn in the lock.

'Hugh,' she moaned, throwing herself against the door. She gave a sob. Inside there was silence. After a while she returned to her bedroom where she fell on the bed and cried.

The sense that she'd ruined everything was overwhelming. She'd accused her husband of something of which she had no proof, only an intense suspicion. Perhaps she'd done wrong by Jacqueline, who'd been so generous with her time and energy during the last year or so. Maybe she'd ruined her marriage, irreparably. She'd hardly recognised her beloved Hugh in the hard cold man who'd berated her this evening. Perhaps he was right: she was hysterical, irrational, but she didn't think she was. He'd been so unjust, when all she'd wanted was loving reassurance. She could not remember ever feeling so miserable. At that thought she wept some more.

In the morning, when she went downstairs carrying

Lorna, he was eating breakfast alone. He smiled at Lorna but hardly looked at Isabel. 'I've decided I'm going to London this afternoon,' he told her in the chilliest of tones. 'I think it would be best under the circumstances.'

'Oh, Hugh, shouldn't we talk?' she said, unable to stop the sob in her voice.

'I think we've both said enough for now. I rather favour some peace and quiet. Perhaps you'd like to think about what you've said.' He finished his toast, took up his tea and shut himself into his study.

That afternoon, he left for London with only a cold 'Goodbye'.

Chapter 35

Emily

One Friday in July, Emily left for work first thing, planning to swim before getting down to the business of the day, but when she arrived at the swimming baths a notice informed her they were closed because the heating system had broken. Feeling grumpy, she consoled herself with a takeaway pot of creamy porridge from a sandwich shop. She was so early at the office that the receptionist was not yet at her desk and Emily was the only one in the lift as it juddered its way up to her floor.

When the lift door opened she was surprised to see someone waiting to get in – a small, older woman in a neatly tailored blouse and skirt. She looked startled by Emily's appearance, but returned her 'Good morning' in a friendly enough tone as the lift doors closed between them. Emily wondered vaguely who she was. She'd glimpsed her once or twice before.

She went to look at her pigeonhole, but it was too early for the post. She turned and saw from the panel over the lift that it had stopped at one, indicating that the woman had got out at the floor below. That was the floor of the Reference division, she recalled. Perhaps the woman worked there. Emily wondered vaguely what she'd been doing on this floor.

She opened the door to her office and saw she was the first one in, but at once she sensed that someone else had been there. On her desk lay an envelope addressed to 'Miss Emily Gordon', in the same way all the other mysterious envelopes had been. She opened it, her mind still computing connections. Suddenly they all fell into place. That woman she had just seen must have left it here.

She quickly scanned the pages in Isabel's handwriting whilst eating a couple of spoonfuls of porridge, then stuffed the pages back into the envelope and hurried with it to the door, just as Sarah came in.

'You're in early,' Sarah told her.

'Sorry,' she gasped in reply. 'See you later. I've got to catch someone.'

It might sound odd to an outsider that Emily should have worked in a company for almost a year and yet failed to have set foot on one of its floors. But her department operated completely independently from the Reference division, and she had never had any cause to visit anyone there. The first-floor landing, she found, was exactly the same as the second floor in most respects, yet it exuded a different air. There were several posters on the wall here, charts about birds and fish, but these were sad and shabby, the corners curling. Several of the ubiquitous plastic crates colonised the space under the pigeonholes, piled with old reference books no longer wanted in the bright pixelated world of the internet.

Although it was nearly nine now, the place was quiet. How to ask for someone whom she'd only glimpsed for a moment, and whose name she didn't yet know? Still, she prowled the landing hopefully, and was soon rewarded. At the far end, hidden away behind the lift-shaft, a strip of daylight fell across the carpet, drawing her to an open door. She peeped inside but there was no one there, though the occupant had clearly been in the middle of packing books into crates. It was a small office, with a window looking out on the backs of other buildings, but someone had made it their home.

Entranced, Emily took a step inside to admire the lovely old desk, the floor lamp with its fringed shade, pretty cushions on the chairs. On a bookcase by her elbow was a series of wildlife guides, with beautifully decorated spines, that produced a tug of recognition. She put out a hand to withdraw the one which had always been her favourite. It was about creatures of the sea.

'They're first editions.' The voice behind her was low and musical. She looked round in surprise to see a pair of brown eyes, intelligent, amused. They belonged to the woman she had seen upstairs, getting into the lift. She was neat, if plainly dressed, and her grey hair was cut into a schoolgirl bob to frame her heart-shaped face.

'I'm sorry to intrude,' Emily stammered, showing the book in her hand. 'I love this series. My father owns a set. He's always telling us how he bought them with money from his paper round when he was a boy.'

'They're splendid, aren't they?' the woman said, selecting another from the shelves and turning to a beautiful frontis-piece. 'I'm particularly proud of having published them.'

'You did?' These books were a part of Emily's child-hood, and here was the woman responsible for them. There was something amazing about this.

'I was the editor, yes,' the woman told her. 'Quite a labour of love they were at the time, as we had such trouble with the photographs – but it was worth it in the end. They reprint year after year, you know, even now. Can't think why anyone would want one of those wretched ebooks instead. You can't look at those on the shelf, can you?'

'No,' Emily said in hearty agreement. She glanced about the room. 'What an awful business, packing up all of this must be.'

'Yes,' the woman said. 'I'm finding it horribly emotional. The whole of my working life, forty-odd years' worth, is in this room. The files and manuscripts have to go to the archives, and some of the books, but I'm allowed to keep anything they've already got copies of.'

'You're leaving then,' Emily said, passing her the book, 'not just moving offices?'

'I'm leaving, yes.' The woman gave a wistful smile. 'I suppose it's time. I was planning to retire anyway in the next year or two. It's come earlier than I thought, that's all.'

'I don't know your name, I'm afraid,' Emily said, putting out her hand. 'I'm Emily Gordon.'

'I know who you are,' the woman said gravely, shaking it. 'And I know why you've come. I've been waiting.'

'I was right then. It *was* you who's been sending me everything about Isabel. Why? I don't understand.'

'It was indeed me. Come, sit down for a moment.' She scooped up some books from a chair for Emily to sit, then herself sat down behind the desk.

'But how . . . ?' Emily asked.

The woman folded her hands on the desk in a calm pose. 'I'm not sure where to start.'

Emily smiled. 'My granny says always to start at the beginning.'

'That's good advice if one is sure where the beginning is. Well, let me see.' She regarded Emily thoughtfully for a moment. 'You may not know this, but I'm on the circulation list for the minutes of your editorial meetings, and I noticed your name next to Hugh Morton's biography. The biography itself wasn't exactly a surprise. I knew there would have to be one sometime, and then Lorna warned me it was happening.'

'Lorna? You know Lorna?'

'Good gracious, yes. You're surprised. I thought you'd see more of the connections by now.'

Emily felt more and more confused. 'I'm sorry, can we go back a step? I still don't know who you are.'

'Oh, goodness, haven't I introduced myself? I'm Lydia Hardcastle.' Emily recognised the name only vaguely, possibly from some typed list, but certainly not in relation to Isabel. She obviously looked blank, because Lydia said, 'Perhaps it will help you to learn that my maiden name was Barber.'

'Lydia Barber? Then you're . . . ?'

'I'm Isabel's baby sister.'

'Little Lydia?' Emily struggled to accept this. A small girl in a pushchair, far away in time – that was Isabel's sister, not this cultured mature woman sitting across the desk in the offices of a modern publisher.

'I'm sorry,' Lydia sighed. 'I know it's a big thing to take in. There's a great deal to explain, and I must ask you to be patient.'

'Patient?' Emily couldn't help bursting out. 'I don't mean to be rude, but I've been waiting long enough. It's quite creepy and stressful, you know, being sent anonymous packages.'

A shadow fell across Lydia's face and Emily saw she'd hurt her, but it was difficult to regret her words. These last few months had indeed been stressful in a number of ways, and now here was Lydia, whom she had to remember was Isabel's sister. Suddenly the secrecy and the tension were too much. 'Why, for goodness' sake?'

'Please give me time to explain,' Lydia said. She seemed sad now, diminished, and Emily felt sorry for her outburst. Lydia Hardcastle must have been having a difficult time, too, dismantling her life here, coming to terms with retirement.

They were both silent for a moment. Lydia glanced round at the chaos as she struggled to find the right words. 'Do you have the time for this now?' she said. 'All I have to do is continue packing.'

'I'm fine,' Emily said. 'No meetings till eleven. And this is important.'

Lydia settled back in her chair and said hesitantly, 'Have you read any of the material I sent you?'

'All of it. Except today's bit. I've only glanced at that quickly.'

Lydia looked relieved. 'And what did you think about the story so far?'

'What did I think?' Emily considered this. Pictures rose in her mind of a young woman, bright, ambitious, full of vitality, whose life changed dramatically after marriage and having a child. An ordinary story, the story of many women, she supposed, though each story must be utterly individual. 'It was very sad,' she admitted. 'Life didn't turn out as she expected.'

'Most of us can eventually say that,' Lydia murmured. 'Nothing else?'

'I suppose I wondered who it's important to. Isn't Jacqueline Morton trying to suppress all memory of Isabel?'

'Yes,' Lydia said promptly. 'She is.'

'I suppose I can see why. From what I've read, Isabel felt oppressed, but Hugh clearly loved her. Even though he probably slept with Jacqueline. Why did Jacqueline hang about like that? It must have been so demeaning.'

'I agree. Love, I imagine. What else did you glean?'

'Nothing else,' Emily said, then paused. 'I suppose there has to be something, doesn't there? Something I haven't read yet. Is there any more?'

'Not of the memoir, I'm afraid.'

Emily must have looked disappointed because Lydia said, 'But we do know something of what happened next.'

'We? Do you mean you and Jacqueline?'

Lydia said quietly, 'No, I mean Lorna and I.'

'Lorna?' Somehow this had been the last person Emily had expected Lydia to say. Lorna, so quiet and compliant, so much under Jacqueline's thumb.

Lydia looked steadily into Emily's eyes. 'When Jacqueline told Lorna about the biography and who was writing it, we despaired at first. It was plain that Jacqueline had Joel Richards exactly where she wanted him.'

'I think he is a little frightened of her,' Emily said, feeling she ought to defend Joel, even though Lydia had just confirmed her own suspicions.

'I think so too. It seemed my sister would never have justice.'

'Justice? That is a very strong word.'

'When you learn the whole story, you will under-stand. Lorna has ambivalent feelings about Isabel, and in her way she's fond of her stepmother and doesn't like to offend her. Despite all this, she's passionate, abso-lutely passionate, that her real mother is not just wiped out of any account of Hugh. She wants the truth to be told.'

'What truth exactly?' Emily asked, but Lydia had more to say.

'Lorna felt she couldn't speak out publicly, and she would never let me do it, so eventually we came up with the idea of providing you, the editor of the book, with Isabel's story, and you could pass it on to Joel. I say it was our idea, but I suppose it was mine, originally. When I saw those meeting minutes with your name, I wanted to come and speak to you in person, but I couldn't think what you would say. You'd probably have thought me mad, coming along with a garbled story about righting a wrong from long in the past.'

Emily considered this. 'I might have thought you a bit odd.'

'Quite. So I left you Isabel's copy of *Coming Home* on a whim, as a sort of teaser, if you like. And then when Lorna first met you, she liked you very much, saw you as a person of integrity. So we agreed. We'd feed you Isabel's story bit by bit. I already had the file for *Coming Home* in my office. I called it up from the archive some time ago to help with my own research about Isabel.'

'And Isabel's memoir, where did that come from?'

'Ah, now that is intriguing. It nearly didn't survive, you know. Lorna found it after her father's death, together with the wedding photograph. She was deeply troubled by the account and shared it with me. Did you find it interesting?'

'Of course, how could I not have done?' Lydia and Lorna's plan had been a clever one. Emily had become every bit as fascinated as they'd hoped. She looked down at the envelope in her hand.

'You haven't had a chance to read that bit, of course, ' Lydia said.

'No.'

'Well, when you have, let's talk again. I'm not leaving here for another couple of weeks.'

Emily nodded. She stood up to go, then hesitated.

'Information overload,' Lydia said, smiling. 'I'm sorry.'

'There's something you ought to know,' Emily said. 'I've been passing all this information on to Joel, but if you intended me to get him to put it all into the book, then I'm afraid that you'll be disappointed.'

Lydia's expression darkened. 'That's what I feared might happen. How we handle that is one of the matters that we must talk about.'

'There's another thing.' Emily looked down at the envelope. 'You said this was the final part?'

'It was all that we found,' Lydia said quietly. 'I'm sorry. Those are probably the last words Isabel wrote.'

'Oh.'

'But there is something else you can see.' Lydia went to a filing cabinet and opened the top drawer. From one of the files she took a sheaf of paper.

'I typed this myself,' she said, giving it to Isabel. 'It's based on a conversation I had with my Aunt Penelope before she died ten years ago, a very old lady of ninety-five. It was she who found me a job in publishing, you know. She thought it would make up for something. I'd only known the barest details before of what she told me, but she wanted me to hear it all. She still felt guilty, she said, all those years later.'

'Guilty? What of?'

'You'll have to read it to find out. It's quite a story. Read it, and then we'll talk again about what to do next.'

She came round the desk to shake Emily's hand.

Lydia, Emily thought, meeting the woman's warm gaze. It was still difficult to accept that it was her. She already liked the woman immensely; felt there was a connection between the two of them. It was astonishing when you thought about it. Here she was, forging her career, meeting a woman whose work as an editor was nearly done. And like a presence between them was someone else again – Isabel, a young woman whose career, whose very future, had been thwarted.

Chapter 36

Isabel

As good as her word, Penelope telephoned halfway through January. Reginald, she told Isabel, was attending the wedding of his eldest daughter in Hampshire, so she was at a loose end. They arranged that she should pick up Isabel and take her to stay overnight at the beach house, which was nicely warm in winter, Penelope assured her. There was some talk as to whether Lorna should accompany them, but in the end Lily Catchpole offered to look after her, so it was with a rare sense of freedom that Isabel found herself riding beside Penelope in her sleek blue-black car through the wintry countryside. They turned down the narrow road across the marshes to the little seaside town and along the lane to the lonely white-painted house behind the sand dunes.

Once inside, Penelope set about making coffee in the kitchen, whilst Isabel sat stroking Gelert's rough coat.

'That hound's too big for this house,' Penelope grumbled, pushing past him to take down cups from a cupboard, but her tone was affectionate.

Isabel thought how different Penelope was here, more relaxed and talkative. Who'd have thought it, her elegant perfumed aunt with her love of good clothes and city entertainments, at home in this desolate setting with only the sound of the waves, the sough of the breeze across the marshes and the cries of the seabirds for company.

'I have Gelert,' Penelope said, when Isabel commented on this. 'We get along together very well when he isn't under my feet, don't we, my good dog? Perhaps we could walk him along the beach, if you feel up to it.'

The tide was high and they walked by the great waves of an iron-grey sea. The air was cold but still, so that their voices bounced off the cliffs, crisp and clear – not that either spoke much. Penelope walked in front, her head bowed as though under some burden. Isabel shoved her hands deep in her coat pockets in an effort to keep warm and laughed at the dog's comic forays into the sea. And all the while her sense of trepidation grew. Her aunt had brought her here for some reason, but what that was had yet to be revealed.

They walked along the concrete promenade and past the empty pier until they came to a wilder part of the beach, not much visited. Here the brown earth edges of the cliffs were crumbling away and great dead branches of trees lay on the ochre sand where they'd fallen, to be bleached clean by the merciless sea.

'It's like a graveyard of trees,' Isabel remarked at one point. It was the first time either of them had spoken for some time.

'Once or twice it's been a house that's collapsed,' Penelope said. She brushed the sand off a tree trunk and they both sat down on it, looking up at the eroded cliff whilst Gelert ran about before coming to flop down at their feet. 'Everything and everybody is ultimately washed away by the tides of time. And our labours are as naught.'

Isabel glanced up at her aunt in surprise at her bitter tone. She was astonished to see tears in Penelope's eyes, though the woman did her best to hide them.

'Ah, I'm sorry,' Penelope said. 'I was thinking of Pamela.' She brought a packet of cigarettes from her coat pocket and lit one, before saying, 'I know you're wondering what this is all about.'

'I suppose I am.'

Penelope sighed. 'As you know, I went to visit your mother in hospital before Christmas. She'd written to tell me that she was ill again and wanted to see me.'

'I wish she'd let me know, too.'

Penelope laid her hand briefly on Isabel's arm. 'It's very difficult for her. She's a fighter, your mother. But you must let me continue.'

She continued, hesitant at first, then her words flowed more freely.

'Pamela and I for a long time have had little to say to one another. There are things about the way I am that horrify her. And in my turn I've found her and your father hard and unforgiving. Although we're sisters, we do not have much in common these days.'

'But you were once close? That photograph of when you were children,' Isabel said, remembering. 'Your square fringes. You looked so alike.'

'We did, didn't we? Despite being nearly three years apart. Yes, there was a time when we were close. We had to be. It was always us against the world, especially at school. I remember speaking to you once about your grandmother,' Penelope said. 'I'll start by telling you about her. It's a way into the story, if you like. Her own father died young, and being the only child, she was left the family farmlands. Where we were brought up, that was the manor house. Not the original one, of course, but built on the site of the original. What she ought to have done was marry some local landowner who'd look after the place, but instead she followed her heart. Our father was the younger son of a Norwich businessman. He wasn't a bad man, but nor was he a wise one. He inherited none of his own father's acumen. After he invested in some bad business ventures, my parents ended up selling the farmland to get them out of debt. Then in 1916 he was called up, just in time for Passchendaele. He died of injuries sustained in his first week at the front. My mother was left a widow with a tiny pension and two small daughters, and had to beg her husband's family for handouts. The point of me telling you all this is to make you understand about our upbringing. Mummy was always very strict and proper. Although we were never allowed to tell anyone, she worried all the time about money. That was what made things worse, her pride. She was an awful snob. We were never allowed to mix with local children out of school; their parents thought we were stuck-up, and of course that meant our lives were miserable. We were thrown onto our own company a great deal. You can imagine how all this affected us – the secrecy, the isolation.'

Isabel thought about it all. She could imagine her mother as a very young woman, proud, keeping up appearances, suffering in silence, guarding her sister Penelope, whose own aloofness was a form of armour. Yes, it all made too much sense.

'Our gardens backed on to one of the Broads and we had our own mooring and a small sailing dinghy. One day, when your mother was nineteen and I was sixteen, we found a strange boat tied up and four young men sitting on our jetty eating sandwiches. When we confronted them, they said they hadn't seen the Private sign and were terribly apologetic. They were nice boys, Londoners all of them, in their early twenties, but despite their good manners we knew instinctively that they weren't Mummy's type. Pam and I thought them very dashing, especially when they larked about and flirted with us. Right from the start, though, it was obvious that the best-looking of them had his eye on Pamela. Your father was one of those quiet, brooding types then, Isabel – the way I imagined a Romantic poet to be.'

Isabel smiled. It was hard now, remembering him from when she was small, before the quiet brooding turned morose. Mostly it was an impression of gentleness.

'It is a bit chilly,' her aunt said, standing up and tossing her cigarette on the sand. 'I think it's time to go back.'

They walked slowly side by side. Penelope had fallen silent again. Isabel asked, 'What happened next? I mean, I know they went away together.'

'They did, yes. Your grandmother, predictably, kicked up a terrible fuss about Pamela seeing Charles, and Pamela was always stubborn. I often wonder whether, if Mummy had kept quiet, the whole thing would have died a natural death. As it was, Pamela simply would have him, and that was that. There was the most ghastly row and Mummy said she didn't want to see her again. So Pamela went away. I suppose she must have got

Mummy's consent, I really can't remember. I do know we didn't go to the wedding.'

'They lived in Kent, didn't they, by the time they had me?'

'They lived with his relatives in Clapham for several years. Your mother used to write to me from there. It was before the Slump, and your father had what I'm told was a good job at the Post Office, but it wasn't until he was promoted that they could afford to set up house. '

'I wasn't born till later on.'

'Yes – on the tenth of February nineteen twenty-nine. There, I remember your birth date perfectly.'

Isabel smiled. 'You've always been good at that.'

'I have, haven't I?' Penelope stopped for a moment and turned to look out to sea. She murmured what sounded like, 'At least I got something right in my life.'

Whether it was these words, or something else like them, she sounded utterly desolate. Aunt Penelope clearly carried some terrible burden that Isabel had never previously suspected. She waited, hardly daring to speak in case she caused her aunt to close up again, and then she'd never learn whatever it was that she and her sister had spoken about – the thing that had opened up a rift between them.

After a long moment, Penelope called to Gelert and they set off once more. Isabel felt increasingly puzzled as her aunt did not continue with her tale, but instead spoke of Berec's friends Gregor and Karin. Apparently Penelope had had the bright idea of involving Stephen in the campaign to stop the deportation, and Stephen had mobilised one or two well-known writers in their defence. It looked as though the deportation might be stopped.

'Stephen is a good man,' Penelope said quietly.

Isabel remembered what Stephen had said, about knowing Penelope for so long, and she thought of Berec and how he'd introduced her to Stephen, then for some reason she recalled the envelope with Stephen's handwriting that she'd seen in her aunt's kitchen in Earl's Court all that time ago. 'Aunt Penelope,' she said, 'you remember how I got my job at McKinnon and Holt. Was that because of you?'

Penelope smiled. 'No, dear, that was all due to you impressing him. He merely wrote to me for a reference – which I was happy to give.'

'I'm so glad that's all it was,' Isabel said, relieved. 'Thank you.'

They had reached the beach house now. Inside, Penelope rubbed Gelert dry with a towel then started laying out cheese and bread and wrinkled apples on the kitchen table, and poured them both glasses of ruby port. The heavy warmth of the drink spread through Isabel's veins like liquid fire. It made her brave enough to say, 'It's lovely, being with you like this. Oh, I wish I'd seen more of you when I was growing up.'

Penelope laid some cutlery on the table and frowned. 'We lived such different lives, your mother and I. And she was shocked to her little puritan core when I refused to put up with Jonny any more. I still don't think she understands. Just because she stuck with your father all these years . . .'

'She loves him,' Isabel said loyally. 'He can't help what happened to him.'

'Yes, she probably does,' Penelope said with a sigh. 'And, of course, she had all of you to think of.'

'You and Uncle Jonny didn't try to have children?'

'Neither of us wanted them. Anyway, Jonny was too drunk most of the time to do much in that direction.'

Isabel thought of the conversation she'd had with her aunt, when she'd found she was going to have Lorna and her aunt had dropped dark hints about getting rid of the baby. Perhaps Penelope had not been sharing her own experience, after all, just passing on information in case it was useful.

'I can laugh at it now. It's all a very long time ago,' Penelope was saying. 'Life goes on. But not if we don't eat.'

The rest of the day passed pleasantly enough. They had tea in a café in the town and bought fresh herring for dinner, about which there was much palaver as neither of them liked the messiness of gutting fish. They grilled them and ate them with new potatoes and a bottle of crisp white wine, whilst Penelope told amusing stories of her life in London, stories peppered with names Isabel had faintly heard of and others who'd vanished into oblivion.

That night, Isabel slept more soundly than she had done for a long time. This house felt like a sanctuary; it must be something about the wood and its cosy situation, protected from the elements behind the dunes. She woke at one point in darkness, heard her aunt's door open and close, the click of the dog's claws on the floorboards, but quickly sank into slumber once more.

In the morning she woke late to find that she was alone in the house. On the kitchen table was an envelope addressed to her and a key. Puzzled, she opened the envelope. As she drew out the papers within, a five-pound note fluttered to the floor. She picked it up and left it on the table whilst she investigated the rest of the contents. There was a letter and another envelope with her name on it. She started, naturally enough, by reading the letter.

My dear Isabel,

I have taken the coward's way out and gone back to London. Please don't think that I'm not utterly ashamed of myself, because I am, but performing the task that your mother has commanded me to has proved impossible. I hate confrontation of any sort and I cannot bear to see your face when you learn this news. All day yesterday I tried to tell you, but I just haven't been able to do so. I know I'm leaving you without a lift home, so I hope the enclosed will cover the cost of a taxi. Ask at Bunwell's for Eric. He's the son-in-law and I've always found him most reliable.

Now to finish the story I started to tell you on the beach yesterday. After Pamela ran away with your father, I'm afraid things went badly for me. It's quite a burden suddenly to become not only the sole repository of a mother's hopes and expectations, but also the target of her frustrations. I think, looking back, that she must have had some sort of breakdown, for she would often indulge in fits of rage or weeping, which I found terrifying.

When I was eighteen I was sent to live with my uncle's family in Norwich for a year whilst I learned shorthand and typing. Your grandmother wanted me to take a job somewhere respectable locally until I came across 'someone suitable' as she put it, but I got it in my head that I wanted to follow Pamela and move to London. I wrote to her several times about how to do this, and after first trying to dissuade me she told me that I could stay with them for a short time whilst I found somewhere.

In the event I never got there, because of someone I met on the train. His name was Tom, Tom Spencer, and whilst he was definitely from the sort of family Mummy would approve of, he was not, as they say, the marrying kind. I thought he was marvellous, so beautiful and fascinating, and well-connected. I don't know what he saw in me. I was impossibly innocent in those days. Mother never told me a thing about men; she had these wonderful rose-coloured memories of Daddy and that's all she knew. Tom took me in hand right away – I think he saw me as a sort of project, like Pygmalion. He found me a nice little job typing for a literary agent and I took a room with some friends of his, and for the next three or four years my life was a great whirl of parties and cocktails and late nights. Such fun, you'd think, but at the same time it didn't seem at all real. Nobody was very serious about anything, and you only had to look around in London with your eyes open in the 1920s to see just how serious life could be. Even Tom learned in the end. His plane was shot down over the Channel in 1940. He'd made an exceptionally glamorous pilot and I hate to think about the messiness of his end.

The partying ended abruptly for me when I discovered I was to have Tom's child. It's astonishing how my so-called friends melted away. Tom, of course, denied it was his. No one, it seemed, could help me. So I went to the only person I could count on. Not my mother, the shame would have finished her. I went to Pamela.

You were born in a home for unmarried girls in South London. Most of the girls found it terrible, giving up their babies for adoption by couples they didn't know, never to see them again. I was lucky, so they told me. At least my child would stay in the family, be a part of my life, but once I'd handed you over to Pamela I felt an appalling sense of relief.

I'd regained my freedom, you see. And Pamela wanted you. They had no child of their own, and feared they never would. You looked so like my sister. She loved you straight away. You should have seen the light in her eyes when she gazed into yours for the first time. And me? By giving you away to my sister I felt I'd lost all rights to you. It was only fair to let you all alone. I went back to my job with the literary agent but I was an innocent no longer. Not long afterwards I met Jonny, and thought I'd found my chance for security and respectability. How wrong I was.

We never saw the need to tell you any of this, your mother and I. The moment never presented itself. But now it's time. I am truly sorry for the pain this knowledge will give you. I am sorry for failing you over and over again, first as a mother, then as an aunt and as a friend. None of it was planned, it was just how life happens.

Your very affectionate
Penelope

Isabel sank onto a kitchen chair and read the letter through again. She still couldn't believe what it said. Finally she remembered the little envelope waiting on the table. She opened it. Inside was a piece of thick paper which she unfolded. It was a birth certificate. Here was her name, *Isabel Mary*, and Penelope's, *Penelope Frances Lewis* as she was called then, but under *Father* was simply the word *Unknown*. Her date of birth was still 10 February 1929, the place of birth Wandsworth, South London.

It must have been soon afterwards that Charles and Pamela had taken her to live in Kent. A new start, she supposed, where no one would know them. And then four or five years later, the gift of twins of their own, followed eventually by Lydia.

Penelope was her real mother. Everything about the letter and the certificate spoke truth. It was unforgivable that no one had told her this before. Her whole life was not as she'd believed it to be. She didn't want Penelope to be her mother. The woman had never cared for her, never. And now she'd been too afraid to tell Isabel, had run off to hide from her reaction.

She remained at the table without moving for some time, smoothing out the letter to read it a third time, then perusing the slip of stiff paper where her name was clearly written, *Isabel Mary*. Under *Mother* she touched the names *Penelope Frances Lewis* with her finger as though they might dissolve at will, but they remained clear and resolute.

It was difficult to accept the new facts presented to her. Her head knew, but her heart refused to regard the mother she had always known, as being her mother no longer. Penelope was no less emotionally distant for no longer being her aunt. Even her father, despite their difficulties, was still in all ways except the biological, her father.

And yet . . . This great secret was something her mother and Penelope had between them finally decided that she needed to know, now that Pamela was so ill. How had she never guessed? Nothing in all her twenty-four years had ever given her room to doubt the bedrock of her family life. Her mother had always been unwavering in her deep love. Her father had become curmudgeonly, oppressive even, but no more to her than to her brothers and sister; he'd treated them all equally, in this as everything. Had there not been the unmistakable evidence of this paper slip of officialdom with her name and birthdate on it, she might not have believed it.

And yet . . . It left her betrayed. Lied to. Her bedrock had crumbled. The world was now a completely different place, as if it had changed its mind and begun to revolve the other way.

And yet . . . Essentially, what had changed? Nothing. Only her perceptions. She wasn't who she thought she was. Her parents were liars, or at best dissemblers. Her aunt had marked the occasion of revealing herself as Isabel's mother by abandoning her all over again.

Hours passed. Gradually, despite the winter's day, warm sunlight from the window caressed her back and brought her to herself. She rose from the table and started opening cupboards until she found the bottle of port Penelope had opened yesterday. She set down a sherry schooner and very deliberately filled it to the brim with the glowing ruby liquid.

The first sip was like fire, but as she drank it all down she felt it move like molten metal through her veins, numbing her body. After this she felt better. So much better that she poured a second glass, which she took back with her to bed. She drank it, lay down, wrapped herself in blankets and soon fell deeply asleep.

When she awoke, the room was growing dark and she was ravenous. After all, she'd had neither breakfast nor lunch. She got out of bed and went to the kitchen. There was bread and bits and pieces of leftovers in the larder: eggs, cold ham, most of a fruit cake. She switched on a fire in the sitting room and sat with her feet up on the sofa to eat as the night settled in. It was a consolation to be without responsibilities, alone with her thoughts. She thought of Lorna, of course, but knew that she was safe and well, thank goodness, after her illness. Lorna would be all right without her for a while.

The next day she stayed, and the next. She passed the time in long walks, wrapped up against the chill in scarves and gloves of Penelope's. She avoided the town or human company of any sort, except what was necessary to buy food and any small personal items she needed. On her outings she met hardly anyone, except dog walkers or fishermen mending nets down by the harbour. One man always nodded to her as she passed, a big portly old tar who seemed to be out in all weathers repairing an ancient wherry boat that looked as though it wouldn't last another season. She would return the nod and walk on without speaking, but once when she looked behind she saw him gazing after her. Not in an unpleasant way, but as though he was intrigued by her presence.

On the Saturday, five days after she'd left home, she returned from a morning walk to find a strange car parked near the house. As she approached, its door opened and to her surprise out stepped Stephen. He smiled at her uncertainly, passing his hat from hand to hand, and she stared at him dismayed because she was used to her own company now. 'I'm sorry if I'm intruding,' he said.

'Stephen, what are you doing here?'

He shut the car door and leaned against it, then reached into a pocket for his cigarettes, cupping his hand against the wind to light one. 'Let's just say that I was passing,' he said gravely.

'I suppose Penelope put you up to it.'

'She was worried. When you didn't return home, Hugh telephoned her.'

'He didn't come himself then.'

'Clearly not.'

As tears prickled she turned her face away.

'Men have their pride, Isabel.'

'I'd rather not discuss it with you, thank you,' she said, mastering herself. 'Since you're here you'd better come in.'

'Were you really in Suffolk anyway?' she asked, as she poured coffee into cups in the kitchen.

'You remember the writer Harold Chisholm? He lives near Aldborough. He's always good for a bed for the night and it's a lovely spot.' Stephen drank some coffee, watching her.

She gave a short, mirthless laugh.

'I don't like to see you like this,' he said softly.

'I'm sorry I look such a mess,' she said, dipping her head to study her reflection in the teardrop-shaped mirror Penelope had hung by the sink. Her hair was unkempt, and though her face was rosy from the chilly wind, she'd not bothered with make-up and there were dark shadows under her eyes. She didn't care.

'You're not a mess. You look beautiful,' he said, and she stilled, hearing the strangeness in his voice. She heard him put down his cup and sensed him come near. When she turned towards him he caught her in his arms and, pulling her towards him, kissed her. It was an urgent, passionate kiss, and she felt her mouth open under his, couldn't help but kiss him back. He tasted richly of the coffee and tobacco. His jaw grazed her cheek as he kissed her face and her neck and unbuttoned her cardigan to kiss the soft flesh above her collarbone, and she loved the scent of his hair and felt something deep in her start to relax. And in a moment she was crying, actually sobbing, as all her pent-up emotion was released in a great tide.

'My dear,' he said, 'don't,' and he bent to scoop her up and carried her through to the sitting room where he laid her on the sofa and kissed her some more through her tears.

Finally she drew back, then sat up and rubbed her eyes. Stephen reached into his breast pocket and shook out a handkerchief and gave it to her. She stared at it, the memory rushing back. She and Hugh in that steam-filled café in Brighton, when she'd cried and Hugh's handkerchief had been full of sand. The sense of loss she felt now made her start crying all over again.

'I hate to see you so unhappy, dear,' Stephen said, as she blew her nose. 'And I'm sorry, I couldn't stop myself. You don't know how long I've wanted you. It took me a long time to realise. It was when I saw you here last summer . . .'

'I didn't know,' she broke in. 'I'd no idea you felt like that. Oh, I wish you wouldn't. It makes things much more complicated.'

'Yes,' he said, looking very unhappy now. 'It does rather.'

They were silent for a moment, each lost in their own thoughts, then he leaned forward and once again started to kiss her. 'At least we have this moment,' he whispered, in between kisses. He moved his hand and stroked her breast through her blouse. Astonished, as if of its own accord, her body began to respond. It was so long since

Hugh had touched her like this, as though he wanted her desperately, needed her, and here was Stephen, good, solid, kind Stephen, whom she'd always thought of as a rock of strength, needing her in this way. She watched as he peeled off his jacket, loosened his top button and unfastened his cuffs, so she saw the gold hairs curling at his neck and felt a prickle of desire. They clung to one another as though the heat of passion could burn away each other's sorrow.

But as his hands explored, she felt less certain that this was what she wanted. She didn't want it to be Stephen doing this, she wanted Hugh. She couldn't just replace one with the other, it didn't feel right. She pushed his hand away. 'No,' she gasped, then more strongly, 'No, please.'

He drew back. 'I'm sorry,' he said. 'I'm going too fast, aren't I? Forgive me.'

'There's nothing to forgive,' she said. 'I just can't, that's all.' She rose from the sofa and tidied her clothes. 'I meant it when I said I was a mess. Did Penelope tell you everything?'

'Yes,' he said. 'I hope you don't mind. She's sworn me to secrecy. I've never known her so upset.'

'*She's* upset?' Isabel said, outraged. 'I find it impossible to be sorry for her.'

'Perhaps when you've had time to think—'

'Don't patronise me, Stephen,' she cried, angry now. 'Why do you defend her all the time? It's as though you're her poodle. You come here at her command—'

'I came because I wanted to,' he said.

'I can never forgive her. Never. She didn't even have the courage to tell me face-to-face.'

'Isabel, you must try to understand. I knew her when she was cast lower than any woman should be. It's her way of surviving, to be distant. She does care about you, I know she does.'

Isabel sighed. 'Really, Stephen, you're much too decent. That's your trouble. You like to see the best in people. You should have stepped in when Hugh was courting me, told me he was wrong for me.'

'I tried, don't you remember?'

'Did you? I suppose I didn't listen. But none of this is any good because although I'm fond of you, Stephen, and I really am, the fact remains that I'm married to Hugh. And despite everything, I do still love him.'

Stephen looked as though she'd struck him. She felt stronger now, much clearer about what she wanted.

'I think it would be better if you went now. Call in on old Harold, I'm sure he's dying for some company.' She said this gently, trying to make it into a joke.

'You're probably right,' he said humbly. 'I should go. But if you should change your mind . . . Well, you know my feelings now. I'd wait for you, you know.'

'Thank you, but don't,' she said, going to him and kissing him once more. He held her close for a moment, then picked up his jacket and was gone.

She stayed in Penelope's house another few days. Then came gales from the north and the sea was whipped into a torment. She stood on the cliff watching gigantic waves engulf the pier, smash against the promenade below, soaking her in spray, and at last found a kind of peace.

Saturday came and the weather was worse. The wind buffeted the house so it shook. Late in the afternoon she decided. She had a husband whom she still loved and a dear little baby, and she longed to see them both again. Perhaps she was strong enough now to try to win Hugh back. She was ready to go home.

As darkness fell she made her way out in the storm to the telephone box by the church and rang Stone House. When Hugh answered, the line crackled and it was a moment before she heard him properly.

'Hugh? Hugh, it's me.'

The response was not what she had hoped for.

'Isabel, is that you?' His voice was urgent, angry. 'What the heck . . . ? Where are you?'

'I'm still at the beach house. Hugh, forgive me, I'll explain when I see you, but would you come and fetch me? Please?'

'Fetch you? Now? Just a minute, will you?'

The shock came when she heard a woman's voice in the background. The line was bad but she still made out what she said. Not to go tonight, to wait till tomorrow.

'Hugh, hello?'

'Isabel?'

'Hugh, what's Jacqueline doing there?'

Whether he heard her, she never knew. 'Isabel, I'll come tomorrow. The weather's too bad tonight. If it's better in the morning I'll come first thing.'

'Hugh, please, could you not come tonight?'

'Isabel, be reasonable—'

It was then that the line went dead. When she stumbled from the telephone box, all her newfound optimism had evaporated.

Chapter 37

Emily

It was past nine on a Saturday morning, and she was sitting in bed in Joel's apartment drinking his excellent coffee and enjoying a bit of solitude. Joel had had to go out early; a car had come for him an hour before. If she turned on the radio in a moment she should hear him being interviewed about Hugh Morton. There was interest building with the television series coming, and when the day before he'd asked if she minded about him going off, she'd encouraged him to say yes. After all, it was good pre-publicity for the book.

When the doorbell sounded she stumbled out of bed, pulled on Joel's dressing gown, and opened the door to find the postman with a Special Delivery letter, which she signed for. She glanced at the handwriting, thought it faintly familiar, and placed it on a kitchen worktop where Joel would see it.

The programme! She whisked over to the desk, where Joel had left his laptop on, tuned, he'd told her, to the right station. She pressed some keys and sat down in his chair to listen. The interview had started, but only just.

'– on our screens next week, with the gorgeous Zara Collins playing the iconic central character, Nanna,' a woman was saying. 'Joel, you're writing a book about the author, and you've been an adviser on this series, give us a bit of background. This series presents Nanna as a typical nineteen fifties' woman, trying to break free of domesticity. How did Hugh Morton, who one hardly thinks of as a feminist, come to write about her?'

'You have to remember . . .' Joel's voice came across warm, confiding. He was good at this, Emily thought, not for the first time. 'Morton wrote from a man's point of view. He was fascinated by Nanna, but I think he saw her path in life, going against the grain, as progressively self-destructive.'

'The novel finishes with her death, doesn't it?'

'Yes, that's right. The husband tells her story whilst in prison awaiting trial for her manslaughter.'

'Some say that Morton based the character of Nanna on his tragic first wife. What was her name – Isabel?'

Here Emily listened intently.

Joel gave a short laugh. 'It shouldn't be assumed that fictional characters are based, as you say, on real people. Isabel might have inspired Nanna – there are parallels there. Morton met her when his first novel was published. She was his editor, in fact. Nanna is a journalist, so the milieux were close.'

'Fascinating,' the interviewer said.

Joel went on: 'But in many ways Nanna is quite different from Isabel. He quickly realised his marriage was a mistake, you see. After her death he went on to marry a childhood friend, Jacqueline, and they were together for nearly sixty years. The book is dedicated to her, so you could say that she too was an inspiration.'

'Thank you, Joel. Now the fifties' costumes are brilliant and we have the costume designer here in the studio . . .'

Emily hardly heard what the costume designer had to say. She was thinking with astonishment about Joel. He had dismissed Isabel in a couple of sentences. After reading the memoir, after all they had talked about, he was still following Jacqueline's line – that Isabel was an irrelevance to Hugh, a brief wrong turning in his life, the only legacy of which was Lorna. Isabel was unimportant.

'*Zombies and Mermaids,* a new movie coming from the director of . . .' the interviewer continued. Emily pressed a button and the radio cut out. She stared at the computer desktop, thinking, and noticed Joel's document, now labelled *Hugh Morton biography.*

This time she couldn't stop herself opening it. She pulled up a chair, moved the cursor onto the icon and clicked. After a moment the document opened.

She saw very quickly that the book was nearly finished, as Joel had assured her. He'd typed out a Contents page and, when she looked at the final page of the document, she saw he was halfway through a Bibliography. She turned back to the Contents, found a chapter entitled *Coming Home* and started to look for Isabel's name. Here it was: *Stephen McKinnon introduced him to a young woman named Isabel Barber. She was to become his editor, an important influence on his writing and, for a short time, his wife.* The story of Isabel Morton, born Isabel Barber, occupied two chapters. She read, with a feeling of increasing unease, of how Isabel had been 'captivated' by Hugh, had wanted the glamour of being married to a man of letters, but had proved an unfit wife who neglected the couple's daughter and was implicated in the sudden death of Hugh's mother. After Isabel's own death, the impression given was that Jacqueline had brought stability back into his life . . .

The minutes passed. She was still reading when she heard footsteps on the stairs and Joel's voice speaking to someone below. Quickly she clicked to close the document, and waited an agonisingly long time for it to disappear from the screen. She moved away from the computer just as Joel entered the room.

'God, that was a waste of a morning.' He regarded her curiously, standing before him, an uncertain-looking figure engulfed by his towelling robe. 'Are you OK?'

'Yes, of course,' she said hurriedly, but she wasn't really. It was as though she was seeing him for the first time. He looked different, unfamiliar, and yet there was nothing about his physical appearance that could be said to have changed. He was as good-looking as ever, with that same air of self-possession that she had once found so charismatic, but in the space of his short absence he'd lost all attraction for her. Her feelings had changed. How had that happened?

'All that way for five minutes' air time,' he went on. He spied the envelope on the worktop and picked it up.

'I heard it, of course,' she said, recovering herself. 'You were good. Well, except you didn't do her justice. Isabel, I mean.'

Her wan tone made him put down the envelope and move to embrace her, but she stepped aside. She had to have this out with him once and for all.

'Emily,' he said gently. 'Don't keep on worrying about Isabel. It was a five-minute interview. I can hardly put all the subtleties into that. They want soundbites.'

'I know. But it's not just the radio programme, is it?' she said, her voice trembling. 'It's the whole book. All I wanted was for you to tell the truth.'

'I do tell the truth. As I keep explaining, I couldn't corroborate the memoir, don't you see? And all this stuff about Lorna giving it to Lydia to give to you to give to me, it is a little crazy, don't you think?'

'Joel, answer me this: have you actually shown the memoir to Jacqueline and asked her opinion?'

He blustered, and she said again, '*Have you?*'

'No.' He was angry now. 'No, I haven't. Emily, you haven't had to deal with Jacqueline like I have. She's like a block of stone about Isabel. There would be a hell of a row if I were to give her those ramblings. She'd never let me use them.'

'Oh, Joel!' she cried. 'What shall I tell Lydia? Lorna will be devastated if her mother's story isn't told. Surely she has a say?'

'Emily, Lorna was a baby when her mother left. She didn't know Isabel like Jacqueline did. And you'd think she'd show more loyalty to Jacqueline, who brought her up.'

'She has tried to be loyal, but she's conflicted, don't you see? You could still look into the matter deeper in the book, mention Isabel's journal as giving insight. Surely Jacqueline wouldn't mind that.'

'How do you know I haven't?' he answered, sullen.

'I do know you haven't,' she shot back.

'How?' He glanced at his laptop, the glowing screen telling its own story. 'You mean you've gone into my computer and looked?'

She nodded quickly.

'Without asking me?' He stared at her in disbelief as she nodded again. 'Unbelievable.'

'I would have seen it sometime, anyway.'

'When I chose to deliver it to you, you would,' he said, in a voice of steel.

'I know, I'm sorry. It was frustration. I had to know.'

'You've got yourself too involved in Isabel. Why are you so obsessed with her, Emily?'

'I don't know.' She thought for a moment. 'I suppose it's that I feel I know her. And that she's a little bit like me.' Yes, that was it.

'And what about me? Don't I matter? I'm the one who's writing this book, and I thought you trusted me.' He picked up the envelope again and tore it open so violently that the paper inside swooped to the floor. They both reached for it. Emily got there first.

Trust, she thought as she picked it up. That was what was lacking between them. She didn't trust him. And now he didn't trust her.

She stared down at the item in her hand. There was a small compliments slip pinned to a cheque. And the amount on the cheque – her eyes widened – was ten thousand pounds. *For delivery as agreed*, was written on the slip. *With grateful thanks, Jacqueline Morton.*

'Can I have that, please?' Joel commanded, stepping forward. Wordlessly, she passed it to him. So Jacqueline was paying him. No wonder he didn't want to offend her by writing about Isabel.

He glanced at the cheque and laid it on the worktop. 'I know what you're thinking,' he said. 'And I should have told you about it. She offered to top up the advance Parchment paid me, that's all. She's grateful and wanted to be kind.' All the energy had gone out of him now. He looked defeated. She realised she felt nothing for him any more except a sort of pity.

'You're right,' she whispered, sinking onto the sofa, desolate. 'You should have told me. At least now I understand. Ouch!'

Her hand had struck something sharp that was caught down the side of the sofa cushion. She shifted to look, pulled out the object and examined it. It was a large hair-comb with a clip and a pink feathery decoration. Not anything she would ever wear. After a second it came to her where she'd seen it before. It was Anna's – the blonde woman downstairs with the tap she couldn't turn off.

'I wonder how this got there,' she said lightly, standing and holding it out to him. He looked down at it with a frozen expression on his face.

'I – it's not what you think,' he started to say, but she didn't want to hear any more. She laid the comb down on top of the cheque.

'I'd better get dressed,' she said, trying to stop her voice wobbling. 'I'm sorry, Joel, but it's probably time I left.'

Chapter 38

Emily

Three months later

There could be no doubt that Jacqueline Morton was more frail now than when Emily had last seen her, almost a year ago. The old lady stooped and had to lean on a stick as she and Emily followed Lorna into the dining room at Stone House. There they found Joel scribbling a note on one of many sections of manuscript he'd arranged round him at the table. Seeing Emily, he rose and came to greet her.

'Hello,' she said quietly, shaking his hand. She met his nervous gaze with a direct and friendly one and he looked relieved. It was the first time they'd met face-to-face since the day she had walked out of his flat. They'd been in contact since then, they'd had to because of the book, first by text, then in a cool, but remarkably civilised phone call, during which they both found that they were willing to continue working together. He'd delivered the manuscript to her by email the week before.

She had been surprised, but grateful, that they'd snapped back into a professional relationship so easily. After the break-up she'd been upset, of course, but not as badly as she'd been after Matthew. It was clear to her now that the relationship had been on the rebound from Matthew and largely based on physical attraction. She'd been charmed by Joel and the world he moved in. Now she knew that all those things were of little importance since she couldn't trust him in all sorts of ways. She wondered about Joel's feelings. He'd never said he loved her and she sensed he wasn't hurt much, except perhaps for his dignity. On the whole they were both best out of it. The worst of it, though, was that she found herself mourning Matthew with a freshness she hadn't believed possible. Thank heavens work was so busy at the moment – it stopped her dwelling on her unhappy personal life.

'Come and sit here by me,' Jacqueline commanded. Emily found herself set opposite Joel, with Jacqueline at the head of the table between them, a position that implied control. Today, however, Emily was determined not to let her dominate. She and Lydia had met up as planned and had decided on a new way of putting pressure on Jacqueline.

'I'll make coffee,' Lorna said brightly from the doorway and went out to the kitchen.

'Shall we make a start?' Jacqueline suggested.

'Won't Lorna be joining us?' Emily asked in her mildest voice.

Jacqueline contemplated Emily for a moment. 'If you think she ought to, then I don't see why not.'

'I think she should.' She was surprised that this first part of Lydia's plan had worked without a fight. Perhaps Jacqueline really wasn't as hearty as she used to be.

After a conversation with Lydia a week or so before, Emily had come here determined to take charge. Not that she'd be rude about anything, indeed they'd decided that charm often worked best.

'Thank you so much for having me here,' she told Jacqueline now whilst they were waiting for Lorna. 'I know you and Joel have been discussing the script so I thought it might be useful to have me too. Joel, is the draft you've got there the same as the one you sent me?' It was important that this was clarified.

'Yes, of course,' he said, guarded.

'I've read it twice now,' Jacqueline said. 'I must say you've done a splendid job, Joel.'

Joel smiled his thanks, but still looked wary.

'Yes, it's magnificent,' Emily told him. 'And I sent you both that complimentary report from the Cambridge professor. Joel, you're so good on Hugh Morton as a writer, but I got a real sense of him as a man, too. Not that I ever met him,' she added hastily. 'You're the expert there, Jacqueline.'

Jacqueline gave a gracious nod of acknowledgment. 'One only ever sees one side of people, even when you know them very well, but I think Hugh would have been pleased. Yes, very pleased. There are a number of points I've been raising with Joel. I expect that you'll have a few, too, Emily.'

'Yes, I've got my list here.' Emily brought her copy of the script out of her bag together with some typed notes. 'I think Joel showed you earlier drafts of the book too, didn't he, so I hope I won't be going over old ground.'

Joel, looking from one woman to the other, caught the implication. Emily might be reopening dangerous areas. He mumbled, 'Jacqueline has been kind enough to give me advice from time to time.'

'Hardly kind – I asked to see it,' Jacqueline said, at her most imperious.

'Well then,' Emily said with a crocodile smile, 'perhaps there won't be very much more that you'll want to raise.'

'There are one or two matters,' Jacqueline said, 'but perhaps we should consider your concerns first?'

She put out her hand for the notes, but Emily stayed her. 'Shall we just wait for Lorna? I'd really like her views.'

As well as to Lydia, Emily had spoken to her boss, Gillian, about this whole conundrum, telling her how uncomfortable she was with the amount of control Hugh Morton's widow had over this book. Gillian was less bothered than Emily, though, and reminded her that the biography was being advertised as authorised by Morton's estate, and that permission to quote from Hugh's books and private papers was completely dependent on Jacqueline's agreement. 'You must try to negotiate with her, but if she's not happy there'll be no book at all,' was Gillian's view. This calmed Emily's fears a little, but did not dampen her sense of mission.

Emily then explained to her about Isabel and the memoir. Gillian was fascinated, particularly about the connection with Lydia, whom she knew only slightly. 'If you could persuade Jacqueline and Joel to put more in about Isabel, then that would add saleability to the book. What's it like otherwise?'

'Really good. Joel writes so vividly and analyses the books so interestingly. It's just he's put in so little about Isabel. It's very frustrating.'

Emily remembered that the conversation had ended with Gillian telling her she wanted to have lunch with her soon to talk something over. It was typical of Gillian to make the whole thing sound ominous so she was left worried.

At last Lorna returned with a heavy tray. She poured coffee into fragile cups.

'Emily would like you to stay, Lorna,' Jacqueline said. 'She thinks you might be useful.'

Jacqueline and her stepdaughter regarded one another intently. 'Thank you,' Lorna said quietly and sat down next to Emily.

'Now, if you wouldn't mind looking at these.' Emily handed round copies of her notes. Jacqueline ran her finger down the first page, and opened her mouth to speak, but Emily got there first.

'Jacqueline and Lorna, I could have emailed these notes to Joel and asked him to discuss them with you, but since there are one or two delicate matters I wanted to raise, I thought it would be easier for us all to discuss them face-to-face.'

'I'm sure you're right,' Jacqueline murmured. 'Though these are very minor points.'

'The ones on the first page are,' Emily agreed, 'but there's something bigger I want to talk about. First of all, I'd like to repeat what a fabulous job Joel has done with this book.'

'I'm longing to read it,' Lorna said. Joel and Emily looked at one another, surprised.

'Of course, I want you to,' Jacqueline replied quickly. 'But it wasn't worth you seeing early drafts.'

'I didn't know you hadn't read it,' Emily said. 'Jacqueline, don't you think it necessary that Lorna does? She is after all an interested party.'

'I was going to give it to her when it was ready.' The old

woman's hand shook, rattling the cup as she replaced it in its saucer.

'Mother, I'd like to read it now, please.'

Jacqueline shot Lorna a look Emily read as *Don't Embarrass Me by Arguing in Public* and was shocked that Lorna, a woman of sixty, should be bullied in this way.

'There is something that is particularly relevant to Lorna. Gillian and I . . .' Emily said, hoping her boss would not mind being used to bolster her argument, 'are surprised that there's so little in the book about Isabel. We're left with an unbalanced feel, given what we know, that Isabel was married to Hugh, and was Lorna's mother.'

She and Lorna exchanged smiles.

'And what is more, there does seem to be plenty of evidence that Isabel directly inspired the character of Nanna in *The Silent Tide*, Hugh's most important novel.'

'What do you mean by evidence?' Jacqueline asked, looking thoroughly put out. 'Isabel wasn't a newspaper journalist like Nanna, she worked for a publisher. And Hugh can hardly be said to have killed Isabel.'

'No, of course not,' Emily soothed. 'But scholars such as our Cambridge expert have made the connection, as he points out in his report. Isabel gave up her work when she became a wife and mother, and by all accounts she found this very frustrating.'

'I think you'd best show her, Emily,' Lorna said in a low voice.

'Show me what?' Jacqueline demanded.

Time seemed to still in the room as Emily reached into her bag and brought out a folder. She laid it on the table and slid out Isabel's memoir. She placed it before Jacqueline.

Joel made an impatient sort of noise, leaned back in his chair and folded his arms.

Jacqueline examined the first page and her face changed. 'How did you get this?' she asked Emily in a quavery voice.

'I gave it to her, Mother,' Lorna said.

'*You?*'

'I found it in Daddy's study. You sent me to look for something once after he died. It was under some letters in a drawer.'

'You took it? Your father's private papers?'

'It wasn't just his, and it certainly wasn't ever yours. It's mine, now. Neither you nor Daddy have ever remembered me in this. And I don't care if you're angry, you have no right to be. I read it all – I've read it many times now. And then I thought about what to do . . . I knew Joel wouldn't be the right person to give it to.'

Joel's face was a confused mix of emotion.

'So I worked out a way of giving it to Emily.'

'Lorna!' Jacqueline was astonished. 'You – you traitor!' In her weakened voice, this didn't sound as devastating as it might, but it still upset Lorna.

'Mother, please, it's not about taking sides. It's about writing the truth, the truth about Isabel. You and Daddy would hardly ever talk to me about her, and if you did it was to say something unpleasant. Why do you still hate Isabel so much?'

'Lorna, she abandoned you. What kind of mother would do that to a child?'

'But why? Why did she abandon me? No one ever explained. When I read those pages I began finally to understand.'

'I'm sorry, but I read them, too, years ago, and they confirmed my opinion of her. Your father was so upset by finding them that I insisted on him sharing them with me. I wanted to destroy them then, but he wouldn't let me.'

'*Destroy* them? Would you have done that after he died if I hadn't found them first?'

'I don't know,' Jacqueline admitted.

'It's my turn to confess,' Joel broke in. 'Emily showed them to me. I should have told you, Jacqueline, but . . . they didn't seem important.'

Jacqueline gave him an icy glare.

Joel rushed on. 'Emily didn't know at first where the memoir had come from. I had no way of testing its veracity.'

'I guessed that would be his reaction,' Lorna told Jacqueline. 'You've been so black and white about Isabel he was too nervous even to ask you about it.'

'It wasn't that . . .' Joel started to say.

'I think it was,' Emily said softly. 'You didn't want to have anything to do with it, did you? You knew Mrs Morton wouldn't like it. And since she's paying you for part of this project . . .'

'Don't be ridiculous,' Joel replied. 'That wouldn't have influenced me.'

'Please.' Jacqueline's tone was so heartfelt that everyone was silent. 'There's no need to quarrel. It's true that I've given Joel money. Publishers' advances are not generous, Emily. It's also true I was not keen for Joel to dwell on Isabel. She made my husband and me deeply unhappy, not to mention Lorna here.'

'I don't remember her, so how could she have made me

unhappy?' Emily was surprised at the passion in Lorna's voice, at her courage in finally speaking out.

'No, but you felt the lack of her, Lorna. How was I to deal with Isabel objectively? I felt it better not to speak of her much at all.' The pain in her face was so obvious that for the first time Emily felt a little sorry for her.

'I suppose I disappoint you,' Jacqueline said to Emily.

'Not exactly,' Emily lied. 'I don't want to be tactless, but I could see from Isabel's papers that you and she weren't close.'

'I tried so hard with her, but she resented me so much.'

'She saw you as an interloper, didn't she?' Emily said quietly.

Jacqueline sighed. All her harshness was gone now. 'She thought I was trying to get between her and Hugh, but I wasn't. Lorna, I always had a soft spot for your father. Ever since I was very young. But we both married other people. Hugh didn't realise he loved me until after the failure of his marriage and Isabel's death.'

Emily wondered if Hugh and Isabel's marriage could be said to have failed exactly, but could hardly say this to Jacqueline.

But Lorna, gentle, obedient Lorna, was speaking. 'He never loved you in the way he loved Isabel, did he? That's what you couldn't get over.' Emily was shocked by this brutal accusation. Jacqueline flinched, but quickly recovered.

'He did love me,' she said, 'but in a different way to how he loved Isabel. I was determined to be strong and reliable, the sort of wife he needed. The woman behind the man. A helpmeet. Isabel was never that.'

'Perhaps she would have been, if she had lived,' Lorna persisted.

'I doubt it. She was too selfish.'

'You mean she wanted to be her own person, too? You've read what she wrote, how depressed she became, especially after having a baby. And as for Granny, Isabel makes her sound a real tyrant.'

'Hugh's mother never liked her, no. And of course Hugh always felt that Isabel should have called a doctor, the night that she died.'

Joel cleared his throat. 'I've written all about this, in my chapter about the marriage.'

'Yes,' Emily put in, 'but from Hugh's point of view. You don't put Isabel's feelings into it. Evidence from her account would give a more rounded picture.'

'I've told you before. This book is about Hugh, not Isabel. It's not surprising that I should write it that way. Hugh would not have your twenty-first-century perspective, Emily. Isabel was an unusual young woman for the times. Hugh was simply out of his depth with her.'

'I don't think she was that unusual,' Emily countered. 'She didn't match up to society's expectations of women, that's for sure, but—'

'Oh, all this is fiddle-faddle,' Jacqueline interrupted. 'None of you really understands. It's all more personal than that.' She looked sad now, sad and diminished, as though Lorna's rebellion had breached every one of her defences. 'I'm the one who lived through it, and I remember it as clearly as if it were yesterday.'

Emily was surprised to see her eyes shining with tears. Jacqueline's haughty demeanour had worn thin, whether from age or grief, or both, and Emily at last glimpsed the vulnerability beneath.

'I wish you would explain, Mother,' Lorna said, her

hands palm-upturned on the table. 'Then we might all understand. I need so much to understand.'

They all waited for Jacqueline's answer.

After a long moment she said, 'I'll tell you my side of the story, if that satisfies you, but I will not have it all raked over in the book. I simply will not.'

She glared at each of them. Joel, unnerved, started shuffling papers. Lorna rubbed her face tiredly. Only Emily looked directly back at her and nodded.

Jacqueline closed her eyes and began to speak, hesitantly at first.

'Hugh and I were happily married for fifty-eight years.' She stopped for a moment, and her lips moved soundlessly, but then she gathered strength and went on. 'I'd known him since I was a child, and there came a time when I must have known I loved him. I wasn't a fool, though. Even as a teenager, I could see Hugh didn't return my feelings, but this didn't stop me hoping that he would change. I lost that hope for a time after he fell in love with Anne. He was different with her, so devoted. It was so painful for me, as though I was invisible to him. It was soon after this that I met Michael and he was so courteous and attentive that I was flattered. No one had treated me in that way before – you know, made me feel special. And so I married him. Too late, I saw the kind of man he was. There was nothing bad about him, don't get me wrong, but he was not, shall we say, comfortable with intimacy. That side of things was, well, not successful. With Michael away at the war I had plenty of time to dwell on this and I came to the conclusion that he had married because he thought he ought to, that he had a position to keep up. I didn't mind playing to that, and he was away so much that at first I didn't find it a great strain. Until the end of the war, after Anne was killed in that air raid, and I saw more of Hugh again. Of course, I was married, and anyway I could see that his feelings towards me were unchanged. To him I was just a friend, but I thought I could be happy if I just saw him from time to time.' She paused before saying, 'And then he met Isabel.

'From the first time I saw her, at a party Hugh held in his new flat, I knew she was wrong for him. She was too interested in talking to the men. Had nothing to say to the ladies there and hardly a word for me. I couldn't say anything to him, though, he was obviously smitten by her. I thought she was one of those bright, pretty sorts who have no thought for anyone but themselves. I'm sorry, Lorna, but there it is. I suppose I was seeing her in a jealous light, because I liked her better once I got to know her, and after they were married I came to see she was unhappy stuck in Stone House with Hugh's mother glowering at her all the time. What was difficult was that Isabel kept me at arm's length. She knew she needed my help with you, Lorna, but she wasn't grateful, oh no. Poor Hugh. All he wanted was a peaceful household so he could get on with his work, but peace was the last thing she gave him.

'I did my best to help. If I was in London and Hugh was up for a few days, we might do something together, just for company – go out to dinner or to the theatre. It didn't do any harm, though some people had nasty minds. Again, I can assure you that nothing untoward went on.

'Emily wasn't sure she believed her.'

'I wasn't unhappy with this situation. I could tell that

Hugh was starting to rely on me – oh, in all sorts of ways – and I liked that feeling. On a practical level, you see, I kept the household going for him. My being there settled old Mrs Morton, too. I knew how to stay calm, and they appreciated that very much. Especially when Isabel took to her bed, which she sometimes did, and wouldn't get up to deal with Lorna. Poor Lorna, there were times, dear, I found you red in the face and exhausted from all your crying.'

'I don't think Isabel could help it,' Emily murmured. She was shocked by Jacqueline's resentful tone, her jealousy of Isabel after so many years, but there was no stopping the woman now. It was as though she'd forgotten she had an audience.

'There did come a time when I became terribly sorry for her. Her mother was ill and Hugh was so angry with her about his own mother's death. He simply wouldn't see reason about that – it was the grief, you see. But nothing could forgive what Isabel did next. Her aunt was partly to blame, of course. Sowing ideas in Isabel's head, I'd say, vicious ideas, particularly about me and Hugh. It was Penelope who helped her leave. She had this holiday house on the coast. We used to take you to the beach there, Lorna, until Isabel died. Anyway, we were originally told that they'd spend the night there, and that Penelope would bring her back the next day, but when the time came she telephoned from somewhere in the town to say she wasn't coming home. And that's the last we heard of her for nearly a fortnight. You were quite distraught, Lorna, I have to say. You kept asking for Mama and I had no idea what to tell you.'

'I wish I could remember,' Lorna whispered, 'but I

don't. I used to look at the photographs in Daddy's album and think that I did remember her, but now I realise that the photographs became my memories.'

'What do we remember of people we've lost?' Joel suddenly said, so sadly that Emily wondered whether there was a whole side of him she'd never even begun to know. 'Today we're surrounded by photographs and videos to remind us of everything that happens, but it's still hard accessing our actual memories of how people we loved looked and sounded and felt.'

Emily's thoughts flew to Matthew. She had a very clear picture in her mind of him sitting in his dressing gown, his hair sticking up, waving a piece of toast about as he explained a point. The memory made her immeasurably sad and she almost missed what Joel said next.

'But you heard from Isabel again, didn't you?'

'Once more,' Jacqueline agreed. 'It was ten days later.'

'The thirty-first of January nineteen fifty-three. The night she died,' Joel said and she nodded.

'What happened?' Emily whispered.

Jacqueline fiddled with the papers in front of her, then she closed her eyes and continued.

'I was staying here because after she'd left there was no one to look after Lorna, and of course I was the first person Hugh turned to. Anyway, early evening the telephone rang and it was her. Hugh answered the phone. I . . . I couldn't help hearing their conversation. It seemed as though she'd decided to come home and she wanted Hugh to drop everything and leave that moment to get her. We hadn't eaten yet, and the weather was atrocious, so this made me angry. Why should he be at her beck and call all the time? I could tell that he was prepared to go out at once, but I didn't see why she couldn't wait until the next morning, so I interrupted him and said so. I still think it was completely reasonable under the circumstances, and in the end, that's what was agreed. He told her that he'd fetch her as soon as seemed sensible the next morning and ended the call. It was the last time he ever spoke to her.'

She was silent again, gathering her thoughts.

Emily eventually asked, 'How did you feel, about her coming back, I mean?'

'How did I feel? What did that matter? I could see that Hugh had mixed feelings, for he wouldn't settle all evening. He was relieved that she wanted to come back, he confided in me, but worried, too. Worried about how she'd be. When we went to bed that night, we had no idea of what terror would await us in the morning.'

She paused and Joel took up the tale. 'Let me explain. Several natural phenomena came together that awful night. Powerful northerly winds caused a tremendous surge of seawater funnelling round from Scotland into the North Sea. This heavy sea, followed by an unusually high spring tide, caused devastating floods along the east coast. Several hundred people were killed. It was declared a national disaster.'

'As I say,' Jacqueline went on, 'the weather had been dreadful all day. I lay awake for what seemed like hours, listening to the wind buffeting the house, rattling the windows. In the end I must have slept, for when I next woke it was getting light. The wind had lessened, but there were other sounds, animal cries, and I got up to look out. I'll never forget the sight that met my eyes. Half the garden and the marshes beyond were underwater. One of the donkeys was braying, but I couldn't see it. I put on my dressing gown and went to wake Hugh, who got dressed and went out to see if he could rescue the wretched beast. He shouted up to say the scullery was flooded so I came down, too. I turned on the kitchen tap to fill the kettle and the water came out foul and salty, then Hugh came back to say that the poor beasts were marooned on the muck heap but that the water was retreating.

'At seven o'clock we switched on the wireless. It was only then we learned something of the extent of the tragedy that was unfolding and Hugh went to the garage in a panic to see if he could start the car up. He could, and set off at once. I did not see him again until the evening.'

Lorna made a little noise of despair, but Jacqueline carried on. Her eyes were closed again and Emily was of the impression that she was reliving that day nearly sixty years ago.

'When he returned, he had an awful wild look about him. His shoes were encrusted with mud, and his clothes were in a dreadful state. It took me quite some while to calm him down enough to find out what had happened.

'The town, he said, had virtually become an island. The sea had come up over the marshes, and although the worst was over, everywhere was impassable. The main road was flooded and they were turning vehicles back all over the place just to get emergency services through. It was complete chaos, he said. No one knew what was going on or what to do about it. There were awful stories circulating about all the poor people who'd been drowned or were missing or whose homes had been washed away, but no proper information – and since no one was being let through, it was impossible to find out.

'It wasn't until the afternoon that he managed to hitch a lift on a tractor and found the hall where survivors had been taken. Then he went to the hospital – oh, I don't like to think what he saw there – but there was no sign of *her* anywhere. The lane down to the house was completely cut off and the buildings all destroyed. He could tell by the way people looked at him that there wasn't much hope and there was simply nothing he could do. It was getting dark so he thought he'd better come home and go back again in the morning.'

There was complete silence in the room. Jacqueline opened her eyes, but she looked distant, still lost in the past.

'He was distraught. There was nothing I could do to comfort him. He kept saying over and over again that it was his fault. If only he'd gone to fetch her the night before, if only he hadn't listened to me. I tried to reason with him, but it was no good, no good at all.

'He went back again in the morning. I begged to go with him, but he simply wouldn't let me near him. It was the most terrible day, waiting and waiting for news. And there was none. The search for survivors had become a search for bodies. There were ever so many people missing or unaccounted for, and every day the paper had news of some who'd died and others who'd been found safely staying with relatives, unaware that they'd been feared drowned. But we knew Isabel had remained in the house that night, and as time dragged on I simply hoped that they'd find her soon so that we could put her to rest. They never did, though. There were others, too, who were lost and who were never found. The sea can be terribly cruel.

'I tried my best to support Hugh through this and we grew closer. The following year *The Silent Tide* was published and he and I were married.'

Jacqueline leaned back in her chair, her story finished. All that could be heard in the room was the clock ticking on the mantelpiece.

She'd told it movingly, Emily thought, and clearly believed her version of events, but it was a version of the truth, just as Isabel's was. There were parts she'd understandably skated over, such as how intimate her relationship with Hugh had been while Isabel was alive; Emily felt that Isabel had been right in her suspicions, but it was hardly possible to ask Jacqueline that one. Did she know what Penelope had told Isabel, that had made Isabel remain at the beach house so long? Possibly she did now, but presumably she didn't then, and it certainly hadn't stopped her believing still that Isabel was selfish and had abandoned her husband and daughter. The tides of resentment had washed away her ability to reason about Isabel.

Emily wondered what other secrets remained untold. It would be a hard task negotiating with the old lady about presenting Isabel's side of the story. She would just have to do her best.

Chapter 39

Emily

So much had happened in a single year, Emily reflected two weeks later. After all the upheavals of recent months, it was her turn to fill crates with books and scripts, to empty her desk drawers. Her filing cabinet, her lamp and her computer were festooned with fluorescent labels telling the removal men where they were to go. Everything was coated in a layer of fine dust from an ancient Jiffy bag that had exploded during the packing.

'You won't know what to do with all the space in your new place,' Sarah said as she helped Emily drag the heavy bag to the door to join two others for collection.

Emily wasn't moving very far, just to the other side of the floor – to George's old office, in fact. An office of her own – she still couldn't believe it – and it was nice to hear, too, that George had recently secured a job at her old firm.

Shortly after her visit to Suffolk, Gillian had taken Emily out for the much-feared lunch, and over a glass of wine had offered her a new job in the department. They were starting up a new imprint, fiction and non-fiction, and she wanted Emily to run it. It took Emily ten seconds to decide she'd accept, but she forced herself to be cool, to ask a lot of questions and ascertain the salary before she told Gillian her decision. She was already sketching out ideas in her head.

'Everybody's impressed by the projects you've taken on,' Gillian told her, and named several of her new authors. 'The buzz is building about Tobias's novel, and Joel Richards looks as though he'll be a real star. Are you happy to go on working with him? It's no shame if you'd rather hand him on to someone else.'

After recovering from this second shock, Emily saw that Gillian was trying to be helpful. Why was she so surprised that her boss knew that she'd become close to Joel? She coloured up.

'I've been there myself,' Gillian confided, and Emily suddenly glimpsed a different view of this striking, stern and powerful woman. Perhaps Gillian had a soft centre, after all.

The series *The Silent Tide* was being broadcast at a prime time over Christmas. An edition of the novel with a huge picture of Zara and her co-star Jasper on the front was piled on bookshops' front tables. Publication of *Catching the Tide: A Life of Hugh Morton* had been brought forward to the spring. The publicity machine was already starting up.

Since it was a Friday today, and the move would take place over the weekend, Emily couldn't go home till everything was packed up. And she had work to finish.

At seven o'clock she was still there, all on her own, everyone gone home. It was dark outside. She finished writing a last email, switched off the computer and found a place in a crate for one last file. Beyond the window, the square was busy with people and traffic, and she watched for a while, struck by a memory. It had been a year ago that she'd sat here looking out into the night as she waited for Matthew. That was the night that she'd found the copy of *Coming Home* in her pigeonhole, the book that had started the search for Isabel.

Coming Home had been given back to Lydia and the old Morton files returned to the archive, no longer needed. In the end, Jacqueline, astonishingly, had agreed that the chapters about Isabel might be expanded. Joel had quoted selectively from Isabel's memoir, though not the more jealous assertions about Jacqueline – those would be left for some biographer in the far future to make of what they would. Hugh's papers were to be archived at Duke's College – Joel had arranged this for Jacqueline. Lorna had insisted on keeping Isabel's memoir for the moment, but eventually it would join the archive, too.

Emily had felt close to Isabel this past year, reading her words, learning about her life; had been moved that she died so young, and in such awful circumstances. Sometimes she wondered what might have happened if she'd been reunited with Hugh. It was, of course, impossible to say.

Lorna had recently been in touch. She was coming to London to stay with her cousin – Lydia's daughter Cassie – and she'd asked to meet Emily for lunch on Monday. There was talk of wanting to show her something. All very mysterious, but Emily was free so of course she'd said yes.

Watching from the window, she caught herself

scanning the people passing, as though looking for someone in particular, but she was expecting no one. It dawned on her finally that it was Matthew. She was looking for Matthew. How pointless. She turned away, remembering now the anxiety of anticipation, how annoying it had been that he was late so often, but she couldn't help recalling, too, how beautifully he read his poetry, the soft lilt of his voice, spell-binding, musical. She thought of his passion for his writing, remembered so many things about him: the gentle touch of his fingers, the clean soapy scent of him . . . and a deep sense of loss washed over her. He would have finished his studies now, she supposed. He'd have done well – Tobias always spoke highly of him. She sometimes wondered if she should get in touch, but then she'd recall seeing him that time with the girl in the white shirt and wasn't sure she should.

She should stop being maudlin and go. One last check that the shelves were empty, then she restacked a precarious-looking heap of papers in one of the crates and swept up some paperclips from the desk. A new life would begin for her on Monday. She switched off the lamp then, thinking that she might as well be helpful, crouched down to unplug it from the wall.

The back of the desk, where it met the partition, had a wooden modesty panel to hide one's legs if positioned in the middle of a room – and beneath the panel a triangle of paper peeped out. She should have checked before whether anything had fallen down there. Forgetting the plug, she got up to pull the desk out an inch or two. Then she checked underneath once more. Several items caught behind the panel had now fallen to the floor – nothing interesting: a stained teaspoon, some curled-up scrap paper and what looked like a piece of white card, the size of a small postcard. She reached in and gathered all of this up. The bit of card was thicker than she'd first thought and was actually an envelope. It bore her name on it in a flowing script.

She frowned as she lifted the flap, wondering how long it had been there. Inside was a handmade card, pretty, with a cut-out heart – a Valentine's card, she realised with surprise. She opened it to see handwriting she knew – no name, of course. For a moment she was so amazed that she couldn't make sense of the words. She switched on the light again to examine it properly. Yes, it was definitely a Valentine's card. There was a folded piece of paper too. The writing on the card was Matthew's.

I hope you love the flowers, he had written. *They speak for themselves. My letter says the rest.*

Red roses. She'd never found out who gave them to her. She hadn't suspected Matthew for a single minute; he'd never given her flowers, ever, had been contemptuous of Valentine's Day. But this card had come with the roses. Red roses, for true love. A tender pain stabbed cruelly through her. Her hands shook as she unfolded the letter.

My very dearest Em,

I write in great humility to tell you that now I've had time to think about it, I realise that I've made an awful mistake in finishing things between us. Em, I am simply not happy without you. I miss you all the time, I miss everything about you, even your views about poetry and when you get antsy about the mess in my kitchen. I have no expectations – I simply don't deserve to – but if you'd at least agree to meet up, perhaps we could talk.

With hope and love, Little Bird
Yours ever,
Matthew

She felt at first a great relief. Matthew had tried to get in touch with her. He did love her. But then peace was replaced by horror. It was too late, the letter had been written back in February, nine months ago! She'd had no idea who'd delivered the flowers to her desk, but the envelope had obviously not been secured to the cellophane properly. It had slipped away and fallen down behind the desk. And now it was November. All that lost time. How shattering to think of Matthew waiting and hoping, never knowing why she hadn't called. How he must hate her now. Or have forgotten her altogether. She'd seen him with that girl. It was all too late. She covered her face with her hands.

For a long time she sat there, thinking of reasons and consequences, the quirkiness of fate, the way huge events could turn on small coincidences. In the end the answer came to her.

She must follow her heart.

She wasted no time. She bought a card in Oxford Street on the way home, a reproduction of a beautiful Elizabethan youth reading. The right choice was vital, even more so what she wrote in it. She must make no assumptions. She could only honestly tell of the lost card, her despair that he'd never had an answer. She supposed, she wrote, that it was too late, but if there was any chance of meeting up, she'd like to do so very much. She dropped the card into the box on Saturday, then, too late, wondered if maybe he'd changed his address, but after a moment's panic she reasoned it was likely to reach him eventually. The rest of Saturday crept by, then Sunday at her parents'. Maybe on Monday he'd receive it.

Chapter 40

Emily

On Monday Emily paused on the way up the central staircase at Fortnum & Mason to take in the scene. It was Lorna who had suggested meeting for tea. Emily rarely had cause to come here, but she loved the dark wood fittings, the feel of old-fashioned luxury, the exquisite boxes of biscuits and sweets, the rich aroma of ground coffees and chocolate all around. Hanging down from the ceiling into the atrium was a mobile: hundreds of tiny lions and unicorns on dazzling threads. Emily looked up to see Lorna waving to her over the rail on the floor above and hurried up the stairs to meet her.

'I haven't been here for years,' Lorna told her after they'd been shown to a table in the ice-cream bar. 'It's different now, of course, but still lovely. I've bought Mother some special tea. She's always complaining that tea doesn't taste the same as it used to. This is the one she used to like best. I expect she'll still complain, you know.'

'I expect she will!' Emily agreed, laughing easily with Lorna. Isabel's daughter seemed different these days, more lively, less diffident. Jacqueline might be diminishing, but Lorna was expanding into her space. She was dressed more smartly today, still a Liberty-print blouse but a tailored jacket and skirt with it, and prettier shoes. A triple string of pearls gleamed softly above her collarbone.

When the waitress returned, Emily asked for peppermint tea, but Lorna said, 'Would it be awfully indulgent to have ice cream?'

'Of course not!' Emily was amused by her guilty expression. When the ice cream came, all covered in strawberry syrup and nuts, she enjoyed the sight of Lorna eating it like a small girl out on a treat.

'It's always been a weakness of mine,' Lorna sighed and slid another spoonful into her mouth.

Emily was still wondering why she had been invited here, when Lorna laid down her spoon, checked her watch and leaned across the table confidingly.

'I hope you don't mind, but I've invited Lydia along. And there's someone I'd like you to meet.'

'Lydia. That would be lovely – I haven't seen her for ages. But who . . . ?'

'There's something I need to tell you about first. Or show you, rather. Hang on, I don't want to get it covered in ice cream.' Lorna pushed her sundae dish away, and delved in her handbag. She brought out a package in a white envelope.

'It's the most extraordinary thing,' Lorna confided. 'I can't really make it out.'

'What is it?' Emily asked, her gaze fixed on the envelope.

'I need to explain. You know Granny's old glory-hole, the room beyond the box room she used to keep locked?'

'Yes.' Emily remembered Isabel's fascination with the

room, and what she had found in it. 'Is it still full of your grandmother's clothes?'

Lorna shook her head. 'After Daddy died, Mother got a vintage clothes expert in. The woman paid an awful lot for them – because of the good condition, she said. No, it's something else. Recently Mother said she had found a few things of Isabel's there she felt I should have. This necklace was one.' She fingered the pearls.

'They're gorgeous.' Emily was a little shocked that Jacqueline hadn't even given her Isabel's pearls before. It had taken the recent events to soften the old woman's stance.

'She also gave me this,' Lorna said, passing over the envelope. 'Look at the name on the front.'

Emily took it from her and stared hard at the handwriting, which was foreign and ornate. It was not easy to make out the words, apart from *Stone House* and at the bottom, *l'Angleterre*. The stamp, too, was French, but old, priced in francs instead of euros, though the date of postage had faded beyond legibility. The name on the front was harder to read: probably *Morton*, possibly *Madame*.

'Madame J. Morton,' Emily guessed aloud. 'Or it is an L?'

'You don't know either?' Lorna said, and Emily saw her relief. 'It was sent in nineteen eighty-five, soon after I got married, you'll see when you look inside. Mother claims she opened it by accident. I . . . I wasn't sure whether to believe her, but if you're not sure either . . .'

'It could be a J,' Emily said, turning the envelope over. There was a return address on the flap, in Paris, *deuxième Arrondissement*. 'What's in it?'

'I'll show you.' Taking it back, Lorna drew out some papers and photographs and laid them on the table.

'I don't know what to make of it all,' she said. 'I wondered what you thought. Here's the covering letter.' She unfolded a fragile page. 'It's in French, of course, but Lydia knows a bit of French so we've worked out what it says. It's from a Madame Eleanor Sorel.' She slid the letter between them, and they pored over it together.

Lorna said, 'We reckon it says, "These documents enclosed were found amongst the belongings of my friend Mademoiselle Vivienne Stern, who I am sad to relate died recently after a short illness. It is directed that they be sent to Mademoiselle Lorna Morton, who may comprehend their significance".'

Emily nodded. The handwriting wasn't very clear and her French not all that good, but Lorna's translation seemed plausible.

Next, Lorna passed her a photograph. It was of two elegantly dressed women, past their youth, but only just, sitting at a table outside a café. They laughed as they posed for the camera. The colour had faded, but the smaller woman definitely looked familiar. Lorna picked out another of her, older this time, thin and ill-looking, standing arm-in-arm with a very French-looking man in a suit in front of a cathedral. She looked to see *Rome, 1976* scribbled on the back in an English hand. There was a postcard addressed to *Dear V* and signed *I*, extolling the virtues of the food in Sicily and referring to someone called 'Raoul', and finally an Order of Service dated 22 November 1976. It was for the funeral of 'Isabel Lewis'.

'Isabel,' Emily whispered, hardly believing her eyes. '*Isabel.*'

'I know,' Lorna said, her eyes round and solemn. 'Of

course, the surname was her mother and Penelope's family name.'

'But Isabel died – I mean, she died in nineteen fifty-three!'

'So we've always believed, but they never found a body, remember.'

'No, but I still don't understand.'

'Nor do I, Emily.'

Emily looked at the envelope again. 'Jacqueline – I can see how she might have opened this, thinking it was for her . . . But she didn't show it to anyone?'

'She says she didn't even show it to Hugh. I don't think she could cope with it. Didn't want to stir everything up again. That's what she says, anyway. Part of her has always refused to accept it. After she read it she put it all away and dismissed it from her mind.'

'Oh my goodness! If Isabel was still alive, that would have meant . . .' Emily stopped.

'What?'

'No, it's tactless. Sorry.'

'You mean that if my mother had still been alive, it would have made my father a bigamist and his and Jacqueline's marriage invalid?'

'Yes.'

'Funnily enough, she didn't spell that out to me.' Lorna started packing the items back into the envelope. 'We must remember that Jacqueline never felt that she was quite as loved by my father as Isabel was. Oh, she was valuable to him, of course, and he was immensely fond of her, relied on her utterly. I dread to think how he'd have coped if she'd died before he did. But a deep, passionate love? No, I think he always grieved for Isabel.'

Emily thought there might be some truth in this. Jacqueline had been the one he'd turned to when he'd lost the other women he'd loved: his pale first love, Anne, then his mother, then Isabel. Jacqueline had been his tower of strength. It had been a good marriage, but perhaps Jacqueline felt jealous of Isabel still. She remembered what Jacqueline had said about Hugh's remorse after Isabel was believed dead. He wouldn't have been the first man to have put the first wife whom he'd betrayed on a pedestal after he lost her. And now, extraordinarily, it seemed that she might not have died after all.

'How can you find out more?' she asked now.

'I don't know,' Lorna replied. 'I'm still getting used to the idea. The packet was sent twenty-seven years ago. Is there anyone left who'd know anything?' She sighed then said, more animated, 'I looked up Vivienne Stern on the internet. There's lots about her. She was a very successful scientist. Based in Paris but worked a lot in America, too. That made me wonder, how would Isabel have earned her living?'

'I'll bet it was books.'

'I wouldn't be surprised, you know,' Lorna said and they smiled at one another.

Suddenly, something across the room caught Lorna's attention. 'Oh, they're here!' she cried, jumping up.

Emily turned to see Lydia's neat figure coming towards them and behind her followed a willowy girl with long dark-red hair and a creamy complexion. Lorna greeted each of them with an enthusiastic hug.

'Emily, how lovely to see you,' Lydia said, leaning to kiss her. 'Emily, may I introduce my granddaughter, Olivia?'

'Hello,' Olivia murmured, looking up shyly from under thick lashes. She was very lovely, a girl on the cusp of womanhood.

'Olivia's mother Cassie is my goddaughter,' Lorna explained eagerly.

'I know – you're the one who likes reading!' Emily cried, remembering Lorna buying the fantasy paperbacks.

'Yes, Mummy is always calling me a bookworm,' Olivia said, smiling.

'Shall we all sit down?' Lorna suggested.

After they'd ordered, Lorna told Lydia, 'I've been showing Emily the package from Paris.'

'What did you think of it, Emily?' Lydia asked in a serious tone.

'If it is the same Isabel as ours, it's absolutely extraordinary,' Emily replied. 'But what do you make of Jacqueline keeping it from you and Lorna all these years?'

'It's unforgivable,' Lydia growled, her face darkening. 'No, I'm sorry, Lorna, but it is.'

'It is, I suppose,' Lorna said. 'But I think she was – I don't know, frightened.'

'I can imagine the whole thing being overwhelming,' Emily said. She was touched by how forgiving Lorna was of her stepmother. 'Assuming in the first place that she understood the significance of the material.'

'Of course she would have,' Lydia said. 'Nothing would escape Jacqueline.'

Olivia glanced from one to the other, consternation in her big brown eyes. 'Who are you all talking about?' she asked her grandmother. Emily was finding it difficult to think of Lydia, so recently retired, being a grandmother.

'Oh, Isabel again, darling,' Lydia said, and Olivia

nodded. She was clearly used to these conversations. A phone chimed in her handbag and she took it out and began texting while the grown-ups talked.

'Not even to mention it to Hugh,' Lydia grumbled. 'That woman is the limit.'

'She *is* the limit,' Lorna said, 'but I think I understand her. And, I've thought about this a lot, Lydia – maybe my mother didn't want to be found?'

Lydia stared at Lorna for a moment in amazement, then murmured, 'I hadn't considered that. You may be right.'

Emily thought Lorna *was* right, but didn't like to say anything to come between the two women, still grieving over the loss of Isabel all those years ago. Perhaps the mystery would never be solved. How could Isabel have escaped the flood, for a start? And what made her change her mind and not return to her family? There were still so many questions unanswered.

'We could go to Paris and look for her grave,' Lorna was telling Lydia now. 'I'd like to do that. I should be angry with her, you know, but for some reason I'm not. Perhaps it's because I feel I understand her. But we need to be prepared for the fact that we may never learn all the answers.'

'One day the two of you should write a book about it,' Olivia said brightly, putting away her phone.

'Maybe,' Lydia said gently. 'Ah, your ice cream's coming.'

Whilst Olivia ate ice cream and the others sipped tea, Lydia told Emily, 'I especially wanted you to meet Olivia, as she has something to ask.'

'Oh yes.' Olivia laid down her spoon and licked her lips. 'It's to do with school. I'm at sixth-form college now, and we've been told to get work experience. I so much want to do something with books and reading and—'

'Would it be a real nuisance, Emily,' Lydia broke in, 'to take her for a week or two? Show her the ropes? She's very good with people.'

'I'll do anything,' Olivia cried, her eyes sparkling.

Emily, watching her, smiled and thought of the miracle of the thread that connected the nineteen-year-old Isabel and young Olivia now. She couldn't work out the family relationship easily, but Isabel being Penelope's daughter and Olivia, Lydia's granddaughter, they must be some sort of cousins, and there was something about Olivia's looks that reminded her of the black-and-white photographs of Isabel. Those large eyes, the intelligence, the eagerness.

'I'm sure we could sort out something,' she said, smiling at the girl. 'You'd have to do a lot of reading, mind.'

'That would be amazing,' Olivia whispered and Emily laughed at this lovely fresh enthusiasm.

That very evening, on the bus home from work, Emily's BlackBerry plinked softly. Matthew's name came up on the screen. A text. She opened it, hardly daring to breathe.

Chapter 41

Emily

They agreed to meet in the café of a bookshop in the Charing Cross Road the following evening, but although she'd been thinking about it all day, at the last moment Emily had to deal with a crisis at the office and consequently rushed into the shop fifteen minutes late, hoping for once that Matthew wasn't on time.

But he was, sitting alone at a table, engrossed in a book, and for a moment her courage faltered. He was wearing glasses, which he never used to, nerdy black-framed ones that lent him a serious air, and his hair was shorter. Then he ran his hand across the nape of his neck in a familiar gesture, and in this and the rapt concentration as he read, as though the words played music in his mind, she knew he was her own dear Matthew and she was filled with longing. Just then he glanced round, and on seeing her stood up too quickly, snatching off his spectacles and almost knocking his book to the floor.

'Em. Hi! I was beginning to wonder if I'd got the wrong time again.'

'No, it was my fault – sorry,' she said, finding her voice.

And then they were hugging one another and she felt so happy.

He bought coffees, which they hardly drank; instead, they smiled and threw each other shy glances.

'I like the specs,' she told him. 'They really suit you.'

'They're only for reading,' he said, prodding them on the table. 'Those late nights squinting at the computer did for me.'

'It's over now, your course?'

'Yes. I've just heard from Tobias, in fact. You're now talking to Matthew Heaton MA.'

'That's wonderful!' she cried. 'You worked so hard. Oh, congratulations!'

'Thanks.' He beamed with pleasure. 'And Tobias told me something about you – your promotion. That's fantastic, Em.'

'Thank you. Tobias's book helped towards that, you know.'

'He sounds elated by how it's all going, I must say. I dropped in on him recently to ask him about a reference. I'm applying for jobs, you see.'

They chatted easily. It all felt so natural, so right, Emily thought, but all the while she was aware of the deep lake of unsaid words that lay between them.

At last he said quietly, 'It was quite a shock getting your card yesterday.'

'I'm sorry. I felt terrible. I had no idea that you sent the flowers. You must have hated me for not replying.'

'I could never hate you, Em.' He pushed his coffee away half-finished and rubbed his face wearily.

Something about the sadness of his expression alarmed her. The memory of Matthew and Lola, arms round each other, came unbidden.

'I visited your college to see Tobias once,' she said, watching him carefully. 'In June, it must have been. I saw you, but you were with someone so I didn't try to say hello.'

He looked at her, puzzled. 'Who?' Then the penny dropped.

'She's pretty, Lola. You looked very happy together.'

She waited. A world hung on his response. Finally he spoke.

'We're not together any more, Em. Lola is lovely, terribly sweet. We had fun for a while but it was never any more than that.'

The relief was immeasurable. 'I was with someone for a bit, too,' she said, 'but that didn't work out either.'

'I've missed you, Em,' he whispered, and reached out his hand to take hers.

'I missed you too,' she managed to say. Their eyes locked. 'How did we mess it up so badly?'

'Everything got on top of me that term,' he said. 'But it wasn't just that.'

'It was me, wasn't it, pushing you places you didn't want to go?'

'A bit,' he admitted. 'But if I hadn't been so selfish . . .'

'Me, too.'

'Not as much as me. Em . . . darling, I'm ready now. If you'll have me back.'

Happiness flooded through her, but something made her hesitate. 'We should take it more slowly, perhaps,' she said finally.

He saw at once what was wrong. 'You're frightened, aren't you? I'm sorry. I did that to you.'

'I did it to myself.' She saw more clearly now what had

gone wrong, how in all sorts of little ways she hadn't given him enough space, not allowed him to come to her at his own rate.

'Let's do it properly this time,' he said, taking her other hand.

The time for worrying was over. He leaned forward, almost knocking the cup over as he kissed her.

The café was shutting up, so they strolled hand-in-hand into Soho looking for somewhere to eat, but principally where they could sit and be with one another.

'There's a brasserie I remember that isn't too expensive,' Matthew said, taking them north across Oxford Street.

Emily glanced at a road sign. 'Rathbone Place,' she said and then she remembered. Let's go up here,' she begged. 'There's somewhere I want to look at.'

'Sure, if you like,' he said, puzzled.

They passed restaurants, houses and offices, but she hardly took them in. And then they came to the crossing with Percy Street where the road jinked in a sort of elbow, and the buildings were grouped in a quiet square. Emily had never studied it properly before. She recognised the name of one of the pubs.

She looked about, half-expecting to see the sign for McKinnon & Holt, but of course there wasn't one. A corner building it had been, with a few steps up to the door. 'This must be the one,' she whispered. There was no plaque of any sort to indicate the business conducted there now, and only one downstairs light was on.

In the soft lamplight that blurred everything, it might have been today or sixty years ago or longer.

'This was the office where Isabel worked,' she told Matthew and he nodded, remembering. 'There's the Fitzroy Tavern, where they used to go, and over there must have been the café where she sat with Hugh and talked about his book.'

She could see it all in her mind's eye, almost imagine the door to McKinnon & Holt open and a small neat figure in a sherry-coloured coat and hat, carrying a bagful of scripts, trip down the steps. Isabel. What had really happened to her in the end? Perhaps Lorna was right and they'd never know.

'There's so much to tell you,' she said. 'Such a story about Isabel.'

'And I look forward to heaving it. But right now, Little Bird, there's something else I want to do.'

And beneath the lamp post, Matthew, very much real and alive, drew her into his arms and kissed her, and they were lost to time and place.

Epilogue

Isabel

Isabel slipped drowsily from the collapsing house down into the freezing water where, jerked awake, she gasped and struggled to breathe. Then something dug at the back of her neck and she found herself lifted up and flung over the side of a boat, strong hands hauling her in. She lay in the boat's bottom, flapping and heaving like a dying fish. 'You're all right,' said a smoky voice. She heard the splash of oars. The boat surged forward. She knew no more.

When she awoke, she was warm and dry in a bed heaped with blankets. Her head hurt and when she put up a hand to explore, she found a bandage round it. She stared at her sleeve, orange brushed-nylon with lace at the cuff, an old lady's nightgown, then pushed herself up, though it made her head throb, and looked around. She was in a large room with wood-slatted walls, and beams across the sloping ceiling. It smelled, not unpleasantly, of tar. There was no door, which was peculiar, but pale daylight gleamed comfortingly through a small skylight above her head. Rain pattered on the roof. There was little furniture apart from the bed, just a chest of drawers, a wardrobe and a chair. Upon the chair lay a pile of neatly folded clothes. On top sat a handbag, the only thing familiar in the room. She knew nothing, not who she was or where she was or how she got there, but she wasn't worried. On the contrary, she felt peaceful and safe.

She lay down again, but as she sank into a doze, there came a knock from under the floorboards, then a trap-door opened up near her bed and a man's grizzled head appeared, like a walrus through an ice hole.

'Ah, you're awake,' he said in a country accent. He heaved himself up into the room. 'How are you?'

'I don't know,' she replied. She had a faint feeling she'd seen him before somewhere. His weathered face was friendly, his eyes when he smiled almost lost in wrinkles.

'Where is this?' she asked him.

'It's where I live. And where I work. A boathouse, I suppose you'd call it.'

'How did I get here?' she whispered.

He looked puzzled. 'There was a flood,' he said, 'don't you remember? I rescued you.'

'Did you?' She thought a moment. 'Thank you,' she said simply. 'I'm afraid I simply don't remember.'

The old man's name was Saul and she stayed with him for some while, a week, maybe two; she couldn't track the passing time. He was very solicitous. The nylon nightdresses belonged to his late wife, Doris, and crack-led with static. He brought Isabel huge meals she couldn't eat – fish, thickly buttered bread, heavy slabs of cake – and changed the dressing on the large bump on her temple. He didn't say much. She sensed that he was glad to have her here, someone to look after. He plainly missed his Doris, and the couple had not been blessed with children.

After a few days she got up and dressed in the clothes he'd left her – baggy skirts and blouses and thick woollen stockings, also Doris's. The old man looked over her up and down, his eyes filling with tears. She sensed that he'd like to keep her here, but also that he wouldn't force her, so she wasn't frightened.

She still couldn't recall much. Often she took out the contents of the handbag and looked at it all, wondered at the fact it survived the water intact. There was quite a lot of money in a purse, some letters, a birth certificate from which she learned her name, Isabel Lewis. She thumbed the blank pages of the engagement diary, tried out the lipstick and the powder compact, dissolved an aspirin for her headache, watching it fizz in the glass.

As she handled her possessions and read the appointments in the diary, shadowy memories started to dart like fish beneath the tranquil surface of her mind. She was Isabel but not Lewis. She had a husband, Hugh, and a child, Lorna. There was some reason she couldn't see them – here her memory stuck like a gramophone needle on a scratch. They'd been taken away, that was it. The name Jacqueline sounded in her dreams. Jacqueline had taken them. She found she didn't mind. They were safe with Jacqueline. She was free now.

One of the letters in her bag was from a woman who lived in Paris. Isabel read it over and over again, liking the sound of Vivienne and noting the phrase '*You must come and stay with me here.*' Gradually she discerned what she wanted to do.

The day came when she told Saul it was time for her to go and could hardly bear his distress. She thanked him and hugged him. He stood sadly watching as the bus pulled away. She was to catch a train from Halesworth, he'd instructed.

When she alighted at Ipswich, she automatically followed the crowds to the exit, feeling the pull of home, but then she paused as people flowed round her. A woman's voice was playing in her mind: '*Don't go, Hugh darling*,' it said. '*Leave it till tomorrow.*' Jacqueline. Hugh and Lorna were safe with Jacqueline, she told herself. Now which was the right platform?

She climbed into the train for London, her mind already on the future. She was Isabel Lewis now, she would shed her old life like a dead skin. She'd arrange a passport and a ticket to Paris, but first – she looked down at Doris's old skirt and cardigan – she really must buy some new clothes.

Author's Note

The books of Diana Athill, especially *Stet* and *Instead of a Letter*, have proved invaluable in my imaging of Isabel's professional world. Jessica Mann's *The Fifties Mystique* offered some fascinating domestic detail. David Kynaston's *Austerity Britain 1945–51* and *Family Britain 1951–57* provided wider historical context, and Muriel Spark's novels painted marvellous pictures of genteel London bedsit-land. Anne Sayre's memoir *Rosalind Franklin and DNA* helped with my portrayal of Vivienne.

Thanks to Dr Ann Stanley for medical advice.

I'm immeasurably grateful to my agent Sheila Crowley and her colleagues at Curtis Brown, also to my editor Suzanne Baboneau and the team at Simon & Schuster UK, particularly Clare Hey, Carla Josephson, Florence Partridge, Kerr MacRae, James Horobin, Dawn Burnett, Ally Murphy and my copy editor Joan Dietch.

Finally, much love and many thanks are due to my husband David, to Felix, Benjy and Leo, to my mother Phyllis, and to all the friends who encouraged me through the difficult bits.

RH
2013